FAKE OUT

A Long Beach Mystery

FAYE BAYKO

Fake Out
Copyright © 2024 by Faye Bayko

All rights reserved. No part of this publication may be reproduced, distributed, or transmitted in any form or by any means, including photocopying, recording, or other electronic or mechanical methods, without the prior written permission of the author, except in the case of brief quotations embodied in critical reviews and certain other non-commercial uses permitted by copyright law.

Tellwell Talent
www.tellwell.ca

ISBN
978-1-77962-479-6 (Hardcover)
978-1-77962-478-9 (Paperback)
978-1-77962-480-2 (eBook)

For Robert, who laughed at all the right places and stood by me in the dark when my characters wouldn't speak to me.

PARADISE LOST

Though fictional, this series is set in the historical location of the original Wickaninnish Inn, built in 1964 by Robin Fells, and the Wickaninnish Lodge, established by Joseph Webb in 1950. These original businesses were located on the south end of Wickaninnish Bay on the west coast of Vancouver Island, Canada.

Robin built the original inn intending to create a paradise home for his growing family and a business to take him and his family into the future. Unfortunately for Robin, the federal government had set its sights on Wickaninnish Bay becoming Phase I of a large west coast national park. By April 1970 the provincial and federal governments had signed a cost-sharing agreement that would see the purchase of private land within the park boundaries, and homes and businesses removed. The inn, which had opened July 4, 1964, was shut down by the end of December 1977, and the main portion of the building was demolished two years later. The lounge with its swayback roof was left standing, the lone reminder of what had been a landmark inn.

The federal government, in spite of its previously expressed policy of no commercial businesses within the park's boundaries, reopened the lounge as a restaurant in May 1980. Meanwhile, spending cutbacks kept the newly constructed shell of the promised Wickaninnish (interpretive) Centre, which had been attached to the new restaurant, unfinished until 1984. In 2011, the building was renamed the Kʷisitis Visitor Centre.

The present Wickaninnish Inn, located on the north end of Chesterman Beach, opened in 1996, through the efforts of Howard McDiarmid, a local land developer, former doctor, and politician.

NOTE:

At the time of the series the whole of the beach at Wickaninnish Bay was known as Long Beach, the present-day Wick Road was Long Beach Road, and the former Kʷisitis village site was IR9 and its frontage was Lismer Beach.

Historical attitudes and language have been kept in the story to ensure an authentic depiction of the period, and to inspire debate.

Some locations have been fictionalized to accommodate the story.

THURSDAY, APRIL 25, 1968

PROLOGUE

The old man rolled the rock chip around the palm of his hand as he examined the milky vein running through it. After licking his finger, he used its wetness to rub away the gritty surface dirt and expose the yellow material embedded in the quartz.

"Hmm." He moved the rock in and out of the sunlight streaming through the forest surrounding him, checking its colour. Then, he used his fingernail to pick at the gold. A flake came away and was caught by the breeze. *Fool's gold.* He let out a sigh, tossed the rock into the underbrush, and returned to his digging.

The sun's warmth was surprising for a cloudy April afternoon, and its heat had glued his shirt to his back. He shrugged his shoulders to release the tension. His body was betraying him. Each year, the stiffness crept further into his joints and muscles. Soon, he would no longer be able to scramble up the steep bank from Lost Shoe Creek onto the rock shelf where he had built his shack. He didn't want to think about a future without the sounds of the wind rustling through the trees above or the skittering of curious forest creatures in the brush below.

He loved the freedom prospecting afforded him, but it was a hard grind. Working in a rainforest on the west coast of Vancouver Island meant he had to appreciate the dry days when they came. He removed his shirt. Although worn through in places and caked in the mud of his toil, he could not yet afford a new one, so he folded it and set it on the crown of a nearby salal bush, careful not to crush the pinkish, urn-shaped blooms. He needed the berries they would produce in the late summer. Prospecting was a passion he was too old to give up, even if it often meant an empty dinner plate.

He was about to pick up his shovel again when human voices interrupted the sounds of the forest. Two. Male. He froze, focused on identifying the direction. North. A third voice joined in. Female. He shifted, careful not to make a sound, and scanned the surrounding forest. If he was lucky, they were just hippies who had wandered from the path down to the beach at Wreck Bay, a mile to the west of him. If he wasn't, well, he might have a serious problem.

The intruders didn't seem to be coming any closer, yet they weren't going away either. He could see nothing but trees in a forest gone silent except for the raised voices of the three humans. Cautiously, he started climbing the bank.

He came on them suddenly, almost giving himself away. They were standing together about a hundred yards from the edge of the embankment. He crouched, hiding behind the tangled screen of salal and fern undergrowth surrounding two Sitka spruce, and listened.

"I tell you, Rod, she's right. That shack is perfect," said the shorter of the two men. "It's down the bank, surrounded by trees. No one can see it from this path." He waved his hands. "No one comes here. I don't think anyone even remembers what the road was originally built for, and the entrance is masked by brush on both sides."

The old man didn't recognize either of the men, but knew the sound of impatience when he heard it. He settled deeper into the undergrowth, curious.

"And you've checked on the claim? It's not active?"

Rod, thought the old man. From the authority in his voice, Rod was the one the other two needed to please.

"Hasn't been worked in at least ten years," the short man said. "I heard the family left the area."

"It's all I could find, Rod."

The conciliatory tone of the woman's voice ground on the old man's nerves, and he frowned. *I know that voice.* But try as he might, he couldn't put a name to it. He chanced a glance out from behind his screen. The three of them stood facing each other. The shorter man wore the work clothes commonly seen in the area: flannel shirt, denim pants, heavy wool socks pulled up over the bottoms of the pant legs, and leather work boots. The other was dressed sharper: dark leather jacket, jeans, and high-top boots. The woman, whose back was toward him, wore a green rain slicker that came down to her knees, where blue jeans flared over black rubber boots. Her hair was hidden by a baseball cap and the hood of her slicker crumpled around the base of her neck. He could only see the side of her forehead and cheek, which teased at the edges of his memory.

His knees began to protest his squat, yet he didn't dare stand. He bit back a groan as he shifted his weight to ease the tension. He had no idea who the men were, but his gut told him he didn't want them to discover he was watching. The girl, however, gave him a warm feeling of familiarity, which frustrated him. Having lived in the area between Tofino and Ucluelet for several decades, he'd watched generations grow up. Plain old age kept him from matching her voice to a name.

Right now, her identity wasn't the question that worried him the most. *Why are they interested in the old Johnston claim?*

The neighbouring claim was a placer claim, like his. It dated back at least two generations, and as far as he knew, its registration had been kept up to date. Although it wasn't unusual for a claim to be abandoned. Prospectors often had several claims, their attention easily drawn from one to another. The old man wondered if these three were thinking of buying up the claims above Wreck Bay. *Why?* He barely covered expenses working his claim, and there hadn't been news of any large strikes in the area since the early nineteen-hundreds.

If they were planning on buying up the Johnston claim, maybe they would be after his own. Thinking of what he had left exposed at his shack, anxiety gripped him, and he carefully made his way back down the hill.

FRIDAY,
MAY 10, 1968

1.

Sandy stood where the path exited through the hedgerow of salal bush and wind-stunted Sitka spruce and gazed out on Long Beach for the first time. It was better than she had imagined. The steady roar of the surf frightened and soothed her at the same time. A stack of surf-polished logs lay jumbled in front of her, part of a massive group tossed helter-skelter at the top of a beach that ran for miles to her right. To her left, similar piles were amassed at the base of volcanic rock that held a beautifully rustic inn as if on a pedestal. The inn and the ancient rock on which it stood jutted out from the hedgerow and forest behind as if trying to create an island of itself. At high tide, Sandy could easily imagine the inn accomplishing its wish, with a crashing surf pounding it on three sides. Luckily, it wasn't high tide.

Shading her eyes against the brilliant afternoon sun, she felt Geoff brush past to launch himself at the jumbled stack of logs in front of them, skipping barefoot from one sun-bleached perch to another, his attention focused on the surf rolling in off the Pacific Ocean. She laughed in appreciation of his grace. He looked back and gave her a mock salute, then suddenly went down hard on the log in front. The pounding surf swallowed his cry of pain. Sandy cringed in sympathy.

She had been about to make her first tentative attempt at crossing the logs but was discouraged by Geoff's fall. He gathered himself, stood, turned, and waved at her.

"Akaw!" he shouted and motioned to the ocean. "Outta sight, man!"

Sandy laughed. "I don't understand!"

He shook his head, gesturing with his hands to indicate he couldn't hear her over the thunder of the waves. Then he spun to face the ocean once more.

Sandy stood transfixed by his beauty. Framed by the shimmering blues of ocean and bright sky, the sun turning the soft curls of his hair into spun gold as it floated above his bronzed shoulders in the sea breeze, he was the male version of Sandro Botticelli's *Birth of Venus.* Of course, the psychedelic swim trunks turned the image into more of a Wes Wilson poster.

She had never hung out with a surfer before and found it hard to voice an opinion of the waves, if that was what he'd shouted at her, but the artist in her drank in the beauty of her setting. The brilliant blue of the sky made the cotton ball clouds look like painted stage props hanging by invisible wires. The ocean rolling toward the beach, by contrast, was front-of-stage liquid drama. Ultramarine violet swirled into cobalt blue, drawing in the occasional Windsor green and indigo, before swelling, cresting, transforming to a frothy Chinese white that crashed and spread out into a lacy froth on the sienna-blushed beach.

She had taken a chance by hitchhiking from her home in Victoria at the southern tip of Vancouver Island to this remote beach on the wild west coast of the island. But she'd been lucky. The first two rides she'd caught on the trip up-island had been with young families, where her only challenge was avoiding the children's sticky fingers. Then, a mile outside of the small town of Port Alberni, where she'd spent the night in a cold church hall, Geoff had answered the universal gesture of hitchhikers and pulled his van over in a cloud of dust. He was everything her father would have warned her about if he'd known what she was doing—which he did not.

Geoff was young, gorgeous, and a hippie. From the moment he leaned over the front seat of his van and opened the passenger door for her, fixing her with his liquid-blue eyes, she trusted him. She had climbed in knowing that, with him, she had nothing to fear while crossing the fifty miles of gravel logging roads standing between them and their destination.

Geoff had filled the two-hour road trip with chatter about his surfing exploits in California and his excitement at trying the west coast of Canada's cold-water surfing. His enthusiasm for the sport was infectious, and Sandy found herself wondering how hard it would be to learn it. The journey came to a quick end when they reached the bottom of Long Beach Road, both driver and passenger dusty, sweaty, and itching to get out on to the beach.

Sandy cheered as Geoff jumped from the final log and raced over the sand to the edge of the surf, scattering flocks of feeding seabirds as he went.

The breeze teased her hair and played with the hem of the cotton minidress she wore over her bikini as if encouraging her to join in the fun. She slipped off her moccasins, leaving them where they lay, and stepped out onto the first log. It shifted slightly as it took her weight.

She balanced, took a second step, and then a third. Her crossing wasn't as fast or as graceful as Geoff's, but she avoided falling and soon found herself stepping down onto the beach. Legs shaking, she collapsed onto the log.

She dug her toes into the warm sand and breathed deeply, feeling her lungs and throat expand as if for the first time. The briny, earthy scent of the ocean air eased the tension from her shoulders. This was the edge of the world—or of Canada, at least. After so desperately wanting to escape her predictable life in Victoria and the expectations of loving but overly protective parents, she'd finally done it. She had let go. Shrugging out of her dress, she uncovered the yellow bikini she'd purchased as part of that separation. Her parents would have been shocked at how much of her body she was exposing to the world—or at least to those in the inn.

She glanced up at it. The golden honey of the cedar cladding had weathered to a deep, warm brown where it faced the ocean. The building appeared as if it had grown naturally from the rock, sand, and forest of its setting, yet stood out sharp against the sky, daring the gods to deny its place on the beach. *It would make an impressive painting.* Sandy wished she hadn't left her art supplies at home. Then her eyes settled on the outline of a man who seemed to be staring out at her from a one of the inn's windows. Surprised, she quickly ducked her head, her cheeks flushing.

"Man, that's cold!"

Sandy turned and caught her breath. Geoff was running out of the surf, droplets flying in the wind as he shook the water from his hair. The man was even more beautiful wet. A gasp of pleasure escaped her lips before her sex-addled brain registered what was happening. He was barrelling across the beach toward her, arms outstretched. She knew what that meant. Having grown up with a younger brother she was painfully aware of the prankster element that seemed part of being male. She took off to the left, running parallel to the surf.

She didn't make it far before Geoff caught her, wrapping her in wet arms made ice cold by the spring breeze. His laughter floated over her protests as he turned toward the surf with her pinned against his chest, her feet no longer touching the ground.

Sandy stopped struggling. Her bikini would not survive the effort, and she feared it had already shifted to reveal even more of her body than she'd intended. Geoff carried her to the edge of the surf, and Sandy steeled herself against the chill of the water. Surprisingly, he didn't toss her in. He relaxed his grip, her feet found the sand, and she stood braced against him, facing the ocean.

"Isn't it beautiful?" he whispered, his breath sending shivers down her neck and along her shoulder. Sandy felt herself melt against him. The icy chill of the surf ebbing and flowing around her ankles disappeared as she stood wrapped in his arms.

"Yes," she sighed. "It is."

2.

Tom stepped back from the window, drained the scotch from his glass, and turned his attention back into the lounge. The inn's lounge offered guests a panoramic view of the Pacific Ocean rolling onto the long, lazy curve of Wickaninnish Bay, part of a twelve-mile stretch of sand commonly referred to as Long Beach. The view was what had prompted Robin Fells, the owner of the inn, to build his dream hotel perched on top of the rocky outcrop in 1964. Four years on, Wickaninnish Inn was attracting a steady stream of visitors from across Canada looking for a beach holiday without the roughness of camping.

Tom smiled. The large windows that lined the front and side walls of the lounge provided a perfect vantage point for watching people, and today he had witnessed a young couple's foreplay. Somewhere, a mattress would soon be getting a workout.

He crossed the lounge, gathering empty glasses from the tables as he passed. The afternoon crowd was light. Most of the hotel's guests were outside, enjoying the view from the deck or exploring the beach below. He set the dirty glasses behind the bar, pulled a fresh glass off the counter, and filled it with water. It would act as a chaser without diluting the buzz of the whisky. He set the drink to the left of the sink, under the lip of the bar. It was going to be a long day. Usually, he only worked the evening shift, Monday to Saturday, but that morning, Brent, the afternoon bartender, had asked him to cover his eleven to three shift so he could drive out to Port Alberni. He then promised to cover both their shifts the next day, which meant a rare, full weekend off for Tom.

Taking a job as a bartender at the inn had been his father's idea. Tom certainly hadn't wanted to move away from the parties and fast lifestyle of West Vancouver, but after his father had bailed him out from a string of arrests, he was given no choice. It was either accept banishment to the end of the Earth or join his father's real estate company. Tom couldn't see himself driving well-heeled but extremely boring clients around West Vancouver, so he'd opted for the banishment.

It wasn't that the job was bad. He was naturally a social person and, at twenty-one, he fit in with most of the staff. He was just bored. Spring and fall bus tours provided the inn with a steady income, while a growing reputation among middle-class vacationers looking for an edge-of-the-world escape filled the summer. However, nothing in the area provided the high-energy city vibe Tom was used to. The inn's no-television, no-radio, and no-newspaper atmosphere often left him feeling bored, cut off, and very alone.

He glanced out from behind the bar. A family, who had wandered in off the beach, sat at a table near the window, and a regular sat at the bar.

"Did you hear? The police picked up two teens for last month's fire."

Tom turned toward the speaker, a man named James, who slouched on a bar stool, as he did almost every Friday evening, drinking two Boilermakers before heading home. At least that was the routine Tom was familiar with. "You're early today, aren't you, James?"

"A delivery of materials didn't show up as planned. I had nothing to do, so I booked off early."

Tom pulled a Lucky from the bar fridge, uncapped it, and set the bottle in front of James before pouring the whisky shot. "What's this about a fire?"

"Remember the boathouse that burned down behind the old marina in Ucluelet about two weeks ago?"

"Oh, right."

James knocked back the whisky, set the shot glass down on the bar, then guzzled half the beer before continuing. "Turns out two kids sneakin' a smoke caused the fire."

Tom waited as James took another long slug of his beer. "Are they going to be charged?"

"Not sure, but that's not why I mentioned it. Seems everyone thought the owner abandoned it years ago, you know, and the town had taken it over. Turns out the guy had been sitting on it, waiting for the market to improve. He finally sold it to someone from Vancouver. The scuttlebutt about town is that the new owner was set to transport fish to Vancouver over the new road. The boathouse was going to be their base. Now, who knows?"

"I thought the fishermen already started some sort of shipping company when the road first opened in '59."

"Guess it didn't get off the ground. Or maybe this guy's coming in as competition."

"Was the boathouse empty?"

"Yeah. The guy was bringin' a truck—" James coughed. "He was bringing a truck up the following weekend to start the business. The fire changed things." He shook his head. "I was so sure those damn hippies set the fire."

Tom tried not to smile. Everyone knew how much James hated hippies. "Another?" Tom asked, already reaching into the cooler for a fresh beer.

"Yeah."

When Tom set the fresh beer down, James seemed lost in thought. Tom reached for the whiskey to refill the shot glass and found James' eyes on him. "The draft dodgers and hippies have taken over Wreck Bay again."

Tom leaned against the back of the bar, and waited.

"It's not even the long weekend yet." James shook his head, staring down at the newly filled shot glass. "Can you imagine how many of those lazy no-goods will be here by midsummer?"

Tom didn't bother answering. James would continue his one-sided conversation whether or not he replied.

"They're asking for trouble."

Tom tried not to groan. He wasn't in the mood to listen to one of James' tirades.

"You won't remember 'cause you weren't here, but they started showin' up last year, strutting around naked, doing all sorts of who knows what in those log lean-tos they've thrown together on the beach. And there were kids there too! Can you believe it? Little ones seeing body parts that shouldn't be out, danglin' about at eye level!" James shook his head, then sucked back on his beer. "I heard they've already started spreading out to other beaches. A buddy of mine told me he seen a couple of lean-tos set up against the dunes at Long Beach."

"That should prove interesting, with the number of kids racing their cars across the sand by Green Point campground." James was leaning slightly to the right, and Tom was about to tell him when the man righted himself.

"A group of us got talking at the Legion last night, and we decided we're gonna teach them lazy bastards a lesson or two."

"Which? The kids or the hippies?"

"What? What are you talking about? The kids? The hippies, of course!" James turned to look out at the beach through the lounge's wall of picture windows. "Pretty soon, they'll be campin' right outside here. Bare butts and all."

"So, what happened?"

James turned back to face Tom, anger etched on his face. "Someone snitched; that's what happened. Next thing we know, the cops show up at the work site this morning for a little chat. Law-abiding citizens, us, all with jobs I might add, are given a what-for, while young men who refuse to fight for their country come into ours and live off our welfare system! And we get told to back off for trying to do something about it?"

As Tom set his empty water glass in the bar's sink he was distracted by the sudden change in music filtering through the speakers in the lounge. It was not a subtle change, and he grinned. Steppenwolf's *Born to be Wild* had been replaced by Handel's *Water Music*.

"What're you grinnin' about? You think it's funny we got raked over by the cops?"

Tom turned to see James' glare. "What? No." Tom scrubbed his fingers through the thick waves of his dark hair, then quickly stopped. A girlfriend had once told him the habit made him look nervous. The last thing he wanted was to appear nervous—or worse, high. If it got back to his father that he was using again, there was no telling where he'd be shipped off to next. "No. The music changed. Didn't you notice?"

"What's that got to do with anything?"

"It's broadcast throughout the inn. I was laughing because it's become a bit of a game between the staff and Robin. We sneak our cassettes into the player in the office, and then Robin comes in, takes them out, and shoves in his classical music." Tom paused. "He must be in the office."

"How's Robin doing?"

Tom looked across at James. "All right, I guess."

"He doesn't talk to you?"

Tom frowned. "Just about work. Why would he?"

"Just wonderin', that's all."

Tom glanced at the step-through doorway to the dining room. One of the hardest aspects of living in a remote community was that not only did everyone know everyone else's business, but they thought they had a right to that knowledge. He had tried his best to stay out of all the small-town gossip, mostly because he just wasn't interested, nonetheless it had caught up with him a couple of times when he was in the wrong place at the wrong time. Since then, he had started paying cautious attention. "Why?" he asked. "What have you heard?"

James glanced around as if checking for eavesdroppers. "There's been some talk about the proposed new park's border comin' down as far as Wreck Bay and all the residents bein' kicked out."

Tom frowned. Wreck Bay was south of the inn. If the border came down that far, then all of Long Beach, including the inn, would be part of the proposed national park. "That'd be a huge park. Why do you think they'd kick everyone out?"

"There's talk the government won't allow any commercial businesses inside the park boundaries."

"That's crazy." Tom laughed. "Why would they close the inn? There are hotels in other national parks. Look at Banff and Jasper."

"Who knows? I'm just sayin'." After a pause, he stood. "Well, I gotta get goin'." He set a five-dollar bill on the counter and walked out of the lounge.

Tom picked up the bill and cleared away the glass and bottle, pausing to consider the views of the wild ocean beyond the picture windows. While he didn't plan on staying past the end of the season, he had thought the inn would continue operating for years. It was only four years old. *How can anyone consider closing it?*

The laughter of two women entering the lounge from the lobby brought Tom out of his reflection. He hated politics. Flirting was much more fun. "Good afternoon, ladies. What can I get you?"

Sandy glanced at Geoff as they crossed the parking lot next to the Wickaninnish Inn. They had moved the van from its earlier parking spot at the bottom of Long Beach Road to a space at the inn. Geoff wanted to bring it closer to a path he'd been told would take them to Wreck Bay, where he hoped to run into a fellow surfer he knew from California.

The parking lot ran south along a rocky shelf about twenty feet above the beach. A scrub forest, which had been cleared for the parking lot, continued across the shelf and down to the edge of the beach. In that forest, they had been told, they would find the path they were looking for. The space between the inn and that forest drew Sandy's gaze. No trees blocked the view at the edge of the shelf facing the sea, and the tide had gone way out. Sandy paused to appreciate the dramatic scene.

"Are you coming?"

Startled, she turned to find Geoff waiting at the entrance of a laneway. Although no longer a water god in wet splendour, the body-hugging drainpipe jeans and blue T-shirt worn under an open purple and orange paisley shirt still caused a jolt of newly awakened desire. She was suddenly aware of her soft cotton blouse brushing against her nipples and the sway of her denim maxiskirt against her bare legs. She took a deep breath and started to run across the gravel to him, but the soft leather of her moccasins slowed her to a less painful pace. Geoff turned away without waiting for her and entered the shade of the forest. Sandy followed, concerned by his aloofness. He seemed to have left the jokester, as well as the psychedelic swim trunks, behind.

He hadn't spoken since they'd left the van, and he didn't look back at her now. His behaviour didn't make sense.

They'd spent the afternoon in the back of his van, and she could no longer claim to be a virgin. She was okay with what had happened, but had been surprised and embarrassed by the blood. She hadn't known there would be blood. It seemed to have surprised Geoff as well, although he was very kind about the mess. Even using the precious supply of water from the camper's storage tank for the necessary sponge bath hadn't seemed to concern him. But then, afterward, he had been aloof. When she reached for his hand as she exited the van, he'd taken it but held it loosely. She eventually let go as they walked across the parking lot.

She considered not following him to Wreck Bay, slowing her pace until she was walking several paces behind him. He didn't seem to notice. She stopped. He noticed that, and stopped, a question in his eyes.

"Look," she said. "I'm sorry about your sheets. I'll buy you new ones."

"It's not the sheets."

"What then?"

Geoff glanced at the trees edging the parking lot as if they could give him the words he sought. Finally, he looked across at her. "You should have told me."

"Why?" Sandy crossed her arms to hide the emptiness she felt. "What would it have changed? Would we have skipped the sex and just played cards?"

"I don't know." Geoff paced back and forth in front of her. "I just—well, yeah, I probably wouldn't have brought you back to the van." He stopped and faced her. "I know how important it is for girls. I mean, weren't you waiting for marriage?"

"What?" Sandy was suddenly so angry that she could've kicked him. "First off, you could've stopped at any time. I wasn't forcing you to have sex with me. Second, where do you get off telling me what I should or shouldn't do with my life? This is 1968! If I want to have sex, I'll have sex!"

A giggle behind her made her swing around. Two girls were walking across the parking lot toward them. One gave her the peace sign as she and her grinning friend passed.

Sandy turned back to Geoff, who now had his back to her. He was staring at the inn. She sighed. "Geoff, it's okay. Really." She placed her hand lightly on his arm. "Look, I came here to experience the whole"—she swung her arms open as if to embrace the entire scene—"thing." She laughed. "I expected to have sex with someone. I'm glad it was with you."

Geoff glanced down at her. "Are you sure you're okay with it?" He traced the curve of her cheek with his finger.

"Yes, I'm okay with it! Okay?"

Stepping back, he grinned. "Yeah. Cool. I was just worried, you know. I have three older sisters and I couldn't imagine—"

Sandy burst out laughing and punched his arm. "What are you? Catholic?"

Geoff grimaced. "Well, yeah."

"Well, yeah," she mimicked. "Well, I'm not the Virgin Mary, and I'm sure your sisters aren't either—or they don't want to be, at least."

At Geoff's shocked expression, she laughed again. Then she darted around him to run along the laneway.

Geoff ran after her. "You haven't met them yet!"

3.

Sandy slipped around Geoff. *Thank God! Sunshine! Sky!* She had begun to worry she'd never see either again. The path from the end of the laneway by the cottages to the top of the ridge looking down on Wreck Bay had taken almost an hour of trudging through a thick rainforest that, at times, had closed in above them like a leafy cave. The sandy beach that lay below them was about a third the size of the one they'd left behind at the Wickaninnish Inn, still its gentle curve pulled in an equally dramatic surf, and instead of cars and campers parked along its length, there were makeshift lean-tos, the odd canvas tent, and people. People were everywhere: standing in small groups, seated around campfires, sunbathing on the beach, or sitting on surfboards bobbing on the rolling sea.

Only a few of the sunbathers were nude, which surprised her. From what she'd heard about the beach, she'd expected everyone to be naked. Even more surprising were the children running and playing among the camps, some very young. All nude. Their tiny, perfect bodies showed no tan lines. *No diapers, then.* Sandy cringed. Somehow, she had never thought about the possibility of children while envisioning the hippie lifestyle. "Wow," she said.

Geoff smiled back at her. "This is so much better than I imagined."

"What were you expecting?"

"A replica of California, I guess. But this is wild. California is like a carnival." He took a deep breath and slowly let it out. "I can hardly wait to put my board in the water."

"Why'd you leave it strapped to the top of your van, then?"

"I'll get it when I move the van closer."

Sandy frowned as she scrambled down the steep drop to the beach behind him. How, she wondered, was he planning on moving his van closer when the laneway had swiftly narrowed to a rough path? She was about to ask him when his hand whipped out and caught a Frisbee mid-air. He tossed it back to the group on the beach who'd been playing with it.

One player called out, "Hey, man, want to join us?"

Without even looking at her, Geoff ran off to join in.

"You go ahead. I'll just watch," Sandy called after him. When he didn't appear to catch her sarcasm, she turned and walked down the beach, taking in the scene. The art program she had attended used live models, so she wasn't a stranger to nude bodies, but for some reason, seeing them casually strolling a public beach was quite different. More than once, she caught herself staring. She told herself it was the play of the late afternoon light on the different skin tones that fascinated her, but she knew it was just plain curiosity about the human form in all its various sizes, shapes, and colours that kept drawing her eye from those who were clothed to those who were not.

The nudity around her, though, made her feel comfortable about being braless. It had been a spontaneous, last-minute decision before leaving the van. Now she was glad she'd made it. Somehow, it seemed wrong to wear a bra in this place—and the freedom felt good.

As she strolled, she noticed people cooking food on campfires, and her stomach started grumbling. Not purchasing supplies in Port Alberni before walking to the edge of town to hitch a ride to the coast was a city-girl mistake; she'd assumed there would be stores close to the beach. She sat on an unoccupied log, pulled her shoulder bag off her arm, and began searching through it for a stray chocolate bar. Nothing. She would have to ask Geoff for the keys to the van.

"Want a toke?"

Sandy glanced up. A beautiful blonde girl, naked except for a shawl knotted at her waist, held out a joint.

"Sure." Sandy smiled, accepted the joint, and brought it to her lips.

The girl settled on the log beside Sandy. "Where're you from?"

Sandy handed the joint back as she exhaled. "Victoria." She looked out at the ocean. Next to the girl's casual nudity, Sandy felt overdressed. When the joint was passed again, she drew in a long drag and paused a moment to let the sweet smoke fill her lungs before returning it to the girl. "I'm Sandy."

"I'm Angela, but everyone here calls me Angel." A small smile played across the girl's cupid's bow lips.

Sandy glanced away. The girl's emerald eyes held a wildness that made her feel as if she'd glimpsed something feral. "How old are you?"

"Fourteen and a half. Well, almost three-quarters." Angel laughed. "Why? You looking to shag?"

A deep blush sprang to Sandy's cheeks, and she had trouble answering. The girl didn't wait for one. She jumped up and sprinted down the beach into the arms of a fully clothed male well into his twenties. Sandy returned her attention to Geoff and the others tossing the Frisbee. Someone's dog had joined them, barking in protest whenever one of the guys caught the flying disk before it did.

The animal's frustration was painful to watch for Sandy, who was a dog lover, and she turned away. Movement on the sand caught her eye. Several bugs were creeping along the sand in front of her. She lifted her purse from their path and set off a cloud of tiny fleas, she jumped up and away only to discover the log had its own population of insects. She swatted at her legs and butt, hoping to get rid of the pesky things.

The joint had only made her hungrier. She glanced over at Geoff; he had just done a face plant into the sand, much to the amusement of the others. She called above their laughter, "Geoff, can I borrow your keys?"

He turned in her direction and squinted. For a moment, Sandy thought he didn't recognize her. Then he smiled. "Give me a bit and I'll walk back with you."

"Not too long. I'm starving!" Sandy shouted back, but Geoff had already returned to the game.

"If you're hungry, you're welcome to share our meal."

The offer came from a man in his late twenties sitting in front of his lean-too about ten feet up the beach. The tantalizing smell of roasting salmon rose from his campfire. He smiled.

She responded with a half-smile before turning back to Geoff. He was no longer chasing the Frisbee. He stood at the edge of the surf, talking with a group of surfers, apparently in no hurry to return to the van. She headed up the beach toward the man who had invited her to dinner. "If you're sure you have enough," she said.

"There's always room for one more at our table," he answered, fixing her with deep-set eyes the colour of melted dark chocolate. She quickly looked away, focusing on their surroundings, wondering where the others were.

The young man acknowledged her confusion. "They'll be here soon. Sit. Enjoy the view. My name's Mark."

"Mine's Sandy." Her attention was drawn to the fish he was cooking. Two had been split open and stretched by thin spikes of wood woven through the flesh; a stake stuck in the sand held them at an angle before the fire. Mounds of pan bread sat on a log, their centres showing a patchwork of golden and blackened crust. "Looks amazing," she said.

He motioned toward the log next to him. "Sit. Sit."

After her recent experience with the beach's insects, Sandy pulled her poncho out of her shoulder bag and spread it on the log before sitting.

"Did you just arrive?"

"Yes. I hitched from Victoria and I'm starving." Sandy laughed. "I didn't plan this trip very well."

Mark passed her a bottle of beer. "You don't have to worry. Here on the beach, we share what we have with anyone who needs it."

Sandy liked his laid-back attitude. "How did you learn to cook fish like that?" The few times she'd been camping was on school trips where the fish had been thrown in a frying pan with a slab of butter, usually ending up as burnt flakes.

"From the local Aboriginals."

"Are they also the ones who taught you to carve?" Sandy pointed to the carved plaques resting against the driftwood lean-to behind them.

"In a way. I did some carving in high school. Experimenting." Mark swept his hand in front of him. "When I came up here and saw what the area Aboriginals were producing, I was inspired. I love the complexity of meaning and the geometric precision of their carving. I've been trying to learn their technique."

Sandy picked up one of the plaques and examined it. She could see a style influence, but the end result was very different from any Indian carving she'd ever seen. "I just dropped out of art college," she said as she returned the plaque to where she'd found it.

"Why?" Mark gestured for her to pass him the plates stacked on her side of the log.

At the sound of the plates being lifted from the stack, two guys separated from the group playing cards at the next camp and stepped up. "Hey," they said in unison.

Mark placed pieces of pan bread on the plates and made the introductions. "Neal. Jim. This is Sandy from Victoria." He then passed the plates back to Sandy to hold while he pulled a staked fish away from the fire and laid it on a flat piece of cedar. Dividing the fish, he placed a share on each of the plates Sandy held.

Sandy couldn't help staring at Jim as he leaned down to take one of the plates she held out. She'd never seen a man with such long hair before. It hung like a black cloak around his shoulders, and it took her a moment after both men had returned to their card game to realize she had no recollection of what the second man looked like. She'd been so entranced by Jim.

"Plates?" Mark was kneeling by the fire, waving two golden-brown pan breads.

Sandy blushed and quickly pulled the last two plates from where they'd been stacked. "Looks delicious."

Mark divided the last fish between them and rose to take a seat beside her on the log.

"I don't want to keep you from hanging out with them." Sandy pointed to where Jim and his friend were sitting.

"You're not. I sold a carving in town today, so I bought some salmon off the dock in Ucluelet. Neal and Jim shared their meal with me last night, so I returned the favour tonight." Mark tore away a piece of pan bread and folded in a bit of salmon, then paused and waved his hand to include the whole beach. "It's all about peace, love, and rock'n roll. Right?"

Sandy chuckled. "Cool. Thank you." She did her best to scoop the fish into her mouth using the pan bread, as she saw the others do. When she could speak around the food, she asked, "What brought you out here?"

Mark turned to look out at the wide expanse of sand. "It's a hell of a lot colder here than California or Hawaii, even so the waves come in slower, so you have a better chance to improve your surfing. In Hawaii, the waves are so powerful there are no second chances. Plus, the surf's so crowded you spend most of your time dodging heads or flying boards." Mark grinned. "Besides, you Canadians are so polite."

"You're American?"

"I was born in Maine, but my parents travelled a lot. Dad's a biologist, and we were always packing up to head off somewhere for his next research project."

"That's why you don't have the American accent?"

Mark shrugged.

Sandy examined the makeshift camp behind them. The lean-to was basic. The side posts, cross beams, and roof beams were all driftwood. A sheet of plastic had been tied with twine across the roof, while tree boughs filled in the two sides. From what she could see of the interior, Mark had set up a cot for his bed along one side of the lean-to and on the other, he'd used crates to create shelves to hold a couple of books and some dry goods. "Are you planning on staying on the beach for long?"

"It's been fun, but if you're serious about surfing, you have to move on. Sort of like those guys in *Endless Summer*. Did you see it?"

"No, I didn't," she said, glancing at her empty plate. "Was it about surfing, like *Beach Party*?"

"Not like *Beach Party*." Mark's chortle was joined by Jim's as he stepped up to return his and Neal's dirty dishes.

"*Endless Summer* was a documentary," Jim explained.

Mark jumped in. "It was about two guys who travelled the world, following the sun and searching for the perfect wave. No singing."

Sandy set her plate on the sand. Still hungry. "Cool."

"What's cool?" Geoff asked, dropping down on the log beside her.

Sandy shifted over. "We were talking about a movie."

"Do they have a movie house up here?" Geoff asked Mark.

"Not sure, pal."

Geoff glanced at the stack of dirty plates by the log. "Hey, you wouldn't have any food left would ya?"

"Sorry, mate. You just missed it." Mark paused when he spotted the frying pan. "There's a bit of pan bread left."

"I'll take it." Geoff accepted the bread. "It's still warm!"

"Do you want a beer to wash it down?"

"Do you have a juice?"

Mark stood and walked to the cooler at the front of his lean-to. "I've got a cola. Would that do?"

"Choice!"

Mark passed the soda to Geoff, who set it in the sand by his hip, then reached into his pocket and pulled out a pouch with a joint in it. "Look what I got for us." Grinning, he started searching through his pocket again.

Mark reached down to the base of his log, picked up a pack of matches, and tossed it to Geoff.

"Thanks, man." He lit the joint and sucked deeply, exhaling slowly, letting the smoke rise in a veil across his face. He closed his eyes against the sting and passed the joint to Sandy, leaning in close and whispering, "How's my spooky little girl?"

Sandy shifted on the log to put some distance between them before taking a quick drag and passing the joint to Mark. She didn't know what she felt for Geoff, exactly, but she didn't like that he had left her alone for so long. She had left Victoria to experience the whole make-love-not-war thing, but she hadn't thought about what to do with the guy afterward. Her stuff was still in his van. If she waited until later to get it, would he expect her to have sex with him again? She wasn't sure if she wanted to. This weekend was turning out a lot more complicated than she had thought it would be.

SATURDAY, MAY 11, 1968

4.

Conny took a long draw from her bottle of beer and watched the people gathered around the beach bonfire. At two in the morning, the party on Wreck Bay was in full swing, but she had only sold half the supply tucked into her purse, and nothing of the sample product her boyfriend had brought over from the mainland. Usually, by this time, she'd have sold out and people would be clamouring for more.

She glanced around, looking to see if another dealer was working the party. She recognized several locals, but most of the partiers were outsiders attracted to the freestyle party life of the beach. She walked along the edge of a retreating surf, and scrutinized faces revealed by campfire light or by the flash of a match held to a cigarette. None had the look of someone with product to sell. She turned back to join the group at the main bonfire.

As she approached, her attention was caught by talk of a placer claim. She stopped and looked toward the speaker. It was unusual to hear the term. She only knew it because one of her mother's boyfriends had considered himself a prospector.

The speaker was standing on the opposite side of the bonfire. His hair hung to his shoulders in a knotted mess. Maybe he was more attractive than the average longhair, but he was still a longhair. His jeans rode low on his narrow hips, and his blue T-shirt was heavily wrinkled.

He waved a prospector's pan like a fan as he spoke. She didn't know if he was drunk or just enjoying the attention of the small audience gathered around him.

"I didn't know I had prospector's blood in me, but isn't it cool?" He took a swig of his beer and scrunched up his mouth as if he'd tasted something foul. He held up the beer, eyeballing its contents through the brown glass of the bottle. He then tossed the bottle in a high arc into the fire. He was distracted from the impact by a question asked of him. The voice didn't carry across the general noise of the party, but Conny heard the longhair's answer.

"Yeah, gold. I can't remember when, but my cousin told me it was discovered here at Wreck Bay." The longhair held the prospector's pan like he was dipping it in water. The flat, shallow pan caught the firelight and emphasized the movements. "He said they would find a spot and scoop out some sand from the river bottom and then swish water around until the gold was revealed."

"Sounds simple," Conny shouted across the fire, but the longhair didn't hear her. He had turned toward a cute brunette leaning in close to whisper in his ear. Conny shook her head. The prospector boyfriend of her mother's had drunk away her mother's welfare cheques while filling her head with dreams of riches. Those dreams never came to fruition, and her mother soon replaced him with another man, who drained her in a different way.

Conny weaved through the crowd, working her way around the fire to get closer to the longhair. When she was next to him, she drew his attention from the brunette by asking to see the pan.

He turned, grinning widely, and handed it to her.

"It looks very old," she said.

"It used to belong to my grandfather."

"Where did he pan?"

The longhair looked at her and gave her a crocked smile. "Around," he said.

Conny returned his smile. He was already starting to think with a prospector's suspicion. She held out her hand. "Hi. I'm Conny. That's Conny with a *Y*."

The introduction seemed to relax him; he took her hand and shook it enthusiastically. "Geoff."

"I knew someone who prospected around here." Conny kept her face relaxed, not wanting to give away the lie. "I was just wondering if your claim was close to my friend's. Was it on the creek?"

"I'm not sure." He pointed to the top of the clay cliff behind them, which reflected the golden hues of the bonfire. "Up there. I think. My cousin's going to tell me more tomorrow night. We're meeting for supper…I didn't know anything about this part of my history."

As Conny lowered her glance from the cliffs, she caught sight of an old man whose gaze followed where the longhair had pointed. She recognized him from the inn, where she worked as a chambermaid. She'd seen him in the lounge sometimes when she stopped for a drink after her supper. Tom, the bartender, had pointed him out as a Friday-night regular and said he always ordered a glass of wine—white, always white—and sat by himself at one of the corner tables.

She watched him turn and walk into the darkness.

"Where does your friend have a claim?"

Conny turned back to the longhair and laughed. "Not here!" She paused to take a sip of her beer. "So, what are you going to do with the claim?"

"Not sure. My cousin thinks we should sell it. There's a new interest in the area. He heard Japan was buying our copper and gold. And there is a BC company with a new way of processing the black sand of Wreck Bay."

Conny looked him over. He was very attractive, if you liked the surf-bum type. Tendrils of soft, doe-coloured hair curled around his face invitingly. "You don't look like someone who'd be interested in business."

"Hey, man, that's cool. No judgment." He reached out and poked a finger at her hair. The double layer of hairspray she had applied that morning resisted any attempt at damage his finger might do. "You don't look like someone who would be interested in the beach." He withdrew his finger, grinning.

Conny stared at him, unsure if his remark and gesture were meant as an insult. She thought about her own recent venture into business and how much she was depending on its success. She'd only recently started selling drugs, but her new boyfriend and supplier had promised big returns. She was counting on those returns to get her away from the small-town culture she was drowning in. She wanted to move to Hollywood and live the life she'd dreamed of since she was old enough to buy movie magazines.

After Geoff's very animated storytelling, he quieted right down. His audience offered a few good luck wishes as they dispersed and blended with the general party goers. She reached into her pocket and pulled out a blotter of acid, holding it so Geoff could see. "Do you want to score?"

Geoff shook his head. "No, man. I don't do that stuff." He turned and walked away, weaving slightly.

Conny watched him go, then glanced up at the cliffs and wondered where exactly his claim was. When she turned back to see if he was still close by, he had disappeared.

Sandy rolled over, pulling up the sleeping bag to block out the morning chill creeping up the shoreline. She didn't want to get up yet, but her bladder was insistent. She wiggled deeper into the sleeping bag, trying to distract her body from the urgent ache. She didn't want to walk into the surrounding bush alone. Last night, people were awake and partying when she discovered the reason for the shovels stuck in the sand and the reality of camping rough on the beach.

She peeked out of the sleeping bag and then sat up. A fog had settled on the beach, softening the darkness. She looked back at the cliffs, where a faint glow was starting to show over the forest crowning them. She couldn't see much further than the other side of the damp and blackened campfire pit, but she could tell that a few of the people who had gathered around the fire the night before had found sleep where they'd sat.

Sandy turned her attention back to her own situation and reached into the depths of the sleeping bag, feeling for the wristwatch she'd taken off. When she found it, she pulled it out and buckled it to her wrist. *Five o'clock.* She groaned. Too early for any of last night's partiers to be awake.

From the steady snoring coming from within the lean-to a short distance from the fire, Mark was still very much asleep. She wondered what had happened to the flashlight he had left leaning against the side of the entry. She glanced around but couldn't see it. Not that it would do much good in the thick fog. She reached to the bottom of the sleeping bag again, this time to retrieve her poncho. She slipped it over her peasant blouse. She'd shed her skirt during the night, finding it too uncomfortable to sleep in. She wiggled out of the warmth of the sleeping bag, stretched her stiff muscles, and then considered how to brave the cluster of bushes at the bottom of the cliffs—and the dig-and-bury option hidden within.

She was tired and dirty, and her skin itched as if a thousand sand fleas had feasted on her. She wanted a shower, but the closest was at the end of a very long, lonely walk to the inn.

She searched for her moccasins. They were nowhere to be seen, so she slipped on a pair of sandals she found by the edge of the dead campfire.

The fog-shrouded bush lining the beach looked forbidding. She turned toward the surf, which she could hear but could only see hints of white foam reflecting the weak sun rising slowly over the trees at the top of the cliffs behind her. Fog drifted in whisps across the expanse of sand exposed by a low tide. It was far enough away that maybe she could have a pee and get clean all at once. It would be better than walking into a forest filled with the refuse of last night's partiers. Not all who ventured to the beach respected the dig-and-bury courtesy, leaving the provided shovels unused.

She glanced around quickly. Everyone was asleep. *Dare I?* Sandy quickly slipped out of the sandals, her poncho, shirt and underwear. The cool mist chilled her as she stood naked on the beach. Taking a deep breath, she ran across the sand, feeling crazy and brave at the same time, not slowing even when her feet splashed through the icy surf.

She kept pushing forward until she was waist-deep in the water. It gently rocked her, forcing her to quickly step backward or forward to keep her balance. Gradually, her body released the pressure in her bladder, and she relaxed. The rising sun shone on the rippled, surging surf playing peek-a-boo with the fog. *Why aren't I scared? I should be scared.* Instead, her senses expanded and she closed her eyes. The mist's moisture beaded on her lips, her hair danced with the teasing breeze, and her nipples hardened with the chill of the rocking surf.

A rogue wave rode that surf silently toward her. Sandy opened her eyes as it crested. It hit her hard, plunged her backward, and dragged her along in its churning response to the moon's demand that it reach the shore. When it let her go, she crawled up the beach, the retreating surf sucking the sand from under her knees.

Slowly, she gained control and stood, her legs weak. Forcing herself to move, she started slowly up the beach, just as a figure emerged from the fog at the top of the beach. She stopped. "Geoff!"

The figure made no move to acknowledge her call, walking across the beach and disappearing among the swirling clouds of fog drifting on the morning breeze. Unnerved, Sandy stumbled up to Mark's campsite. She slipped first the peasant blouse, then the poncho, over her damp skin. Rummaging through the sleeping bag, she found her denim skirt and used it to quickly dry the rest of her body. She was suddenly anxious to be dressed before anyone else woke. With the skirt finally wrapped and buttoned around her waist, she took a deep breath, appreciating the comfort and warmth her clothes provided.

Looking across the beach to an ocean bejewelled by the dawn, a shiver went through her, as did a new respect for the power behind the beauty. She turned away and looked toward the trail head, wondering if her mind had played tricks. If the figure had been Geoff, why hadn't he responded to her call? If it hadn't been Geoff, then where was he?

She glanced across the beach, unsure if she should venture into the swirling mists that floated around and over the sleeping partiers. *Where is he?* She hadn't seen him since he'd left Mark's campsite the previous evening. She had spent the evening chatting with Mark and a few others who had joined his campfire. Evening had deepened into night, and the night had grown noisier as more and more people joined the party.

She had walked the beach a couple of times looking for Geoff but hadn't found him. Without him or his key, she couldn't get her stuff out of his van, so she had returned to Mark's campsite, where a heated discussion on the validity of the Vietnam peace talks drew her attention for a while. Mark brought out his sleeping bag for her to crawl into, and she had fallen asleep with her head in his lap and the debate raging around her.

Maybe Geoff had returned to his van without her. She looked up at the forest's edge and shivered. The fog still clung to the ground, making the area feel creepy. Her decision to come now seemed rash. She turned, gradually taking in her surroundings. The sand was littered with garbage, and the air was filled with the stench of human waste. *Is this really what I want?*

When she'd decided to run away to the hippie haven of Wreck Bay, she hadn't expected the area to be so far away from everything, nor had she anticipated the depth of darkness at night. Back in the city, the light of the street lamps always guided her home after dark—or to the welcome security of a taxi.

She pulled her purse out of the sleeping bag. The suede pouch and fringe were undamaged. A quick glance around the campsite confirmed that the matching moccasins were nowhere nearby. She hoped exposure to the sea air and fog hadn't damaged the soft leather, but when she found them behind a log by the next campsite, water-stained and half-buried in the sand, they were obviously ruined. Another decision she hadn't thought through. Like the purse, the moccasins were an impulse purchase after seeing a model in a magazine fashion section wearing similar items. She thought they would suit her new hippie lifestyle. She couldn't have been more wrong.

After picking up the moccasins, she drained the sand and tried to force her foot into the hardened leather. She stifled a cry as it pinched her foot. The fog had begun to lift, but the sand was still wet. She decided to carry the moccasins and started walking along the beach, her eyes scanning over the clusters of people who had spent the night on the beach. *Where are you, Geoff?*

Sandy returned to Mark's camp and gathered up his sleeping bag, frustrated at not being able to find Geoff after an hour of searching. She did, however, get a tip from a camper on how to revive her moccasins until they were flexible enough to wear. They were still ruined, but at least they would protect her feet until she got to the inn.

"Are you off?" came Mark's groggy voice from inside his lean-to.

Sandy walked to the entrance, knelt, and peered inside. Mark, hair standing out every which way, sat up on his makeshift bed, the blanket sliding down to reveal a well-muscled chest with a light covering of dark curls.

"I'm going to check if Geoff's at his van. I've checked the beach but didn't find him." Sandy paused and then added, "I'm going to head back to Victoria."

"Wow. I hope we didn't scare you off with last night's party." Mark's eyes clouded with concern. "The weekends tend to be a bit crazy with all the tourists and townies coming out, but during the week it's pretty chill and laid-back. Why don't you stay?"

Sandy shook her head. Whatever she had been looking for when she left Victoria, she hadn't found it on the beach. "Thanks for loaning me your sleeping bag."

"Let me walk you out. The path's still a bit dark under the trees, and cougars and wolves prowl the area."

Sandy turned away, afraid her face would give away her surprise, her naivety. Yet another stupid mistake. She hadn't considered the possibility of wild animals along the path. When she'd walked it the afternoon before, the forest had seemed friendly, hiding nothing more sinister than a mouse or two. But then, she'd been focused on Geoff and the beach they were looking for. Once she gathered herself, she faced Mark. "Thanks."

Mark slipped into a flannel shirt as he half-crawled out of his lean-to. "Are you going to hitch back to Victoria today?"

"I was thinking about it." Sandy stepped back to give Mark space to stand.

"We should check at the Wick first. If someone there has to make a run down to Port for supplies, or something, maybe you could catch a ride."

"The Wick? Port?"

Mark laughed. "The hotel you parked beside. The Wickaninnish Inn. Everyone calls it the Wick. And Port is Port Alberni."

"Oh." His laughter and smile unnerved her, and she lowered her gaze. She was afraid he'd see how attracted to him she'd been the night before, how protected she'd felt with her head on his thigh and his arm cradling her. The memory caused her body to respond as if to a chill quite different from the one she'd experienced during her morning battle with the ocean.

Mark had grown quiet, causing Sandy to look up. He took her hand and started toward the path that would take them to the inn.

5.

When Sandy and Mark emerged from the dense rainforest close to an hour later, the sun cast a rosy gold light on the fog still hanging low over the beach stretching on three sides of the inn, bringing the white foam of the surf into sharp focus. Sandy caught her breath, overwhelmed by an edge-of-the-Earth feeling; the inn looked very much like a magic castle guarding its kingdom. At that moment, she couldn't think of a place she would rather be.

Mark broke the spell. "Where's Geoff's van?"

Sandy pointed at the wildly painted vehicle with a surfboard strapped to its roof and marched over, determined to pound on the doors loud enough to wake the dead. Then she stopped. "It's been moved," she said. "It was closer to the inn when Geoff parked it yesterday."

Mark walked up beside her. "Are you sure?"

"Yes!" Sandy glared at Mark. "He scared me. He parked so close to the edge, I thought he was going to drive right over it. The drop to the beach was right in front of it." She indicated the wide patch of beach grass presently in front of the van. "This is not where we were parked yesterday."

"Maybe he went for a drive last night."

Sandy walked around the van. The inside window curtains were still drawn like they'd been the afternoon before. She tried peeking between them, but she couldn't see inside the back.

"So, he's camperized it?" Mark asked.

"He told me he bought it like this in Vancouver." Sandy continued to circle the van, knocking on the windows as she went. "Geoff! Open up!" No response. When she came to the passenger door, she paused her pounding. Through the window, she saw her bikini laying on top of her backpack. She had left it hanging on the door's mirror. She had also left her backpack sitting on the driver's seat. It now sat on the passenger seat. She couldn't see her sleeping bag. She tried the door. Locked. She stood on her toes to see if she could see into the back of the van, but the curtains behind the front seats had been drawn.

"Must be a heavy sleeper," Mark said. He moved to the side doors and tried opening them.

"Everything's locked up," Sandy said.

Mark pounded on the panel of a door. "Hey! If you're in there, open up!"

The only answer was the screech of an eagle circling above them.

"Damn it, open up! I need my stuff!" Sandy beat her fist on the side window.

Mark grabbed her hands, but Sandy pulled away.

"You could hurt yourself if you break the glass," he said.

Sandy turned away, not wanting him to see her so close to tears. "I just want my stuff."

"Maybe he's having breakfast at the inn," Mark suggested. "I know I've been able to get a coffee before they open at eight."

Of course. Sandy felt like a fool and took a quick peek at her wristwatch. *Seven-thirty.* "Let's try." She turned and headed toward the inn's front entry.

Mark followed. They found only a handful of people in the dining room; Geoff wasn't among them.

"He must still be down on the beach somewhere," Mark reasoned.

"I checked." Sandy slumped into a chair. "I need my stuff, Mark."

Mark put his hand on her shoulder. "How about we have a coffee and maybe some toast? Afterward, I'll help you get into the van."

Clouds of mist clung to the ground as Sandy walked the road leading up the hill, away from Long Beach. After their coffee, she and Mark had broken into Geoff's van using a wire coat hanger provided by the front desk clerk. Geoff was not inside.

Sandy grabbed her backpack, stuffed her bikini and purse inside. She had not found her sleeping bag. Bidding Mark a quick farewell she set off.

When she reached the top of the hill, the mist drifted lazily across the road. The sun sent beams of light between the trees that flashed like strobe lights against the side of her face as she walked. Though warm on her cheeks, the sun hadn't warmed the air enough to disperse the mist or for her to remove her poncho. She tried not to get spooked as the mist shifted into banks of thick fog that enveloped her like a blanket, muffling sound and blocking the sun. Each time she walked out of the fog, she searched the edges of the cleared landscape for clues as to how far she'd travelled, but although the air was clearer and the sun fought hard to encourage her, she soon lost all sense of direction.

Reaching down to gather her poncho closer for comfort as well as to fend off the chill, Sandy considered turning back. Then she spotted something in the water-filled ditch. At first, she thought it was a bundle of abandoned clothes. Venturing closer, her mind gradually made sense of what her eyes were telling it. The bundle of clothes became lumps separated by water reflecting a veiled sun. She recognized the curve of an ear, the soft down at the nape of a neck, and the caramel shade of the hair floating in the water. Geoff was lying on his stomach, his face turned away from her and his body partially submerged in the dirty ditch water.

"Oh, god!" Sandy dropped her backpack and stumbled into the ditch. She sank to mid-shin in icy, muddy water. She grabbed his arm and pulled. The action unbalanced her, and she fell back against the bank with Geoff's head and shoulders resting in her lap. "Geoff! Geoff!"

He lay face-up, unmoving and cold.

She brushed his hair away from his neck and searched for a pulse, wishing she had paid more attention during the first-aid classes she had taken in high school. She could find nothing. "Geoff! Geoff, wake up!"

He remained silent. She lifted his wrist, searching for a pulse. None. She tried his neck again. Still none.

"Geoff, please, please, please," she murmured as she slapped his cheeks. Half crying, she brushed the wet hair from his face. "Please wake—"

His half-open eyes stared up at her with spooky cloudiness. Stifling a scream, she scrambled out from under him and away from his stare, leaving him to slip partially back into the ditch.

The sound of a car approaching brought her to her feet, her scream no longer locked in her throat.

6.

RCMP Corporal David Moore tilted his head to the left to release the tension in his neck before leaning back over the steering wheel, squinting through the shifting patches of fog floating across the road. He and his constable were searching for the scene of a reported hit-and-run on Long Beach Road.

"It's got to be around here somewhere," Constable Halden Evans moaned. "They said it was about a mile off the Tofino–Ucluelet Highway."

A ghost light appeared out of the fog, waving back and forth, with the spectral form of a man backlit by a larger, harsher light. Moore slammed on the brakes, tossing Evans forward.

"Jesus!" Evans cursed, shifting back into his seat. He rubbed the arm he'd stretched out to keep his head from striking the windshield.

Both men looked out as the ghostly form solidified into a human. "Boy, am I glad to see you!" it shouted.

Moore motioned for the man to lower the beam of his flashlight. Once he did, Moore could make out the scene behind him. A dark blue vehicle was parked at an angle across the road, blocking any oncoming traffic approaching the scene from the beach. The back door was open, revealing a young woman sitting on the edge of the seat, a grey poncho clutched tightly around her, and a barefoot peeking from beneath the hem of a denim maxiskirt. She was staring off to his left where the vehicle's headlights revealed the top half of a body lying on the side of the road. The bottom, Moore hoped, was just shrouded by the thick fog.

Halden picked up the handset. "Dispatch, we've arrived."

Moore turned to Evans. "Ask how far away Constable Nelson is. We need a roadblock at the top of this road as soon as possible. We don't want anyone coming down here and landing on top of us!"

After asking the man to step away from the patrol car, Moore backed away from the scene and parked at an angle, blocking the road. Leaving the lights on to warn any drivers coming down the road from the Tofino–Ucluelet Highway, he turned off the siren, grabbed his flashlight, and exited the vehicle. "I'm Corporal David Moore of the Ucluelet detachment."

The man accepted Moore's hand and gave his name as Ian Walker.

"Very well, Mr. Walker. How are you involved with this?"

"Oh! Not at all. My wife and I were just on our way out for breakfast, when this young woman flagged us down. She told us to go to the inn and call the police, as there'd been an awful accident." He pointed to the body by the side of the road. "As you can see, the young man died. I'm glad I dropped the wife at the bungalow resort we're staying at next to the inn. She—my wife—would not have been able to handle this."

So, not a participant then. Moore asked for his contact information and dismissed him when he saw his constable approaching. "What do you have, Evans?"

"Nelson should be here any moment, sir."

"Good. We need that roadblock." He lowered his voice. "I'll go check on the victim and you"—gesturing toward the girl in the car—"talk to her." A shiver rippled through the girl, and she pulled her poncho tighter around her shoulders. "But before that, move her to the patrol car and get a blanket from the trunk. She's cold."

Evans nodded and turned toward the girl. "Come on, let's get you somewhere warmer."

Moore strode to where the victim lay, relieved to see that the bottom half was indeed still attached to the top, though from the knees down, it was submerged in ditch water. Pulling out his notebook, Moore surveyed the scene, sketching it as he walked. He found no skid marks or broken glass. The ditch was narrow and deep, filled with grass and bordered by bush. The fog still danced across the surface and clung in clumps to the far bank.

Kneeling, Moore noted that the victim's clothing and hair were damp. When he did a quick check for a pulse, the skin was cold. The lack of a pulse didn't surprise him, as one look into the clouded eyes told him the man was dead. Still, the scene felt off. He'd only worked one other hit-and-run case, and that had been back in Alberta when he was first starting out and too green to ask questions; he now wished he had. That victim had been a ten-year-old boy hit while riding his bike home from an afternoon spent at a friend's farm. He had ended up in a wide, shallow, hay-filled prairie ditch. His body had looked much different than this one; the trauma had been evident. Moore scanned the body in front of him but spotted no visible trauma. Maybe the size of the victim was the difference; the man's body able to absorb the impact. Or maybe the difference was in the impact itself. The boy's body had taken a full-on hit. Perhaps this man was only clipped by a car's side mirror.

Moore lifted the victim's right-side hip to access his back pocket and found the jeans not just damp, but wet. He reached into the pocket and pulled out the victim's wallet. Flipping open the wet leather revealed waterlogged bills, two twenties and a fiver. A small piece of equally waterlogged paper was plastered against the back of a California driver's licence, a smudged note with what might have been an address written across its front. The licence identified the young man as Geoff Turner, 22. But when Moore checked the University of California student card, showing a similar photo, he found a different name, Geoff Johnston. Closing the wallet, Moore stood and crossed to where Evans was tucking a blanket around the girl sitting in the backseat of the patrol car.

"He's dead." Moore handed him the wallet. "Call the Tofino office and ask them to look up his next of kin. There's two different IDs in there; one is obviously a fake. My bet is the driver's licence, so tell them to try the university first. They should have a next of kin on file."

Evans rose. "This is Sandra Chambers."

"Sandy," she corrected.

"Yes, of course. Sandy." Evans glanced at the girl, then returned his focus to Moore. "She said she discovered him while she was walking along the road, coming from the inn."

Moore waited for the girl to add a comment, but she had closed her eyes. He was unsure if it was an attempt to shut him out or gather strength. "Did she see who hit him?"

"No."

"Did she see any cars on the road before or after she found the victim?"

"His name's Geoff." The girl, whose eyes were now open, cut in. "I didn't see any cars except the one I flagged down."

"Do you know him?" Moore indicated Walker, now sitting behind the steering wheel of his car.

"Him? No."

"Right then. Thanks." Moore turned from the girl, waving Evans away. "Go radio Tofino." Then he changed his mind. "Hold on a minute. When you're done with Tofino, grab my camera out of the trunk and record as much as you can from the scene. With any luck, there'll be skid marks or headlight glass somewhere." He frowned at the fog. "The driver probably thought he hit a deer or a dog and kept on driving."

Leaving Evans to deal with the girl, Moore headed once more across to her guardian angel. "Okay, Mr. Walker, I'm sending you back to your wife." The man appeared reluctant to go. Moore wondered if it was genuine concern for the girl or a desire to be seen as part of the team. Probably the latter. He took his arm and walked Walker toward his car before firmly instructing him to leave.

Moore slid into the driver's seat and adjusted the rear-view mirror so he could see the girl in the backseat. Wrapped in the blanket, her hair hanging in a damp, tangled mess, and her face free of make up she appeared vulnerable. Tears tracked down her cheeks. "Did you know him?"

She looked up and quickly wiped the tears from her cheek. "Yes," she said. Then stopped. "No." She looked back at him through the mirror and Moore was struck by the deep blue of her eyes, dark like wet denim, set off by brows that ran straight as if a felt marker had been used to slash a golden streak across the top of both eyes.

"He gave me a ride from Port Alberni yesterday," she explained. "I didn't know him before that."

Not local, then. He pulled his notebook from his breast pocket. "You were hitchhiking?"

"Yes. First time." She turned away and looked out the window. "I don't understand."

Moore followed her gaze to Evans, now kneeling beside the body as his camera's flash froze moments in time. "Accidents are like that."

"I know *that*," she snapped, facing him again. "What I don't understand is why he was *here*. If he had to go somewhere, why didn't he take his van?"

"His van?" Moore twisted in his seat to look at her. "What van?"

"The one he was driving yesterday. The one he picked me up in."

Of course. Hitchhiking. Moore shook his head. He should have caught that. "Do you know where his van is now?"

"It was at the inn the last I saw."

Moore straightened in his seat so he faced forward. Evans was now walking along the road, searching its edges, taking pictures as best he could in the fog. Moore looked back at the body. He hadn't found keys in the pockets when he'd looked for identification. He tossed his notebook on the passenger seat, opened the door, and called Evans over. "You haven't seen a set of keys, have you?"

"Keys?"

Moore twisted around to look at Sandy. "What type of van?"

"A camper. Volkswagen."

"Colour?"

"All sorts. The painting was roughly done." She closed her eyes. "The main background colour was a powder blue. There were bright yellow sunflowers painted near the back, and the words peace and love in bold red and pink along the one side. Left, I think. Yes, left. And a hand giving the peace sign on the other side." Opening her eyes, she half smiled. "Geoff told me he thought it'd been painted during a party when everyone was high. It was kind of ugly, but he said he didn't care. He'd bought it because the inside had been beautifully done."

Moore turned to Evans. "Did you get that?"

"Yeah."

Moore glanced around. "Does it look like the fog is lifting a bit? Or am I imagining things?"

"It does seem to be thinning, sir. Do you think Constable Nelson will be long?"

As if summoned by the mention of his name, the sound of a siren announced the constable's approach from the top of the road. "Here he is now," Moore announced.

A moment later, Constable Monty Nelson pulled his patrol car behind Moore's. Evans waved and called out to

Nelson as he exited his vehicle. "Good to see you! I feared the corporal was about to leave me in the dark."

"Nelson!" Moore cut into the banter. "Turn around. I told dispatch I wanted you to set up a roadblock. I don't want anyone coming down this road and landing on top of us or messing up the scene before the coroner gets here."

Chastised, Nelson lost his grin. "Sorry, sir. I thought I should check in first." After dropping back into his patrol car, he turned it around and sped off.

The mention of the van unsettled Moore. *Why was the victim walking on the road when he had a vehicle at the inn?* He paused to gather his thoughts. "Okay," he said. "The coroner should be here soon. I'm going to take Miss Chambers back to the inn. I'll set up an interview room there. You and Nelson come down as soon as the coroner finishes up here." He waved and rolled up the window before retrieving the radio handset and pressing the release. "Dispatch?"

"Yes?"

"Get a tow truck out to the Wickaninnish Inn as soon—"

"You found the suspect's vehicle?"

"No!" Moore scowled. "Just tell the driver to find me when he gets there." He was about to sign off when he changed his mind. "Is the coroner on his way?"

"He said so, sir."

With a sigh, Moore signed off and glanced again at the young woman in his back seat. Fresh tears glistened on her cheeks. He reached under the passenger seat for the canvas bag he'd stuffed there that morning, pulled out a thermos of coffee, and passed it back to her. "Here.

This'll help to warm you up." Noticing how her hands shook as she poured the hot liquid, he turned his attention to getting them to the inn, a short mile down the road.

"Right then, Miss Chambers, when we arrive, I'm going to ask that you stay in the car while I run inside to organize things. When I come out, you need to tell me how you ended up walking along this road."

She shifted in the seat. "I was going home."

Her voice was clear and strong. All trace of the earlier emotion and tears had gone. "And where's that?" he asked.

"Victoria."

"How did you intend to get there?"

"Hitchhiking, once I got to the main highway."

"In this fog? The cars would have been on top of you before they'd even seen you!"

A sob burst from the girl, and she turned away from his gaze. Moore groaned. "I'm sorry, Miss Chambers—Sandy. I shouldn't have shouted. It's just that hitchhiking is dangerous enough without trying to do it in the fog."

"It wasn't this bad when I left the inn."

He shifted back into driving position. "Well, now you know how quickly things can change on the coast." He put the car in gear and pulled away from the scene.

The fog had definitely started to lift. Visibility had improved, leaving a good portion of the forest around them and a fair distance of road ahead clear, allowing Moore to increase his speed. Glancing in the rear-view mirror, he ventured, "Mr. Turner wasn't giving you a ride back?"

"Do you mean Geoff?"

"Yes, Geoff." *So, she didn't know his last name.* Moore wondered if Geoff had deliberately withheld his full name, or if it was just an example of the informality of the younger generation.

"No, he said he was staying for the summer. He also said he was looking for a friend from California he thought was surfing up here."

"Did he meet that friend?"

"I don't know."

"So, you weren't with him last night?"

"No."

"You weren't with him at all last night?"

Her eyes met his in the mirror. "Well, yes. I was with him for the afternoon, but when we got to Wreck Bay, he went off with some Frisbee players and I didn't see him till later."

"Later that afternoon or evening?"

"Evening."

"So, where were you during the afternoon?"

Her pause drew his eyes to the rear-view mirror again. She had turned to look out the side window. When she realized he was watching her, she met his gaze. "We checked out the main beach and then his van."

Moore understood the inference; the new generation's casual attitude toward sex baffled him. "What did you do while Geoff was playing Frisbee with his new friends?"

"I explored the beach. Then I was offered supper at a campfire."

"Do you have the name of the person who offered you supper?"

"Mark."

"Last name?"

"He didn't tell me."

Moore refocused on the road, slowing for the curved descent to beach level. He took the left-hand turn onto the inn's driveway, which led up a short rise to a wide, gravelled front entry. He pulled to the side and parked before turning to face Sandy. "I'll be right back."

7.

When Moore pushed through the Wickaninnish Inn's lobby door, the crowd inside turned as one to face him and went silent. "Good morning, everyone. I'm Corporal David Moore of the Ucluelet detachment. As you know by now, there has been a serious accident on the road out to the highway, and the road has been closed until things are cleared up. In the meantime, I need to speak with anyone who travelled that road late last night or early this morning. If you could leave your name at the front desk, I'll speak to you as soon as I can."

"What about the bus?" A young woman with a clipboard stepped out of the crowd. "It's already ten-thirty! We have a tour group waiting to leave and another arriving soon."

"Once the road is opened, I'm sure things will proceed as they need to."

"How long?"

"It's hard to say. I would suggest your group make use of the extra time to enjoy this beautiful setting."

Moore crossed to the office and asked the clerk for a spare room he could use for interviews. She passed him a key and gave him directions to the main-floor room. He thanked her and slipped back through the crowded lobby and out the door, ignoring the questions shouted after him.

Moore was happy to see that Sandy had remained in the vehicle. Taking a deep breath, he picked up his notebook and turned to face her. "I agree with you, Miss Chambers. It does seem strange that Geoff was on the road without his van. Can you think of any reason he would leave his vehicle behind?"

A frown creased her brow. "All I can think of is that somehow the man he met left him on the road. Or he was walking back from wherever he ended up."

Moore nodded. Both were possible. "Let's go back to when you were offered supper. You mentioned you saw Geoff later. Where?"

"At Mark's campfire. He came around six or seven. We'd just finished eating. He asked if we had any food. The only thing left was pan bread, which he ate. Then we just sat and listened. Everyone was discussing the peace talks."

"Everyone? There were others at the campsite?"

"Yes. About five or six. They just started dropping in after supper."

"Did you know any of them?"

"No."

"Did you hear Mark call any of them by name?"

Sandy shook her head, then stopped. "Yes. I remember there were two guys he introduced me to when they came to pick up their meal. Neal and Jim. But only Jim came back after supper. I don't know his last name. He had very long hair, dark, almost black."

"So, when did Geoff meet the man you mentioned?" Moore found this part of his job a bit frustrating. The endless questions. He glanced back at her; she seemed to be waiting for him. He repeated the question.

"I said a little after seven." She seemed to recognize his frustration because she didn't wait for the next question.

"A guy who had been playing Frisbee with Geoff earlier came up and told him that someone was asking around and wanted to meet up with him. So, he left."

"Geoff left with the Frisbee guy?"

"Yes."

"Did you go?"

"No."

"Did you see where he went?"

"Yes. I wanted to keep an eye on him because I still needed to get my stuff out of his van."

"You left your stuff in his van?"

"Yes."

So, she intended to see him again. "Where did he go?"

"I stood up so I could see above the people sitting on the other side of the campfire. He went down the beach a way and stopped on the other side of the stack of wood they were building for a bonfire. They met the guy there. The messenger left."

"Did you recognize the man Geoff met with?"

"No."

"Can you describe him?"

She closed her eyes. "He was big, bigger than Geoff in height and weight. I think he was wearing a jean jacket, jeans. He looked like a logger. Not a hippie, for sure."

"Could you tell what they were doing?"

"Just talking, then they walked away."

"Where?"

"I don't know. It was very crowded on the beach, and by then the bonfire had been lit, attracting a lot of people."

"Did you see him again?"

"No. There were so many people. Once the sun set it was quite dark, it was hard to tell who was who. The campfires lit the people sitting around them, and there were a few lanterns, but people were moving from campfire to campfire. He could have come back to the beach, and I wouldn't have known."

"Did you leave your contact information with Constable Evans?"

"Yes."

Moore considered the information she had given him before closing his notebook. It supported the hit-and-run scenario if Geoff was walking back from a meeting with the man he met, who was probably the friend he'd been looking for. "Right then. That'll be all for now." Moore got out of the patrol car and opened the backseat door. When she held up his thermos, he told her to leave it on the seat. She shed the blanket and gathered her backpack, which had slipped down onto the floor behind the passenger seat. The grey poncho had slipped over one shoulder, exposing a hint of white cotton underneath, but it was her bare feet peeking out from under a still-wet denim maxiskirt that caught his attention. "Are you going to be okay?"

"Yes."

He shook his head as she stepped out onto the gravelled driveway. She caught him looking and stood straighter. "The ditch water was pretty awful, and the mud sucked my moccasins right off my feet."

Moccasins? Why would anyone bring soft leather shoes to a beach? Then he froze. *She was in the ditch!* He grabbed her arm to stop her leaving and pulled her against him. Embarrassed, he released her. "Sorry. Are you okay?"

"Yes. Yes." Sandy leaned against the hood of the car and sent him a puzzled look.

"I just thought of a question I should have asked." Moore paused. "What'd you do when you found him?"

"I don't understand."

"Your clothes are wet. His clothes are wet. He was in the ditch when you found him, not on the side of it?"

"Yes. I thought he might still be alive."

"And you jumped in to try and save him?"

"Yes."

"Damn!"

Sandy jumped at his outburst.

"Sorry. Sorry." He reached out and patted her arm, trying to reassure her. "Everything's fine." Shaking his head, he started to walk away, mumbling, "I saw, but I didn't see."

"What?"

Moore waved away her question. "Nothing. I made a stupid mistake." He had assumed that she had found the body in the position it was in when he and Halden had arrived. Pulling his notebook from his pocket, he asked, "Was he face-up or face-down?"

"Down. That's what panicked me. I wanted to get him out of the water. But as soon as I dragged him out I saw his eyes, and I knew he was dead."

"So, you didn't attempt reviving him?"

"No. His eyes were all cloudy. They totally creeped me out!"

"What'd you do after bringing him out of the water?"

She hesitated and Moore looked up from his note-taking. "Miss?"

Taking a deep breath, she raised her eyes to his. "I'm ashamed to say I let go of him and he slid partway back into the ditch."

"Where we found him?"

"Yes."

"Right then. Thanks, Miss Chambers."

He watched her leave until the low rumble of an engine revving to take the slight rise of the inn's driveway drew his attention. The tow truck he'd ordered pulled up beside him and stopped.

Tom stumbled, took a moment to right himself, and then started forward again. He couldn't remember coming in the night before. *Must've had a good time.* He squinted at the morning sun filtering through clouds riding low on the ocean. It was a short walk from the staff housing in the lodge to the inn, but his eyes were burning, making it difficult to see. Conny pounding on his door had woken him from a deep sleep a little after ten-thirty. She told him to get up and get to the inn. Why the staff were being gathered, she didn't say, but after making sure he was up, she'd left, confident he'd follow, if for no other reason than to satisfy his curiosity. He stopped to calm the wave of dizziness threatening to embarrass him in front of a cute brunette who had just exited a Dodge Charger. He offered a weak smile but didn't stick around after a very bronzed boyfriend got out of the driver's side.

As he approached the inn, he realized the gathering wasn't for a staff meeting. A police car was parked where the tour bus usually sat, an officer leaning against the hood talking with a barefooted blonde he recognized from somewhere but couldn't place. *Did I sleep through the siren?* Tom looked up the lane. No tour bus. *Where is it?* Saturday was usually the turnover day. He spotted Conny speaking with Susan from the neighbouring bungalows. He smiled but kept walking. Susan had proved a pest after he'd made the mistake of taking her out at the beginning of the season.

On entering the inn's small lobby, he found it full of guests and staff milling about. He spotted Tish, one of the chambermaids, sitting on the staircase that led to the second floor. He squeezed through the crowd and went to sit beside her, but she got up and walked away. "Tish!" he called after her. "What's going on?"

Ignoring him, she continued through the crowd to stand with the two teenaged, weekend chambermaids. He frowned. He thought they'd been getting along lately. He couldn't think of what he'd done to make Tish angry this time.

"Someone found a body on the side of the road."

Tom turned to see a man in his forties standing next to the lobby door, his suitcase leaning against his leg. He recognized him as a guest he'd served in the bar the night before. "A body?" he asked. "What body?"

"I don't know. A police officer came in and asked anyone who drove the road last night or this morning to wait to be interviewed."

Tom understood now why Conny had woken him. He pointed toward a thirty-something couple backed up against the inn's office, their hands clasped as if welded together. "Did they find the body?"

The man shook his head. "No, it was some girl." He turned to look out the glass lobby doors and pointed. "I think it was that one. The one who's walking across the driveway."

Tom moved around the man and realized he was talking about the barefooted blonde he'd passed on the way from the lodge. This time, he recognized her. She was the one he'd seen enjoying a bit of horseplay on the beach the day before with a long-haired guy in psychedelic swim trunks. He wondered if his was the body she'd discovered. "Did they say who the body was?"

"No. But the road's closed till they clear things up."

That explains the absence of the tour bus. Tom turned away from the window. "Did the police say how long that would be?"

"No."

"Thanks." Tom patted the man's shoulder and left to find a much-needed coffee.

Sandy's insides were churning to the point she was afraid they'd burst. She didn't want the embarrassment of throwing up beside the police car or in front of the crowd of people milling around the inn. Stepping gingerly, she crossed the gravel driveway toward the inn's entrance, but she had to stop and brace herself against a tree as another wave of nausea swept over her. Her backpack slipped to the ground when she closed her eyes against the vertigo. *Please, don't let me get sick here.*

Slowly opening her eyes, she glanced around, searching for some clue where the nearest toilet would be. A woman was staring at her. Sandy looked away, embarrassed. She must look a mess if she was inviting such open curiosity. She crouched down to gather her backpack, but lost focus and fell forward.

The woman who had been staring walked over and offered her a hand up. "Are you all right?"

Sandy shook her head. "I think I'm going to be sick. Bathroom?"

"Come with me."

Her rescuer took her by the arm and led her to the inn, through the double glass doors of the lobby, crowded with people all talking at once, and down a hallway. Her rescuer let go of her and pointed, indicating a door marked LADIES.

Sandy gasped a quick thank you, pushed through the door, and rushed into a cubicle. The contents of her stomach exploded into the toilet basin.

"Sorry," she mumbled to no one in particular before tearing at the toilet paper dispenser. Shredded paper filled the air, but not one full sheet appeared.

"Are you all right?"

The voice startled her. "I thought you'd be gone," she said.

"I wanted to make sure you were okay."

Flippin' hell! Sandy closed her eyes, took a deep breath, and nearly choked. Leaning forward, she spit the remains of her embarrassment into the toilet and wiped her mouth with what scraps of tissue she could gather. Standing, she flushed the toilet and exited the cubicle. The woman was standing beside the counter.

"My name's Conny," she said. "With a *Y*."

"Mine's Sandy."

Conny pulled a set of keys out of her pocket and unlocked the cabinet under the sink. Removing a towel, she set it on the counter with a small bar of soap.

Sandy quickly washed the mess from her face and hands. "I'm sorry."

"Don't worry about it."

The woman was younger than Sandy had first thought—maybe only a couple of years older than she was. Her shoulder-length, auburn hair was back combed high on the crown of her head, then swept and hairsprayed back and down to her shoulders, where a stylish flip accented her strong jaw line. Black eyeliner had been applied with a bold stroke along the lashes, framing grey-blue eyes accented by dramatically plucked eyebrows. The cake makeup she wore hid any imperfections, and dark red lipstick provided the illusion of plumpness where Sandy could see none existed.

Her own reflection revealed someone not nearly so put-together. Her strawberry-blonde hair was a tangled mess that shortened it from its usual mid-back length. She ran her fingers through it, trying to bring it into some sort of order. She glanced at Conny, then quickly back to the mirror. The contrast was stark. Her face was bare of makeup, revealing skin that had been exposed to too much sun and sand. Her un-tweezed brows formed a thick slash above her eyes with none of Conny's manicured artistry. Sandy took the towel and wiped away the evidence of her earlier tears. Conny looked so cool and calm; she'd probably never thrown up all over a hotel bathroom.

Sandy blurted, "It's just...I'd never seen a dead body before."

"It must've been awful."

"Yes, it was."

Conny glanced at her watch. "It's only eleven, not quite lunchtime, and the dining room's crazy with guests waiting for the road to open. How about I get you a tea in the lounge? Are you feeling up to that?"

"Yes, but my backpack. I need to change. This skirt is still wet—"

"Of course. Wait here."

Sandy watched her, feeling a fool for not grabbing her backpack before allowing herself to be led inside. She ran her fingers through her hair once more, and Conny reappeared with the backpack.

"Thank you!" Sandy dashed into a cubical and started stripping.

"You'll need shoes," Conny called through the door "Do you have any?"

"I lost my moccasins in the ditch by the road." Sandy stepped out from the cubicle feeling fresh in a green tie-dyed T-shirt and bell-bottomed jeans.

"I'll see what we've got in the lost and found box."

Sandy followed Conny out into the hall. "What do you do here?" Sandy asked.

"I look after the cleaning staff."

At the end of the hall they entered a dining room filled with chattering guests and bustling waitresses. Conny pushed through, ignoring the curious stares. Sandy meant to follow but her attention was caught by the sight of rolling surf viewed through a panel of windows running the length of the room.

"Are you coming?" Conny called.

"Yes!" Sandy did a quick sidestep to avoid colliding with a waitress carrying a full tray before rushing to join Conny as she descended three steps into a chalet-style lounge. Sandy gasped. An expanded view of the scene she'd witnessed in the dining room opened before her through large picture windows set along the width of the front wall and a series of smaller ones set along the far side wall. The elevated perspective offered by the pedestal of rock on which the inn sat, lowered the horizon, and expanded the sky.

"Wow," Sandy gushed. "It so different than being down on the beach."

"Yeah. We get a lot of people who come here just to sit and watch the waves."

"I can see why." Sandy turned away from the drama to face her hostess. "The sunsets must be amazing!"

"They are."

Sandy took in the rest of the room. The rustic décor gave the place a beach-hut feel. The roof trusses had been painted brown, but the chipboard wall panels had been left their natural pine colour. A large river-rock fireplace took pride of place between the entrance from the dining room and the exit to the outside deck.

Sandy ran her hands over the stones as she passed, following Conny to the bar.

"The fireplace is double-sided," explained Conny. "The outside fire is used to cook special meals, like salmon. It's quite a show for the guests"

"I bet it is." Sandy gestured toward the dining room. "Is it always so busy?"

"Today's an unusual day." Conny filled the kettle and plugged it in. "Normally, it's only open eight to nine-thirty for breakfast and twelve-thirty to two for lunch. That way the girls get a chance to clean and set up for the next meal service."

Sandy had never thought about how much would go on behind the scenes in running a restaurant. As she slipped onto a bar stool, her attention was caught by the long wood carving covering the back wall of the bar. It appeared to be telling a story, but the figures and symbols were unfamiliar to her.

Conny glanced up. "That has an interesting story."

"It's the perfect size. Was it made for the bar?"

"It was. Although it wasn't a commission. A guest made it for Robin after vacationing here."

"Robin?"

"The owner of the inn."

"Did the guest carve it here?"

"No, he went home and made it, then returned with it, complete with an explanation of the story it's telling." Conny started searching the drawers behind the bar. "There should be a copy of it somewhere. Robin made a bunch to hand out to guests because so many were asking about it." Giving up on the drawers, Conny started opening cabinets. "It tells of the meeting between Chief Wickaninnish, who is the figure in the centre, and Captain John Meares, an Englishman who traded with the Indians for otter furs, back in seventeen hundred and eighty something. There are two guards posted on either side of the chief, who are there to protect the much treasured copper kettles he received from Meares."

"Is that who the inn is named after?"

"Sort of. The bay in which the inn sits is named after the chief, as is an island up by Tofino."

"I thought the beach was called Long Beach."

"Long Beach is what the whole twelve-mile stretch of sand is called. The bay that the beach is cradled by is named Wickaninnish Bay." Conny gave up her search, unplugged the kettle, and made tea. "I don't know much about the history. The library would have books, I'm sure, if you're interested."

"Who's the artist?"

"Arthur Hardy. I think he's from Richmond."

"On the mainland? Vancouver?"

"Yeah." Conny slid a cup of tea across the bar. "I heard you knew the guy."

Momentarily confused by the change in subject, Sandy took a quick sip of her tea before answering. "I met Geoff yesterday when I was thumbing for a ride outside Port Alberni. He was very nice." Sandy rolled and unrolled the napkin she had pulled from the stack on the bar. "Polite, you know?"

Conny nodded. "I know what polite is. I just haven't experienced much of it." She poured herself a glass of water. "Don't get me wrong. Working here, I get treated right. But out there"—she waved her hand to indicate the world outside the inn—"that's another story. Loggers. Fishermen. Paving crews. Sometimes they forget how to treat a girl."

"There must be other types of guys who come up here," Sandy said, thinking of Mark.

"The longhairs? Never! No matter how polite he is, a man without a job is useless to me."

Sandy was surprised by Conny's tone. "Longhairs?"

"Hippies."

Sandy wasn't sure how to react so reached for her tea again.

Conny leaned against the back of the bar. "You didn't know the guy who died?"

"No. I guess not." Sandy inhaled the comforting scent of the beverage, trying to relax the sudden tension in her shoulders. "He gave me a ride, and we hung out a bit."

"Did you come up here to surf or vacation?"

Sandy looked across the bar at Conny, trying to figure out if she was making conversation or looking for information. "Just a break," she said. "In Victoria, where I'm from, you hear a lot about Long Beach and all the freedom. I guess I just wanted to see what it was like." A memory of Geoff running across the beach threatened to bring tears. Sandy ducked her head. *He also left you to fend for yourself. Remember that!*

"But you were leaving, weren't you? I thought I heard you were hitching back home."

"I was. How'd you know?"

"Oh," Conny said, "news travels fast here. Small town, you know."

Sandy answered with a quick bob, even though she didn't know what Conny was getting at.

"Why'd you decide to leave after only one day?"

Sandy shrugged. "I made a mistake. I've never slept rough on a beach before. At home, when I read about the hippies, their lives sounded so wonderful, so free. But last night…" Sandy scrubbed her fingernails against her skirt. They were still marked with the stains of a night spent on the beach. "I just didn't realize it would be so dirty. Or that there'd be so many bugs."

"Hey, Conny." A petite brunette, her hair in long pigtails, came through from the dining room and stepped up to the bar.

"What do you want, Tish?" Conny moved out from behind the counter.

"Another officer's shown up. The road's been opened but no one's allowed to leave until they've been interviewed. So, we've got guests who can't check out. Some are in the lobby with all their luggage; some are still in their rooms. Can you talk to the officer? It's getting too crowded in the lobby, and Bobbie's going crazy at the front desk."

Without a backward glance, Conny followed Tish out of the lounge.

8.

Tom's lack of sleep was catching up with him. He stifled a yawn as he exited the inn. After setting his coffee on a chair by the lobby doors, he pulled a cigarette pack from the inside pocket of his jacket.

"Got another one of those?"

Tom turned to see Roxanne, a waitress from the dining room, had followed him out. She was a beauty worthy of wet dreams, but she was strictly hands-off. Keeping his mind out of the gutter, he held out his pack and watched her slender fingers pull out her selection. "How'd you escape the thirsty horde?" he asked.

Roxanne laughed. "If coffee keeps them happy, I'll serve it." After removing his coffee cup from the chair and handing it to him, she sat. "I've been rushed off my feet. I needed some fresh air." She glanced at the lobby doors. "I don't think he knows I've left." She smiled up at Tom as she leaned in to put her cigarette to the flame he held out for her.

She was referring to the inn's chef, whose temper was well-known. Roxanne, with her easy-going personality, was often able to calm him. She sat with her legs crossed, the hem of her waitress uniform riding high on her thigh. Tom suspected she controlled the kitchen beast with more than her attitude. The bright orange of her cotton minidress with its tie-dyed starburst pattern suited Roxanne's dark colouring and drew more than a few admiring glances as she manoeuvred around the dining room's tables, her long braid swaying with her hips. "Have the cops talked with you yet?"

"No. I've been too busy taking care of all the people waiting their turn—or who are just plain snoopy."

"What are you doing here today? I thought you had weekends off."

"One of the girls phoned in sick."

Tom drew a deep drag off his cigarette. "I hope this doesn't take long. I've got a date tonight, and I want to make sure I get my beauty sleep."

"You look like you could use it. Where were you last night?"

"The beer parlour in Ukee. At least that's where I started out." He grinned and winked. "Then we hit Janet's."

"Well, you look rough. Who're you going out with?"

"Would you believe I can't remember?" Tom took another deep pull and then exhaled a series of smoke circles. He loved playing with the smoke as it left his mouth. It prolonged the pleasure—plus chicks seemed to find it sexy.

"Wait a minute. I think she gave me her name." He pushed himself off the wall and handed Roxanne his cigarette. Slipping his left arm out of his leather jacket, he pulled up the sleeve of his cotton shirt. "She was quite a sweet talker." He winked at Roxanne. "A very talented tongue." The raised sleeve revealed a series of smudged ink markings that ran from his wrist to the inside of his elbow. "Does that look like 'Cheryl' or 'Carol'?"

"It looks more like 'Susan' to me."

"Shit."

"Excuse me?"

Tom looked up to see an RCMP officer approaching. "Sorry," he mumbled, stepping back from Roxanne. He rolled his shirt sleeve down over his smudged arm and put his jacket back on. "I wasn't saying it to you." He was always amazed at how cops could appear out of nowhere. He turned to Roxanne and took his cigarette back.

Roxanne stood, tossed her unfinished cigarette to the ground, and crushed it out with the toe of her shoe. "Good morning, David." She smiled at the officer before turning and slipping back into the inn's lobby.

Tom noticed the officer's eyes follow Roxanne, and he grinned. "So, you know Roxanne?"

The officer's eyes hardened as he refocused on Tom, and he drew himself up, squaring his shoulders, emphasizing the slight height difference between him and Tom's five foot eleven. "That," the officer said slowly, "is none of your business."

Tom had encountered enough cops to know when not to push. Instead, he leaned back against the wall, taking a long draw on his cigarette. *Play it cool.* Last thing he wanted was to get tangled in anything that would prevent his return to West Vancouver.

The officer allowed the silence between them to stretch, but he didn't take his eyes off Tom. When he did speak, his voice was low and firm. "I'm Corporal David Moore. Who are you?"

"Tom Robinson."

The corporal nodded toward the beach stretched out to the side of the inn. "Beautiful. I'd never tire of looking at that."

Tom glanced over at the view, wondering what the cop was up to.

"Do you work here?"

Tom straightened. "Am I being interviewed?"

The cop pulled out his notebook. "I don't believe in wasting an opportunity."

"I work the bar."

"And where do you live?"

"Staff housing. The lodge."

"Where's that, sir?"

Tom looked at the officer, trying to figure out if he was joking. From Roxanne's familiarity with him, Tom had assumed he was a local. "The largest cabin in the group over there." He indicated the cluster of cabins amid the trees at the opposite end of the parking lot.

"Where were you last night?" The cop looked at Tom expectantly.

"I worked till midnight, then drove into Ucluelet, to the beer parlour." Tom dropped his cigarette to the ground and stubbed it out.

"Until what time?"

"About one-thirty, I guess. Then I went over to a friend's house." *Damn.* He hadn't meant to add that bit.

"Who and where was that, Mr. Robinson?"

Maybe his bringing it up was better than the cop finding out through some other source and wondering why Tom hadn't told him upfront. "Janet's in Ucluelet." Tom gave the officer Janet's address. The officer gave no indication that he knew the name or the address, even though Tom figured he was probably familiar with it. Janet's was not a place you dropped in for tea and an evening of social gossip. You came with a pocket full of cash and left with a baggie of weed and maybe a little extra something.

"How long were you there?"

Pulling another cigarette out of his package, Tom offered the pack to the officer, who shook his head. Tom lit his and took a quick pull. This time, he let the smoke exit in a soft, slow cloud. "I'm not sure," he said, "I didn't keep track. Is it important?"

The cop looked up from his notebook, his brown eyes boring into Tom's. "A young man lost his life, so yes, I'd say it's important." He paused. "I'm speaking with anyone who travelled that road over the last few hours. I was told you had. Did you come back last night or this morning?"

Tom felt chastised and reacted defensively. "Sometime this morning. Probably around three, three-thirty. That's usually when I get back from a night in town."

The officer's eyes left Tom's, focusing on the notes written on his pad. "Did you drive yourself?"

"Y-yes." Tom froze, mad at himself for stammering. He hadn't been ready for that question. "I usually do."

"I'm not interested in what you usually do. I asked what you did."

"I drove."

The sound of a call coming over the radio in the patrol car caused the officer to pause his note-taking before continuing. "What type of vehicle do you drive?"

Tom frowned. "Shouldn't you get that?"

"Just answer the question, sir."

"A '64 Mustang."

"Did you notice anything unusual on the road?"

"No."

"No one on the road? Nothing unusual?"

"No."

The corporal closed his notebook and gave one quick bob of his head. "Okay, sir. We need you to stay in the area until we've completed our investigation."

Tom remained where he was for a moment after the corporal left. Then, he crushed out his cigarette and headed to the lodge, worried about the lies he had just told. The trouble was, he couldn't remember anything after he had walked to Janet's and taken that first drink— or was it after a hit? Janet always supplied top-of-the-line drugs, never any slicing and dicing. He couldn't blame his lack of memory on a bad trip, could he? He could feel a difference in the hangover.

Though he'd said that he hadn't noticed anything unusual on the road, he couldn't even remember coming back to the beach, let alone anything he might have seen on the way. He must have driven, yet he couldn't remember doing so. His black Mustang sat in the lane beside the lodge as if to taunt him. He needed to find out how he had made it back to the inn, and he needed to find out fast. But how? Janet wouldn't be up yet. She rarely rose before late afternoon.

A vague image teased the edges of his memory, pushing hard at the fog clouding his brain. When it cleared, he turned back to the inn.

Sandy lingered at the bar, uncertain of what to do. Conny had not returned after leaving with Tish. Sandy didn't want to go out to the lobby for fear that the crowd would crush her bare feet. She pushed her tea away and was about to leave when a sound made her look up.

"Hello."

A man about her own age came in from the dining room and slipped behind the bar. Setting his coat on a hook, he turned and looked at her expectantly.

"Sorry," she mumbled, sliding off her stool. "I was just leaving."

"Wait. You don't have to go. I'm just a little late for my shift. You can keep me company while I get the bar ready." Reaching for her teacup, he smiled. "Conny told me you'd be here. Why don't I get you a fresh cup?"

With the carpet tickling her toes, she was reminded that Conny was going to check the lost and found for a pair of shoes. Maybe she should wait for her to return. She climbed back onto her stool.

"You're the one who found the body, aren't you?" He pulled a fresh tea bag from the box, dropped it in her cup, and then plugged the kettle in.

She sighed. "Yes, I am."

"So, why were you leaving after only one day?"

Why does everyone want to know why I'm leaving? And how does he even know that I am? "Does it matter?"

He chuckled. "No. I guess it doesn't."

"Why do you want to know why I only stayed one day?"

He picked up a towel and started wiping the glasses drying on the drainer by the sink. "I guess I just get tired of it. So many people come up here only to turn around and go back."

"What do you mean? There are lots of people living on the beaches! That's all we hear about in Victoria."

"Yeah, but they've created their own little community. They haven't become part of ours."

When she didn't respond, he extended his hand. "My name's Brent. Just ignore me. I get melancholy every once in a while. The curse of being a musician."

A flash of him sitting on stage, bent over a guitar, cigarette smoke drifting around him made her grin, and she accepted his hand. "Mine's Sandy."

Brent's eyes twinkled. "Anything else I can get you, Sandy?"

He has a beautiful smile. Heat rose in her cheeks. "As a musician?"

"As a bartender."

"What about being a musician?"

"I just—"

"Shoes," Sandy blurted. "You can get me shoes. Conny was going to check the lost and found for a pair."

Brent laughed, dropped the towel on the counter, and unplugged the kettle. "I can do that for you. What size?"

"Seven."

"Fine. I'll be right back."

A few minutes later, he was back with a pair of bright pink flip-flops. "They're the best I could do."

After accepting the offering, she slipped them on. "They'll do. Thank you."

Brent returned to the bar and busied himself drying and stacking glasses. His dark-blonde hair was just long enough to brush the tops of his ears and the collar of his shirt. *Not like Geoff's.* The way the soft curls framed his face brought back memories of the afternoon spent in Geoff's van. *Was it really only yesterday?*

Brent looked up and caught her staring. Her blush deepened as she watched his hazel eyes darkened to a forest green. "You should consider staying," he said.

She was saved from responding by a young couple breezing into the bar and asking if it was too early to get a drink. Brent put down the glass he was drying and gave them a look that broadcasted his disbelief. "Let's see some ID." The couple changed their minds and asked for sodas. No sooner had they moved to the bench seating along the windows than a large group from the lobby came in and placed their order.

When she had Brent's attention again, Sandy blurted, "I can't spend another night on the beach!"

"You don't have to. Tish's given notice. That means there'll be a chambermaid's position open. If you want, you can work the rest of the season here. It would include a room in the lodge."

A chambermaid? Is that how I want to spend my summer?

Brent seemed to pick up on her hesitancy. "Look. Why don't I make you another tea?" He glanced over at the kettle that had long been forgotten, then back at her. "This time, I promise to finish the process." His face brightened when she laughed. "Look, you go outside on the deck, away from all this craziness, and have a good think. I'll bring the tea when it's ready."

His expression of concern seemed genuine, but she had to ask. "Why do you care if I stay or not?"

"I don't. I mean, um, look, this is a remote area. Tourists come here to get away from their ordinary lives.

They swim, camp, party. But then they pack up and go home, leaving us to deal with the mess they leave behind." He paused as if searching for words. "Sometimes I just wish they'd stay and see this place for what it is. Enjoy it in all its seasons."

Sandy stared at him. *Is he for real?* "You're quite the salesman."

"My dad sells used cars." He winked at her, then headed for the other end of the bar to turn the kettle on again.

A waitress approached the bar and ordered two glasses of white wine. As she waited for Brent to fill the order, she flirted openly with him. Sandy studied her, wondering how hard it would be to waitress. Maybe that could be an option. She glanced at the clock. It was just past noon. If she worked the bar, she would have the mornings to herself.

She watched the waitress' easy grace as she balanced her tray while climbing the three steps into the dining room. Sandy groaned. She could never be that graceful. She would have spilled the drinks halfway up those stairs.

Her attention returned to Brent. "Think about it," he said.

Tom found Tish on the second floor of the inn pulling sheets out of the maid's cart. He was surprised to see her working. Weekends were usually her days off. He grabbed her arm, startling her.

"What?" she demanded, sounding more surprised than angry.

"You drove me back here last night, didn't you?"

Tish frowned. "Don't you remember?"

"Not much."

Tish jerked her arm out of his grip. "Of course you wouldn't remember. What was I thinking? Yeah, I drove. So what?"

Tom followed her into the room where she was remaking the bed. "The cop asked how I got home last night, and I told him I drove, but then I remembered you did. Have they spoken to you yet?"

"Yeah," she shot back. "And I told him I drove."

The sound of the sheet snapping in the air as she shook it out over the mattress warned Tom to tread carefully. He was well aware of her lightning-quick mood swings. They had hooked up a couple of times for surprisingly enjoyable encounters, but he didn't consider them serious. He watched her bend to smooth the wrinkles and fold in the bottom corners. *Crisp military corners, just like Conny likes them.* "I didn't know I was lying," he said, "because I only just remembered you were driving."

"Tell them, then." Tish pushed him aside so she could move to the top of the bed, where she folded down the sheets and laid out matching pillows. When she turned back, Tom was in her way again. She shoved him aside, stooped, and pulled up the bedspread.

"I can't. They'll think I lied on purpose."

Tish stood, her hand brushing the bedspread to smooth it out. "What do you suppose they'll think now, with both of us saying we drove?"

"Christ!" He dropped to the edge of the bed and put his head in his hands.

"Tom!" Tish hit him and he jumped up. She quickly smoothed all trace of him from the bed, then sighed.

"Look, just go tell them you were too wasted to know that you weren't driving."

Facing her, his own emotions rose. "Oh, that'll really sound like I know what I'm doing!"

Tish walked around the room, making sure things were straight and shutting off all the lights before holding the door open for him. "Are you coming?"

As he passed her, she wrinkled her nose. "You reek of stale booze and BO, Tom. You need a shower."

Tom turned away, not wanting to see such obvious disgust on her face. *I didn't have time. Conny told me I had to come right away.*

She pushed the maid's cart to the next room, stopping to look back at him before going in. "You know, there was a time when I would've asked what you're thinking right now," she said. "And I would've cared about your answer. But I no longer give a shit." She rolled her eyes. "You probably don't even have the brainpower to think."

She disappeared into the room. *Chicks can be so cruel.* He kept his face neutral and followed her. "Do you remember hitting anything last night, Tish?"

Tom was surprised by how quickly she spun around, and he was not expecting the force of her anger. "Did you even hear a word I said?" She grabbed an ashtray off the bedside table and chucked it at him. He ducked, and it bounced off the wall. "How could you think I'm the type of person who would hit someone and just drive away?"

Tom looked at the chip in the wall where the ceramic ashtray had hit, just inches away from his shoulder. Robin wouldn't be pleased. She must be extremely angry to deliberately cause damage to Robin's inn. She worshipped the man. Tom couldn't think of a thing to say.

"I can't believe I had such a crush on you. I fell for those oh-so-soulful, lonely eyes and your bad-boy reputation."

Her confession confused him. He'd always thought they were on the same page. That things were casual. "Keep your voice down, Tish," he pleaded. Glancing at the open doorway, he hoped no one was outside hearing Tish's tirade.

Tish didn't seem to hear him; she paced and mumbled. Finally, she stopped and faced him. "I saw the way you were eyeing up the new nurse from Australia at the party last night." She gagged. "Then you assumed you could come crawling up my skirt after she rejected you."

Tom saw her scan the room and instinctively stepped outside the room, ready to use the door as a shield. "And now you tell me you don't remember any of it?" she ranted. "Well, I've had enough of you not respecting me. No more! No more!"

"You couldn't have been that mad at me, Tish. You drove me home."

Tish stopped and stared at him. "I drove *us* back. Us. You forget; I live here too!"

He shook his head. "You never let me forget. You follow me everywhere."

"Follow you?" Tish sat on the unmade bed, then jumped back up. "Well, you don't have to worry about that anymore. I'm leaving. I'm going home."

"What?" He grabbed Tish by her shoulders as she passed and forced her to stop. "Back to your parents? You don't want to go back to Calgary!" Remembering all their late-night discussions about shared experiences of having controlling parents, his concern grew. "It won't be good for you. You'll climb the walls."

Tish took a deep breath and wiggled out of his grip. "I don't care." All the fight seemed to have drained out of her.

He stood in silence, his hands feeling very empty.

"Go tell the police, Tom. Get it over with." Tish grabbed a dust cloth from the cart and started wiping down the counters and end tables.

He watched her for a moment before walking out of the room. If she was determined to leave, he wouldn't stop her. *There are plenty of girls out here to keep me entertained.*

Tom took the stairs two at a time. Tish was right. The sooner he let the police know about his mistake, the better things would look for him. It was already almost noon. When he entered the lobby, he saw the police car still parked out front, with a second one behind it. He glanced across the lobby to the office and saw Conny speaking with the same cop who had interviewed him. *Great.* He certainly wasn't going to admit to his mistake while Conny was around. He bypassed them by walking around a group of guests talking in the centre of the lobby, then rushing down the hallway to the lounge. It was busier than he'd ever seen it. If Brent spotted him, he'd be asked to help, so he fled, leaving the inn by the side entrance and taking the boardwalk around to the front of the inn.

The fog had thinned, leaving a few low-hanging clouds drifting among the Douglas fir and hemlock clustered at the back of the inn. He breathed a sigh of relief as he put on his sunglasses. If the cops were interviewing other people, they must not consider him a potential suspect. He decided to return to the lodge and catch up on his sleep. As he crossed the parking lot, a tour bus pulled up. The road must be open. He laughed and picked up his pace. The nap forgotten.

Staff could park their cars along the side of the lodge, leaving a small space for pathway access to the building. His Mustang was the second vehicle in, and still covered in shade. He opened the driver's door and climbed inside. The bucket seat creaked slightly as it accepted his weight. He ran his hands around the steering wheel, remembering the day he had driven it into his parents' driveway. His dad had stormed out of the house, yelling for him to get the noisy scrap off his property. That was the moment he knew he loved this car. The guttural rumble of the Mustang's muffler had vibrated off the fortresses of West Vancouver every time he returned home from a night out.

He turned the key and shifted the stick into reverse, backing out of the small driveway and into the inn's parking lot. He did a hundred and eighty-degree turn and gunned it down the inn's driveway, then turned right on to Long Beach Road. His swim trunks were in the back. A quick swim at Kennedy Lake, though chilly at this time of year, would solve the odour problem Tish complained of, and he'd follow it with a run into Ucluelet where he could drop in at the RCMP detachment to correct his mistake.

9.

The thunder of the pounding surf instantly replaced the chatter of the growing crowd inside as Sandy stepped out onto the inn's deck. And the expanse of sky and ocean nearly unnerved her. The beauty was expected. The uncontrolled wildness, the sense of danger was not. It was something she'd never experienced. Victoria's coastline, though the same ocean, somehow seemed tame, protected, safe. The horizon was defined by land: the San Juan Islands, Port Angeles, and the Olympic National Park. As she looked to the horizon here, though still veiled in a thin sheath of fog, no visible land marked the boundary between an open, heaving ocean and a moody sky.

Turning away from the expanse, she sat in one of the weather-bleached wooden lounge chairs. She shivered. The night of partying and sleeping at Wreck Bay, followed by that long, lonely forty minutes on the side of the road with Geoff's body, had brought home just how remote the area was.

The sound of the patio door opening made her turn. Brent stepped onto the deck and set her tea on the weather worn table beside her. "I don't know," she said.

Brent crossed to the railing and studied her for a moment. "Look, by the time the police finish up here and open the road, it'll be too late for you to try and hitch all the way back home today. Why don't you stay another night?"

Sandy shook her head. "I won't sleep on that beach again, and I can't afford this place."

"You can crash on the couch at the lodge. I've done that many a time when I was too drunk or tired to drive home. You can meet everyone. Then, tomorrow, you can decide if you want to stay. After all, you've come all this way."

Her jaw clenched, resenting the feeling of being pressured. "How do you know how far I've come?" When Brent started to answer, she held up her hand. "Stop. Don't tell me. Small bloody town!"

Brent shrugged and turned to look out at the ocean. Sandy immediately regretted her words. People were offering to help her out of a situation she had put herself into, and she was acting like a bitch. "Sorry," she mumbled.

"It *is* like a small town," he said, his attention still focused on the waves. "And people *do* know your business, often before you do. But you'll find that their hearts are in the right place. You'll experience a generosity of spirit here that's hard to find in the city." He turned and walked back into the lounge, closing the door softly.

Sandy stared out at the ocean. Geoff had been so happy to arrive at the beach. She wondered if he had found the friend he'd come looking for. Then, suddenly, she had the sensation of his head resting in her lap, as it had when she dragged him out of the water-filled ditch. She jumped up, rocking the table beside her. Her teacup shattered on the deck. For a second, she was staring down into Geoff's cloudy eyes. A cold sweat broke out across her chest and arms. She struggled to breathe, and a sob broke from her lungs as tears tracked down her cheeks.

"Are you okay, miss?"

The soft voice broke the spell, and she turned to see an elderly man standing in the doorway to the lounge, concern etched across his face. "Yes," she answered, stepping back and sitting down on the chair once more. "Yes, I am. Thank you."

"Well then." He returned to the lounge, the door closing behind him with a sharp click.

Sandy was too embarrassed to look inside. She didn't want to see how many others had witnessed her fright. Shards of china were scattered at the bottom of the table. She gingerly picked up the pieces of the ruined teacup and saucer and, careful not to cut herself, dumped the shards into the wastebasket by the door.

Turning away from the picture windows, she went to the railing and looked out over the ocean. The memory of holding Geoff made her wonder if anyone had notified Geoff's family. Did they live in California or Vancouver? She couldn't remember what he'd said. Suddenly, she missed her own family. She had left without letting them know where she was going. If she got hurt, or disappeared, while she was up here, would they even know? How would they be notified? Would they drive up to find her?

She looked out over the expanse of sand and ocean. Though beautiful, its bareness emphasized how very far away from home she was. *Isn't that what I wanted? To get away? To stand alone?*

She no longer knew.

Her father's words still stung. She knew he held outdated opinions, but when he'd told her that going to college was a waste of money and time for a woman, she had seen red. She had defied him and registered with the University of Victoria, determined to prove him wrong. Now, a year and a half later, she was proving him right. She had quit university, stuck out her thumb, and sought a lifestyle of complete freedom.

None of which solved her problem.

After the first year of an art degree, it became obvious that it didn't suit her. She had no idea why. And now, one night of the hippie lifestyle she'd fantasized about taught her the same thing.

So, what do I want?

She watched the waves roll into the long, curved shoreline as if caressing it, and she inhaled deep breaths of the sea air. Closing her eyes, she realized what she wanted was time—time to sort out what she wanted to do with her life.

Sandy headed back into the lounge. It was busy. A waitress was directing people to keep their luggage with them whether they were stopping in the lounge or the dining room. Brent was busy pouring drinks, and he didn't look up as she passed the bar. Sandy weaved her way through the crowded hallway to the lobby. Tish was nowhere in sight, so she headed up a staircase that wrapped around a driftwood log standing on end, like a piece of modern art. The dried bark twisted around stubs of amputated branches reaching upwards as if to a heaven beyond the roof that sheltered it.

Sandy found Tish in the second room she checked. "I understand you're leaving. How would I apply for your job?"

"You just did!" Tish stopped making the bed and looked Sandy over. Her eyes lingered on the pink flip-flops, then lifted. "Conny's a bit of a dragon,' she said, "but if you pull your own weight and show up on time, she'll be fine."

"Conny's the manager?"

"No. She's our supervisor. Robin, the owner, manages the hotel, but he's been busy lately." She glanced at Sandy's feet. "You'll need to wear proper shoes."

"Oh, yes." Sandy gestured to her feet. "My moccasins got ruined, and Conny said she'd check the lost and found." She sighed and looked straight at Tish. "When should I start?"

"I'll have to run it past Conny, but I'm sure she'll start training you tomorrow if you want."

Sandy considered. "Okay. Brent said it came with a place to stay."

"The lodge! The lodge, of course. You can have my room when I'm gone." Tish started pulling at the bed linens again. "When I'm finished here, I'll take you over."

"I'll meet you downstairs," Sandy said. "I left my backpack in the lounge."

Sandy found Tish waiting for her outside the inn's front entry, a small paper bag clutched to her chest. "Here," she said. "I found these in the upstairs supply closet."

Sandy accepted the bag and unrolled the top to see a pair of green, flat-soled runners.

"I figured you wouldn't mind what colour they were. They may be a bit big, but you can just tighten the laces."

Sandy closed the bag and smiled. "Thank you."

Fog tendrils continued to shift in the air, hiding the details of the surrounding landscape. Tish led Sandy across the parking lot, taking them away from the beach side to the back corner of the lot, where they entered the same laneway Sandy and Geoff had walked the day before.

"This is the way to Wreck Bay," Sandy said.

"Yes, but the lodge is here too."

They passed a small cabin on their right, just inside the trees. "I noticed yesterday that there are several cabins here," Sandy said. "Whose are they?"

"They're all part of the inn's property. The one we just passed and four others were part of the package when Robin worked out a deal with the lodge's owners to build the inn."

Sandy stopped at a driveway that ran through the trees. "One cabin seemed newer than the others and quite different."

Tish smiled. "With a steep roof? That's Robin's cabin. He built the A-frame for his family the year after he built the inn."

"Does he also own the cabins on the north side of the inn?"

"No. They're part of the Long Beach Bungalow Resort."

Sandy was so focused on walking the dusty road that she missed Tish turning up a driveway on their left. She quickly backtracked and was right behind Tish as she climbed the porch stairs.

The horizontal cedar siding matched that of the two smaller cabins Sandy had seen, but the building was much larger. Below the roofline, the building's siding had been painted a rusty brown; above, it was ecru. A pitched cedar-shake roof topped the structure.

Inside, the fogged landscape outdoors muted what light shone through the large picture window on the front wall, giving the living room an intimate, closed-in feel. It failed, Sandy noted, to subdue the impact of the river-stone fireplace set against the central wall separating the room from the kitchen. Like the one at the inn, the fireplace was the room's standout feature; but unlike the inn the rest was pretty basic. Brown panelling covered the walls, the wood-plank floor was painted rust brown to match the exterior, and the ceiling was plaster.

Tish stripped off her sweater, flinging it onto the back of one of two overstuffed armchairs flanking the fireplace, and walked through to the kitchen. Sandy laid her backpack on the equally overstuffed couch set between the two armchairs, facing the fireplace, and walked past a pool table to the rough wood bookcase that spanned the width of the side wall. Various board games were stacked on the bottom shelves, while the middle shelves held a variety of fiction and nonfiction books. A mix of knickknacks and found objects occupied the upper shelves. Her eyes landed on a stack of art supplies tucked to the left side of the third shelf from the top.

Tish came up behind her. "An odd collection. I was told some of it came with the original building." She handed Sandy a soda and then took a long draft from her own. "The lodge was once a section of the hospital set up at the RCAF base during the Second World War. The Tofino Airport is there now."

Sandy turned in a slow circle to survey her new home; everywhere, the panelled walls were covered with posters displaying popular bands: The Stones, The Byrds, The Doors, The Beatles. She took a quick drink of her soda before following Tish into the kitchen. A large wooden table occupied the centre of the room, with six mismatched wooden chairs tucked around it. Fitted cupboards, roughly painted grey, ran across the plastered back wall. A fridge stood between the counter and the lodge's back door. Dish-towel curtains covered a small window in that door as well as the window over the kitchen sink. An old-fashioned wood-burning range sat to the side. Grey-checkered linoleum covered the floor beneath scattered braided rugs that looked homemade from brightly-coloured scraps of cloth.

"Everyone's responsible for their own food, but we mostly just get takeout from the inn," Tish explained. "There're five bedrooms." She swept her hand across the room, indicating the closed doors flanking the kitchen area. "As you can tell, it was set up for communal living. Conny and I each have a bedroom. The others are taken by Tom, a bartender; Edan, a chef; and Roxanne, a waitress. Don't worry, they're not all here at the same time. You and Conny will work the same shift Monday to Friday, eight to three—maybe a little longer, depending on how booked the inn is. You have weekends off. A couple of schoolgirls from Ucluelet come in for that shift."

"Wait a minute. You and Conny were working today."

"Yes, but today was different. The two girls we get to come in on weekends are just teenagers. There's no way they could've handled today. You saw the chaos. It's crazy. You'll find the staff here pitch in wherever and whenever they're needed." Turning to face the doors on the left, she continued her tour. "Tom works the late bar, six to whatever time people leave, usually before midnight. He sometimes parties afterward, so he'll probably still be sleeping when you leave for work. He and Brent trade days when one wants a day off."

"Brent told me he sometimes sleeps on the couch."

"That's right," Tish said. "He shares a place in Ucluelet with a couple of friends, but when he trades shifts with Tom or works a double, he crashes here. Not tonight. You don't have to worry. I'll make sure he knows." She paused.

"He already does."

Giving a quick nod, Tish continued. "Edan is the head chef, so he works basically all the time. He has two assistants, and kitchen help who come in from town as needed. They have friends who live up the road, so they crash there when they don't feel like hitching back into town. Roxanne works whenever and wherever she's needed. She's saving up to go to university in the fall, so she takes as many shifts as she can handle. She's who Conny calls if she needs extra help with the rooms. I'll be here for a couple more days, so you'll have to make do with the couch until then."

Sandy scanned the room, trying to absorb all the names and schedules.

"That"—Tish pointed to the third door on the left side of the room—"is the bathroom. It has a tub with a shower."

Sandy was pleased. "Looks great."

Tish walked back out to the living room. "I've got to get back to work. It's going to be a long day, but I'll bring back supper."

Sandy went to sit on the couch, but the cushions were covered by Hollywood fan magazines. Tish rushed over to scoop them up and stack them on the coffee table. "Conny's obsessed with the idea of moving to Hollywood and being discovered." Tish struck a pose, causing Sandy to laugh. "You know, like Lana Turner….You can keep your stuff in my room and use it to change. It's the second on the right."

Tish glanced at her watch. "It's past noon, so you should have the place to yourself until three when, hopefully, I'll be done. Edan and Roxanne will also be off-shift around then. I think Tom's got the day off, so you might see him around." Tish handed Sandy a set of keys. "You can use my keys for the afternoon."

"Is Conny okay with me working here?"

"I told her, but she was busy helping Bobbie at the front desk. I'm not sure if she heard me." Tish turned toward the door. "I've got to get back to work. Don't worry about Conny. She'll be fine with it."

Freshly showered and changed, Sandy stood in the centre of the now-empty lodge, suddenly feeling very alone. She glanced around. It would be at least another two hours before anyone working at the inn would return, and she had no idea who or where Tom was. If she stayed inside, she'd only think about Geoff and how he had died. *What was he doing walking along that road? And why hadn't he let her know he was leaving the party? Was there another path from Wreck Bay?* She walked over to the bookshelf.

No maps were stacked among the books, but she found a sketchpad and a box of artist pencils. She flipped through the pages of the sketchpad. Someone had attempted a couple of portraits, but the rest of the pages were unused. The familiar feel of the paper made her think of the sketchbooks she'd left at home—and her reason for not bringing her own art supplies with her. She had envisioned living in a driftwood lean-to on the beach and spending her summer learning to surf. No room for sketch pads and pencils. But the night before had taught her a hard truth about fantasy and reality.

She took the sketchpad and selected a pencil, determined to hike back to Wreck Bay and see if any other paths branched off the main one. If there were, she could create her own map.

Slipping on the runners, she left the lodge and headed down the laneway. She had walked only a few steps when someone called her name. She spun around and found Mark coming from the direction of the inn. "I was just looking for you," he said.

"Oh?"

"I heard what happened and wanted to see if you were all right."

"I am."

An awkward silence stretched between them until Mark broke it. "Where are you going with the sketchpad?"

"I was going to see if I could find any more paths from Wreck Bay that would explain how Geoff ended up on the road the way he did. I just don't get why he didn't take his van."

"There are a couple of paths from the bay. Where was he on the road?"

Sandy opened the sketchpad, planning to show Mark by drawing, but closed it again and gestured toward the lodge. "Do you want to come in? It'd be easier to draw on the table."

"Is this where you're staying?"

"Yes. I've decided to take a job at the inn."

"So, you're going to be here for the summer?"

"I hope to be."

"Um"—he lifted the bag he held—"I was on my way to deliver some of my carvings to a lady who's opening a new shop in town."

"That's great!"

"Well, the shop isn't open yet. She just wants to get an idea of what I do."

"I'm sure she'll love your work."

"The road is open again, and I only have the use of my friend's car for today. I should get going." Mark paused. "Did you want to come?" Sandy's eyes dropped to her sketchbook. Mark added, "I know about the paths at Wreck Bay. I could help you with that after I make my delivery."

"Will there be time for shopping? I need to pick up some things I should've brought up here with me."

"Sure!"

10.

It was four o'clock by the time Moore walked through the front doors of Tofino's hospital, and he was in a foul mood. He had left Constable Evans to track down and interview residents along the road. So far, the time Moore had spent only emphasized how impossible it would be to find the guilty driver.

With the only hospital in the area located in Tofino, he had to travel at least half an hour from wherever he was in his Ucluelet jurisdiction to get there. It ate up a lot of his time.

He strode down the central hall of the small, single-story hospital, pushed through the door at the end, and descended to the basement. The morgue was only large enough to hold one body, so it wasn't unusual to find extras lying on gurneys in the hallway. Moore ignored the single draped form as he passed.

Inside the morgue, he tossed his jacket on the counter by the door and walked to where his friend was reading a file. He kept his eyes away from the body laid out like a museum display in the middle of the room. He never got used to this part of the job. In an area composed of small communities and villages, the bodies he saw rarely belonged to strangers. "Dispatch said you had something to tell me."

"Yes, yes." Dr. John Martin removed his reading glasses and stood. "The young man you sent in. How sure are you that it was a hit-and-run?"

Moore frowned. "Scene. No witnesses. Why?"

"Because I don't think that's what we have here."

Moore lifted his eyebrows. His friend had been the area's GP for ten years and rarely expressed doubt. He was one of the most confident people Moore knew, and they had developed a strong working relationship because of it. Moore stood aside and let John lead him to Geoff's body. "I did a quick external exam, and I think we're going to have to send him to Nanaimo."

Moore groaned. Sending the body to Nanaimo for an autopsy meant that John suspected a serious crime. It also meant that Moore would lose control of the case. RCMP policing came under strict jurisdictional control. Local detachments, like his in Ucluelet, handled everyday policing incidents, but specialist units, like those operating out of Victoria and Nanaimo, handled major crimes. "Show me," he said.

John lifted the sheet covering Geoff's body, exposing his legs. A network of red marks covered his thighs. "At first glance," John said, "given where and when the body was found, it could have easily been assumed that this was a hit-and-run. But a car didn't cause these." He used the pencil he'd pulled from his breast pocket to point to a cluster of light bruises. "Their pattern is chaotic and inconsistent with vehicle–body impact injuries."

Moore couldn't keep the surprise from his voice. "What caused them?"

"I'm not sure. But he was already dead when he got them."

Moore leaned in and looked closely at the marks. "There's little bruising, and the skin isn't broken or indented much. These weren't done with much force."

John nodded. "I don't think it was a frenzied attack for that same reason. But most puzzling is why do this at all?"

Moore examined the marks once more. "The majority are long and narrow. Any idea what type of weapon did this?"

"Not sure. But there's something else." John moved to Geoff's head.

Moore followed. Even in death, the victim was unusually attractive. *He must've been the subject of more than a few young girls' fantasies while he was alive.*

John brushed a stray lock of hair from the dead man's forehead with a gentle intimacy. "I knew the family," he said. "His grandparents were among the original settlers here in Tofino, but their son moved his family down to Seattle when Geoff was quite young."

Moore had grown to admire and depend upon his friend's local knowledge. John could rattle off the family lineage of seemingly every Tofino resident at the drop of a hat. "He had ID under two different names. Turner and Johnston."

"Yes. I saw the note Constable Evans sent with the body." The doctor looked across at Moore. "His father's name is Johnston; his mother's maiden name was Turner. When I saw the two names together, I knew who he was."

So, the driver's licence was the false one. Moore scribbled the information into his notebook before looking back at his friend. "Seattle? He had a student card and licence from California."

"Kids move away from home."

"So, what brought him back here, I wonder?"

"That'll be for you to find out. For me"—John tapped his head with his pencil—"I got curious. Why would someone go to so much trouble beating up a dead body? If they were trying to make it look like he'd been hit by a car, they didn't know anything about such impacts. What were they trying to cover up? It didn't take long for me to solve the mystery." John rolled Geoff onto his right side and lifted the hair at the nape, revealing a raised red welt at the base of the neck with an egg-shaped area of bruising around it. "Do you know what that is?"

Moore shook his head.

"An injection site. Either he did a horrible job of administering the drug himself, or someone else did. Notice the bruising and swelling. The needle went in at an angle, and hard."

"A strange place."

"Not as strange as you might think, for a drug addict." The doctor rolled the body back to its original position. "But I don't think that's what we're dealing with here. I searched the body for other injection sites and found these." John moved the sheeting, revealing the victim's lower abdomen and three small bruises with a red dot in the centre of one.

Moore leaned in to get a better look. "Quite different."

"Your victim was self-administering a drug. Notice the slight bruising. These weren't done by force but by someone unsure of himself. Legal or illegal, I'd say his drug-use, at least by this method, was within a day or two. And he was new to it."

Covering the victim, John signaled Moore to follow him. "There were also fresh scratches and bruises. Not quite like he'd been in a fight, maybe a struggle. It's hard to tell." He stopped at his desk. A pile of neatly stacked clothing lay on top.

"I also found this." John showed Moore a patch of dried goop on the inside of Geoff's paisley shirt collar. "Given that he was in the ditch, we're lucky to have it. The rest probably washed away."

That looks familiar. Moore smiled at John. "Looks like what ends up on my shirt after my six-month-old refuses his supper."

"I don't think a baby was involved. However, you're right this is vomit, which, with the needle marks, leads me to believe a drug overdose was involved."

"So why the beating? Was it to make it look like he had been struck by a car?" Moore paused to think through the consequences of what he was being told. "Are you saying he was murdered?"

"I can't go that far without opening him up and doing toxicology tests, but it's suspicious enough for us to lose jurisdiction. I have to send him to the pathologist in Nanaimo. He'll do the autopsy and give you Geoff's blood work."

Moore took a deep breath. "Has the coroner mentioned an inquest?"

"Yes. He was in earlier. He did not have a jury with him and said there won't be one following. As you know jurors no longer have to view victims' bodies." The doctor returned the shirt to the pile. "I imagine the inquest will be held in a couple of days."

Moore sighed. It was rare for the local coroner to go beyond the obvious. "I wish you were the coroner."

John smiled. "I don't have the right type of friends."

Moore groaned. Coroners were elected members of the community, usually possessing, at the very least, an interest in law or medicine. Theirs did not. He was a local man with his fingers in many pies and very little time to devote to the job. "Anyway, it won't be me the lab will give their report to. It'll be someone sent up from the General Investigation Section in Victoria." Moore paused. "What about the time of death?"

The doctor glanced down at the notes on his desk. "I'd say somewhere between midnight and early morning."

"You didn't find a set of keys on him, by any chance?"

"Keys?"

"To his van. We have the vehicle but no keys," Moore explained.

When his friend shook his head, Moore picked up his coat and notebook and tried to control the emotions rolling over him. "Give me a shout at home tonight if you think of anything else." He threw open the lab door so forcefully that it slammed against the interior wall. After calling a brief apology to John, he stormed down the hallway and exited the hospital through the basement.

This new information meant he had spent the morning asking the wrong questions. The cause of death wasn't a senseless accident but a murder. He and Evans had to get back out to the inn and focus on tracking the victim's movements the night before, and he needed to stop at the Tofino detachment office to have a constable assigned to the body for transport to Nanaimo.

11.

Moore's stop in at the Tofino detachment meant he was a half-hour late meeting Constable Evans at Wreck Bay, which didn't improve the young constable's mood as they looked down on the scene. This was no holiday beach; it was built for those who wanted to escape the world. With steep clay cliffs overlooking five miles of sand and rock, access wasn't easy. One had to approach via a path off the inn's parking lot, involving close to an hour's walk through a thick rainforest, or by a narrow, two-track, rutted dirt road, accessed off Long Beach Road about a mile from the inn. Though it risked the patrol car's undercarriage, Moore and Evans had chosen the latter option. An overgrown path led toward Lost Shoe Creek and then to the beach, but they had taken the other, clearly marked one, which led to a junction with the path coming from the inn just before it descended to the beach.

Squatters and weekend partiers were scattered across the beach, some alone, others clustered around campfires. Someone gently strummed a guitar, its notes floating in the air above the rhythmic crash of the surf. Other than the occasional burst of laughter from those tossing Frisbees, the energy was slow and lazy.

The beach's population usually doubled during party nights, but this was supper hour and too early for the late-night crowd. So, while Moore estimated over a hundred squatters were on the beach, he knew at least the same number who had been on the beach the night before were now back at home in neighbouring communities or in tents pitched at official or unofficial campsites along the coastline. He would have to put a call out over the local radio station asking those who had attended the party to contact their local RCMP detachment. That would endear him to his fellow officers.

Moore heard Evans' deep sigh and turned to the younger officer standing beside him. "There's no getting around it," Moore said. "This is going to take a while."

"We could use Constable Nelson, sir," Evans whined.

"I'm not calling him early for his shift. He had three call outs last night so didn't get much sleep. He'll probably be busy all night tonight as well."

"Yeah." Evans sighed again.

David placed a hand on Evans' shoulder. "Dispatch has contacted a couple of auxiliary officers. They should show up soon." He gave Evans a double pat then led the way down the path. Once on the beach, they headed toward the nearest group of young people, who watched them approach. "I think this will go faster if we split up," Moore said. "I'll look for the Mark who Miss Chambers mentioned in her statement."

When Evans opened his mouth to protest, Moore pushed one of the photocopies of Geoff's driver's licence photo at him. "Keep it short and focused. Collect contact information. Ask if they knew the victim or noticed him at the party. Get details of what he was doing and who he was with."

The constable nodded and moved toward a group gathered around a small campfire, while Moore joined the group that had watched their approach. "Good afternoon," he said. "We're wondering if you recognize this man from the party last night." He pulled out his copy of the Geoff's driver's licence photo and his notebook.

The group proved cooperative, but none had known Geoff or noticed him at the party. They did, however, point out Mark's lean-to. When Moore walked over, he found the campsite neat and organized. The fire pit was cold, with kindling and logs stacked under a tarp next to it. He ducked for a quick peek into the lean-to and found it equally neat with no sign of the man he sought.

"Who are you?"

Moore stood up to find a skeletal youth in a ragged grey T-shirt, and cut-off jean shorts that hung low on his rail-thin hips, sending an intense glare across the camp at him. Moore squared his shoulders. "I'm Corporal David Moore of the RCMP Ucluelet detachment. I'm looking for Mark. I was told this was his lean-to."

"He's not here, man."

"I can see that. Do you know where he is?"

The youth gave Moore a slow once over. "I ain't no snitch."

The youth's deep blue eyes were unsettling. They appeared almost black beneath the fringe of his tangled, red hair. "I'm not asking you to be. I just want to talk to Mark. Do you know where he is?"

"Naw."

Moore turned away, frustrated, and scanned the beach for Evans, spotting him several campsites further down the beach. He was surrounded by nude hippies.

Moore grinned, imagining the young officer's blushing cheeks.

"Whatcha want to talk to Mark about?"

The youth had come up beside him, his head barely reaching Moore's shoulder. Up close, his body appeared shriveled like an old man's. "How old are you?"

"Seventeen."

"What's your name?"

"Buzz."

"Buzz? That's your real name?"

"Aye, man. You gotta problem?"

"No." Moore held up his hands in surrender, then reached in his pocket for the photocopy and his notebook. "Did you see this guy at the party last night?"

Buzz pulled the paper from Moore's grip and studied the image of Geoff. "Aye. I seen him." He handed the paper back. "Tossed a Frisbee around a bit."

Moore stopped writing. "Were you the one who came to this campsite and delivered a message to him?"

"Aye. I tried to warn him that the guy he was meeting was trouble."

"In what way?"

"He belongs to a group that harasses us, trying to get us to leave the beach."

"Do you know his name?"

The teen shook his head.

"Where was the meeting?"

"At the bonfire."

Moore frowned. "Where was that?"

Buzz pointed toward the south end of the beach. "Down there about halfway."

Moore noticed a tremor travel down Buzz's arm before he lowered it, and wondered what Buzz was coming down from. "Are you okay?"

Buzz waved the concern away and stepped toward the surf. Moore grabbed his arm to stop him from leaving but let go immediately when a look of raw pain creased the youth's face. Momentarily shocked, both froze. Moore's mind raced. *Is he sick, not high?* "How long have you been living on the beach?" he blurted.

"Just leave me alone!" Buzz shouted and ran off.

Moore watched the receding figure. He had no wish to enter a foot race this late in the day. He refolded Geoff's picture and placed it as a marker in his notebook before trudging through the sand to where his constable had moved on. This time those gathered around him were fully clothed.

Evans stepped away from the group and faced his boss. "Any luck, sir?"

"He wasn't there."

"Nothing to report so far here either. I could use some help. Are the auxiliaries going to show up?"

"I'm sure they'll be here soon." Moore paused, then faced the group. "Do any one of you know a Mark from the campsite over next to the path?"

"I do." Moore scanned the faces and found a man in a beat-up fedora looking directly at him. The man rose from where he had been sitting cross-legged in the sand and placed the guitar he'd been cradling against a log before approaching the two cops. "We hang out sometime. Is there something wrong?"

"Do you know where he is? He's not at his camp."

"Last I saw him, he was on his way up to the inn to see some girl he met at the party last night."

Sandy. "What time was this?"

"Afternoon. Early, I think."

Moore scribbled a quick note in his book and a memory flashed. He flipped back to his interview with Sandy and found the name of the man whose striking appearance she had commented on, Jim. When he looked up the guitar player had returned to his place and resumed the melody he'd been playing. Clearing his throat, Moore addressed the group. "Do you know of anyone named Jim? He has dark features and very long hair."

A girl who looked no more than twelve stood up from where she was cooking pan bread on the campfire. "Jim's camp is down by the creek. It's the one with the totem pole in front."

Suddenly everyone was talking and pointing down the beach.

"Isn't he the one with the pregnant wife?"

"If he's not there, he's probably playing cards with Neal."

"He could be surfing. Did you check the waves?"

"I thought he went to Ukee!"

"Whoa! Whoa! Whoa!" Moore shouted. "Enough!" He waited while the group quieted then indicated Evans, who squared his shoulders. "We are investigating a serious incident that occurred on Long Beach Road early this morning. Constable Evans has been handing around a photo. If you recognize the man in the photo and have any information on his activities over the last twelve hours, or who he was with, let the constable know." Turning to

Evans, he informed him that he was going in search of a totem pole.

Moore maneuvered around the blackened remnants of the large bonfire and tried to determine where Geoff and the man he met could have disappeared. All he saw was canvas tents tucked in among the storm-tossed logs piled against the brush marking the base of the clay cliffs. Interspersed among these were rough structures made of driftwood, bits of plywood, and plastic. He was about to give up when he spotted the totem pole, and next to it a nude man sitting on a log sharpening a stick with a very large knife. As he approached, the man looked up and smiled. "What can I do for you, Officer?"

"Is your name Jim?"

"Yes." Jim tilted his head, and the wind whipped his long black hair across his face.

Moore was surprised by the length. It looked as if it would reach to his hips if the wind stopped blowing it about. The man appeared to be in his early thirties but his eyes held the intensity of a much older man. Moore could see why Sandy had found him memorable. Moore stepped forward and introduced himself. "We're looking into a suspicious death that happened last night on Long Beach Road. I'm told you shared a meal with a guy named Mark last night."

Jim stuck the knife point-down in the sand, set the stick on the log beside him, and brushed the shavings off the blanket he used as a cushion. He shook his head to free his face of the wind-blown strands, then set his deep-set, mocha-brown eyes on Moore. "Yes, I did. What does that have to do with the hit-and-run on the road?"

Taken aback by Jim's knowledge of the situation, Moore answered honestly. "I'm trying to trace the victim's movements." He passed Jim a copy of Geoff's image. "I'm told he came down to the beach to meet with someone. So far, no one has been able to tell me who." Moore paused. "Do you know about what time you were at Mark's camp?"

"Around five. Mark likes to pretend he doesn't care about time, but he has a set routine. He eats at five when he's here."

"Did you notice anyone else at Mark's campfire?"

"A girl. Pretty. Long hair, a light red, almost blonde, and the most incredible blue eyes. I think it was her first time on the beach. She looked a little nervous and overwhelmed."

"Name?"

"Sandy, I think. Somehow appropriate for a beautiful girl on a beach."

Moore smiled. This was his second season dealing with the transient hippies who squatted on the area's beaches, and he was beginning to realize they weren't always what they seemed. "Do you remember *that* young man with her?"

Jim examined the photograph before passing it back. "Not the first time I met her. Later, though, when I rejoined Mark's camp.…Mark often attracts an interesting crowd, and there's usually at least one rousing debate. I'm pretty sure that guy dropped beside Sandy and started making some moves on her. Mark didn't seem happy about it. First time I'd seen him interested in a member of the opposite sex."

"Did he mention his name?"

"He didn't but she did. Geoff."

"Was that the only time you saw him last night?"

"Was he the victim?" When Moore didn't answer, Jim let it slide. "I think I saw him later. At the bonfire."

"What time was this?"

"Oh, way later, about two-ish. Something like that." Jim pointed toward the area Moore had just come from. "My wife's close to nine months pregnant and the baby's been very restless. We end up walking a lot at night. A big group was gathered around the bonfire, with the usual storytelling going on. And one of those storytellers was that guy, I'm pretty sure. According to him, his cousin had just told him their grandfather had some old placer claims on the land above the beach." Jim pointed to the cliffs that loomed over them. "He went on about how he'd be rich one day because some BC company was showing interest in the area's minerals, including gold."

Jim paused, his gaze probing Moore's. "Apparently, the government's also interested. They want to bring in a national park. The guy was waving a prospector's pan around, making sure everyone noticed him. He seemed excited by the idea of prospecting. At the time, I wasn't sure if his story was all campfire posturing. You know how it is." When Moore didn't respond, Jim added, "The booze, the acid, whatever."

The casual mention of drugs made Moore check Jim's arms for tracks. He saw none there or anywhere on the man's lean body.

"Anyway—"

The force behind the word drew Moore's eyes back up to Jim's face, where he found a smile. Moore's cheeks flushed.

"Anyway," Jim repeated. "I was going to track him down and ask him about the claims today, but when I went looking for him this morning, I couldn't find him."

Moore's brow furrowed. "Why track him down?"

Jim stood and indicated that he'd be back in a moment, then disappeared into his tent. Moore could hear him rummaging around. A minute later, he came out with a clear glass tube, which he handed over. The tube was a quarter full of what looked like tiny flakes of gold.

Jim sat again. "Thought it was a bit of a coincidence."

"Is this gold?"

"I haven't had it to an assay agent yet, but from what I can tell, it is."

Moore handed the vial back to Jim. "Where'd you get it?"

"I've been panning Lost Shoe Creek."

"Lost Shoe?" Moore asked. "Isn't that the creek just there?" He pointed to the wide fan of rivulets etched into the sand a few feet away.

"Further up." Jim gestured to indicate where the stream emerged from a wide cut in the cliffs that edged the beach. "You have to know what to look for. Black sand was my first clue. Then I found out some claims had been worked in the area."

"Claims as in the ones Geoff was talking about?"

"I'm not sure. That's why I wanted to speak with him." Jim looked down at the tube in his hand. "When I was exploring the creek a couple of days ago, I found an old prospector's shack. It was locked up pretty tight."

"What day was this?"

"Wednesday."

"Did you see anyone?"

Jim shook his head. "No. It looked like it hadn't been used for a while—at least not by a prospector."

"What do you mean?"

"The place looked old, abandoned, but a new padlock secured the door, and the windows had been blacked out and screwed shut."

That had Moore's attention. "Not what an old prospector would do."

"No. And I saw remnants of a campfire....Also a couple of cigarette butts. Filtered."

"Filtered?"

"Yeah. How many bushmen smoke filtered cigarettes? Not anyone I know. Cash is too tight. It's hand-rolled, no filters."

"The campfire and cigarettes could indicate that someone was guarding it at one point." He scanned the area around. "Have you seen any strangers around?"

Jim raised an eyebrow. "You're kidding, right?"

Moore groaned. *Of course, the party.* "Anyone who wasn't in party mode?"

"They were pretty much all into partying. It was Friday night on the beach....But there was one guy. He wasn't a stranger, though. He's been down on the beach before. Part of the group that regularly comes down to harass us."

Moore wrote a couple of quick notes in his notebook before looking up again. "Do you know his name?"

Jim shook his head.

"Can you describe him?"

"Big. Looked like he grew up chopping trees. Not the type you'd want to meet in a dark alley."

"That describes half the logging and paving crews in town," Moore said. He considered the vigilante angle as he wrote the description. As a motive, it didn't fit. If they wanted to scare the hippies off the beach, why leave the body on the road, away from the beach?

Jim set the container of gold dust on the log beside him, but Moore could tell it meant a lot to him because he kept glancing at it. "Tell me a bit more about the gold. It sounds like more than a bit of curiosity. Are you a prospector?"

"No. But before I came here, I was working toward a degree in geoscience at Caltech. I've always loved rocks and the history they tell us." Jim's fingers wrapped protectively around the container. "Then I got my draft notice. They were going to ship me off to a war I didn't believe in."

Moore frowned. "I thought students were exempt from the draft."

"That's true in a way. A couple of years ago the U.S. government got rid of *that* deferment and introduced the Selective Service Qualification Test which, according to them, helped select the best recruits to draft into the war. If you received a high enough mark on the test then you got a deferment. It's just another system set up to favour the privileged, so I protested."

"You gave up completing your degree to come here?"

"I can always complete it later, here or there."

Whether they were hippies or draft dodgers, Moore struggled to understand what motivated the young men who flocked to the rough life on the beach. He surveyed the campsite, taking note of its neatness and organization. "So, you're going to be a father."

"Any day now."

Moore paused. *How are you going to handle being a new parent while living out of a tent*? There would be no way his wife, Samantha, would agree to such a lifestyle. He shook his head and changed his focus. "Do you think it's more than a coincidence that you found gold in Lost Shoe Creek and then heard about Geoff's claims on the neighbouring land?"

"Not really, no."

Moore closed his notebook. "I'll check into it. Do you know who the prospector's shack belongs to?"

"No. But that wasn't the only one I found. Last month, when I was following the path in from the other way, you know, from the highway, I ran across a shack farther up the creek and well-hidden in the bush. An old guy's working that claim."

"Did he know anything about the locked-up shack?"

"I don't know. As soon as he saw me, he grabbed his shotgun. I didn't stick around."

"How close to the other shack was this?"

"About a half mile upstream."

"We'll check it out."

Jim stood, and the wind caught his hair, causing it to momentarily float like wings spread out from his shoulders. Moore was reminded of a painting he had seen once of an Indian standing on a hilltop. Jim's dark complexion, long nose, and square jaw could easily mark him as a member of one of the local tribes. It made him wonder about the California story.

"Can I see your driver's licence?"

"I don't have a driver's licence. I have no car. I have a passport."

No licence? No car? What're you going to do when the baby's sick? Moore forced himself to keep his concern to himself. "Can you get it, please?"

Jim turned and slipped into the tent, returning moments later with a small envelope. Inside was an Italian passport for a Giacomo Ricci. Moore frowned. "I thought your name was Jim."

"It is, in English. In Italian, it's Giacomo."

"Don't you have to be an American to be drafted?"

"I hold dual citizenship. Or I used to. I gave up my American citizenship when I came up here."

Moore wrote the details of the passport into his notebook and passed it back. "Were you on or near Long Beach Road in the early hours this morning?"

"No."

Moore reached into his shirt pocket and pulled out a card, realizing too late the awkwardness of what he was about to do.

Jim grinned and held out his hand. "You were about to offer me your card, but realized I have no pockets to put it into."

Moore laughed. He was beginning to like this Italian. "Well, I'll give it to you anyway. Just in case you find a pocket somewhere."

Jim returned the smile and accepted the card.

12.

With a population of just over a thousand people, Mark explained, Ucluelet was double the size of Tofino. It was obviously nothing like Victoria, Sandy thought, as she cast a critical eye over the few shops there were. Mark parked the Ford Falcon in front of a small café, where they agreed to meet in a half-hour. He left to market his carvings and she started on a circuit of the town centre.

It was in the second shop she came to that she found a cute pair of brown loafers, which she happily showed off to Mark when they met at the café as planned. Mark shared the news that the new shop owner had accepted all the carvings he'd brought. Sandy congratulated him and they settled down to discussing the various scenarios that would put Geoff on the road where she'd found him, based on the map of pathways Mark had drawn.

"None of the paths seem right," Sandy groaned as they examined Mark's map for the third time. "We must be missing something."

"How about we give it a break."

Sandy agreed. "Do we have time for me to do some more shopping? I could use some work clothes, and I should pick up some groceries."

"Let's go!"

It was after five o'clock before they arrived back at the car, and Mark offered to buy her supper. She accepted and threw her bags in the back seat. Slipping in front with him, she felt prepared for her summer adventure. "Wow, we did okay, didn't we?"

Mark pulled out on to Peninsula Road, then turned left on Main Street, which dropped to the waterfront. Halfway down its steep grade, he slipped into a parking spot in front of a two-storey building that sat flush to the sidewalk, its signage declared it to be The Innlet. Sandy made to comment but found Mark had already exited the vehicle and was halfway around the car.

He gestured to the sign above the front door. "You have a choice of a cocktail lounge, a dining room, or a beer parlour. What do you feel like?"

Sandy cast a critical eye over the jeans, cotton top and poncho she was wearing. "I don't think I'm dressed for a lounge or dining room. Maybe we should stick with the beer parlour."

Mark looked her over. "This town is supported by fishermen and loggers. I doubt what you're wearing would cause a problem. In the dining room you could order a meal, in the beer parlour it'll be sandwiches."

"Still, I'd rather not," Sandy insisted.

Mark accepted her decision and led her toward the side of the building. Sandy relaxed. It had not been her appearance that had caused her concern, but rather the altered birth date on her driver's licence. She had been afraid it wouldn't stand up to the scrutiny of a lounge or a dining room waiter.

When Sandy spotted the side entrance marked LADIES & ESCORTS, she stopped "Do they still separate us? I thought that went out in '63."

"Maybe they just haven't had time to change the sign. Last time I was here I didn't notice any division, except by the pool table."

The moment she pushed through and saw the crowded, noisy room, she let out a sigh. *This will do.* Mark led her to a table near a low divider that ran three-quarters of the width of the room. Mark caught the eye of a waiter, who hurried over.

"I'm sorry, miss. I'm going to have to ask you for your ID."

Taking a deep breath, Sandy fished out her wallet. She had turned twenty in April but had been using a false ID showing her age as twenty-one since entering university in September. On campus it was almost expected that students lied about how old they were. But this wasn't a university campus. This was the real world. Sandy squared her shoulders and held out her wallet, open to show her driver's licence. The waiter barely glanced at it before taking their orders and disappearing.

"You should consider it a compliment. You're a beautiful woman who will carry her youth well into old age," Mark said.

Sandy blushed. "Are you sure you're not a politician?" Glancing around the room, she added, "Are there babies to kiss now?"

"They're coming later." He laughed, then changed the subject. "Do you play pool?"

"I've never played."

"Well, it's time you learned." He stood and made his way around the barrier to where a bar of lights highlighted a single pool table. He placed a quarter on the edge of the table and returned to her.

"Why'd you do that?"

"To let the people playing know that we'll play the winners or take the table next if they don't want to play anymore."

Sandy glanced at the four men playing pool. They looked very serious—not the sort with the patience to allow a greenhorn to learn. "I don't know. Maybe we shouldn't."

"Relax. Stay cool."

She let out a slow breath and told herself it'd be all right. "You said last night that you traveled a lot with your parents. Did you grow up wanting to be a biologist like your dad?"

"No. My brother is following that path."

Their waiter returned, placed their beers on the table, and disappeared into the crowd once more. Mark lifted his glass and waited for her to do the same. "Here's to forging our own paths." After touching her glass to his, Sandy took a quick sip and wondered if she should ask the question she wanted to. *Are you a draft dodger?* Over the last couple of years, many men had crossed the border between Canada and the United States to avoid the draft or as deserters from the military forces engaging in the Vietnam War. Sandy's father was very vocal about his feelings toward these men. He had fought in the Second World War and could not understand why men wouldn't want to fight for their country. Sandy had a hard time believing that the young men being sent to Vietnam were being sent to protect their homeland.

Before she could ask her question, the waiter returned with their sandwiches. The hot beef looked juicy and the bread fresh. They had just taken their first bite when a man's shout interrupted them.

"Hey, girly. This your quarter?"

Sandy looked toward the voice. Its source stood beside the pool table, holding up the quarter Mark had set there. The man's black hair was clipped close, accenting a long nose and the harsh angles of his face. He was a large, barrel-chested man, dressed in a red-and-black striped polo shirt and dull-brown chinos. The man started tossing a coin in the air with his right hand and catching it with his left as he walked toward the table.

Another man joined the first, and Sandy started to get nervous. Both men sneered down at Mark, and Sandy realized their question hadn't been directed at her. She shifted to look across the table at him and found his attention was on her.

"No, Sandy," he said quietly. "Don't react." He stood. "Yes, it is," he said, a forced lightness in his voice.

The man tossing the coin stopped. "Then you're up. Heads or tails?"

The other man burst out laughing, pausing enough to repeat the question. "Heads or tails? That's a hoot, Rod!"

Rod tossed the coin high in the air. "Call it!" he demanded.

"Heads," Mark answered.

Rod caught the coin as it fell with his left hand and swiftly clapped it down on the top of his right. He grinned at Mark and slowly lifted his hand to reveal the coin beneath. "You break," he said, and tossed the coin to Mark.

Mark pocketed the coin and walked over to the rack of cues, taking his time in choosing one.

Rod winked at Sandy before joining Mark at the table. "So, how many hippies does it take to screw in a light bulb?"

When Mark didn't answer, Rod said, "None. Too much like work!"

Rod's friend laughed again, but Mark kept his focus on the shot he was lining up. He sighted down the length of the pool cue to the white ball resting in the centre of the head string and took his shot. The ball slammed into those resting at the foot end of the table, scattering them across the table, but none sank in the pockets.

Mark stood back and waited to see which of the men he'd be playing against. Rod stepped up. Mark glanced at Sandy, who offered him a bolstering smile.

Rod's shot sank the nine ball in the corner pocket. "Stripes," Rod said, then took his second shot, which missed.

Mark faced Sandy and extended his cue. "Your turn."

Sandy stood and started to cross the distance to the table.

"Looks like we're playing a pair of girls," Rod called out.

Mark dropped his extended arm, and the cue butt came to rest on the floor by his foot. Sandy stopped in her tracks.

"What's the matter, girls? Lose your nerve?"

Mark pulled up the cue and laid it on the pool table before approaching Sandy. "I think we'll take our dinner to go."

After wrapping the sandwiches in foil Mark got from the waiter, they headed out the door to the sound of Rod calling, "Look, the girlies don't want to play anymore."

13.

Leaving Evans to continue the beach interviews with the assistance of two auxiliary officers who had finally shown up, Moore returned to his patrol car. If he hurried, he wouldn't be too late for dinner and would, hopefully, avoid a lecture from his wife. He knew he should feel lucky to have her at all. Married men weren't recruited for the Force, and single men had to wait at least two years before they were allowed to take on the commitment of a wife. He had blown that restriction by a year when Samantha got pregnant, and they quickly married.

The birth of their first son changed everything. His world became brighter. Before that, he had been completely focused on his job and a steady climb through the ranks. After his son arrived, all Moore could think about was his role as a father. He envied his wife's ability to stay at home and watch their son grow up.

It wasn't until the previous year, when their son turned fifteen, that Moore discovered his wife's discontent.

Advertisements requesting applications from those with nursing qualifications, circled and torn from Vancouver newspapers, started appearing on the breakfast table. No discussion. Just the clippings. Moore figured she would explain eventually. Over the years, he had learned not to push her. But then the second pregnancy had come along, and the bits of newspaper with their quiet messages stopped appearing.

With the birth of their second son, Moore felt as if he'd been given a chance to correct the mistakes he'd made the first time around. At the top of his to-do list was settling down. No more transfers. He was going to stabilize his family, and the west coast of Vancouver Island was where he wanted that to happen. He finally understood his father's decision to remain in a municipal police force rather than move into the national RCMP, where continuous transfers were the norm.

Samantha, however, didn't seem as enthusiastic. Since giving birth for the second time, she had become more subdued, less interested in going outside. Gone were the hints about restarting the career that had never truly begun, since she'd become pregnant with their first child while she was studying to become a nurse. Often, he found her silently crying as she rocked the baby to sleep. When he asked what was wrong, she shook off his concern, saying, "Just a bout of maternity blues."

Maybe it was time to arrange a babysitter and take her away for a weekend.

The problem was that he loved his job—even more so since taking his present post. West Coast people were, on the whole, hard-working, honest, and fiercely independent. The area was wild and breathtaking. He could see raising a healthy, happy family here. And the Long Beach murder was exactly the type of case he had been waiting for. It would provide the opportunity to prove his skills and gain the promotion he hoped would convince his wife they could make a life where they were.

As he approached his vehicle, a flicker pulled his attention to his windshield. A piece of torn cardboard stuck beneath his wiper caught the breeze. Moore opened the driver's door and reached across the front seat to pull a pair of gloves from the vehicle's cubbyhole. He then pulled the cardboard from under the wipers. It turned out to be a piece of a cereal box with a message in pencil scrawled across it: NOT ALL THAT GLITTERS IS GOLD.

14.

When the door to the beer parlour swung shut behind them, Sandy and Mark found themselves standing on the empty side-street bathed in the garish neon light of the hotel's signage. "Why didn't you stand up to them?"

Mark stopped, bewilderment written on his face. "Did you see the size of them?"

"What? Were you afraid?" As soon as she said it, shame heated her cheeks. She quick-stepped away, turned and started to walk, not wanting him to see the confusion written all over her face.

"And what would've happened, Sandy? They would've pounded the shit out of me, and then they would have come after you." He caught up to her and grabbed her arm, spinning her to face him. "I'm sure you can imagine what that type of guy would've done to you."

Sandy stared down at the gravel road. "But now they think you're a girl."

"It doesn't matter." He threw his sandwich in the garbage bin by the corner of the hotel.

Sandy thought about doing the same, but she was too hungry to do it.

"Look," Mark continued. "I don't care what they think of me. If they think I'm a girl because my hair's longer than they think it should be, so what? That's their problem, not mine."

"Don't you want people to like you?"

"Of course I want people to like me." Mark took her hand and started walking toward the car. "But I'm not going to change who I am to gain their approval. Isn't that what our generation's all about? Pushing expectations? Being ourselves?"

When they reached the car, and Mark opened the door for her, Sandy thought about her own expectations as she slid into the seat. When he'd settled in behind the wheel, she asked, "Is that all we're about? Pushing expectations? I mean, are we being different just to be different?"

Sandy watched the play of emotion on Mark's face and found that she enjoyed being with him for that reason. She could see his mind working. When he spoke, it was softly. "I came up to Canada because your government doesn't force its citizens to fight in an undeclared war. If I had stayed, the American government would've forced me into becoming a killing machine."

Mark looked out the window, back toward the beer parlour. "Those gorillas back there? I couldn't care less what they think of me. Since moving here, I've had the time to get to know who I am. I believe in living in peace, walking in peace. It's not a slogan to me. It's a way of life. And sometimes that makes other people angry, crazy, or both."

Sandy didn't know what to say. When Mark started the car and headed toward the highway and the inn, Sandy looked to the sky, which, though darker, was clearing. The colours of a hidden setting sun shone their magic on the soft edges of the remaining clouds. The moon was still full and rising from the east. Mark switched on the car's lights, a precaution for the ride back to the lodge in the dusk of the early evening.

She didn't want to be what others thought she should be, either, and she believed in the peace movement. *So why am I so disappointed that Mark didn't take on those two goons?* "I'm sorry. I guess I'm a bit confused," she said, turning to Mark. "On the one hand, I believe that, as a woman, I should be able to do anything I want, including having a career. But I guess I still expect a man to fight for me, as if"—she paused, ashamed of the realization—"as if I were a little girl."

"There's always a price to pay to get what we want," Mark answered. "But first, you need to figure out what that is."

15.

Moore exited the Wickaninnish Inn as a burgundy Ford Falcon drove past, Sandy in the passenger seat. He followed the vehicle to where the driver parked facing the ocean and waited as Sandy unfolded from the passenger seat. "Good evening."

Surprised, Sandy looked up. "Oh! Hi. What are you doing here?"

"I need to ask you a question. Do you have a few minutes?"

Sandy moved out from between the parked vehicles and motioned to where the driver was exiting the car. "This is Mark."

A stocky man dressed in frayed jeans and a grey Doors concert T-shirt, stepped forward, accepted Moore's offered hand, and met his inquisitive gaze without wavering. "How can we help you, Officer?"

Moore introduced himself and assessed the shorter man. *Confident.* A uniform wouldn't intimidate him. "I'm glad you're here Mark. I was looking for you on the beach earlier."

"Sandy and I went into town to do some errands."

The sound of laughter rang out and the three stepped back against the car. A pickup truck passed them, its driver searching for an open parking spot while the teens in the back played a game of keep-away with what looked like a girl's bikini top. Moore shook his head. "Maybe we should find someplace private to talk."

"Let's go to the lodge," Sandy offered. "I'll just grab my bags out of the back seat." Sandy touched Mark's arm. "Could you grab the groceries from the trunk?"

With arms loaded, the two men followed Sandy into the lodge, where she directed the unpacking of the purchases. When Sandy paused to read a note left on the table, Mark suggested they move to the living room.

After settling into one of the armchairs, Moore pulled out his notebook while Mark chose a spot on the couch. "I understand Miss Chambers spent the evening at your campfire last night."

A slow smile spread from Mark's lips to his eyes. "Yes, she spent time at my campfire."

The clatter of dishes and cupboard doors shutting in the kitchen momentarily confused Moore. He had expected Sandy to join them. Finding his place in his notes, he continued. "Tell me about last night."

"I shared my dinner with her because the guy she came with left her on her own."

"That would be Geoff Johnston?"

"Geoff? Yes. I'm not sure about the last name."

"What time was this?"

"I don't know. We don't keep track of time on the beach. We eat when we're hungry. We sleep when we're tired."

Moore stifled a groan. *Not another rant on the evils of modern society.* "Was anyone else with you?"

"Jim and Neal came to get their share."

"Jim Ricci?"

Mark shrugged. "You'll find that most people don't use last names on the beach. A lot of reasons for that.

Privacy is a big one. Jim hasn't shared his last name with me, and even if he had, I wouldn't tell you."

"Good thing I've spoken with Mr. Ricci already then. What about the other one, Neal? Where would I find him?"

"He left."

"When?"

"This morning. He said he was going to hitch back to Vancouver, then maybe out to the Okanagan."

"The Okanagan? Why there?"

"Said he was done with the rain."

"Last name?"

"Not a clue."

Moore fought the anger Mark's attitude inspired. "I am conducting a police investigation. If I feel you are hindering that investigation in any way, I will not hesitate to take you into the station. Do you understand?"

"I do." Mark looked him directly in the eye. "But I respect my neighbours' privacy."

Moore glared back. "Your last name and place of residence."

Mark's lips curved. "Smith, and the beach."

Moore took a steadying breath. "Driver's licence?"

Mark reached into the back pocket of his jeans and pulled out his wallet. "Wilson. It's Wilson."

Moore took the driver's licence and wrote the number, as well as Mark's name and address. *Encinitas, California?* He'd never heard of it. He returned Mark's licence. "Do you own a vehicle?"

"No."

Moore looked up. "What about the Falcon?"

"A friend's. And, no, I'm not giving you his name."

Moore ignored the comment. "Were you on Long Beach Road at any time last night, or early this morning?"

"No."

"You said Miss Chambers was at your campsite for dinner. What time did she leave?"

"This morning, early. I walked her to the inn."

Moore looked up from his notes. "She spent the night with you?"

"Not in the way you're thinking. I loaned her my sleeping bag, and she slept out by the fire."

"So, you can't confirm that she was there the whole night?" Moore glanced up from his note-taking when Mark's answer didn't come right away.

Mark saw his glance and shifted so that he sat taller. "Well, no, I guess not. But there were at least three others crashed by the fire."

"Names?"

"Again, haven't a clue."

Moore paused. "What about Miss Chambers? Was she alone?"

"What does Sandy say?"

"I want to hear it from you."

"There's not much to say. Geoff showed up at the campfire just after we ate. Tried to push in on Sandy, but she wasn't having any of it."

"Did you know Mr. Johnston, er, Geoff, previously?"

"No."

"Then how'd you know who he was?"

"Sandy introduced him to everyone."

Of course she did. He jumped to another question. "What time was this?"

When Mark didn't answer, Moore looked up from his notes. Mark sent him a sideways grin. "Oh," Moore said. "Let me guess, you don't know."

"Right."

"Did he stay?"

"No. Sandy was angry—"

"Angry? When?" Both men looked up to see Sandy carrying a tray with steaming mugs of tea and a plate of fig newton cookies.

"I was just saying you were upset with Geoff because all your stuff was locked in his van at the inn, and he had promised to go back with you or give you the keys."

Moore looked to Sandy. "Did he?"

"Did he what?" Sandy set the tray on the coffee table, then chose a mug and cookie before taking the empty space on the couch.

"Give you the keys."

"No." Mark answered for her. "And then a guy showed up, and they left together."

Moore frowned. "Miss Chambers left?"

Sandy placed a hand on Mark's shoulder, stopping him from continuing. "No, Geoff left with the Frisbee guy."

"Ah. I've met him," Moore said.

"Where?"

Moore waved away Mark's question. "Can you describe him?"

Mark paused, then shook his head. "To tell you the truth, I didn't pay him much attention. Skinny. Too skinny." Mark lifted one eyebrow. "You know what I'm saying?"

Moore nodded. *A heavy drug user.*

"Red hair," Mark offered, "but darker. Bleached on top. Short." He motioned toward his jawline. "I think he was wearing swim trunks and a T-shirt." Mark paused. "No. I seem to remember sleeves." He paused again. "Maybe not." He shook his head. "I can't remember. I was just glad Geoff was leaving."

"What do you mean by that?"

Mark leaned forward and picked up a cookie, examined it, then shoved it in his mouth, chewing as he answered. "I don't know. Geoff had a nervous energy about him I didn't like. It was almost like he was high… but his eyes didn't show that he was high. He just gave off a strange vibe."

Moore considered Mark's observation, mentally comparing it to what his friend had shown him in the morgue. "Did you see where Geoff and this other guy went?"

"They walked off down the beach."

When Sandy leaned forward, about to coach him, Moore held up his hand. "Don't. I want what Mark saw."

Sandy sat back.

Moore continued. "Did you see who they went to meet?"

"All I could see was that they'd stopped just the other side of where the logs had been stacked up for a bonfire. The guy they met wasn't that much taller than Geoff, but he was heavier." Mark extended his arms out to his sides to indicate a wide body.

Moore took a moment to consider his next question. "I want to ask you both if either of you can remember

Geoff mentioning anything about finding gold in the area? Or knowing prospectors?"

Sandy and Mark shook their heads in unison.

"Right." Moore rose and pulled two business cards out of his shirt pocket and placed them on the coffee table. "If you think of anything else, call me."

Mark stuffed a card into the pocket of his jeans. "It wasn't a friendly meeting."

Moore, who had closed and pocketed his notebook, pulled it out again. "What do you mean?"

"I'm not sure. It just wasn't the usual handshake or punch-on-the-shoulder-type thing."

"I agree."

Mark sent a quick glance at Sandy, then turned back to Moore. "Geoff stopped a few feet away from the other guy, and they seemed to argue for a minute before walking away together."

"Did the Frisbee guy go with them?"

"He left as soon as the two started arguing."

"Anything else?"

"No."

"Okay, you have my card." When Sandy went to stand, Moore waved her down. "I can see myself out."

Tom gave a polite wave to the officer as he walked past. He recognized him from the morning's interview but could not recall his name. Taking a moment after parking his Mustang in its usual spot by the lodge, behind Edan's Jeepster and Brent's red MGB roadster, he focused on the Mustang's rear view mirror and watched the image of the officer continue down the lane to the inn. *What were you up to?*

There was only one way to find out. He jumped out of the Mustang and headed for the door. The interior of the lodge was flooded with light, and the turkey-strut beat of the Rolling Stones' *It's Only Rock 'n Roll*. Conny must be in. She was the serious Stones fan. Tom crossed the living room to the picture window, where the stereo was perched on a cabinet, and turned down the volume.

"Hey, what'd you do that for?"

He was wrong; it was Tish. He glanced over his shoulder to see her standing in the walk through to the kitchen with the girl he recognized from the morning's incident. She was even more attractive up close, but he refocused his attention on Tish. "Don't worry, I won't be staying." He returned to the stereo and raised the volume.

"That's more like it!" Tish shouted.

The new girl smiled as she manoeuvred around Tish and entered the living room. "Conny's just gone up to the inn to get us supper. We didn't realize you'd be home. I'm sure there'll be enough to share if you'd like. I've already had a sandwich—"

"Who are you?"

Tish stepped up beside Sandy. "This is Sandy. She'll be staying here for a while."

Great. Tom smiled. He recognized a great buffer when he saw one. Tish glared at him as if she'd read his mind. He met her glare. "I won't be staying." He wasn't into another shouting match. "I just came to get a coat." He knew his coat was already in the back seat of the Mustang, but the lie had just slipped out.

He was halfway to his room when he heard Sandy's sarcastic, "He's sociable."

Tish replied, "Don't mind him, he's a prick."

Tom took a deep breath and faced them. "Now, that's a matter of opinion," he said, striding into the living room. He winked at Sandy. "I've changed my mind. I'm going to stay in tonight." He gestured toward Tish, who had dropped into the overstuffed chair by the fireplace. "After all, there's such a short time left to enjoy your company."

When Tish ignored him, he sauntered into the kitchen and opened the fridge. "I feel like a beer."

Tish shook her head. "I heard you had a date tonight!"

Tom froze. He'd forgotten about the date, and he was pretty sure the swim in Kennedy Lake had washed away the name written on his arm. He pulled up his sleeve and did a quick check. Nothing. He decided the reminder would give him the perfect excuse to return to his original decision to avoid an evening in the lodge with Tish's anger. "Okay, it's one beer and I'll be off!"

He pulled a Lucky from the fridge and returned to the living room, where he joined Sandy on the couch. "What have you got there?" he asked, indicating the sketchbook she was flipping through.

"A map. I was going to walk to Wreck Bay this afternoon. I wanted to see if Geoff could have taken another path from the beach. I can't understand why he was on that road. He would have had to walk right past his van to get there."

Tom sat back and took a pull on his beer. "Oh, right. You're the one who found the dead hippie on the road."

"Tom!" Tish yelled. "Don't be so crude. She knew the guy."

Tom caught Sandy's frozen expression. *Was the dead hippie who he had seen her on the beach with the day before?* "Did you know him well?"

Sandy closed the sketchpad. "He gave me a ride from Port Alberni."

Tom hesitated. He didn't want to admit that he had watched their horseplay on the beach, nor voice his suspicion about what they'd done afterward. "I heard they thought it was a hit-and-run. Is that what the cop was here for?"

Sandy frowned. "No. He wanted to talk to Mark."

"Mark?"

"A guy I met on the beach yesterday. He took me into town today."

"Ukee?"

"Ucluelet," Tish explained. "It's what everyone here calls Ucluelet."

"Then, yes, we went into Ukee."

Tom scanned the room. "Where is he now?"

"He went back to the beach."

"This beach?"

"No, Wreck Bay."

Tom felt Tish's glare from across the room. He shifted to make more space between himself and Sandy. "Why are you so interested in how the hippie got to where he was?"

Sandy refocused on her sketchpad. "I'm just curious why he didn't take his van. You know, if he was going somewhere. Mark told me about a couple of paths he could have taken."

"Finding the body," Tish interrupted. "That must've been awful."

Sandy sighed. "It was."

"What do you think happened?" Tom asked.

Sandy opened her mouth to answer, but the front door opened and Conny burst in, carrying three covered plates. "Dinner's here," she called.

"Great!" Tish stood and started toward the kitchen.

Tom jumped up from the couch and grabbed Tish's arm. "We need to talk." He glanced down at Sandy and turned his back to her, whispering, "I dropped into the cop shop this afternoon."

Tish pulled her arm out of his grip and glared at him. "Well good for you," she whispered back.

Tom shifted out of Sandy's way as she rose and made her way to the kitchen. When he figured she was out of earshot, he continued, "I told the officer on duty that you were driving my car because I was too drunk. I told them we didn't hit anyone and saw nothing. The trouble is, I think there's something else going on. I think this might be more than a hit-and-run."

Tish raised her eyebrows. "Did they say what it was?"

"Not really. It was more the questions he asked. He wanted to know if I had seen the guy's van on the road or in town that night." Tom raised his voice and directed his next question at Sandy, "You mentioned your guy had a van. Did the police ask you about it?"

"No, I told them about it."

Tom glanced at the abandoned sketchpad. "Did you find the road that goes to Wreck Bay? He may have come up that way. Maybe he was walking back to the inn."

Sandy left the table and retrieved the pad from the couch. "Mark told me about one that went beside a bog."

"It's little more than a track made by some old homesteaders years ago," Conny said. "It's rough and overgrown. I doubt Geoff would have known about it, let alone found it." She turned to Tom. "And it doesn't go all the way to the bay."

Tom frowned and tilted his head. The road was rough and easily washed out, but it was well-used by locals. "He may not have known about it, Conny, but if he hooked up with a local, he could have walked out that way." Turning back to Tish, he whispered, "I told the cop I didn't even know the guy had a van. He asked if anyone at Janet's place had asked about him. I told him I didn't remember anyone mentioning him. Do you?"

Tish shrugged and gave him one of the smiles he never knew how to read. He lowered his voice and leaned in. "The cop had me write out my statement. Did you have to write out a statement?"

"What are you two whispering about?" Conny demanded.

"Tom says the cops asked him some strange questions." Tish joined Conny and Sandy, who had returned to the table. "He thinks it might be more than a hit-and-run."

At Sandy's gasp, Tom turned to look at her and noticed Conny frowning down at her dinner. "Did Edan screw up your order, Conny?"

Looking up, she gave her head a shake. "No. Everything's fine."

Tom stared at her. His gut told him she had just lied to him. She had never been one to share her feelings, but she had always been straight with people. He walked to the table and challenged Tish. "I need to talk to you. Can we go outside for a minute?"

"My dinner will get cold. Go away. I have no interest in talking with you."

Frustrated, Tom threw his hands up in the air. "You might want to change your mind since, from what the cop said, so far, we're the only two people they can put on that road around the time that guy was hit…or murdered."

Sandy grabbed his arm. "Murdered? They think Geoff was murdered?"

Gently, Tom pried his arm from her grip. "I don't know. It's just a feeling."

Tish's eyes narrowed. "A feeling? You don't have feelings!"

Tom took a deep breath. There would be no getting through to Tish until she calmed down. "Don't worry, I'm leaving."

Tom fought a bout of homesickness as he watched the rolling surf wash over the golden sand, its white froth gliding toward the dark, jagged rocks at the base of the inn. Tom's toes curled against the sharp chill of the skim of water and he quick stepped back to the dry warmth offered ahead of the incoming tide. The sun was already splashing its fiery reds, royal purples, and orange-rimmed yellows against the soft edges of the dark, moody clouds jamming the sky, even though sunset was close to two hours away. Tom sighed. As beautiful as his present surroundings were, he wanted to go home. He missed the energy and hidden secrets of the city.

He sank onto a large log and set down his shoes beside him. Two surfers straddling their boards were backlit by the sun, like black buoys bobbing among the swells. He'd often thought of trying the sport. The inn kept a supply of boards for guests or staff to use; he'd just never taken the opportunity. He wondered now if he ever would.

He had decided not to drive into Ucluelet, just in case the girl who had written her number on his arm hadn't been as drunk as he was and was waiting for him to take her out. His memory of the night before offered no clue who she might be. He only hoped her memory was just as foggy.

He stood and continued his walk barefooted. A few lean-tos and tents were set up against the top of the beach, their occupants off partying somewhere else. In Vancouver, he would never have socialized with such people. If he had seen them on the street, he would have looked the other way or made some disparaging remark to his companion of the moment. The idea of conversing with them would never have crossed his mind. Or if it had, he would have been disgusted. Even Tish. If he had met her in Vancouver, he would never have given her a second glance. But here on the wild west coast of Vancouver Island, things were different.

Sea birds skittered across the sand, advancing and retreating with the surge of the tide. Life seemed so simple on the beach. Tom wondered what it would be like to escape his life as the hippies seemed to have done. Would he be able to give up his life in Vancouver and live here on nothing more than found or recycled items?

He laughed at the absurdity. *No, I wouldn't.* His complicated family often drove him crazy, but that family had provided a comfortable lifestyle he wasn't about to throw away. He just needed to figure out how to prevent his involvement in the present police investigation from interfering with his planned return to Vancouver.

SUNDAY, MAY 12, 1968

16.

Moore leaned back in his chair and closed his eyes. Dawn had just broken, and birdsong filtered through the small window beside his desk. Usually, the office was quiet and empty on a Sunday, especially in the morning, but not this week. Four officers, two his own and two auxiliaries, had come in for a six o'clock case briefing.

"So." Moore's eyes remained closed. "What we've got is an overkill. There's too much happening with the body in this case: the beaten legs, a syringe-punctured neck, and a possible drug overdose. Does this make sense to any of you?"

He opened his eyes to see three of the four officers shaking their heads, and Constable Evans staring into space before bringing his gaze down to look at him directly. "I get the feeling that the killer didn't expect the victim to die."

Moore motioned for him to continue. It had taken a lot of work since arriving as the new head of the detachment to inspire enough confidence in his officers that they'd express their opinions without fear of reprisal. His management style bordered on conflicting with the rigid, military, top-down style of the Force, but Moore had persisted. "What makes you think that?"

"I don't know. Just a feeling."

"Well, let's keep that feeling in mind as we review what we know. Sometimes our guts pick up on hidden aspects of a case before our brains do." Moore stood and handed out the case notes he had typed up earlier.

"The coroner viewed the body yesterday at the scene and later at the morgue. As expected, he agreed the situation is confusing and has delayed holding an inquest, pending further investigation by us and the receipt of a pathologist's report." Moore leaned against the front of his desk and faced the group. "The body's being shipped to the pathologist in Nanaimo this morning so any blood work will be done there." Moore sighed. "I've got a call into that office, hoping to get a copy of the results sent here as well as to Victoria."

Constable Evans looked up from the handwritten witness statements he had been gathering into a neat pile. "Won't Victoria be sending someone up here?"

Moore smiled. Evans was the more ambitious of his two constables, always looking for his next posting. He wouldn't waste the opportunity of working with a member of Victoria's Major Crimes Unit, part of the General Investigation Section. "They will, but that doesn't mean we're shutting down our investigation until they get here." Moore gestured to the notes his officers held. "What do we have? Battering the victim's legs seems to have been an attempt to redirect our attention. Was it planned or improvised on the spot?"

Evans was quick to answer. "I'd say it happened on the spot. That's why it's so overdone. If this was premeditated, they would have figured out how to make the marks look like they were caused by a vehicle instead of just hammering away at the legs."

"Good," Moore acknowledged. "What happened to our victim? Why was he killed? Why was there an effort to disguise it? What was he doing out on that road when he had a perfectly good vehicle parked at the inn? Ideas?"

"A fight with his girlfriend? And she leaves him by the side of the road?"

Moore turned to the speaker, Timothy Owens, one of the auxiliary officers, and brother to Terry, owner of Owens' Garage. "Possibly. You're thinking the girl who found him was his girlfriend? Or is there someone else?"

"I was thinking of the girl who found him." Owens opened his notebook. "Sandy. It would explain why the victim was on the side of the road even though he had a vehicle parked at the inn. She was familiar with the vehicle and the victim. Some of the partiers said she had been looking for the victim—"

"Geoff. His name was Geoff," Evans mumbled.

"Fine. Geoff," Owens corrected, glancing at Evans, his brows creasing, before returning to his notes. "According to witnesses, she was looking for Geoff to get his keys so she could remove her stuff from his van. Maybe they argued as they walked back to the van. He dies. She drives the body out on the road, then returns the van to the parking lot."

Moore took a long sip of his coffee. "You're thinking it was an emotional attack?"

"Yes."

"Anyone else think Miss Chambers is our attacker?"

Nelson cleared his throat. "I'm wondering about the injection. If it was an emotional attack, then the injection doesn't fit. The killer would have needed the syringe ready and primed. Don't you think? That suggests premeditation, doesn't it?"

Unlike his teammate, Nelson didn't possess an abundance of confidence. He often needed reassurance. Moore offered it. "Yes, it could, Constable. Good catch."

"There's a lot of drugs on the beach this year, sir." Alex Doukas, the second auxiliary officer, jumped into the discussion. "New stuff. Not just the usual marijuana and hash."

"So, you're thinking there's a drug or gang-related motivation for this murder?" Moore was surprised by Doukas' information. He or his constables should have noticed the presence of new drugs.

"There could be. It all depends on what else we find."

Moore sighed. "As you all know, Victoria's MCU, as part of the GIS, handles all major crime on the island, so I was required to contact them. I did so yesterday afternoon. They're rounding up an officer who will head this investigation. They're also contacting an identification specialist operating out of Nanaimo, who will manage the forensic evidence." Moore chose not to share that Victoria had implied it could be midweek by the time someone was available to assist with the investigation as several of their officers were in Vancouver for training. An island-based drug squad was being developed and training had started in anticipation of a major, province-wide shuffling within the ranks. It was expected more specialist squads would be developed. An internal memo about the new squad and the opportunities it would present had arrived the week before. He had posted it on the notice board by the coffee machine and discussed it with both his constables. Evans had shown great interest, his eyes firmly set on a transfer to a major city.

Nothing like the present to remind him of his current position. "When we're done here, I want you to head over to the garage and make sure the victim's van is secured," Moore ordered.

"I'm sure it would be—"

Moore held up his hand to stop further interruption from the auxiliary officer, before continuing. "Then I want you to return here to develop our scene photos and go through them, logging what you see. I'll review them when you're done."

Moore casually leaned back. "When I spoke with Miss Chambers yesterday morning, she told me she had only met Mr. Johnston, Geoff, the day before, when he picked her up hitchhiking outside of Port Alberni. Do I believe her? I'm not sure. If it was just a chance meeting, then her involvement is minimal. Did any of you speak with anyone on the beach who knew her? Or him?"

"No one I spoke to remembered either of them. They all claimed to have been too focused on enjoying the party to notice what anyone in particular was doing," Evans said. "I think most of them were still high when we spoke."

"We found a lot of the same," added Doukas. "The majority were still in weekend party mode, and those who weren't were preparing to be." He flipped through a couple of pages of his notebook until he found what he was looking for. "One guy said he threw a Frisbee around with someone who matched the description we gave. The only reason he remembers him is because later that night, he came over asking if they had any food. He couldn't confirm it was our victim because they hadn't exchanged names." The constable closed his notebook and put it back in his pocket.

"So, none of them admitted to driving the victim to where he was discovered?" Moore asked. "Or hearing anyone talk about seeing anything odd on the road down to the party?"

All four men shook their heads.

Moore looked up at the ceiling, cursing the blindness of crowds. "Okay, I'll speak to Miss Chambers again. In the meantime, I've put a notice in the paper and on the radio asking anyone who saw or heard anything to come forward. As you know, the local paper doesn't come out until Thursday. That's four days away. Hopefully, the radio will provide us with what we need before then."

He turned his attention to the two auxiliary officers. "I appreciate your help yesterday, and your willingness to come in today for the briefing. I'll let you get on with your day."

Once the auxiliary officers had left, Moore focused on his constables. "I want to thank you, as well. I know yesterday was long and challenging." Moore paused. "I want to keep our focus on this case because, as I said earlier, it is our case until we hand it over. With all this in mind, we need to be prepared for more long days. Monty, when you come back in for your shift tonight, I want you to go through all the statements and pull any information that wasn't brought forward this morning. Also, make notes of anyone or anything you feel we need to follow up on."

Nelson's head bobbed as he scribbled notes, then looked up. "Speaking of my shift, I've noticed an increase in call-outs to Long Beach. There are just too many people camping and driving on that beach. It's getting dangerous."

"I have too," added Evans. "And the summer hasn't even officially started yet."

"I know. All we can do is do our best." Moore sighed and brought the tired constables up to speed on his beach interviews, asking at the end if the search for gold could be behind the murder.

"Aren't those claims dead?" Evans asked. "I heard all the gold had been taken out in the late 1800s, early 1900s."

"Mr. Ricci claimed to have found gold recently. Then there's the fortressed shack."

"What I don't understand"—Nelson piped up—"is why anyone would kill to pan an old claim?"

Moore paused and looked at Nelson. "There may be no connection at all, but I want to check those shacks out tomorrow." He picked up the piece of cereal box from the top of his desk and read its message out loud. "Not all that glitters is gold." He dropped the paper on his desk. "Either someone believes the gold connection is false and is trying to help us, or this is another diversion."

Nelson shook his head. "Is there a gold connection?"

"That's what we need to find out." Moore toyed with the piece of cardboard. "Maybe beach gossip included such speculation." Setting the cardboard down, he continued. "Anyway, I dropped into Tofino Hospital and talked with the GP. The victim's family was from there originally; they moved away when Geoff was about seven. We need to know why Geoff returned. Was it just to check out the surf, or is there a reason that will connect to a motive behind his murder?"

"It's going to take sheer luck to find anyone who noticed the movements of one long-haired hippie among a sea of long-haired hippies." Drumming his fingers on his desk, he considered how to direct the case. "We don't know where the victim died. It may have been in the van. It may have been on the trail somewhere. What we do know is that it wasn't in the ditch, and it wasn't by hit-and-run." Moore glanced at his watch. "It's about eight o'clock now. We've got a lot to do. How about we meet again tomorrow morning? If the GIS officers arrive by then, we'll have more to give them."

"Sir?" Evans stood. "Did you see the statement left in the file from last night?"

"No."

Evans reached over and pulled the sheet from the file. "The bartender from the inn dropped in to say that he didn't drive himself home on Saturday morning like he'd told you. He mixed things up. His roommate, Miss Phillips, drove."

Moore read through the statement. "No matter who drove, they were still both on the road around the same time as the victim."

"Interesting."

"Yes." Evans placed the statement back in the file.

"So, now their statements match." Moore nodded slowly as he absorbed the new information. "Either they're both involved and are lying, or they've just helped us narrow down the timeline."

17.

Conny walked slowly through the room, her eyes scanning for missed details. She pointed at the edge of a pillowcase peeking out from under a wrinkled comforter. Sandy rushed over to tuck in the errant linen, then stood back while Conny continued her inspection. Conny smiled. She always enjoyed this part of her job, when the girls who came to work at the inn were focused on trying to please her. In the beginning it was always "Yes, Conny. Anything you say, Conny." It would eventually change, sometimes to where she'd have to reassert her authority. But this girl showed promise. Conny turned to Sandy, waiting at the door. "Good job."

The girl visibly relaxed. Conny was about to suggest a celebratory drink since it was the end of their shift, when they were joined by Tish.

"All done," Tish announced. "How'd things go here?"

Conny glanced once more around the room. "Good."

Tish beamed. "Great!" She looked first at Sandy then back to Conny. "I think I'll make tomorrow my last day."

Conny felt a stab of disappointment. She had hoped Tish would stay for another week to allow the new girl to adjust. She silently cursed Tom and glanced at the new girl. *If he so much as sniffs at her*, Conny decided, *I'll chop his balls off.* No way was she going to hire another girl before the end of the season.

"I think I'll take a walk along the beach," Tish said. "Do you two want to join me?"

"Where are you going?" Sandy asked.

Conny interrupted, "I think we'll go back to the lodge. It's been a long day, and there should be a couple of beers left in the fridge."

"I won't be long. Should I bring supper?"

"There are leftovers in the fridge we need to finish," Conny said.

Tish rolled her eyes. "Yes, Mother."

Conny watched Tish turn and leave. She would miss her. She had been the closest to a girlfriend she had ever had. They had worked well together. If only Tom had kept his mitts off her.

"Shall we go?" Conny pointed to the door. Sandy waited while Conny locked the guest room door behind them, then followed as she pushed the housekeeping cart to the end of the hall and tucked it into the storage room. She showed Sandy which of her new set of keys to use to lock the door.

As they walked down the stairs and out the front entrance of the inn, Conny felt quite smug about her decision to hire Sandy. It could prove to be the solution she had been looking for.

A gentle sea breeze brushed her face as they exited the inn, and she inhaled deeply, relaxing. She was about to ask Sandy what type of clothes she had brought with her when she caught sight of Rod, her boyfriend, standing beside his Firebird. "Hi!" she shouted and waved. Turning to Sandy, she said, "I've got to go."

Without waiting for Sandy's reply, Conny ran across the parking lot toward Rod. As she approached, Rod's expression changed, and she stopped, suddenly unsure.

"Get in," he said. He opened the door and Dwayne, a business associate of Rod's, got out of the passenger seat, turned, and tipped the back of the seat forward. It took a moment for Conny to realize he wasn't going to slip into the backseat; he was waiting for her to get in. She looked across at Rod, who only repeated, "Get in."

Alarm bells started clamouring inside Conny's head, and she took a step back. "No. I think I'll stay here. Sandy and Tish are expecting me to have supper with them."

Dwayne grabbed her arm and shoved her toward the open backseat. "He told you to get in."

"You're hurting me. Let go!" She swung around, trying to run back toward the inn. Sandy had continued crossing the parking lot, oblivious to her struggle. Conny twisted again, trying to free herself, but Dwayne grabbed her other arm and pulled her tight to his chest. He leaned down and whispered, "Shout like that again and you won't like what happens to you." Conny stopped struggling. "Now get in the car like a good girl. Rod wants a word."

Conny ducked her head and slipped into the back seat. She was surprised to see she would not be alone. A man she recognized from one of the parties Rod had taken her to in Nanaimo sat on the far side. She sent a tentative smile his way as she settled in, but he only grunted and turned to watch Rod and Dwayne get into the front seats. Conny had never ridden in the backseat of the Firebird before. Her place was always beside Rod in the front. The back didn't offer much room, and because the car was a two-door, she couldn't get out unless Rod or his passenger moved. She tried to calm her breathing. Rod had a temper. She had known that when she first met him, but her life had always been full of angry men, so Rod hadn't stood out. Over the six months they'd been dating, she had only seen his anger directed toward others. This was the first it had come her way. She wondered at its cause. She swallowed, trying to moisten her mouth. The last thing she wanted was to squeak. "Rod," she said. "What's up? Why am I back here?"

Rod put the car in gear and spun out of the inn's driveway, taking them up the hill and onto Long Beach Road. He opened the Firebird up, and they tore off down the narrow lane. Conny hoped there were no other cars, because she didn't want to be trapped in the backseat if they hit one.

She relaxed when Rod geared down, and the vehicle slowed. Maybe the short burst of speed had spent his anger. Then Rod made a right turn and they were bumping over a rutted track into the trees. Conny recognized the spot. They were in the woods above Lost Shoe Creek, which emptied into Wreck Bay.

18.

Rod stopped the car and got out. He pulled the back of his seat forward to allow the man beside her out. Then Dwayne exited and pulled his seat forward, allowing her to climb out. Conny had just uncurled herself when he grabbed her arm again.

"Hey!"

He ignored her protest and dragged her around the car to Rod, where he let her go but stood behind her, mimicking a soldier's at-ease stance. Rod remained silent, gazing into the forest beyond the small circle of rutted mud they were parked in. Without a word, he started walking down a narrow trail. The goon behind her pushed her with his palm. She stumbled forward and followed Rod.

"Do you remember our business arrangement?" Rod asked over his shoulder.

"Of course," she said.

"Remember how after the fire destroyed the boathouse, you said that you knew a place where our product would be *safe* until we were able to establish a new permanent storefront?"

Conny paused. Had something happened to the product? Dwayne pushed her to keep walking.

"Well." Rod headed off the path and into the scrub before stopping on the crest of a hill and pointing down through the trees. "What the hell's this?"

Conny came up beside him and looked down at the shack she had found for Rod as temporary storage. The small building stood halfway down the hill on a lower ridge. A path half-buried by overgrown salal led up to it from Lost Shoe Creek. They were above and behind the shack, so she couldn't see the front, only the windowless back. An abandoned garden was tucked in the far back corner against the edge of the ridge. A large pile of cast-off material sat in the near corner, leaving a small pathway circling the shack. The shack had been abandoned years earlier, but it shouldn't have the degree of abandonment she was sensing now. The hairs on the back of her neck started to stand up.

"Where's the guard?" she asked.

"Exactly. Where's the guard?" Rod snarled. Grabbing her arm, he dragged her stumbling behind him as he strode through the underbrush down the hill. When he brought her around to the front of the shack, she saw why he was angry. The door hung loose on one hinge, the lock cut and lying in pieces on the front step. She fought Rod's grip. "I had no idea, Rod! You can't believe I had anything to do with this!"

A metal box the size of a small suitcase, its lid twisted and mangled, sat open on a roughly made table inside the door. She didn't have to look inside to know the stash was gone. The box had been purchased two weeks earlier to store the shipment of drugs Rod had brought across from Vancouver. That was the last time she'd seen it. She hadn't visited the site since, confident in the arrangements she had made with a local fisherman to act as the night-shift guard and Rod's assignment of one of his many lackeys to the day shift. Neither guard, as far as she knew, had been told what they were guarding. She'd told the fisherman he was guarding office supplies.

Conny had seen no sign of the day-shift guard as they'd come down the hill. She considered the anger Rod was directing at her. His man should be the one standing here answering his questions. One glance at the rigid set of his jaw and she knew it would be dangerous to point that fact out. She understood his anger, though. There had been at least five grand's worth of product in the strongbox stored inside, and more arriving with Rod's return from the mainland the day before. Suddenly, a cold sweat swept over her. "When did this happen?"

"You tell me, Conny."

"Last night?" she guessed.

"Bingo! Give the girl a Kewpie Doll!" The goon laughed.

Conny almost fainted. The goon's response meant the shipment Rod had said he was bringing up from Vancouver the day before had been delivered, doubling the amount of stash stored in the shed overnight. *Ten thousand dollars!*

Rod stepped up as if to steady her, but he gripped her throat instead, lifting her slightly upward. She had to stand on her toes to keep from being choked. "Who else would do this? Who else knew about this?"

"N-n-no one, Rod! I didn't tell anyone!" Conny swallowed hard. Her toes ached, and she was unsure how long they would hold her. Rod grinned, revealing how truly ugly he was. "Please," she begged. "Let go."

Rod's eyes narrowed. "Let go? I could." He dropped his arm but kept the grip on her neck. Conny almost cried in relief when her feet relaxed against the ground. "Or not." Tightening his grip, he raised her even higher, until only the tips of her toes touched the ground. Clawing wildly at his wrist, she fought desperately for air. "What's that you say?" Rod shouted. "Can't hear you!"

Conny passed out.

19.

Sandy stretched her arms above her head and yawned. The lodge's couch was comfortable, but she had spent too much time on it, and she needed to get up. She tossed her sketchpad to the side. On it was a rough sketch of a short road and a path Mark had drawn. He had told her about the various pathways in the area, but only one route would have taken Geoff from Wreck Bay to the road where he was found, and that was along an overgrown path that climbed up the hill from Lost Shoe Creek to join a muddy, rutted road that came in off Long Beach Road and ran alongside a bog. Not a natural choice for someone unfamiliar with the area, Mark had told her.

She paced the living room, wishing for someone to talk to. Tish was out for a walk. Roxanne had left the afternoon before to spend the balance of her weekend with friends in Port Alberni, and Conny was with her boyfriend. As for the rest of her roommates, she had no idea.

The clock on the wall read four o'clock. With a few hours of daylight left, maybe she could do some sketching. Drawing had always relaxed her, even as a kid, or so her mother had told her. She selected a few more pencils from the box on the bookshelf before retrieving the sketchpad and heading for the door.

Sandy followed a short path from the lodge to the beach and came out south of the inn. The tide was on its way out and the skim of water left on the sand mirrored the cloudy sky. The effect was magical, but she didn't want guests at the inn to watch her. She turned south and headed to the series of rocks that marked the end of Wickaninnish Bay. As she scrambled over them, she discovered a cove on the other side. The beach was small and the surrounding land rocky—neither as open nor as flat as the beach at the inn. Rocks, large and small, poked up through the sand in groupings that hid tidal pools lined with starfish and tiny crustaceans. The receding tide alternatively plunged forward and backward over and between the rocks in frothy madness. The tang of wet seaweed and salt water cleared her sinuses and she took a deep breath. Victoria had the ocean on three sides, yet the air there didn't have the earthy richness of this wild place.

Sandy evaluated the area for the best vantage point before selecting a large rock on which to sit. After throwing her beach towel over it she discovered that she was at the perfect height to comfortably sketch the scene. No shore birds skittered around the rocks, but the cries of the seagulls sailing overhead provided the perfect music for her to immerse herself in her first sketch.

Time passed. The air cooled and the tide changed. Sandy looked up when she heard the scrape of a shoe on a log. A man stood about twenty feet behind her. He seemed frozen halfway through a jumble of logs and rocks at the top of the beach. "Oh," she gasped. "I didn't see you."

A black lab came bounding out of the bush behind him but stopped as soon as he saw her. The man signalled the dog, and it moved to sit at his side. "Sorry," he apologized. "I wasn't expecting anyone to be here. Usually, it's just me and the dog."

The angle of the sun created a stained-glass shine to his brown eyes that complimented the honey brown of his skin. Sandy responded with a tentative smile. "That's okay. I was just sketching."

The man returned her smile, revealing deep dimples in his cheeks and crow's feet at the corners of his eyes. "It's a very inspiring place." He signalled the dog, which jumped up and raced ahead, chasing seagulls and sniffing at the bull kelp washed ashore by the tide. As the man walked past, Sandy realized his hair wasn't short but pulled back at the nape of his neck in a ponytail that reached mid-way down his back. The sun highlighted streaks of silver in his otherwise coal-black hair. *He's older than I thought.* The man continued toward the beach, using the toe of his shoe or the stick he carried to separate items from the base of the rocks or buried in the sand. He examined them, tossed them away or placed them into the woven basket he held.

Sandy looked down at her drawing paper, unsure what to do. She could feel herself getting nervous. She had never been around Indians before. She'd certainly never spoken to one. She had no idea what to expect. *Should I stay? Should I leave?* She glanced up. He had moved closer to the water, where his dog was digging in the sand. She leaned the sketchpad against the rock, placed her pencils on the sand beside her, and stood. Raising her hand to shade her eyes, she studied the man. The colour of his chinos and his short-sleeved shirt had faded to an uneven grey that stood out against the dark green of the wet seaweed clinging to the rocks he was silhouetted against. The man and his dog seemed so much a part of the scene that she suddenly wanted to draw them. She grabbed her sketchpad and pencil and began making quick, confident strokes on the paper.

The man turned back, and the dog, after a moment of hesitation, bound across the sand toward her.

Sandy stood awkwardly as dog and master approached. "Would he allow me to pet him?"

"His name's Spike. We've already had an hour of exploring beaches, so he's a bit muddy. Be careful."

Spike looked back at his master as if insulted, then spun and ran off across the beach again. Sandy giggled.

"I'm Steve."

"I'm Sandy."

Formal introduction complete, Steve shifted the basket to his right hand and started heading up the beach. "Have a good afternoon."

"I like your basket!" she blurted.

"Thanks." Steve stopped and held it up proudly. "My grandmother made it for my mother, and now I use it."

"I was trying to figure out what you were collecting."

"My treasure?" He chuckled. "Just this and that. Whatever I think I can use in my work."

"You're an artist?" Relief washed over her. *A fellow artist.* "What type of work do you do?"

"Some weaving, but mostly carving."

"I tried carving once. It didn't work out."

Steve smirked. "It requires a lot of patience."

"Well, that explains my failure." Sandy offered a lopsided grin. "Patience? I'm not good at that."

"What are you sketching?" Steve stepped forward.

"I was trying to catch the water surging through the rocks but I'm having trouble getting the perspective right."

"Here." Steve set his basket on the sand by his feet and reached for Sandy's sketchpad. "Let me try."

As she passed it across to him, she realized it was still open to the sketch she'd done of him and his dog.

Steve paused, then looked at Sandy. "This isn't the one you were having trouble with perspective, is it?"

"N-no. It isn't. It's the next page."

"Good-looking dog you captured there."

Her cheeks burned.

Steve flipped the page. "Ah. Yes, I see." He sat and studied what she'd drawn, then looked at the scene she had sketched. Sandy was about to comment when Steve reached for the pencil she still held in her hand. She let go and he used it to make swift, bold lines across her drawing. When he finished, he handed both pad and pencil back to her. "Try that," he said as he stood.

Sandy studied the lines he'd drawn then looked at him. "You fixed it!"

"Sometimes it just takes another set of eyes to solve a problem." He picked up his basket and whistled for his dog. Spike raced across the beach, sped past them, then circled around and came to a bouncing stop at Steve's side. Steve bent to settle the dog, then looked up at Sandy. "This place has inspired many artists, both local and well-known. You should make sure to check Arthur Lismer's work when he comes in August."

"Arthur Lismer comes here?"

"Yes." Steve straightened, his hand remaining at the base of the lab's neck, fingers curled around its collar. "He's been coming to this area since the early fifties."

"The Group of Seven artist? Seriously?" Sandy couldn't help being impressed. The famous group was part of the university curriculum she hadn't stayed long enough to study.

"Yes."

"In August?" Sandy looked at the surrounding landscape with renewed interest.

"He and his wife come for six weeks every summer. They stay at the cabin by the inn. He often holds an open house at the end of his stay. If you're still around, you should check it out." Steve released the dog's collar and started walking up the beach.

Sandy looked around and tried to imagine the artist sketching there. "I will be around. I work at the inn."

Steve stopped at the top of the beach and looked over his shoulder at Sandy. Spike took the opportunity to run back toward the water. "That's good. It seems nobody wants to stay here anymore." Steve called Spike back from sniffing around a tidal pool. Spike ignored him. "Even that poor boy who was struck on the road on Friday night. He didn't stay."

"I found him," Sandy blurted.

"Oh. Sorry. I didn't know."

Sandy shrugged.

"I heard that the girl who found him was a hitchhiker. Where were you hitching from?"

"Victoria. Geoff picked me up outside Port Alberni on Friday."

"Did you know each other?"

"Not before then, no." She turned away from Steve's gaze and watched Spike as he followed a scent trail weaving around the rocks to the brush line.

"Spike! Come!" Steve shouted. The dog bounded back toward him, tail wagging, then stopped when his attention was drawn by movement in a tide pool. Steve sighed. "I saw him," he said. "He was walking along the path."

"Here?"

"No." He pointed to the trees lining the beach. "On the path that runs along this beach."

"When? When did you see him?"

"About three yesterday morning."

Sandy considered this new information. "How do you know it was him?"

"I knew him when he was a boy."

"In California?"

"No. When he lived here."

Sandy sank heavily on her rock. Geoff hadn't told her that he'd lived in the area before. She was sure he had said the friend he was hoping to meet at the beach was a surfer from California. Maybe she had misunderstood, and the friend was local. "Was he with anyone?"

"Friday night? There were lots of people on the path."

"Then what made you notice him?"

"Because he looked so much like Allan—"

"Allan?"

Steve looked out at the ocean. "He was a friend who drowned recently."

"Oh, sorry."

Steve swatted at a mosquito circling his exposed arms, finally killing it where it landed near his elbow. Satisfied, he returned his attention to Sandy. "As soon as I thought of Allan, I realized the guy couldn't be Allan's kid. Allan's son doesn't look anything like his dad. So, it must've been his nephew. I couldn't remember his name, but you called him Geoff." He paused as if reliving some memory. "He was such a happy kid when he was little, always laughing, joking."

"Did you talk to him?"

"No." Steve looked down at his feet and then back at her. "I wish I had."

"Oh."

Steve suddenly appeared uneasy, and looked for his dog. Spike had his nose buried deep in a crevice between two ridges of rock. "Spike!" Steve whistled. The lab raised his head, hesitated a moment, and then ran in great leaps through the incoming surf to his master.

Sandy watched them move off the beach and onto the ridge that ran along it. "Wait! Did you tell the police?"

Steve looked at her. "We don't talk to the police." He then turned and disappeared where the path entered the bushes.

Sandy watched him go, then turned back to the water ebbing and flowing around the rocks. *Who did he mean by "we"? And why wouldn't they talk with the police?* She squinted at her sketch but couldn't concentrate on it. She kept thinking about what Steve had said about Geoff being on the path in the early hours of the morning. The sighting meant that he hadn't taken any of the other paths. He must have been returning to the van to sleep.

She stood, no longer wanting to be alone on the beach. After gathering her sketchpad and pencils, she made her way along the shoreline to the lodge.

20.

The sudden absence of motion woke Conny, and she was momentarily confused by what she saw. *Red?* The colour filled her vision. She blinked, trying to clear it. Then she spotted a line of stitching and realized she was seeing the back of the Firebird's front seats. A groan escaped her lips as the memory of Rod's fingers gripping her throat flowed over her. Suddenly, her head was snapped up, and pain seared through her scalp as she was hoisted into a half-seated position.

"Ack!" Her arms searched for leverage to counter the upward pull of the fingers tightly threaded through her hair. "Let go!"

Releasing her, the goon beside her leaned against the seat, his hand sliding from her scalp to her shoulder, his finger tracing a circle on the exposed skin. "The princess awakens."

Conny slapped his hand away and sat fully up, shifting so she was as far away from the man as the small confines of the Firebird's back seat would allow. She wondered how long she'd been lying unconscious on the goon's lap and how she'd got there.

"Good," Rod said from the front seat. "I want you awake for this."

Stifling a groan, Conny glanced out her side window. It was overcast, but the light still made her squint. They were no longer in the forest above Wreck Bay, meaning she had been out long enough for them to have driven into either Ucluelet or Tofino. They were now parked on a neighbourhood street. *But which neighbourhood?* None of the houses lining either side of the street were familiar. She looked at the scenery behind the houses, trying to get a sense of the skyline. Tofino and Ucluelet occupied opposite ends of the hammer-head of land that sat broadside to the Pacific Ocean; Tofino on the EsowistaPeninsula, Ucluelet on the UcluethPeninsula. And while each was surrounded by ocean on three sides they were laid out differently. The skyline, Conny realized, indicated they had driven to Ucluelet. So, she hadn't been out of it too long. Ucluelet was less than eight miles from Wreck Bay.

She gently massaged her scalp, expecting to see blood when she pulled her hand away, but there was none. Tucking both hands beneath her thighs to hide their shaking, she looked at Rod. "What do you want?" she croaked, throat aching from his brutal grip.

"I want you to tell me where the goods are."

"I don't know." This time her voice definitely squeaked. She clamped her mouth shut and considered her situation. The goon's mistreatment worried her. Such behaviour should have drawn a swift and violent reprimand from Rod, but he ignored it, even as the goon reached across and brushed a stray stand of hair from her face. His hand came to rest at the base of her neck, where his fingers caressed the bruised flesh. She brushed it away.

The man's boldness suggested she was no longer under Rod's protection.

She closed her eyes and turned to face the window, trying to swallow her fear. When she opened them again, her gaze picked up the movement of a woman gardening in her front yard. Conny tried not to show her excitement or draw attention to what she had spotted. If she could just get out of the car, she was sure she could run the short distance to the woman and escape whatever punishment she feared was about to happen.

"If you're thinking we're done, we're not." Rod shifted in his seat. "Look at me!"

Conny slowly turned her head and met his icy glare.

"Tell me where my stuff is," he demanded.

"I don't know!" Conny sucked in a quick breath, her mind racing. "When did it happen?"

"Thanos discovered it this morning."

"What's Danny say?"

Rod shifted so he was facing forward once more. "Why don't we ask Danny?" He paused, as if considering the question, then burst out laughing. Dwayne and the goon joined in.

Conny gripped her knees, her nails piercing the skin, stopping the sudden tremors rippling through her body. *Breathe! Breathe!*

Rod stopped laughing. "Your sweetheart was gone."

Conny darted a glance at the goon next to her. He gave her a lop-sided grin. "Looks like you're on your own." His eyes bore into hers. "Your guy's done a runner."

"He wouldn't!" Turning to Rod, she repeated, "He wouldn't!"

Rod took a deep breath, opened his door, and got out. Leaning in, he glared at her. "Maybe these two will be able to convince you to start telling us the truth."

"No!" Conny pleaded.

Rod tossed the car keys to Dwayne in the front seat and slammed the door. Conny watched him walk away, waving at the woman in her garden as he passed.

21.

Sandy searched the cupboards, wondering where her roommates would keep wine glasses. She finally found two tucked behind a glass juice jug on the bottom shelf. She straightened and turned toward Mark, holding up her prizes triumphantly. "I found two!"

"Good thing that's all we need. You didn't find a corkscrew in your search, did you?"

"Give me a minute." She rinsed the glasses and set them on the table in front of Mark. "I'm glad it's just the two of us. It's been a crazy day."

Mark had shown up at the lodge with a bottle of wine just after her return from the beach. He was a welcome distraction. She had been brooding, angry with herself for not asking Steve his last name or where he lived. His revelations about not just knowing Geoff, but seeing him on the path the night he died, had stunned her. Now she had so many questions spinning around in her head, and no way to get them answered.

All that frustration disappeared when she saw Mark standing at the door, the deep blue of his plaid shirt setting off the deep brown of his eyes. She had found it hard to look away long enough to invite him in. The search for glasses had provided her with an easy escape.

"So," he said. "A crazy day? Sit down and tell me all about it."

"I will. I just need to—Yes!" Grinning, she tossed the corkscrew to Mark, who caught it as it sailed across the kitchen table. "I'd planned on an evening curled up on the couch reading, but this is better."

"Good thing I turned up. Saved you from a boring night." Mark applied the corkscrew to the bottle and soon had the cork out. "Here we go," he said, reaching for a wine glass.

"I was surprised to see you at the door. I thought you would be surfing or working on your carving."

Mark smiled. "I wanted to celebrate your decision to stay on the beach." He passed one of the glasses of wine to her, and took a seat at the table. "Cheers."

"Cheers." Sandy pulled out a chair and sat across from him. Mark was staring at her. "Do I have food on my face?"

Mark took a sip of his wine. "No. I'm just glad you're back."

Unsure how to take his comment, Sandy took a deep gulp of her wine and nearly gagged. Her mouth puckered, and she rushed to the sink to pour herself a glass of water.

Mark laughed. "Not used to wine?"

"I've never had it before. My parents were more into the hard stuff. Mom liked her cocktails."

Mark smiled. "No wonder you made that face." He held up his glass so she could see the rich, dark burgundy colour of the liquid inside. "Syrah may be a bit too big of a first step."

Sandy's cheeks heated. She didn't want to seem like a child. She took another sip. This time, she was prepared for the earthy tang and found it less harsh on her tongue.

She looked across at Mark. "It's fine when you get used to it."

Mark leaned forward, elbows on the table, his right hand holding his glass by its stem as he examined the wine within it. "My father, as I told you, was a biologist, and we travelled a lot. That's how I got to learn about food and wine. We spent three years in France." He looked across at her. "That's where this is from. My parents like to buy wine by the case. This came up with my brother last month when he visited."

"I've never been anywhere." Unable to put her elbows on the table after years of being yelled at for doing so, Sandy sat back in her chair, her elbows tucked against her sides, hands cupping the wine glass. "My dad's been an English professor at the university in Victoria all my life. My mom stays home and spends her life caring for us. I've never heard either of them express a desire to go any further than Vancouver."

"There's value in staying in one place," Mark said. "Not everyone wants a life of continuous moving."

"I would!" She smiled. "At least for a little while."

Mark took a deep breath. "You miss out on friendship. In the beginning, I was always excited about making new friends, but after awhile, I stopped being excited. What was the point? As soon as I started to like someone, I'd have to say goodbye."

"I never thought of that. I have a couple of friends I've known since first grade, and there are others I've made since beginning my art studies. Did you keep in touch with the friends you made from travelling, like pen pals?"

"I've had a couple, but they've fizzled out over time."

Sandy couldn't think of anything to say. The kitchen was filled with the sound of the ocean and the birds in the trees outside the open window. It became a comfortable silence until a knock on the front door broke it.

They both stood. "Are you expecting anyone?" Mark asked.

"No."

The knock came again. Sandy moved around the table and went to answer the door.

A grey-haired couple stood on the porch, holding hands and leaning into each other. Sandy recognized Geoff's eyes in the woman and his cleft chin in the man.

The man took a deep breath and asked, "Are you Sandy?"

Sandy motioned for them to enter. "Please, come in."

A tear silently rolled down the mother's cheek, but her eyes never left Sandy as her husband guided her inside. They stopped when they saw Mark standing by the table.

"You're Geoff's parents," Sandy said softly.

"Arthur and Marta Johnston," Geoff's father stated.

"Johnston? I thought…"

"You thought Geoff's last name was Turner." He smiled, and the smile reminded her of Geoff too. "It seems our son used a fake driver's licence to cross the border. Turner's his mother's maiden name. We didn't know about the fake ID until the pathologist in Nanaimo requested that we confirm his identity as well as his body."

Glancing at the couple, then Mark, she stammered, "Mr. a-a-and Mrs. Johnston, this is Mark."

Mark stepped forward to shake their hands. "I'm so sorry about your son."

"Thank you," Mr. Johnston said.

"Here. Please, sit down." Sandy rushed to the couch, swept the blanket out of the way, and picked the book off the cushion. She tossed both to Mark, who dropped them in the kitchen on the table.

The Johnstons sat slowly, almost painfully, on the couch.

"Would you like some tea or wine? Some water? I might have beer—"

"We won't be staying. It's been a long day." Mr. Johnston put his arm around his wife and gently squeezed her. Her head tilted, coming to rest on his shoulder.

Sandy took a seat in the chair opposite.

Mark stepped forward, then stopped. "Look. I'm going to go."

"Oh. Um." Sandy rose and walked Mark to the door.

"Are you going to be okay?" he asked, as he slipped on his sandals.

"Yes. It's just a little strange."

Sandy closed the door after Mark left and returned to her unexpected guests.

"We saw our son," Mr. Johnston said.

Sandy hesitated a moment as she passed the couple on the couch, unsure how to respond. She perched on the arm of the overstuffed chair and leaned forward, waiting.

"Had to do it in Nanaimo. Formal identification." He shook his head. "After that, Marta wanted to see where it happened, where he died."

"Oh." Sandy sat back, surprised.

"We understand you found our Geoff," Mr. Johnston said.

Tremulously, Mrs. Johnston asked, "Was he? Did he…?"

In a stronger voice, Mr. Johnston explained, "I think what Marta is asking is…did he suffer?"

Sandy's heart caught in her chest. "I don't know. Didn't the police say what had happened to him?"

Anger battled the sorrow on Mrs. Johnston's face. "They didn't tell us anything except that he was dead. We could tell *that* from looking at him on that horrible table!" She rummaged through her jacket pocket for a tissue, then blew her nose. "They didn't tell us where he was found or by whom. They didn't even tell us that he was murdered. We had to find that out from the taxi driver!"

Her husband pulled her against his shoulder once more, accepting her rage and tears. He looked at Sandy. "We flew in from Nanaimo. Didn't want to chance the road. A taxi picked us up at the airport and drove us here."

"To me?"

"No. The inn." Geoff's father half-smiled and Sandy was jolted by how much that smile resembled his son's. "The driver started talking about it." His hand gently squeezed his wife's shoulder. "He didn't realize we were the parents. He was just making conversation, like cab drivers do. That's how we found out that you had found Geoff, and that his death is now considered a murder. He also told us where you were staying. Was the driver correct about you finding our son?"

"Yes." Sandy's throat constricted, and she was unable to give anything more. She put a hand to her neck. She didn't know how to feel about being the subject of taxi conversations. *What else are they saying about me, about Geoff?* She glanced at his mother, fearing what she expected of her. Would she want a detailed description of that morning?

"Did you know my son?"

"N-n-no."

At the surprise on their faces, Sandy took a deep breath and sat forward, her hands braced on her knees, and answered in what she hoped was a respectful manner. "He gave me a ride up here from Port Alberni on Friday."

"So how did you end up finding our son?"

Sandy faced Geoff's father. "I was walking out to the main road to hitchhike back to Victoria."

Mrs. Johnston sat forward, mirroring Sandy's position. Her eyes, so much like Geoff's but with no sign of his gentleness, bore into Sandy's. "Did you trade sex for the ride?"

Sandy blinked and searched for words that wouldn't come. Mr. Johnston's cheeks were pink with embarrassment. "U-u-um," she stammered.

"I guess that means you did!" Mrs. Johnston snapped.

Sandy stood. Though she was raised to respect her elders, she was at a loss on how to answer this one politely. "I didn't trade sex for a ride. That's gross!" she protested. "We made love. Afterward. No strings." Sandy instantly regretted her words; they sounded trite even to her own ears.

"Whore!" The word floated out so softly Sandy wasn't sure she had heard it correctly, but the impact of it lifted Mr. Johnston out of his seat, pulling his wife with him.

"I think it's best we go now. I'm sorry. I'm sure she didn't mean it. It's been a long day."

His wife pushed away from him. "Of course I meant it!" Turning to Sandy, she shouted, "What kind of girl hitchhikes alone and gives herself freely to a man she doesn't know?" She darted to the side of the couch when her husband attempted to grab her arm. "Did you abandon my son to die alone while you chased other men? Is that why he was on the road? Was he looking for you?"

Sandy shook her head. "I don't know why he was there, but it didn't have anything to do with me."

When Mr. Johnston took a step toward her, Mrs. Johnston moved closer to Sandy. "My son deserved better!"

Mr. Johnston caught his wife in a hug before the hand that had whipped out to slap Sandy's cheek could connect. Pinning his wife against his chest, he marched her to the door. "We're leaving. Now!"

The action was so similar to the one his son had used on her, Sandy was momentarily overcome with the memory of it. Shaking, she rushed to open the door for them and stood behind it as they passed. "We've booked into the inn," Mr. Johnston told her. "I'm sure my wife will wish to apologize to you personally when she's feeling more herself."

"I will not!" Mrs. Johnston screamed as the door closed. "I never will!"

Sandy, dazed, dropped into the comforting softness of the couch and cried as the memory of standing on the beach wrapped in Geoff's arms flooded over her.

"It's beautiful out there!"

Startled, Sandy sat up to see Tish in the entry hall, hanging up her sweater.

"What?"

"The moon's so full and bright, peeking out from behind wisps of cloud. It looks so mystical!"

Sandy shifted so Tish could sit beside her and glanced at her watch. *Six-thirty*. "It's not sunset yet."

"No, but the moon is still rising bright and beautiful?" Tish pushed a pillow out of the way.

"Well, I guess that explains it."

"Explains what?" Tish dropped down beside Sandy.

"Just…," Sandy searched for words to describe her evening. "It was strange. Geoff's parents came to see me."

"As in the guy you found on the road this morning?"

"Yes. I was…I wouldn't have expected them to drop in."

"They got here fast!"

Sandy could smell alcohol on Tish's breath. She must have stopped at the bar on her way home from the beach. "They flew."

"So, why did they come here to see you?"

"The taxi driver told them I was the one who found Geoff, and that I was staying here." Sandy silently cursed the driver's chatty nature. "They wanted to know if I knew anything about what happened," she said. "But then she called me a whore."

"Why would she call you that?"

"Because I had sex with a man I didn't know." Sandy pulled the blanket off the side of the couch and wrapped it around her shoulders, suddenly cold.

"Geoff, you mean?"

Sandy nodded.

"Why would you tell her that?" Tish jumped up, not waiting for an answer. "Never mind. How about I make some tea? Or would you like something stronger? I see an open bottle of wine on the table."

"Tea would be fine." Sandy shrugged. "It was just…a weird conversation."

After Tish placed the kettle on the stove to boil, she returned to Sandy. "Look, Geoff's mom is probably just hurting over her son. She probably didn't mean it." When Sandy started to shake her head, Tish rushed on. "And even if she *did* mean it, you know what moms are like. They come from the dinosaur era when women were men's property, and chastity was their main currency."

Sandy looked up at Tish, shocked at her phrasing. Then a slow smile spread from her lips to her eyes. "It was almost as if my mom was sitting there."

Tish turned at the sound of the kettle's whistle and rushed to the kitchen in search of tea. "If your mom's anything like mine," she called back over her shoulder, "that's a very scary thought!"

The comment triggered a vivid memory of a photograph in a family album. It showed her as a toddler holding her mother's hand in her grandparents' front garden. They were walking toward the camera, her mother's face half-turned as if responding to her mother, who was coming down the porch steps. Sandy had often thumbed through the album but had never been struck by the expression on her mother's face before. Was it sadness or anger? The memory made Sandy wonder what type of relationship her mother had had with her own mother. She had never asked her.

"Cat got your tongue?" Tish asked as she carried in two mugs of tea.

"No. It's just, well, if you don't like being in the same room with your mom, why are you going back to Calgary to live with her?"

"Who says I'm going to live with her?" Tish squealed.

"Sorry, I just thought that if you were going back home, it meant that you were going back *home*."

"No, I'm moving in with a friend. I couldn't live with my parents again after being out on my own like this."

Sandy took a shallow sip of her tea, wary of burning her tongue. "You know, if I hadn't found Geoff on the side of that road, I would be back home living with my parents right now."

"Well, I'm glad you aren't."

Sandy sat in silence for a moment, considering her reaction to Mrs. Johnston's name-calling. *Am I a whore because I gave up my virginity to a man I'd just met?* She hadn't expected such strong reactions from Geoff or his mother. She had expected that it would be no big deal to lose what she had considered unimportant. "I'm not sure how I feel anymore. I would like to think Geoff is somewhere safe and beautiful, like Heaven." She paused. "But if I believe that, do I then have to believe all the other stuff preached in church, like what women should be or not be?"

"A whore?" Tish looked at Sandy, all sign of humour gone. "No. You're not. I think Geoff's mother just wants to know what happened to her son, and that's for the police to handle."

"They haven't so far, Tish. They didn't tell Geoff's parents anything. Do you think the murderer has gotten away with it?"

"The police will find out who killed Geoff."

Sandy wasn't so sure. She worried that Geoff's parents would take their son home and his murderer would remain free. She looked out the window, through the fringe of trees that stood between the lodge and the shore. The ocean surf pounded the beach and wind stirred the branches.

Tish settled onto the couch and took a tentative sip from her mug of tea. After a moment, she turned to Sandy. "Anyway, you couldn't tell them anything, could you? You just discovered him. You don't know how he was killed."

"That's not exactly true." Sandy set her tea down. "I told the police I didn't touch the body except to pull him out of the ditch water, but I might have done more than that."

"What?" Tish looked at her, eyes wide.

"Well, after I flagged down a car and sent the couple to get help, I couldn't just sit there with Geoff lying dead on the side of the road. So, I kind of checked him out a little."

"What'd you do?"

"Nothing much. I mean he was lying face-down in the water when I found him, and I'd pulled him out because I was going to attempt reviving him, until I realized it was obvious he was dead. He was so cold."

"But that could've been because he was lying in ditch water."

Sandy waved her hands nervously. "I-I-I know. But his eyes. You didn't see his eyes." She stopped, remembering the weight of him across her lap and how the water from the ditch had drained from him onto her, soaking her legs.

She shivered. "When the couple in the car left to get help, I looked down at where Geoff was lying. He had slipped partially back into the water, and I couldn't leave him like that." She looked at Tish for reassurance. "He looked so alone." Tish said nothing. "I-I-I pulled him up so that his head and shoulders were resting on the grass by the road."

"You didn't!"

"I did." Sandy took a reassuring sip of tea before continuing. "His head had rolled to one side and his hair was wet and all messed up. So, I tried straightening it a bit. I found a bruise at the base of his neck, and a welt with a red dot in the middle." She looked at Tish. "I think it was from a needle."

"What do you mean a needle?"

"You know." Sandy pantomimed injecting herself in the arm.

Tish shook her head. "It could've been anything. A scratch or a poke from a thorn bush."

"One of my classmates at university used to shoot up. I know what an injection site looks like. The thing is, Geoff told me he never touched the hard stuff, only MJ."

"And even if he was a regular drug user, that's a weird place to shoot up," Tish leaned forward. "Do you think the police know?"

"I'm not sure."

"So, what're you trying to say?"

"I agree with Tom. There's more to Geoff's death than we're being led to believe. The Johnstons said the taxi driver told them that he'd been murdered. Maybe an injection was how."

MONDAY, MAY 13, 1968

22.

Someone was moving around in the lodge's kitchen. Sandy rolled onto her side and pulled the blanket over her shoulder, doing her best to ignore the noise. She had decided not to open the couch out into a bed the night before and had slept on its narrow seating. Eyes still heavy with sleep, she was just drifting off when her shoulder was grabbed and she was roughly shaken. Her eyes flew open. Tish was leaning over her, expression panicked. "Did you hear Conny come in last night?"

Sandy shifted into a sitting position. "No. I didn't hear anyone."

"I checked her room. The bed hasn't been slept in."

"She probably stayed over with her boyfriend."

"No. Never. Not when she has to work the next day." Tish paused as if deep in thought. "I don't like this."

"Her boyfriend probably dropped her off at work," Sandy said.

"I've already checked. She isn't there, and no one's seen her."

"Okay. Okay." Sandy swung her legs off the couch and leaned forward, rubbing her eyes. "What time is it?"

"Ten after eight." Tish dropped on the sofa beside Sandy. "She's never late. Not once in the four years she's been working at the inn. Something's happened. I know it!" Tish burst into tears.

"Tish! Oh Tish. No." Sandy reached out and rested her hand on Tish's shoulder.

Tish edged away, and Sandy's hand dropped to the couch. "You don't understand. Rod's an asshole. He's big-time bad."

Sandy's breath caught. *Was the man she met in the Ucluelet beer parlour Conny's boyfriend?* If he was, she could understand Tish's concern. Besides looking like a man used to hard labour, he held himself as someone used to being in control, and not in a good way. "What does Rod look like?"

"Big. Aggressive. Like someone who'd use his fists before his brains."

"Conny wouldn't go out with someone like that!" Sandy had a hard time thinking the confident woman she had met and worked with for two days would allow herself to be in a relationship with someone who didn't treat her right.

Tish wiped the tears from her eyes. "You don't know Conny. She's a magnet for assholes."

Sandy stood, searching for the clothes she'd tossed aside the night before. She found her jeans and slipped into them. "How about I help you with the rooms until Conny gets here?"

"That would be great." Tish waited for Sandy to finish dressing. "She's—she's probably just running late. Right?"

Sandy pulled on a fresh T-shirt and grabbed her poncho. "Let's go."

A stray strand of hair tickled her nose and Sandy absently brushed it away as she wiped down the mirror in the guest room's bathroom. The inn was fully booked, and the morning passed quickly. Bathrooms were time consumers, Conny had taught her, but were the first place a guest noticed poor housekeeping. Sandy stood back and scanned every surface, looking for anything she might have missed. Nothing. She gathered her cleaning tools and moved into the main room. She was so focused on the bed, her next task, it took a moment to realize someone was standing in the doorway. She turned to find Conny leaning on the door frame. "Hi," Sandy said.

Conny surveyed the room. "It looks as if you've got things under control."

"Yes." Sandy stole a quick glance at her watch. *Eleven o'clock.* Conny was three hours late. "This is my last checkout. The rest are the bus tour guests, so they only need refreshing. Did you have a good time last night?"

Conny barked a sharp laugh and shook her head. "No."

Sandy frowned. Conny looked like she was still drunk. Her clothes were soiled and wrinkled, her makeup smudged, and her hair a rat's nest. *Did she sleep on the beach?* "Have you seen Tish?" Sandy asked. "She's been worried about you."

Conny shook her head.

Sandy crossed the room, but Conny stepped back before any contact was made. "I can see you don't need me," she said. "I'm going to the lodge."

A foul odour lingered in Conny's wake, and Sandy wrinkled her nose. *Oh Conny. Where have you been?*

"Was that Conny?" Tish had come downstairs and was looking out the glass doors of the lobby at Conny's retreating back.

"Yes. She said she's going to the lodge."

"Did she say where she's been?"

"No, but she looked bad." Remembering Tish's warning that morning, Sandy whispered, "I think something happened."

Tish turned to face Sandy. "Can you finish on your own?"

"Yes, of course."

"My cart's still in the hallway. You'll have to put it away for me." Tish ran out the front door without waiting for Sandy's reply.

Sandy returned to the room she'd been cleaning and had just started stripping the bed when Brent walked in wearing a huge grin. "So, you decided to stay!"

Sandy returned his smile as she bundled up the dirty sheets. "Yes. Your sales pitch was too powerful to resist." Slipping past him, she placed her bundle into the sack on the side of her cart and pulled a fresh set of sheets from the cart's shelf. When she went to return to the room, she hesitated, unsure if he was expecting her to stand and make conversation.

He seemed to realize her discomfort and stepped aside. "Well, I won't bother you. You're working and I should get back to the bar." He threw up his hand awkwardly. "I just wanted to welcome you to the crew."

"Thank you."

Brent bowed and left. Sandy stood a moment, wondering at the strangeness of the day.

23.

Moore watched the newcomer walk up the aisle toward him, a coffee mug balanced on top of the file he was carrying. Jealousy washed over him. The identification specialist was in top physical shape, oozed confidence, and according to the information forwarded from Victoria, was barely in his thirties. Moore pushed himself up from his desk, feeling every bit of his almost-forty years, and addressed his constables. "Gentlemen, this is Corporal Liam McAteer out of Nanaimo, here to handle the forensics of this case."

McAteer nodded at the two constables he passed on his way up the aisle. Moore introduced his team. "The one on the left is Constable Halden Evans. He came to us a year ago after six months with K-Division, stationed in Red Deer, Alberta. The one on the right is Constable Monty Nelson. He has only been with us six months, after almost two years with G-Division in Yellowknife, Northwest Territories." Moore tapped Nelson's desk as he passed. "Thanks for coming in to attend this meeting." Nelson was on his fourth night shift and wasn't scheduled until six o'clock.

A blush bloomed on Nelson's cheeks. "No problem, sir."

Watching the IS officer take a seat at the only empty desk in the room, Moore made a mental note to borrow another desk from somewhere before the expected officer from Victoria arrived. He glanced at his watch. *Three o'clock on the dot.* "Glad you could join us, Corporal McAteer. We were just about to start our briefing." Moore moved to the front of his desk and rested against it. "Maybe you could update us on what the pathologist in Nanaimo has found so far."

When McAteer stood and strode toward the chalkboard, Moore told himself to keep an open mind and relax. It was the first time he had ever had to hand over control of a case, and he was struggling with letting go.

"The body was transferred from Tofino's hospital to Nanaimo's by hearse yesterday morning. The parents, who had been notified Saturday by your counterparts in Seattle, arrived in Nanaimo on Sunday afternoon and identified our victim as their son, Geoffrey Matthew Johnston. The body was then cleared for forensic exam, which only began late this afternoon due to a shortage of staff and holiday scheduling." McAteer paused for a sip of his coffee. "I can report that our victim died sometime in the early hours of Saturday, May 11th, cause unknown."

Moore noticed the corporal's use of the plural and wondered how long it would be before 'our' became 'my'. He had heard rumours from other officers who'd had Victoria come in on a major crime case. It was rarely a cooperative experience. He glanced at the file set on the desk in front of the corporal. "Any idea when the complete report will be available?"

McAteer shook his head. "No. He was unable to tell me much before I left because he'd only just started the examination. Normally, I would have stayed for the exam, but I wanted to make it up here before it got too late in the day. Thank you for moving your usual morning briefing to this afternoon so I could attend." The corporal sent a quick nod to Moore, before continuing. "I called the pathologist for an update just before attending this meeting, and he provided a few more details. He's thinking some form of poisoning happened, but has to wait for the toxicology results. The body showed bruising consistent with a struggle, but the marks on the victim's legs were not consistent with a vehicular impact. They had been done after death had occurred."

Basically, what John said two days ago. Moore made crisp check marks beside the information he had entered after speaking with his friend.

"The pathologist said he was having trouble figuring out what sort of weapon was used to beat the victim's legs, but he stressed that the beating would not have been fatal. He figured that the death occurred somewhere between midnight and five o'clock on Saturday morning."

Moore turned to Evans. "Do you recall seeing anything at the scene that could have been used as a weapon?"

Evans shook his head. "No. But I was looking for evidence of a hit-and-run. I wasn't looking for a murder weapon. I could recheck the photos."

McAteer interrupted, "Better yet, pull them out so we can all review them."

Evans gathered his photos and stood to hand them to the specialist, but Moore stopped him. "Why don't you walk us through what you saw at the scene?"

Evans hesitated, then spread out the photos on his desk. The officers gathered around him as he reviewed what he'd found.

McAteer picked up a photo and turned it over. "You didn't use the office's Polaroid camera?"

Evans sent a quick glance over to Moore before answering. "No, sir."

"How'd you get them processed so quickly, Constable? You obviously didn't send them to one of the Force's labs."

Moore stepped up, motioning Evans to silence. They were all aware of how long sending film to one of the Force's labs could take. "The editor of the local paper allows us to use his dark room, and I've trained both my constables in darkroom processes."

McAteer murmured under his breath and set the photo back on the desk. "So, you found no broken glass or pieces of headlights or fenders?"

"None, sir."

McAteer cleared his throat. "The victim, born February 25, 1946, in Tofino, was just past his twenty-second birthday when he died. According to his parents, they moved to Seattle as a family in the summer of 1953, when their son was seven. After graduating high school, he moved to Los Angeles to attend the University of California and was due to graduate this spring. They had no idea he had dropped out last month, or that he'd moved to Vancouver. Nor did they know he had joined the hippie community living in that city's Kitsilano neighbourhood until they called his dormmate. His parents, Marta and Arthur Johnston, didn't know why he decided to drive over to the west coast of Vancouver Island this past weekend. They had not heard from him in three months. They mentioned that the victim and his father had argued over the Vietnam War. Although his son was not an American,

Mr. Johnston had been pressuring him to volunteer for active duty after he graduated. The son walked out, and the parents hadn't heard from him since."

The corporal returned to his seat.

Moore remained standing at Evans' desk. "The victim has been officially identified and his connection to the area confirmed. Since we don't have a cause of death, we need to look at possible motives. Constable Evans, were you able to find out anything about the girl who found the victim?"

The constable gathered his notes from his desk, shuffled through them until he found the page he wanted, then stood. "Sandra Chambers, who goes by Sandy, was born in Victoria on April 9, 1948. The driver's licence she carries is fake, modified to allow her to pass as legal drinking age. She was enrolled in the University of Victoria's art program. Her father is a professor of English at the same university." He glanced around as if expecting a comment. When none came, he continued, "Her mother is a housewife. There is a brother who will graduate high school this year. The parents filed a missing persons bulletin for Miss Chambers this morning." Evans passed a wire copy to Moore. "Otherwise, she's clean."

"Any connection to the victim?"

"None, according to her, sir, other than the hitchhiking, of course." Evans paused. "What do you want me to do about the missing persons bulletin? Should I call the parents and let them know where their daughter is?"

Moore looked up from his examination of the bulletin. "Contact the initiating detachment and let them know she's here. What were you able to find out from the victim's doctor?"

"I haven't been able to catch up with Dr. Putts."

Moore glanced at the constable. "Well, keep on it." Looking up at the group, he added, "I heard from the superintendent in Victoria this morning. A member of the MCU will be here tomorrow. As his is the unit that investigates all major crime on the island, I'll be handing over the case when he arrives. I expect you to have any witness statements typed and signed, as well as all evidence recorded in the file, ready to hand over."

Disappointment was written across his constables' faces. He understood. It was hard not to feel territorial, but there was no use protesting. He expected they would soon return to regular patrol duty, playing a minor supportive role in the murder investigation.

Moore took a deep breath and asked if anyone had found the keys to the victim's van. At the united shaking of heads, he told them to keep an eye open for them. Turning to McAteer, he said, "The van's been secured at Owens' Garage. I look forward to reading your report on what you find." Pausing, he added, "In the meantime, Constable Nelson can investigate the old prospector's shack above Wreck Bay."

His mention of Wreck Bay reminded him of the torn piece of cereal box sitting in the open file on his desk. He toyed with it a moment before tucking it beneath the top sheet. "I've spoken to a friend at the mines department in Victoria," he said, looking at McAteer, "and he said the claims staked above and around Wreck Bay are old, but that there have been some inquiries recently regarding reactivation. He figures this has less to do with the hunt for gold and more to do with a desire to make a quick buck when the government buys the land for the new national park. "Personally, I can't see a motive for murder there. Whether it's gold dust or park payment, we're not talking a big enough reward. Still, we'll keep that line of inquiry open."

"Could there be a drug connection in this case?" McAteer asked.

"Nothing indicates it so far. We don't have a huge drug problem here—mostly small-time, local distribution of marijuana and hash." Moore paused, remembering a comment made at the previous briefing. "On the other hand, the auxiliary officer from Tofino mentioned that he had seen a lot of new drug activity on the beach recently. Our jurisdictions cover different parts of the beach. It could be that what he's seeing is only related to the north end of the beach or it could indicate what's coming our way."

"Any gang activity in the area?"

Moore knew the corporal was asking questions that needed to be asked, but he couldn't help feeling defensive. "Up till now, the only gang activity has been when the 101 Knights came over from Powell River to party and race their bikes on the beach. So far, nothing in the file connects the victim with either drugs or gang activity." Moore glanced from the corporal to his constables. "Anything else?" When they remained silent, he closed the file on his desk. "Well, we'd better get on with it then." He looked up in time to see McAteer stand and make his way out the door. He sighed and turned to his constables. Evans was making a call while Nelson scribbled notes.

Moore slipped from behind his desk and approached Nelson. "When you're ready to head out to Wreck Bay, let me know. I'll ride along."

The constable looked up and smiled. "That'd be wonderful, sir. Shall we go now?"

Choosing a favourite between constables was never good, but he couldn't help himself when it came to Nelson. Moore had never seen him lose his temper, and his very presence seemed to have a calming effect on people, especially among the Indians. He'd watched the constable inspire spontaneous laughter from faces previously frozen in distrust. Nelson was proving himself to be a real asset to the team, and Moore wanted to keep him as long as he could.

24.

As it turned out, it was after five o'clock before Moore found himself picking his way along the rocky banks of Lost Shoe Creek, his stomach grumbling. He should have grabbed a sandwich before leaving Ucluelet. The climbing was draining him faster than he wanted to admit, and the further away from Wreck Bay they went, the steeper the banks running along the narrow creek became. He had already slid into the creek twice after loose gravel gave way under him. His knee was skinned, and his socks soaked inside his ankle boots. He was not happy. Luckily he had decided to carry his camera around his neck instead off his shoulder. It had remained dry. His sure-footed constable continued to stride ahead with the confidence of someone still warm and dry. "Do you see anything?" he asked.

Nelson stopped and looked back over his shoulder. "No, sir."

"Keep an eye out. It's got to be here somewhere." Moore waved Nelson on. The forest crowded the creek's banks on both sides, slicing the late afternoon sunlight into shafts that illuminated thousands of tiny insects as if they were caught in a search light.

Moore swatted his way through the swarms while being careful where he trod. A third dip in the creek would neither improve his mood nor the state of his uniform.

"I wonder if these companies think they're fooling anyone?" Nelson stopped and leaned against the fallen trunk of a hemlock.

"Companies?" Moore asked as he drew up beside him.

"The logging companies." Nelson spread his arms out to indicate the surrounding forest. "They seem to think that if they leave a fringe of un-logged trees along the roadways, people won't complain about them clear cutting the rest."

Moore surveyed their surroundings. "But this wasn't clearcut."

"Not here specifically. But you don't have to look far in the surrounding forest where they have. Logging continues, even with the possibility of a national park coming in."

Moore realized Nelson was sharing something that obviously meant a lot to him. "What are you trying to say?"

"It's just that this"—Nelson swept his arms wide to indicate the land surrounding them—"is supposed to be preserved for future generations. But, what exactly is being preserved? It's such a fake out!"

"Greed appears in the wilderness just as often as it does in the city."

Nelson sighed. "I've heard there are some who want to use the idea of a national park to have this all dredged or mowed to allow easy access for the rich and their toys."

Moore didn't respond, distracted by Nelson's earlier words. Fake out. It was a term he'd heard the hippies use. It seemed strange to hear it come from Nelson, but somehow it described their situation perfectly—not the logging, but the murder. "A fake out," he mumbled to himself.

"What'd you say?"

Moore shook his head and stepped away from the moss-covered trunk, brushing at the seat of his pants. "Nothing." A sparkle caught his eye, the reflection of sun off glass. "Wait! I think we've found it."

Nelson spun with impressive agility and ran back, not slipping once. *Can the guy do nothing wrong?*

"Where, sir?"

"There." Moore pointed up the bank to where a corner of a window caught the afternoon's light. They were looking up at what appeared to be a small, one-room shed tucked in among a cluster of Douglas fir halfway up the bank. "It looks pretty much as Jim had described it," said Moore. "From here, it's hard to tell if it's occupied, but we should proceed with caution."

"It looks over grown," Nelson said. "If it's abandoned, it hasn't been that way for long."

Moore began to climb the bank, careful where he placed his feet. He was making good progress, until he heard, then saw, Nelson pass him, scrambling up the bank as if it were flat. Moore paused to catch his breath and watch his constable disappear over the crest of the ridge.

By the time Moore reached the crest, Nelson was back and extending a hand to assist him. Moore declined. "Do a search of the area around the shack," he growled.

"I will, sir." Nelson offered, ignoring Moore's tone. "It definitely looks like someone's broken in. The door latch has been forced."

"Any sign of damage inside?"

"I haven't gone in. As far as I can tell, the door is the only damage. Neither side window appears broken. But they are screwed shut, as Mr. Ricci described."

Moore headed for the open front door. Nelson trailed alongside him. Moore tried not to notice that the constable had slowed his pace to match his. He took a deep breath. "Let's see what we can find."

When they stepped onto the flat front porch, Moore held back, forcing Nelson to step forward and push the door wide for him. It was a cheap power move, but Moore couldn't help himself. As Nelson stood holding the door, which was hanging off one hinge, Moore stepped through.

The room seemed larger than the outside dimensions indicated. A black cast-iron wood stove stood to the right of the front door. Wooden crates were stacked to form shelves along the left side, and a simple plank and bucket unit acted as a sink. All were empty. A cot was pushed up against the rear wall, but no bedding covered the mattress. Simple. Functional. Empty—except for the metal box sitting on the plank, its lid open and mangled.

Using the sleeve of his uniform's jacket to avoid contaminating any evidence, Moore grasped the side of the box and tipped it so he could take a good look inside. He estimated it to be about twenty-four by eighteen inches, and by the strength of the metal used to construct it, would have taken a very determined effort to open. If its contents had been the thieves' target, they had left no hint as to what they'd taken.

"A break-in?" Nelson peered around Moore's shoulder.

"Looks like it, yes, but what were they after?" Moore let the lid return to the way they had found it and turned his attention to Nelson. "Unless the box was storing something of value, I can't see why anyone would break in. If it was kids, they'd have trashed the place." He looked around. "I want you to do an expanding-circle circuit of the property. I have a feeling we've missed something."

Moore unclipped the camera case and pulled out his camera. Slowly, he began photographing the interior of the shack. With each flash, the property was revealed as a prospector's shack that had been shut down for the season. If not for the broken door, it could simply have been a case of the owner having lost the key to the box and using extraordinary force to retrieve what he wanted. The door changed everything.

"Sir?"

Moore lowered the camera and turned to see Nelson standing at the door.

"You'd better come see this."

Moore watched McAteer brush dirt from the face of the man still half-buried under the pile of rock and soil. The harsh glare of his flashlight illuminated the damage done to the face by what must have been a savage beating. Moore could only guess what would be revealed when the rest of the body was uncovered. But what he knew—or guessed—was no longer relevant. Corporal Merle Bouton of the Major Crimes Unit now occupied Moore's place at the body's side. He had arrived at the detachment while Moore and Nelson were looking for the prospector's shack. After the discovery of the body, the MCU officer accompanied McAteer to the scene and took charge. The two officers now held their conversations in whispers while Moore held a flashlight for them, and Constable Nelson stood guard at the scene's perimeter.

Darkness was swallowing the surrounding forest, but Moore knew sunset was over an hour away. *At least it isn't raining.* Still, he was glad he'd asked Nelson to bring his trench coat back from the car after he went to report their discovery. The evening was turning chilly. Moore shifted his weight to ease the cramp in his left knee and chance a quick look at his watch. *Eight o'clock.*

"Hold steady," shouted Bouton.

Moore adjusted the angle of the flashlight. The specialist officers had arrived on scene with a tarp and camera, but their portable floodlights had refused to work. That left them with flashlights as their only lighting.

Moore was glad he had taken photos of the scene prior to Nelson informing dispatch about the situation. Over the years since he'd purchased his camera, the act of photographing a scene froze it in his mind. He wouldn't need the physical prints to recall the details afterward. The camera, now hanging from his neck between his trenchcoat and uniform jacket, was a personal item, relieving him of having to share the standard-issue Polaroid office camera. He didn't feel guilty for keeping its existence from the new officers. The newly arrived team had put no effort into building a sense of camaraderie with Moore's on-site team. If Moore had been asked if he had taken photos, he would have answered honestly, but such a question would have implied that the officers were aware enough of him to notice the strange bulge under his trench coat. So, he stood holding his flashlight while the images he had captured earlier ran through his mind like a slideshow:

the ripped cuff of the victim's blue jacket flapping in the breeze like a flag; late afternoon light dappling the torn flesh and splintered bone of an exposed wrist thrust out from the pile of rubble; eyes glazed in death, staring blindly out of a familiar, grit-covered face framed by the mess of gravel and vegetation dug away to reveal them; an empty metal box, its lid twisted out of alignment by an unknown hand eager to get at the contents within; and a set of shiny new wood screws drilled into old window frames as cheap security.

There were several supporting shots of terrain and the structure, as well as the heap under which most of the body still lay. The specialists had dismissed the absence of the victim's hand and the damage to his wrist as animal scavenging, but Moore wasn't jumping to that conclusion. He had taken several close-up shots of the area to make sure he captured details for later consideration. He had not seen the missing hand nor any evidence of scavenging animals.

Moore watched McAteer work at uncovering the body, while Bouton wrote the details in his notebook. McAteer photographed the process with a medium-format camera he'd carried onsite, part of what Moore guessed was his scene toolkit. Moore wasn't sure what he was capturing with each flash of light, but he wondered if the images imprinted on the IS officer's brain. The lack of companionable chit-chat meant he would probably never know. The specialists were focused on the body and each other. *They work well together.* They often completed each other's sentences, like an old married couple. Either they had similar personalities that allowed them to tune in to each other, or they had worked together before.

In either case, their closeness excluded the local officers to the point of rudeness. This irritated Moore and made him glad he had kept the existence of his camera to himself, a small defiance, but the identity of the victim needed to be brought forward. He cleared his throat. "Is it possible for me to see if I recognize him?"

Startled, the specialists looked up at Moore, confirming his suspicions that they had forgotten he was there.

Since neither answered, Moore moved closer, careful to keep his flashlight beam focused on the body. "I just thought, since I'm familiar with the surrounding community, I might be able to identify him."

Bouton stood, and his height surprised Moore into taking a step backward. This close, the half-foot difference was striking. At six feet, Moore was used to being the tallest of his team; it surprised him how losing that distinction affected him. Resisting the urge to puff up his chest, he focused on the body. The face and torso were badly bruised, several areas stained with dried blood where the skin had broken. The man was shirtless under the jacket. Moore knelt and leaned in closer to confirm his first impression. He sat back on his haunches. "It's Danny, Danny Brown." He called over at Nelson. "It's Danny!"

Nelson glanced at Moore, bobbed his head once then returned to his role as perimeter guard. Moore didn't miss the flash of pain that crossed Nelson's face, but he was proud of how he kept his composure. Danny and Nelson played on the same lacrosse team.

"A local Indian?" asked Bouton.

Standing, Moore nodded. "He is, or was, a fisherman who ran his boat out of Ucluelet." Moore took in the damage inflicted on his constable's friend. "He was a good man. Well-liked around here."

"We'll see."

Moore blinked at Bouton. By the look on the man's face, Moore was unsure whether he doubted that the victim was a good man, or if it was more general than that—that Bouton doubted any Indian could be a good man.

Moore was distracted from commenting by Bouton walking over to the transport box they had brought. He watched as the corporal instructed Nelson to give him a hand carrying it over to the IS officer.

McAteer had returned to his position at the head of Danny's body. To Moore, he explained, "Once they bring the box over here, I'll finish extracting the body from the hole and place it in the box. I'll need you to make sure I have the light where I need it. After the body is in the box, I'll seal it and accompany it to Nanaimo." He looked back at the body and sighed. "This'll be a long night."

Moore agreed. He'd known that when he and Nelson first discovered the body. When Nelson had called the detachment office to tell Evans of their find, he'd told him to go home and get some rest so he could spell Nelson off if things went past midnight. Nelson had already worked an extra three hours by coming in for the afternoon briefing. Moore hoped Evans had taken his advice and was now curled up in bed.

Nelson returned to guard duty. It wasn't as if they were expecting anyone to crash the scene, but they were surrounded by a wild forest and its equally wild inhabitants. Bouton approached Moore, a frown furrowing his brow. "Where's the coroner? Didn't you tell me he'd been called?"

Moore kept his expression neutral. "Constable Evans left a message. If the coroner doesn't show, it won't matter; he usually just goes along with whatever we say."

Bouton stared at Moore. "Why is he the coroner?"

Exactly, thought Moore. "If you need a medical opinion, I can call the local doctor."

"The pathologist will provide all the medical opinion we'll need." McAteer stood and looked over at the constable. "Did you contact an undertaker? We'll need him to transport the body to Nanaimo."

Moore used the opportunity to relax the arm holding the flashlight and did some quick stretches to loosen tight back muscles. "He should be here soon."

"Didn't realize you were expecting me, sir."

Moore spun to see Evans emerge from the darkness, carrying two large thermoses of coffee and a bag of sandwiches. "You're supposed to be home in bed!"

Evans grinned. "What can I say, sir. Your wife can be quite persuasive." When Moore opened his mouth to comment, Evens waved him silent. "She also suggested I call in an auxiliary officer to spell Monty. So I called Tim."

Moore sighed. There were times, he knew, he had to face the consequences of his open style of management. "I appreciate your initiative, Constable, but next time be sure to go through me first."

When McAteer knelt beside the body again, Moore resumed his job as light man, and brought his focus back to the scene. Shipping Danny to Nanaimo without the benefit of John's review was disappointing. Moore couldn't help wondering what his friend would have thought of the damage.

25.

Conny closed her eyes and leaned her head against the cushioned bench running along the width of the inn's lounge. She could feel the coolness of the night outside the picture window where the crown of her head touched the glass. The sound and vibration of the waves crashing against the rocks below comforted her. This place, this inn was her home. Or, at least as close to a home as she'd ever known.

As a world-weary eighteen-year-old, she had run away from her life on the streets of Vancouver and hitchhiked across the island in search of the paradise spoken of so highly by the city's hippie community. And she had found it. The beach, the ocean, and the people were all that she had imagined. She'd spent that first spring on Long Beach, smoking pot and giving away for free what she had sold on the streets of Vancouver. Then when the inn she had watched being built at the south end of the beach was hiring staff, she left the beach life and its communal philosophy behind. The new inn's owner didn't care who or what she had been before she walked through his door. He was looking for staff willing to work hard and commit to his vision. It had been the perfect opportunity for Conny to reinvent herself and leave her past behind. The following four years had been the happiest of her life. Now, she feared she had lost it.

"Why won't you tell me where you were last night, Conny?"

Conny opened her eyes and lifted her head so she could face Tish, sitting across the table from her. "Because it's not important."

"But I want to know."

"Why?"

"Because I think something's wrong, and I want to help."

"You can't." Conny could tell from Tish's expression that she was going to sulk. "Look, Tish." Conny waved her hand over the empty glasses covering the table between them. "It's your last night here. See all the farewell drinks people have been buying you. You've enjoyed every one of them!"

Conny settled her head against the window and closed her eyes again, letting her body relax into the afternoon's alcohol-induced buzz.

When Tish had followed her to the lodge earlier, Conny had told her to go back to work. Tish stormed out, and Conny collapsed on her bed, falling into a restless slumber. Rising hours later to the sound of her roommates sharing stories in the living room, she slipped across to the shower to scrub the filth of the night before off a body she felt she no longer knew. Stifling the sharp cries of pain as she stripped off each layer of her clothing, Conny knew there would be no broken bones. The goons were professional monsters. None of the bruising would be visible; not to anyone who saw her clothed, anyway. Inside the bathroom, Conny refused to look at what her naked body revealed. She turned away from the mirror.

She didn't want to know. She stepped into the shower stall, turned the tap as full as it could go, and just stood under the spray. When the water finally turned to ice, she towelled off and darted to her room, where she dressed into a loose-fitting cotton top and pants. She went braless, unwilling to bind her bruised flesh. When she emerged, she joined her roommates for a couple of beers, then told Tish she was taking her out for a farewell drink.

Now, after stretching Tom's bartending skills and her friend's alcohol tolerance, Conny just wanted to curl up in her own bed and think. The evening spent with Rod's lackeys had made one thing very clear—she was no longer safe. She was going to have to change her plans.

She shifted in the chair to ease her stiffening back muscles.

"May I join you, girls?"

Conny looked up as Tom set fresh drinks on the table. "As long as you stop calling us girls," she snapped.

Tom made a mock bow and took the chair between Conny and Tish. "Of course, your ladyship."

Conny shrugged and gazed around the near-empty lounge, thinking of all the times she had dropped in after work for a drink and a chat with various bartenders over the past four years. These men had shared their laughter and kindness with her without expectations. She hadn't appreciated what a gift they'd been until now. Catching Tom's eyes on her, she gave a half-smile.

"So, what have you two been talking about?" he asked.

Conny raised an eyebrow at Tish, leaving it to her to answer since she was the one with a major crush on the guy. When it became obvious Tish wasn't going to say anything, Conny spoke up. "We've just been reminiscing about the past four years."

"Four years? I didn't realize Tish had been here that long." Tom smiled. "You two must have some secrets to tell."

Tish downed the drink she'd been nursing, slammed the glass on the table, and grabbed the drink Tom had set in front of her. Glaring at Conny, as if daring her to stop her, she guzzled half the glass before putting it down again. "I don't know, Con, do you have any secrets you want to share? Isn't that what friends are for?"

"Leave it, Tish."

Tish ignored the warning in Conny's voice and turned to Tom. "Ask her where she was last night."

Tom looked at Tish and smiled. "You might want to take it easy, Tish. I don't want to cut you off on your last night."

"Then don't!"

Conny leaned forward and placed her hand on Tish's. "Tell Tom about the baby."

The distraction worked, and Tish turned to Tom. "You know the pregnant hippie we've seen around? Well, she had her baby on the beach today. And she did it while surrounded by a bunch of naked men!"

"Aren't there always naked men at Wreck Bay?" Tom sat back in his chair and sent a conspiratorial smile across to Conny.

"Well, one of them delivered the baby, right there on the beach!"

Conny was glad the afternoon crowd had moved on and no one was around to hear Tish's tone. She tried to calm her by asking, "Was it a boy or a girl?"

"A girl." Tish relaxed in her chair, eyes half-closed.

Conny wondered if the afternoon of drinking had finally hit her friend. "Did they name her Dewdrop or Star? Don't hippies always name their kids the silliest names?"

Tom shook his head. "I think they really believe in a peaceful future, that there won't be any bullies to worry about."

Tish burst out laughing. "What planet are they living on?"

Conny looked down at her hands, remembering all she had been expected to do with them as she was growing up in the bush outside of Revelstoke. She never had to deal with playground bullies because she had rarely attended school, but her home was full of them. She no longer had the calluses from chopping wood, but hidden scars remained, earned from the chores expected of her by her mother's boyfriends.

She took a deep breath. She hadn't thought of her childhood in a long time. Last night's events must have pried those memories loose. They hadn't, however, pried loose anything about the raided shack. She had no idea who took the drugs, and from the looks on the goons' faces when they finally realized she had no information to give up, she knew her plan to work for Rod until she had enough money to move to Los Angeles was done. She had to find a new plan.

She stood abruptly. "I'm going back to the lodge. I need to sleep." She looked at Tish. "Are you coming?"

Tish looked up at Conny and shook her head. "No. I'm going to stay."

Sandy was disturbed by the sound of loud knocking at the lodge's front door. She had been lost in the Hollywood world of the *Valley of the Dolls,* which Conny had left on the end table. She glanced at her watch. *Ten o'clock. Who would visit so late?* Setting the book aside, she hauled herself up from the couch and approached the door cautiously. "Who is it?"

"Mark…It's Mark, Sandy."

With a sigh of relief, Sandy opened the door. "What are you—"

"I found the logger!" Mark brushed past her and headed for the living room, where he dropped to the couch.

"How?"

"I asked around the beach." Mark glanced over at Sandy as she took a seat at the opposite end of the couch, tucking her feet up under her. "People tend not to talk with strangers, you understand?"

"Yes."

Satisfied that she wasn't taking offence, he continued, "Well, his name is James Johnston, and he lives and works in Tofino as a labourer."

"Johnston? That was Geoff's last name."

"Could they be related?"

"I don't know."

"Well, Johnston is a common name." Mark leaned forward, resting his elbows on his knees and clasping his hands as if to settle nervous energy. "I should warn you, though, James is part of a group of locals who have been trying to kick us off the beach. I'm surprised I didn't recognize him. The lighting must've thrown me, because I've run into him a couple of times. I should've recognized him."

Sandy studied him. He was so focused, so driven. *How could I have thought him weak?*

"In the past," Mark continued, "the group has just written letters to the council or harassed us when we've gone into town. This month, they've started coming down to the beach and handing out job listings or army recruitment notices."

"Real ones?"

"How would I know?" He looked over his shoulder into the kitchen. "Do you still have some of that wine left?"

Sandy went to fetch the wine and glasses.

"One time, they came down with a group of women carrying clothing and lectured us on the sin of nudity. As if there was such a thing. They tried shaming us into getting dressed."

"I didn't realize you went nude."

"Sometimes. It's not a big thing for me."

"Have they threatened you?" She turned to face him. "How far do you think they'd go to get you off the beach?"

"I don't know. Some of them seem more than a little crazy."

Sandy returned with the reopened wine bottle she divided the rest of the wine between the two glasses and handed one to Mark.

"Thanks. Where is everyone?"

"Conny came in a while ago but went straight to her room. Said she'd left Tish drinking up at the inn. Tom is working. Roxanne's out with her boyfriend. And Edan? I don't know where he's at. He could be sleeping. Although I don't think anyone could've slept through your pounding at the door." Sandy set her glass on the coffee table. "Do you think this James could have hurt Geoff during an argument about clearing the beach?"

"I don't know. From what people are saying, James was alone on the beach and looking specifically for Geoff."

"So, it could have nothing to do with the group looking to get rid of—" She leaned forward. "You know what we have to do, don't you?"

Mark stared at her.

"We have to tell Geoff's parents," Sandy said.

"I was on the way to the inn to call the cops. I decided to drop in here first."

"Okay, them too."

"You don't even know where his parents are staying."

"They told me they were staying at the inn." Sandy glanced at her watch. *Ten-thirty*. "We can go now. It'll only take a minute." She stood and started to walk past Mark.

"No, Sandy." He grabbed her hand and held on. "If you're going to tell anyone, it should be the police. *They* can tell the parents." He finished off his glass of wine and placed it on the coffee table. "I'll walk over to the inn and make that call."

TUESDAY,
MAY 14, 1968

26.

The cloudy skies outside the detachment's windows did nothing to lighten the sombre and intense mood as the officers gathered for the morning briefing. The discovery of a second murder victim had the local officers on edge and the specialists excited.

The contrast didn't surprise Moore. He had spent his entire career posted in small towns, so he'd never developed the detachment from a crime's victims that he'd seen in city cops. And although neither he nor his constables had dealt with a murder case before this exceptional week, he believed his constables shared his attitude of seeing victims as humans rather than inanimate puzzle pieces.

However, as Moore surveyed the room, he realized that regardless of their attitude toward murder victims, lack of sleep induced a common reaction amid them all. A series of loud, extended yawns made its way around the room, and he wondered how McAteer had handled the long drive to Nanaimo. It had been close to eleven o'clock before the scene was cleared, and though Moore tried suggesting that transporting the victim to Nanaimo could be delayed until the morning, McAteer had insisted he was all right to escort the body that night. The undertaker had just shrugged. So, they had set off, promising to stop for a break if they needed one.

Moore glanced at his watch. *Six-thirty.* He cleared his throat. "Maybe we should get started, gentlemen."

"Thank you, Corporal Moore." Corporal Bouton turned to address his small audience. "First I would like to thank you and your constables for arranging the extra desks needed for myself and Corporal McAteer. I've been with the Force many years and understand how difficult managing resources can be. That's why I feel you'll understand what I'm about to say." He turned and wrote DANNY BROWN on the chalkboard before facing the group once more. "The discovery of Danny Brown's body last night, has changed things for the team."

Oh, we're a team now, are we? Moore sat forward, wondering where this was going.

"Obviously, the workload has been doubled. And it's this I'd like to discuss before we get into the details of the new case." He paused. "Victoria has informed me they don't have any spare resources to send our way because of the training going on in Vancouver this week. So, on top of your regular duties, you will be working these cases with Corporal McAteer and myself." He looked at Moore. "Any questions?"

Moore quickly glanced at his constables. Halden's face had sprung an ear-to-ear grin. Monty's was buried in his hands. Moore turned to Bouton. "Will we be keeping the shifts or moving everyone to day shift?"

Bouton nodded. "I imagine it'll be easier to keep things as they are for now. We'll use the voluntary services of the local auxiliary officers where we can." He paused. "Have you heard from the coroner?"

"It's in the file, sir. The coroner viewed the body at the scene and will hold an inquest as soon as a jury can be assembled. We're expecting the verdict to be homicide by person or persons unknown."

Bouton flipped through the file on his desk until he found the sheet. "Hopefully, Corporal McAteer will be the only one called before the jury but be prepared just the same. "He glanced at the chalkboard and the points written there then turned his attention to Evans. "Were you able to confirm the ownership of the shack?"

"I'll call today once offices open," Evans stated.

"Very well. Corporal Moore, did you want to report on the next of kin visit?"

Moore considered standing, then decided against it. Instead, he leaned into his chair and folded his hands across his stomach. "After we finished at the scene last night, Corporal Bouton and I informed Danny's mother, Iris, of her son's death. I told her there was no need for the family to formally identify the body as I had already done so at the scene." He wanted to spare her from seeing the shape her son was in when they'd finally pulled him from the pile of rubble.

"She wouldn't have been able to see the body, anyway. Corporal McAteer had already sealed it for transport to Nanaimo," Bouton pointed out.

"I know." Moore tried to keep the defensive tone out of his answer. "But she didn't need to know all that." He took a deep breath. "She just needed to know that her son was dead." He glanced at Nelson. "She came along when we went next door to tell Danny's wife, Lisa. The Brown family are very close-knit. I have no doubt the two women will have the support they need." Moore opened his notebook. "I asked Lisa if she knew why he would have been at a shack by Lost Shoe Creek. She told me Danny had picked up a temporary security job for some company shipping fish to Vancouver. It was night shifts and he expected it to last only a week or so. She said he thought the location was strange, but she didn't know what he had meant by that."

"So, he wasn't involved in the robbery? He was a guard!" Nelson beamed.

"It seems so." Moore took a moment to refocus. "She couldn't remember the name of the company, but she said Danny was thinking of quitting because Marco had warned him off it."

"Marco?" Evans asked. "Who's Marco?"

"He's an old prospector who's been in the area a long time," Nelson explained. "He works several claims in the area." Nelson scribbled a quick note. "I'll check if he has a claim at Lost Shoe Creek."

"That won't be necessary," Bouton said. "Corporal Moore and I will take care of it." The senior corporal turned to Moore. "Do you think the two deaths are connected?"

Moore sent Nelson a reassuring smile before answering, "Not necessarily. I just find it interesting that no sooner do I get my first murder case than a second one appears." He threw up his hands. "We still don't have a cause of death on our first victim. At least the second's was obvious."

"Nothing's obvious, Corporal Moore," Bouton lectured. "The victim took a beating, but we won't know what killed him until the pathologist's exam is complete. As for Johnston, the pathologist should have his toxicology report to us sometime today. The results will, hopefully, confirm the poisoning theory. We'll be treating the two murders as separate events until such time as we find evidence connecting them." He turned to the chalkboard. "What do we know so far about the second murder victim? He was a fisherman. And he took a temporary job guarding a shack in the woods for a couple of weeks. None of this explains why he would end up buried under a cast-off pile behind that shack."

Silence followed Bouton's comments until he broke it. "Could he have known about the box and its contents? Got caught stealing it?"

"Danny wouldn't have—"

"I know he was your friend, Constable Nelson, but we have to consider the possibility," Bouton warned.

"But Danny—"

"It makes sense that Danny was killed *because* he was the guard." Moore stood to break up the confrontation that wouldn't do Nelson's career any good. "We've never had any trouble with Danny. He's a family man and uses his involvement with the lacrosse club to encourage bored youth to get rid of extra energy and pent-up emotions by participating in the sport." Then he turned to face Nelson. "But I think what Corporal Bouton is trying to say, Monty, is that we need to keep an open mind. Once we speak with Marco, we'll have a better understanding of what's going on."

Bouton pointed to Evans. "We can still ask around and get a handle on Mr. Brown's movements over the last couple of days. Constable Evans, do some sniffing around today and see what you can find."

The two constables exchanged furtive glances before Nelson busied himself scribbling in his notebook.

"Okay, let's return to the first murder." Bouton paused while Moore sat. "Yesterday afternoon, Corporal McAteer started his inspection of Mr. Johnston's van." Bouton picked up a sheet of paper from his desk. "His report states that he found blood—"

"Blood? There was no indication that Geoff bled," Moore said.

"Mr. Johnston wasn't the source of the blood," Bouton continued. "He found bloody sheets shoved under the bed. The blood wasn't the victim's, but Corporal McAteer suspects he was involved. From the pattern and colour of the blood, he felt it resulted from a sexual encounter. He took the sheets with him to Nanaimo to be analyzed."

"It was fresh?"

"Fairly fresh, yes. It was less than a day old."

"So, there's a girl out there who was raped?"

Bouton frowned. "I don't know."

A motive? Moore leaned back in his chair. "I guess I'm going to have another conversation with Miss Chambers." He made a note in his book, ignoring the look the senior corporal gave him.

Bouton waited for Moore to finish writing. "Once you're done speaking with Miss Chambers, I'll meet you at the inn and we can check out the other shack."

Moore squared his shoulders and took a deep breath. "Anything else from the van?"

"The van reflected the victim's lifestyle as a surfer. It was camperized with all the usual fittings. However, blood wasn't the only thing that came as a surprise. He also found small traces of vomit, and evidence that the floor and counter space had been wiped down. He didn't find the cleanser used."

Moore whistled. He remembered the spot of vomit his friend pointed out on Geoff's clothing. "So, the van's the murder scene?"

"We'll have to wait for the lab results to confirm that. The sample from the van may be too small or contaminated from the cleaning product." Bouton chalked a large question mark beside VAN on the board, then turned back to Moore. "Corporal McAteer also found a syringe and two vials tucked in the back of a drawer beside the sink."

"Drugs?" Evans asked.

"We'll find out when Corporal McAteer returns."

27.

Sandy tucked the sheet under the mattress, smoothed out the creases, and then pulled the blanket and quilt over top. The repetitive nature of her job allowed her mind to wander, and it kept wandering to Mark. After he'd returned from calling the cops, they had shared a second bottle of wine until one in the morning. She wasn't sure which of them suggested he stay. All she knew was that they stood up from the couch at the same time and started unfolding the bed within.

She smiled at the memory of the soft kiss he'd left her with that morning. Their time together had been different than her time with Geoff, and she wondered if that would be true with each guy she slept with.

Glancing at the view outside, she was drawn to the drama of the clouds and seascape beyond. She crossed the room and opened the patio door, surprised that no guests were enjoying a morning coffee on the balcony that ran along the south side of the inn's second floor. She'd love to just sit and enjoy the view—maybe even attempt to paint it. The cedar railings and banisters could be used to anchor the painting's perspective. Taking a deep breath, she leaned against the cedar siding, and could've sworn the building relaxed around her. She was surprised at how easily she accepted what she sensed as a truth, and let her gaze wander over the beach south of the inn. Unlike the north side, this view offered a shorter stretch of sand ending at mounds of rock crowned by storm-tossed driftwood. Beyond, a cozy cove filled with tidal pools waited for treasure hunters and a famous artist. She wondered if Steve and his dog had been back to beachcomb. She would love to see what he had created with his gathered treasures.

"Hello?"

Startled, Sandy turned to find a RCMP officer standing in the doorway. Recognizing him as the man who drove her to the inn after she discovered Geoff, she returned the greeting.

The officer stepped into the room and glanced around. "Corporal David Moore."

"Yes, I remember." Sandy was taken aback by his resemblance to Paul McCartney of the Beatles. She hadn't noticed when they'd met in his car. Now, the similarity was obvious, except for his chestnut hair, which was military short. Thick brows curved gently over warm, brown eyes, bracketing a strong, straight nose, that capped a small, expressive mouth. It was a very English face.

"Can we talk?"

Sandy moved inside and closed the patio door. The absence of the ocean's continuous roar magnified the sense of unease in the room. Sandy rushed to dispel it by pulling two chairs away from the small table tucked against the wall. "How about here?" She offered one seat to the officer and took the other.

Corporal Moore crossed the room and set the small bag he carried on the floor by his feet. "I've just come from a briefing at the station. We searched Geoff's van, and I need to ask some questions."

Sandy settled into her chair and indicated for him to begin.

"Okay." He unbuttoned his brown, uniform jacket, revealing a light brown dress shirt with blue tie underneath. After hanging his jacket over the back of the chair, he sat. "How well did you get to know Geoff?"

"Not well." Sandy paused. The intense focus of his posture and dark brown eyes added to her nervousness. "Is there anything wrong, Corporal Moore?"

"David. You can call me David." He opened his hands, palms up. "I need to ask how intimately you knew him."

Sandy's eyes widened. "Why?"

"We found some bloodied sheets in his van."

Heat flooded through her, and she quickly looked away. *Oh god!* To give her virginity away in the privacy of Geoff's van was one thing; to discuss it in the cold morning light with a policeman was quite another.

"I don't mean to embarrass you." Moore reached out to briefly touch the hand she rested on the table. "I just need to confirm that you were the one who had sex in the vehicle."

"Yes." Sandy withdrew her hand and squared her shoulders as she faced him. "Yes, I had sex with Geoff in his van."

"When was this?"

Sandy stared at him. She had been sure he'd caught her reference that day in the car when she'd told him she and Geoff had checked out his van. "I told you before. Friday. Maybe two o'clock. It was before we walked over to Wreck Bay."

Sandy saw the officer's cheeks blush before he twisted around to fumble in the breast pocket of his jacket. He pulled out a notebook and pen, and as she watched him scribble notes, a memory of Friday afternoon flooded over her. The soft gold of the sun filtering through the van's yellow curtains, creating a magical light. The taste of the sea on Geoff's surprisingly soft lips. The tickle of his hair brushing her face as he trailed kisses across her cheek, down her neck, and across the rise of her breast as his long, beautiful fingers released the pearl buttons of her peasant blouse.

"Was the blood yours?"

Momentarily confused by the sudden return to the present, Sandy took a moment to answer. "Yes."

"Was it caused by an injury?"

"No."

Her answer seemed to fluster Moore. His pen hung suspended above the notebook's page. Then, as if released from a spell, he set the pen to paper once more. "Is there anything else you need to tell me about your relationship with Geoff or the events leading up to his death?"

"No,"

"I'll need to get your fingerprints—"

"No!" Sandy jumped up from the chair and backed away, suddenly very frightened. "I didn't kill him!"

Moore looked up at her. "I'm not saying you did. I need the prints so we can separate them from any others found in the van."

Blushing deeply, Sandy shook her head. "If I come down to the station, everyone will know it was my blood."

Moore frowned. "How would they even know there was blood in the van? We haven't made that public."

Feeling the impact of the adrenaline rush, Sandy tried to slow her breathing. "Everyone keeps telling me there are no secrets here. It's a small town. Everyone knows everything about everybody."

"Well, if that were true, I'd be out of a job." Moore leaned down and picked up the bag he had brought in with him. "I can take your fingerprints right here. You don't need to go to the station." He stood and started removing items from the bag. "It used to be that all fingerprints had to be sent to Ottawa for processing, which could take several weeks," he commented. "Now, we have local specialist officers who can take on the task and act as experts in court."

Sandy returned to the table and looked down at the ink pad and sheet of paper. "I didn't know I would bleed the first time. Nobody told me," she whispered, then stopped, embarrassed by the naiveté her words revealed. She ran a fingertip along the edge of the paper. "Geoff was surprised and worried. We had a bit of an argument."

"When was this?"

"On the way to Wreck Bay, maybe three, four o'clock."

"Why was he worried?"

"He's Catholic. Or was. Or is?" Sandy paused. "Do you think our faith follows us after death?" At Moore's puzzled look, Sandy stumbled on. "He felt he had taken something from me that was meant for my future husband. I assured him he hadn't." When Sandy saw the look on Moore's face she quickly added, "It's 1968, for Christ's sake!"

"And yet you turned beet red when I mentioned the sheets."

Sandy dropped into the chair. "Just because I believe I have the right to have sex when I want doesn't mean I want the act discussed. I was brought up in a very strict home. There were things I was taught I shouldn't do or say. So, even if I choose to break some of their rules, I still struggle with the embarrassment I might cause my family." She sighed. "I planned on washing the sheets. But things happened."

"Yes," Moore agreed, "they did." He waited for a moment before continuing. "So, as far as you know, you were the only woman to have sex with Geoff in that van before he died?"

Sandy stared at him. "You think there might have been someone else?"

"I'm not saying that. We haven't checked all the fingerprints. I was just asking if you knew if there had been someone. Since you're all liberated and all of that."

Sandy narrowed her eyes. "I know you think we're all into orgies, but we're not. Well, some are, but I'm not!"

Moore sighed. "How about I take your fingerprints now and let you get on with your day?"

He was gentle as he inked and rolled each of her fingertips on the paper, leaving behind a clean imprint. Sandy stared at the black reverse-image prints and thought of how something so simple could have such a large impact on a person's life. As she rubbed the ink from her fingers with the cloth he had given her, she said, "He might have met someone, I guess. He was seen on the path around three in the morning, walking toward the inn."

Sandy and Moore turned at a noise from the doorway. Conny stood there, frozen.

Moore stopped repacking his bag. "Do you need something, Miss Lee?"

"No. I was…I was only checking up on Sandy."

"Sorry for taking her away from her job" Moore said. "I had a few more questions to ask. I won't keep her long."

Conny's eyes did a quick flick to Sandy before she left.

Moore turned back to Sandy. "Someone saw Geoff?"

Her cheeks burning, Sandy worried what Conny had heard. "Yes."

"I thought you said you didn't see him after he left the campfire at seven."

"About seven. Yes. After he suddenly showed up at Mark's campfire. But, like I told you, he left again when one of the guys he'd played Frisbee with showed up. They left together." Sandy fanned her hands on the table to calm herself and slow down her thoughts. Tears burned at the memory of how she had pushed away his advances that night at the campfire. If she'd only played along, he might still be alive. She forced herself to look at Moore. "I didn't see him after that, but I ran into someone who said they did."

"Who?"

"A guy named Steve. He has a dog named Spike. He's an Indian and an artist. That's all I know about him."

"Why didn't you say anything before?"

"I met Steve on Sunday, after you interviewed me." Sandy frowned. "Then I got distracted. It's important, isn't it? It means Geoff took *that* path back to the van, not any of the others. I thought he must have taken a different one because it didn't make sense for him to be on that road at that time when his van was at the inn."

Moore smiled. "I bet you like putting jigsaw puzzles together."

Sandy blinked at him. "What does that have to do with anything?"

Moore offered no answer to her question, asking one of his own, instead. "Does this Steve have a last name?"

"I'm sure he does. I just don't know what it is."

"Can you tell me about the conversation you had with Steve?"

Sandy took a deep breath and described her encounter with the man and his dog.

"That's pretty clear. We should be able to find him." Moore started to close his notebook, then stopped. "Anything else you need to tell me?"

Sandy started to shake her head, then stopped. Glancing down at her hands, then back up at Moore, she said, "I think I know how he was killed"

"Pardon me?"

Sandy took a deep breath and rushed on. "I told you that the position you found him in was the way he was after I dragged him out, but it wasn't. At least not the first time."

"The first time?"

"I couldn't just leave him there. He looked so…so alone."

"He was dead."

"I *know*." She scanned the room. "It was so lonely sitting there with Geoff in the fog, waiting for help to arrive, and I felt bad for dropping him the way I did after I pulled him from the water the first time."

"So, what'd you do?"

"I went over and tugged him a little further out of the ditch. His head rolled to the side, and…well, I saw a needle mark."

Moore sucked in his breath. "A needle mark?"

"It looked like an angry welt near the base of his skull, like the skin had been pierced." Sandy pointed to the location on her own neck and watched Moore closely, waiting for his reaction. None came. "I-I thought it was strange because I distinctly remembered that he'd said he didn't—no, couldn't—take drugs." Except pot, she almost added.

"Did he say why?"

"No." Sandy thought back to their conversation in the van after they'd made love. They'd shared funny stories about parental attempts to control their lives, but nothing specific about the reason behind the aversion to popular drugs. "I think he was just into being healthy. He didn't have any chips or anything like that in the van, just fruit and stuff."

"Have you told anyone about the needle mark?"

Sandy paused, suddenly feeling like she was standing in front of her father, waiting for him to lecture her. "I told Tish."

Moore finished writing and closed his notebook. "I understand that you were studying art down in Victoria."

"Yes."

He sighed. "Things have changed a bit since we first spoke. I want you to draw what you saw when you first found Geoff's body. I want the position of the body and as many details about the surrounding area as you can remember. I also want you to write out exactly what you did when you discovered Geoff, right up to the point when we arrived at the scene. Then I want you to bring both the drawing and your statement into the Ucluelet station. If I'm not there, leave it with the officer who is."

"Okay."

Moore shrugged into his jacket before picking up his bag, then stopped. Rummaging in his jacket's breast pocket again, he withdrew a piece of paper and handed it to her. "And you may want to take care of this as well."

Sandy looked down at the blown-up image of herself and realized it was a missing persons report.

Tom squinted against the morning light streaming through his bedroom window and checked the bedside clock. *Nine-thirty.* He rolled onto his back and stretched, kicking the tangle of bed sheets away from his legs. The beginnings of a headache behind his eyes caused him to groan at the anticipated pain. *Maybe another hour of sleep.*

"Good morning," Tish whispered. She rolled over and moulded her nude body against his.

Tom squeezed his eyes shut as he mentally berated himself. *Shit! Shit! Shit!*

Tish kissed his shoulder as her fingers started tracing circles down his abdomen. She stopped just above the mound of hair that nested his penis. Tom held his breath. He knew the game she was playing and willed himself not to respond. *She's leaving. We're over. This is not a good idea.* Her fingertips started moving again, teasing, tickling, and he hardened in response. He turned toward her.

Tish smiled and shifted until she took his full weight. "So, do you want to give me another going-away present? Or should I give you something to remember me by?"

28.

Back at the office, Moore dropped the fingerprint kit on McAteer's desk. Obviously, the man hadn't returned from delivering Danny's body to the lab in Nanaimo. Evans and Bouton were at their desks, phones at their ears. Moore smiled as he passed. Dropping into his chair, he started flipping through the accumulated paper stacked on his desk. Most involved the usual complaint about speeding cars on the beach, which was difficult to deal with because the offenders were usually long gone by the time he arrived. They could use an officer stationed full-time at the beach over the summer, but so far his requests to headquarters had landed on deaf ears. He set the messages aside and looked through the remaining papers. There were a couple of responses from the radio request for information on Geoff's death, but nothing specific enough for him to follow up on. It was too early to expect anything back from the announcement of Danny's death. He noticed a handwritten note from dispatch that said a Mark Wilson had called with the name of the man Geoff had met with: James Johnston.

The name was familiar. Moore had run into him a few times, usually after Johnston had been drinking and wasn't in the best of moods. The trouble was, he was connected. While living in such a wild and beautiful wilderness had many advantages, small-town group dynamics was one major disadvantage. He ran into it in Tofino, he ran into it in Ucluelet, and he ran into it on the reserves.

James Johnston was connected through marriage to George Hodges, an electrician by trade, who, by his involvement in several community groups, figured he owned Tofino, or at least the people who lived there. He was arrogant enough to feel he could get away with killing someone, and he had the resources to make sure the body disappeared. Which, when Moore thought about it, took him off the list of suspects in Geoff's murder. If this guy was involved, the body would not have been left on the side of a road. It would simply have disappeared. Still, if James had been talking to Geoff, Moore had to tread carefully.

Moore looked up to see Evans was off the phone and was watching him. "Anything important?"

The constable shook his head. "Another speeding complaint from the beach."

Moore was about to suggest Evans join him for the interview with James Johnston, but Bouton ended his phone call and rubbed the back of his neck. "I think I've had my fill of journalists for a while." He looked across at Moore. "Same questions over and over."

Moore was sympathetic but knew dealing with the press was part of the job. "I've got a lead on the guy who was seen talking to Geoff on Friday night," he said. "A local general labourer named James Johnston."

"Does he look good for our guy?"

"I'm not sure. I don't see a motive, but he's probably worth speaking to."

Bouton stood and headed to the exit, calling over his shoulder, "Well, let's get to it."

Grabbing his jacket off the back of his chair, Moore followed. "James is probably at his father-in-law's latest project, the new restaurant in Tofino."

29.

As Moore turned into the driveway, the rumble of the vehicle's tires rolling over loose gravel announced their arrival. He could see James bent over, silhouetted against the clear sky, hammering shingles just off the crest of his cousin's roof. He appeared to be alone. Moore pulled the patrol car as close to the building as he could.

He wanted to push James' boundaries, make him uncomfortable.

They had stopped at the restaurant project in Tofino only to be told James had taken a couple of days off and was reroofing his cousin's house. Moore and Bouton exited the patrol car and stood for a moment beside it, waiting for James to acknowledge them. He had seen James glance at their approaching vehicle.

James stopped hammering, slid his hammer into the loop of his tool belt, and descended via the ladder leaning against the roof's edge. "What's up?" he asked. He didn't offer his hand in greeting.

Given their past encounters, Moore let the snub—if it was one—slide. "Good morning, James. This is Corporal Bouton from the Major Crimes Unit in Victoria. We need to ask you some questions about what you were doing at Wreck Bay on Friday night."

James hesitated. "Will this take long? I promised my cousin I'd finish his roof before it starts rainin' again."

"It shouldn't take long," Bouton answered.

James gestured for the officers to follow him onto the porch with its four bent-reed chairs, their orange cushions adding a splash of colour to the day. When they were all seated, James leaned forward, resting his elbows on his knees. "What do you want to know about Friday night?"

Moore tried to determine if the sweat beading across James' forehead indicated James was nervous or just hot from shingling. "What were you discussing with Geoff Johnston?"

"So, this is about the hit-and-run?"

Moore hesitated, considering whether to correct him.

Bouton took the decision from him. "We're investigating Mr. Johnston's death as a murder."

James sat back suddenly, the colour draining from his face. "Murder? You think Geoff was murdered?"

"Yes," Moore said. "Now you understand why we want to know about your meeting with him on Friday night."

James reached into his shirt pocket and pulled out a pack of cigarettes, his hand trembling as he offered it first to Moore and then Bouton.

"No. Thank you." Moore glanced at the lawn filled with kids' toys. "I'm trying to quit."

Bouton accepted the offer.

James reached into his pants pocket and pulled out a packet of matches. "How long?" He lit his cigarette, then tossed the box to Bouton.

"Trying to quit?" Moore asked. "About six months. The first time was sixteen years ago, when my first son was born. Didn't last. My wife insisted I quit again when my second son came along."

James still appeared shaken by the news of his cousin's death, but the colour had returned to his face. "Do you miss it?"

"Sure. Sometimes." Moore continued to study James. He was a big man, with the muscle tone of the footballer he had once been in high school, but he was softening around the middle.

"*My* wife's tryin'"—James gave a short laugh—"to get me to stop dropping my *G*s. Says it makes me sound like a hillbilly."

Before Moore could comment, Bouton broke in. "So, James, why were you down at Wreck Bay on a Friday night?"

James sucked deeply on his cigarette, letting go with a long, slow exhale. "I went down there to speak with my cousin."

Moore sat forward, surprised. "You and Geoff were cousins?"

"Yeah. Dad's twin brother, Arthur, moved away when he was thirty-something, to Seattle. Caused quite a split in the family. Geoff and I were seven, nine, something like that. We hadn't seen each other since."

Moore removed his notebook from his pocket, and flipped through pages filled with his broad scrawl until he found a clear one. "It must've come as a shock to realize you had a hippie in the family, especially considering your recent activity."

James shrugged. "Family's family."

Bouton shifted in his seat, the reed chair creaking so ominously Moore feared it would burst whatever inadequate pins were holding it together. "So, you're saying you didn't argue with him?"

"Argue?" James looked sharply from Bouton to Moore. "What do you mean 'argue'? Has someone said I was arguin' with Geoff?"

James' flash of anger was more in line with what Moore had expected from him, and he relaxed. This was familiar territory. He'd long since learned that the best way to defuse James' anger was to not react in kind. Choosing his tone carefully, Moore said, "I have a witness who says you and Geoff did *not* approach each other like you were long-lost cousins."

"On the beach?" James waved his hand dismissively, scattering cigarette ash across his lap, the anger visibly leaving him. "On the beach, he didn't know who I was. I didn't recognize him either. So much time had passed. When I started comin', coming toward him, I heard the guy who brought him tell him to be careful as I was part of a group that's been…harassing them. So, Geoff came at me ready to do battle. But once I explained who I was, he was okay."

Moore glanced at Bouton, who had relaxed in his chair and was taking long draws on his cigarette. Moore took his manner as a signal to carry on with the questioning. "How'd you know he was there? Did he contact you?"

"No. A guy I've worked with surfs on his days off. When he ran into me in Tofino on Friday, he said he'd met a guy named Geoff Johnston on the beach earlier that day and asked if he was a relation. I went down to the beach to check him out. I wanted to know if it could be my cousin."

Moore didn't know how much of the story he believed. "Did you stay on the beach?"

"No, I invited him up to my pickup for a beer."

"Your pickup?"

"Yeah, I popped the tailgate, and we sat and talked, caught up like."

"Where was this?"

James hesitated. "There's a road that cuts around the bog and comes out at the top of the cliff midway along the beach. I was parked there."

"It's not much of a road."

"It can be rough. I can't even make it in after a heavy rain, sometimes."

"Is that where you and your buddies park when you harass the campers?"

James exhaled a stream of smoke, his eyes on Moore.

Moore watched the emotions play across James' face. He didn't think James was lying, but he was holding something back. "How long were you and Geoff there?"

"About an hour. I couldn't stay long. It was getting pretty dark, and I had to get back into town. We made plans for supper the next night." James shook his head. "I can't believe he's dead."

An image of a soaked piece of paper with smudged writing on it came to mind, and Moore paused in his note-taking. "Did he know where you lived?"

James nodded. "I gave him my address and phone number."

Moore waited as James stubbed his cigarette out in the ashtray sitting on the patio table. "What else did you plan, James?"

"Nothin'. What do you mean?"

"Apparently, Geoff was telling stories around the bonfire about you two looking to do some prospecting. He was even flashing a prospector's pan about."

"Oh. That. Yeah. I found a family claim on the land above Wreck Bay, and I mentioned it to Geoff."

Moore sighed. "Who told you about the claim?"

"Nobody. I found some papers and a couple of old pans when I cleaned out my dad's place after he died."

"Claim papers?"

"Yeah."

"When was this?"

"When dad died? About three months ago."

Moore blinked. "Oh. Was your father Allan Johnston?"

"Yes."

Moore paused to write a note, annoyed at himself for failing to make the connection. Allan's drowning in February had caused quite a stir, as his wife had drowned two years earlier. Moore offered James a look of sympathy. "A tragic loss."

James nodded slowly.

"So, why tell Geoff?"

"Because it was a joint claim between our fathers. They'd inherited from our grandfather."

"And you didn't know about the claim before this?"

"No."

"So, you found the papers about three months ago. What'd you do with them?"

"Checked to see if they were still active. They brought a lot of memories back, you know, happy childhood memories. Our dads used to take us on hikes in that area. Now I know why." He coughed and looked away.

"They'd take the two of you?"

"Yeah. Our families used to be real close. Geoff and me, we used to do everything together. He was like a brother."

"It seems strange that Geoff's father would move away and leave that claim behind if it was so important to him."

James lit another cigarette and took several pulls before answering. "When Geoff's family moved away, there were no goodbyes—at least, not for Geoff and me. One day they were here, the next they were gone."

Moore wondered if this was leading to a motive for Geoff's murder and leaned forward, encouraging James to continue. "That must've been tough."

"Well, you get over it, don't you? Life goes on." James sighed. "The claim papers weren't the only papers I found. I came across two letters from Uncle Arthur. One hadn't been opened. I read the open one first. I guess it was a response to a letter my father must've sent earlier. From what my uncle wrote, I realized my father must've forced my uncle to move after he caught him trying to seduce my mother. My dad had a hot temper. He threatened to kill my uncle if he ever saw him again."

"That's a pretty strong threat."

"I guess it wasn't the first time something like that had happened. My dad must've mentioned an earlier seduction because when I opened the second letter from my uncle, it was just a bunch of excuses for his behaviour."

"He tried to seduce your mother before?"

"No, someone else."

"Who?"

"Don't know, but my uncle wrote that he wasn't responsible for her suicide."

"Suicide?"

"Yeah."

Moore considered the implications of this information. Had an old family feud caused Geoff's death? He wondered who the second woman could have been. "Do you know if the suicide happened here?"

"No idea."

"Do you know when it happened?"

"Sometime in 1953."

The same year Geoff's parents moved away. "Did you tell Geoff about this?"

"No, but I asked if his parents were still together." James looked at Moore. "He got all defensive and made a big point of how they'd celebrated their last anniversary."

"Do you think that meant he knew about his father?"

James shrugged.

"Getting back to the claim," Bouton interrupted. "Were you expecting to cash in?"

James shifted in his chair. "I thought it'd be fun to see what came out of it. That's all. Geoff seemed up for it."

"So, just a little fun for the two of you."

"Yeah. So what?"

"About what time did you meet Geoff on the beach?"

James hesitated. "I don't know. I wasn't watching the time."

"Why didn't you come forward with this information?" Bouton demanded.

James gave Moore a look. "You know me. You know why."

Moore nodded. James' history with the police made trust an issue. "I will need you to come down to the station and give a formal statement."

James stubbed out his second cigarette. "After I finish the roof."

30.

Sandy stood at the door to the ground-floor suite and watched Conny work. Her movements seemed slow, and she wasn't paying attention to the details as closely as she had taught her to do. Sandy brushed a wrinkle out of the bed's comforter and tucked the corners in properly. Conny didn't even glance her way.

Sandy stepped back and continued to observe her boss. Conny's hair didn't look as if she'd applied the usual layer of hairspray, nor had it been backcombed with any degree of care. Sandy had come down to ask Conny what she had overheard of her conversation with Moore, but now she was worried there was a bigger concern. "Are you okay?"

Conny turned from her dusting, the late morning sun haloing the frizz of untamed hair. "Yeah, why?"

How could Sandy tell her that she didn't seem to be herself when she'd only known Conny a couple of days? But that was exactly what she wanted to say. *You're not yourself.* Instead, she smiled and said, "No reason. Um, it's almost lunch. Do you want to have lunch together?"

Conny turned away and ran the duster over the frame of the picture window. Sandy saw Conny's reflection in the glass. *She looks sad.* Conny had refused to discuss what had happened with her boyfriend, according to Tish. "If there's anything you'd like to talk about," Sandy ventured, "I've been told I'm a good listener."

Conny shook her head and kept dusting. "What do you want, Sandy?"

Sandy took a deep breath and walked across to face Conny. "I just wanted to know what you overheard upstairs. You seemed surprised by something."

Conny stopped what she was doing and looked directly at Sandy. "Did I? I don't recall."

Sandy could have sworn that Conny had been shocked.

"Are you finished with your rooms upstairs?"

Sandy sighed. "Not quite."

"Well, I won't be joining you for lunch, I'm going to spend my break on the beach. I'm hoping the sea breeze will clear my sinus headache."

Sandy returned to her work, wishing Tish wasn't leaving.

It was two o'clock and Sandy was ahead of schedule. She only had one more room to do and she'd be able to put her cart away. She was imagining a walk down the beach, maybe as far as the sand dunes, when Conny walked up. "You've got a call. You'll have to take it in the office."

Sandy couldn't imagine who it could be. She had told none of her friends where she was living or working.

The office, located next to the lobby's entrance, barely had enough room for Paula, the week-day clerk, so communication with guests was restricted to a three-foot by five-foot hole cut out of the wall facing the lobby. Sandy slipped through the door at the side of the hole. Paula nodded to the phone's headset lying on the desk.

Conny stopped just outside the office door. "Drink?"

Sandy gave a quick nod, then took the call. "Hello?"

"Sandy? Oh Sandy. Is that really you?"

The relief and sadness in her mother's voice tore at Sandy's heart. "Yes, Mom. It's me."

"Sandy. We were so worried."

The sound of her mother crying triggered a flood of tears, and she had to turn away from a curious Paula. "Mom, it's all right. I'm okay." Her stomach churned as the full impact her actions had had on her parents hit her. It had not crossed her mind when she took off on her adventure that her parents would worry. She had been so focused on her own anger and hurt at her father's lack of support for her educational goals that she assumed they wouldn't even notice she was gone.

"We didn't know what happened. Where are you?"

Sandy thought of the missing persons poster the policeman had given her that morning. She should have called her parents right away. "I'm up-island, in a place called Tofino."

"That's what the policeman told us, but I don't know where that is." Her mother's crying was interrupted by a shuffling noise.

"Where the hell are you?" her dad shouted into the phone.

"Hi, Dad." Sandy fought to keep her voice calm. The sound of her father's voice had the opposite effect of her mother's, stirring her anger and defiance. "I'm sorry for making you worry."

"That doesn't change anything, does it? Do you know what you put your mother through? She hasn't slept since the school phoned to inform us there would be no refunds for classes dropped by students halfway through their studies. We had no idea you'd left. What the hell's going on?"

Sandy could picture him gripping the phone in one hand and a scotch over ice in the other. She was positive she heard the ice cube drop back against the bottom of the glass after he took a slug. She was instantly transported into that living room, where her mother had insisted they install an extra phone. "The kitchen phone is for the help," her mother would preach to anyone unlucky enough to comment on the two phones. It was a luxury that had always embarrassed Sandy when her friends came over to visit. It was also a means by which her mother could listen in on her conversations—something she didn't mention to her envious friends.

"Well?"

Her father's question made her sigh. She had heard that same tone countless times before, usually when he didn't understand or approve of her actions. Her mother never said anything. Their relationship was a cliché. Her dad brought in the money; her mom looked after the home and the children—or at least bossed around the help who did the hard work. None of the liberated lifestyles of the 1960s had impacted them.

"I'm sorry, Dad." Sandy straightened her shoulders, willing herself to stand taller. "But this is something I had to do."

"What do you mean something you had to do? University is something you have to do. Finding a husband, raising children, those are things you have to do. Running away is not!"

Sandy cringed. "I'll be home in October," she said, then laid the handset gently on its rest without saying goodbye.

Conny, who had reappeared while Sandy was on the phone, handed over one of the two Screwdrivers she was holding. "So, you're here for the season?"

"Yes."

Conny didn't respond, only gazed at her drink.

"Did I make the wrong decision?"

"No!" Conny looked up and raised her glass. "Cheers to the summer!"

Sandy was about to take her first sip, when her eyes met those of Mrs. Johnston as she walked past the lobby office. If looks could kill, Sandy knew she would have dropped to the ground, the rest of her Screwdriver spreading over the carpet.

"What?" Conny asked. "You look like you've just seen a ghost."

Sandy shook her head. "Not ghosts. Geoff's parents."

Conny turned. "Where?"

"They just went down the hall. I think they're going to the lounge."

Conny drained the rest of her drink and gave the glass to Sandy. "I think it's time for me to get out of here."

"Are you going out with Rod tonight?" Sandy asked.

Conny stopped and turned to face Sandy as the lobby door shut between them. The look Conny sent through the glass was chilling. She gave a quick shake of her head before turning and striding across the parking lot.

Sandy stood inside the lobby, watching Conny go.

Tom was polishing wine glasses as the late-lunch crowd filtered out of the lounge. Most were part of the latest seniors' bus tour, so they were probably moving on to a scheduled afternoon activity. Tom picked up a tray and moved out from behind the bar to clear the dirty dishes they'd left behind. A family who had come in from the beach still sat in the centre of the lounge. On his way back to his post, he cleared their empty bar glasses.

It was going to be a long day. Brent had called in sick, cutting short the playtime Tom had been enjoying with Tish. He didn't know how to feel about her return to Calgary. He would miss her. When things were good between them, they were really good.

He was putting the last of the dishes in the washer when a middle-aged couple came in from the lobby and approached the bar. He didn't recognize them as locals, and they were too young to be part of the bus tour. "How are you folks doing?"

"A whisky, neat, for me, and a tall G&T for my wife." The man pulled out a bar stool and helped his wife onto it.

"I stopped serving at two. I'm just cleaning up. The bar will be open again at six. You're welcome to sit and enjoy the view. You can bring in coffee or tea from the dining room." Tom motioned to the seats along the windows.

"Oh." The man glanced at his wife. "We didn't realize."

Tom caught the look of disappointment that passed between them. Instinct told him something deeper than missed drinks was involved. "Where are you folks from?"

Leaning his elbows on the bar, the man wiped a handkerchief across his forehead. "Seattle," he said. His wife fiddled with her purse as if unsure whether to let it drop to the floor at the base of her stool or set it on the bar beside her. She finally chose the latter.

"Did you know him?" The woman looked directly at Tom.

Tom glanced between the man and the woman. "Know who?"

"Our son."

Tom paused, trying to determine if he'd been mistaken about their being locals. Shaking his head, he said, "I'm sorry. I don't recognize you, so I'm not sure who your son is."

"Was," said the man. "Our son died."

"He was murdered!" the wife added. The forcefulness of her statement made Tom's brain fire, and he realized who they must be. "He was murdered, Arthur. Some bastard decided they would take their car and end our son's life and now—" Her grief choked off whatever else she was going to say.

Arthur slipped off his stool and gathered his wife in his arms, pulling her half off her seat. "I know, Marta. I know."

Tom searched his brain for the son's name but came up empty. He'd only ever referred to him as 'the hippie'. He shook his head. "I'm so sorry. I didn't know your son."

The woman's face seemed to crumple. "Nobody cares!"

"I'm sure that's not true," her husband assured her.

Flustered, Tom pulled bottles from the shelf and started pouring the drinks they'd ordered. Geoff's parents stood as if frozen, watching him. When he finished, he slid them across the bar. "Here. On the house."

Arthur looked across at him and gave a quick nod. "Thank you. I think we will take our drinks to a table."

"No need. I'll carry them over." Tom moved out from behind the bar, picked up the couple's drinks, and followed them. They chose a table in the front corner that offered views of the ocean through both the side and front picture windows.

He placed the drinks on the table and turned to leave. Arthur grabbed his arm and held out a couple of bills. "For the drinks."

"It's not necessary. We were all very sorry to hear about your son."

Marta looked up at Tom. "Geoff. His name was Geoff."

Arthur placed the bills on the table. "We tried to find the spot where he died, but we couldn't. Do you know where it happened?"

Tom shook his head.

"We were hoping the young woman who found him would be able to take us, but Marta became too upset when we stopped in to ask her."

Tom glanced at Marta, whose gaze was now fixed on the ocean rolling against the rocks below them. "I could ask her if you'd like."

Tom could tell Arthur was struggling with his response. "No, no. I think it'd be better if it was us."

Tom inclined his head. "I'll leave you to your drinks. Take all the time you need."

"Thank you."

As Tom approached the bar, Sandy walked in. He smiled and greeted her.

"Hi. I'm returning these," she said, setting the empty glasses on the bar and glancing around. Her eyes landed on Geoff's parents and the fresh drinks in front of them. "Isn't the bar supposed to be closed?"

"It is. But they're Geoff's parents."

"We've met."

"Yeah. I heard."

Looking back over her shoulder at him, she sent him a puzzled look. "What do you mean?"

Gesturing toward the couple, Tom explained, "He told me they wanted to ask you to show them where Geoff died, but his wife blew it."

"Oh."

The softness of her response caused Tom to look up from polishing the counter. Sandy was no longer there. She was marching over to the parent's table. He pushed out from behind the bar, rushing after her.

"I hear you want me to show you where I found your son," she announced.

Tom pulled up beside her. "I'm sorry, she just—"

"Yes!" Mr. Johnston answered. "Yes, we do."

"I still have a couple of rooms to finish, but I should be free after four if you'd like to meet then?"

Mr. Johnston didn't even glance back at his wife for confirmation, he just stood and reached for her hand. "Thank you! Thank you very much."

"Okay, then. I'll meet you in the lobby at four."

Tom followed Sandy back to the bar. "Well," he gasped. "That was—"

"I've just had a call from my parents and been made aware of how scary it must be to be one. If something ever happened to me, I hope someone would help my parents find me."

Tom was dumbstruck. *Of course.*

Sandy turned to go but Tom called her back. "Wait." He pulled the keys to his Mustang out of his jean's pocket and held them out to her. "Use my car. I don't think they can handle the walk."

"Thank you. We shouldn't be long. A half-hour tops. I have to be back so I can redo my statement for the police, and they want a drawing as well."

"A drawing?"

"Yes. Long story. I've got to go."

Tom watched Sandy leave, trying to imagine what the police would want her to draw.

"Pretty girl."

Tom turned to see that Arthur had approached the bar and was addressing him.

"Yes," Tom answered.

"Do you get much of a crowd in here?"

"Depends. Right now, the campgrounds are full because the road in isn't too muddy. Last week, the weather was very wet, and it was just me and the bus tour group."

"So, you would've noticed if someone was out of place?"

Tom realized what he was asking. "No. Unfortunately, right now everyone seems to be a stranger. Too many people coming and going. The beaches attract families as well as partiers. This weekend there's a surf competition scheduled, so it's going to be busy."

"So, the police have their hands full."

"I'm sure they're doing everything they can to find out what happened to your son."

A lack of faith in the police was written all over the older man's face. Tom didn't know what to say.

"The road seems to have changed a lot of things around here," Arthur commented.

Tom's brows drew together. "Have you been here before?"

Arthur didn't answer, just strode back to his wife. When Tom looked up again, Arthur was helping his wife from her chair. They walked toward the door of the outdoor patio. As Tom rushed to open the door, Arthur paused and looked at him. "If you think of anything that might help us understand our son's death, please let us know. We're in Room 7."

"You're staying here, then?"

"Yes." Arthur took his wife's elbow, steadying her as they exited the lounge.

Tom had just reopened the inn's lounge for the evening service when James walked in and stepped up to the bar. Tuesday wasn't James' usual day. Another change in behaviour.

The conversation with Geoff's parents had reminded Tom of how their son's death had opened his and others' lives to scrutiny. He looked at James with fresh eyes. *What exactly do I know about him?* He worked at odd construction jobs, usually for his father-in-law. From conversations held over the bar counter, Tom knew the most recent contract involved the construction of a new restaurant in Tofino.

Tom also knew James was part of a group that considered hippies a useless waste of space, and he'd often spoken of how they planned to take the action necessary to rid the area of what he called 'cowardly filth'. For the first time, Tom wondered how far they'd go…and if they'd already started to take that action.

"What are you doing out here, James?" Tom asked. "Are you done with the restaurant?"

"No. I was helping my cousin with his roof all day." James' gaze darted to the side picture window then back. "Just needed to get away."

Tom quickly glanced out the window, but only saw beach and ocean. He returned his focus on James. "The usual?"

"Just a beer."

Tom placed a bottle of Lucky in front of James. "What do you need to get away from?"

"My life," James mumbled. Then, as if he'd said something he hadn't intended, he waved his hand. "I just found out a cousin of mine has died."

"Sorry to hear that. Were you close?"

"We used to be real close, like brothers, before he moved away." He took a long slug of his beer.

"What happened?"

"They thought it was a hit and run."

Tom blinked at him and raised his eyebrows. "You don't mean the guy who was found on the road here yesterday?"

"Yes. That's why I came down. I wanted to see where it happened. Pay my respects, like. I heard it was about a mile from the top of Long Beach Road. Is that right?"

"I don't know."

"I checked it out. I walked quite a ways along the road just to make sure I didn't miss it, but I couldn't see any sign of where it happened." James shook his head absently.

"It's hard to imagine how he could've died where they say he did. It's so open and flat in that section. Now, they think it was murder."

Tom's mind raced. He looked closely at James and tried to read the emotion he was displaying. Was it genuine or put-on? And, if Geoff was a cousin, then James would be related to the parents. He wondered if James knew they were staying at the inn. He considered telling him but then thought better of it. Robin probably wouldn't like him passing on guest information. He was saved from further internal debate by Tish's entrance.

"Hi," she said, eyeing James, then smiling at Tom.

Tom couldn't help but grin back. They had spent a very pleasant morning in bed in spite of his earlier misgivings. "Are you off?"

"Yes. I'm catching a ride to Nanaimo." Tish walked around the bar and opened her arms; Tom stepped into her embrace. "Thank you for last night," she whispered against his neck.

Tom stepped back and looked down at her. She was glowing. He brushed a stray bang from where it had fallen over one eye. "Take care."

Tish sighed. "You too."

Tom watched her leave, surprised by how conflicted he felt. Tish had been one of many chicks he'd bedded since his arrival at the inn. He couldn't understand why he felt he should run after her and tell her to stay. Stepping back, he turned to ask if James wanted another drink, only to find that he, too, had left the bar. Tom cleared the half-empty bottle and slipped the money James had left into the till.

31.

Conny scrutinized the clothes still hanging in her closet. She would have to leave them. She couldn't squeeze anything more into her suitcase, and if she started a second case, she'd struggle to carry the load once she didn't have a car. *Pack light*. There was no guarantee of shelter once she got to Vancouver. She hoped she could just disappear in the crowd, which would be impossible if she were loaded down with luggage.

Travel light and survive.

She lifted the case and judged its weight. Too heavy. Too slow. She set it back on the bed. She'd have to use some of her savings to buy a backpack once she got to Vancouver. It was an expense she didn't want. None of this was. She slumped onto the bed, overcome with frustration, anger, and sadness. Her savings. The money she'd been so sure she could use to finally move to Los Angeles at the end of the season, she now had to use it to escape her life here.

She glanced around. Her room was plain, nothing fancy. The walls were panelled like the rest of the lodge; the linoleum floor worn in places. She'd drawn the paisley curtains to each side of the single window, leaving a framed view of the forest and the lane leading to the next cabin. This room, this lodge, this inn…it had all been her home, her sanctuary, for four years.

Now, Danny was dead, and she was the one who'd brought him into her waking nightmare.

She took a deep breath and stood. Leaving the suitcase where it lay on the bed, she walked out of her room and out of the lodge. She needed to convince Tom to loan her his car.

Tom looked up from the magazine he was reading when Conny walked into the empty lounge—not an unusual sight during a weekday supper hour. She got right to the point. "Can I borrow your car to make a run into Ucluelet?"

He glanced at his watch. "Six-thirty. What do you need to go into town so late for?"

Conny knew how attached he was to his car, but between him, Brent, and Edan, Tom was the most likely to fall for the damsel-in-distress ploy. She feigned embarrassment and launched into her story. "I need some…um, women's supplies. I've run out."

Tom hesitated only a moment before reaching into his pocket and fishing out the car keys. He set them on the bar between them. "Be very careful with it."

Conny smiled. Men were so afraid to talk about anything to do with a woman's monthly cycle. "I will."

Conny gripped the keys in her hand and waved goodbye. Thrilled that her plan had worked, she left the inn and ran across to the lodge, passing Sandy without a glance.

The air was crisp and the sky clear, perfect for a drive.

Conny debated whether she should take the remainder of the drugs from Saturday night with her. If she did, she would have a means of making money when she got to Vancouver. The trouble was, they weren't her drugs. They were Rod's. He supplied them with the understanding that he would get payment for them after she sold them, less a fifteen percent cut for her. If she tried selling them on Vancouver's streets, she increased the risk of Rod finding her though his connections, and that was not what she wanted.

Greed. Greed was what had gotten her into this mess. Greed would not get her out of it. She closed the box and slid the drugs back into their hiding place. She had just stepped out of the closet when Sandy opened the bedroom door. Conny spun on her. "Don't you knock?"

Sandy froze halfway through the doorway. "Um, sorry."

Closing the closet door, Conny took a moment to calm her nerves. "You just caught me off-guard. What did you want?"

"I went to borrow Tom's car, and he said you already had the keys." Sandy scanned the room, her brows furrowing.

Conny turned to see what she was looking at and realized what a mess she'd made. Clothes were strewn across her bed next to two open suitcases, one on the bed, the other on the floor. Facing Sandy, Conny brushed the air with her hand. "Doing a bit of house cleaning." She moved so she stood between Sandy and her view of the mess, "And yeah, Tom loaned me his car. I have an errand to run in Ucluelet."

Sandy stepped around Conny and picked up a blouse from a pile at the foot of the bed. "It looks more like you're packing."

"Honest, I'm not. Just cleaning out my closet." Conny grabbed the blouse away from Sandy. "What did you need the car for?"

"I need to drop off my new statement and a drawing of the scene at the RCMP detachment." Sandy watched as Conny folded the blouse, then dropped it on the bed. "Can I ride in with you?"

Conny considered driving into town with Sandy and pretending to run the errand she had told Tom about, but she didn't want to spend the entire drive dealing with Sandy's curiosity. It was better to adjust. "No. I've changed my mind. How about you take the car and do your errand?" She reached into her pocket and withdrew the keys. "Just leave these on the table when you come back so Tom sees them when he gets off shift."

Sandy accepted the keys but didn't immediately pull her hand away from Conny's. "I don't think you should go," she whispered, raising her eyes to meet Conny's. "Whatever happened, I don't think you should go."

Conny froze, suddenly certain Sandy could see the layers of lies hidden within her. She turned away. "I don't know what you're talking about."

"I think you do."

Conny reached down and closed the suitcase lying on the floor. "You better get going if you want to be back before it gets dark."

Sandy lingered, as if she wanted to say more, then turned and left, closing the door softly behind her.

Conny collapsed onto the bed, wondering if she was doing the right thing. What if she stayed? No. Rod would find her. She knew he would. The price tag on the missing drugs was too high. She closed her eyes, concentrating. Something about the theft had been gnawing at her. She had thought of it just before Rod grabbed her neck. Now, she carefully probed that moment. She had asked him about his trip to Vancouver.

The timing of the theft. It was too perfect.

Conny sat up, mind racing. It had to be someone who'd known about the second shipment and the planned move to the fortified storage the next day. Two names sprang to mind. Slowly she stood up, realization causing her heart to pound. She was in more danger than she'd thought.

WEDNESDAY, MAY 15, 1968

32.

Moore was tired. The investigations were taking a toll on him, not to mention his relationship with Sam and the boys. The long hours he was putting in on the job meant he saw his wife less and less, but that wasn't what had him worried at the moment. Gary, his oldest, had taken him aside that morning to whisper a complaint about his mom. He said she was letting the baby cry until he went in and took care of Matthew himself. He was scared about what happened while he was away at school. He wanted to stay home and keep his brother safe. Moore had reassured his son that the baby would be okay, and their mom was probably just going through some maternity blues. Yet, as he sat staring across the office, sucking back the black coffee Nelson had brought to him at the start of the morning's briefing, worry about Sam consumed him.

"Corporal Moore, do you have any suggestions?"

Moore jerked upright. "Sorry, what did you say?"

McAteer, looking impossibly fresh after what must have been a grueling day driving to and from Nanaimo, sighed. "I asked why the drug was administered to the victim's neck."

Everyone was looking at him. *What'd I miss?* Moore glanced quickly at the chalkboard and to his relief found the answer scrawled there. McAteer must have brought the toxicology report back from Nanaimo.

"Methamphetamine. It's not a drug I've had any experience with, and I haven't seen it in this area."

"Well, according to the pathologist, that's what Mr. Johnston had in his system," McAteer explained. "The drug is commonly taken in pill form, but our victim was injected with it. The question is why?" He paused. "The drug itself isn't lethal unless delivered at high doses, and in this instance, it wasn't. There was just a trace of it in his system. So, why inject him with it?"

"To sedate him?" Evans offered.

McAteer dismissed the suggestion. "The clue to what it does is in its street name. Speed. So, the effect is quite the opposite of sedation. It's a powerful stimulant. The victim would have felt euphoric, energized. And because he was injected, he would have felt the effects immediately. The impact on his system would have been much stronger than if he had taken it in pill form."

Moore thought back to the vomit John had shown him on Geoff's shirt collar. "Could he have been allergic to it?"

McAteer hesitated. "I'm not sure if the pathologist considered that. But after testing the contents of the vials we found in the van and finding them to contain insulin, he believes our victim was a diabetic, which explains the syringe."

"That ties in with what his doctor said." Evans waved his notebook. "I finally got a hold of Geoff's family doctor in Seattle. Dr. Putts said Geoff had only just been diagnosed with diabetes, but not by him. He was diagnosed last week by a Vancouver doctor, who forwarded the information to him."

"Did he give you the Vancouver doctor's name?" Moore asked.

"Yeah, a Dr. Leo Langlois. When I contacted him, he told me that diabetes is very difficult to manage, especially right after diagnosis. Patients find it hard not only to learn how to use a syringe to inject themselves but also to maintain a routine. There's often mistakes in dose accuracy. The consequences can include convulsions, coma, and—in extreme cases—death." Evans looked up from his notes. "Do you think that might have been what happened with Geoff?"

"When the pathologist realized what was in the vials, he said his confusion about what he was seeing in the victim's body made sense. Meth can trigger or heighten the effects of insulin. According to him, the victim choked on his vomit, most likely during a seizure," McAteer explained. "As the victim was unfamiliar with the disease, and perhaps struggling to adapt to a strict routine, introducing meth into his system could have contributed to his death."

Moore looked at Evans, then back at McAteer. "If the killer didn't know about the diabetes, could this have been an accidental death?"

Bouton, who had begun writing the points on the blackboard, stopped and turned around. "Someone injected the victim with methamphetamine in the back of the neck. That was a deliberate act, whether or not they intended to kill him."

"But intent will be a determining factor in the charges," Nelson offered.

"Yes, that's true," agreed Bouton. Turning back to the chalkboard, he wrote INTENT under the previous points. "We'll have to wait until we get a suspect and ask him."

Moore considered Bouton's words, trying to determine who they could consider a suspect. Thus far, it seemed none of the key individuals in the case had a motive. Unless the two cases were linked. He reached for his notebook and wrote BOX in capitals. "Could a supply of methamphetamine have been inside the box in the old prospector's shack?"

"I took that box to Nanaimo," McAteer answered. "They planned to ship it on to the Vancouver lab in the afternoon. I haven't heard if the lab has received it yet. I wouldn't be surprised though if meth had been what was in the box. According to what I've heard, the drug is gaining popularity as well as creating a serious health problem across Canada."

"What about fingerprints?"

"There were several. Most smudged or only partials. I've sent what I could lift off to the national centre to see if a match can be made against a known-criminal's card file."

Moore added the information to his notes.

Bouton referred to the papers on his desk before looking up at the group. "Corporal Moore, how did your interview with Miss Chambers go?"

"She confirmed that it was her blood on the sheets and that it resulted from a sexual encounter, but not a rape." Moore paused. "She also revealed that she had moved the body twice from the position in which she had first found it. I asked her to provide a new statement and a drawing of the body's original position."

Nelson stood and waved a couple of papers. "She dropped into the office last night and left these with me." He handed them to Bouton, then returned to his desk.

The corporal picked up the sheets, scanned them, then handed them to Moore. "Is this what she told you?"

Moore glanced over the statement and drawing, impressed by the skill of the artist. "Yes."

Evans stepped up and took the papers to read through. Bouton glanced around the room. "Does this change anything in our investigation?"

"Not the way I see it, sir." Evans took his seat. "We already figured the scene didn't support a hit-and-run accident. Whether the body was face-down in a water-filled ditch or face-up lying halfway up the bank doesn't change the fact that the situation was not what it seemed. Did the pathologist find water in the lungs?"

"No."

Evans sat back in his chair and crossed his arms. "Then being found face-down in the ditch doesn't change anything."

"It does, in a way," Nelson offered. "It means he was dead before he went into the water. Given the absence of any evidence to support contact with a car, this looks more like a case of body dumping."

Nodding absently, Bouton turned to Moore. "But that's not the point. The fact is, she lied to you."

"She didn't really lie," Moore said. "She just missed some details." Moore caught Nelson's quick glance his way and ignored it.

"Fine." Bouton turned away from Moore and faced the constables. "Corporal Moore and I spoke with James

Johnston, seen talking to our victim at Friday night's party. My report is in the file. Turns out he and the victim were cousins. His alibi has been confirmed by his wife."

McAteer let out a guffaw, drawing the room's attention. "Do you believe her?"

Bouton shrugged.

"James also confirmed what Jim had told me about prospecting possibilities in the area," Moore said. "They were considering working the family's placer claim above Wreck Bay." He paused and then looked over at McAteer. "Did you find a prospector's pan in the van?"

McAteer searched his notes. "We found one on the bed."

"So how did it get there?" Moore asked. "Did Geoff make it back to the van?"

"Or did the killer?" Evans added.

"Miss Chambers mentioned that the van had been moved."

"She also said someone had moved her stuff." Evans held up the copy of Sandy's statement. "The backpack she had left on the driver's seat was on the passenger seat, and the bikini she had left to dry on the side mirror of the passenger door was with the backpack inside the van."

"What does that suggest to you?" McAteer asked.

Evans and Nelson looked at each other, then at Moore. Bouton cleared his throat. "It sounds like you've eliminated Miss Chambers from your suspect list?"

Moore considered. "I don't think she was ever on my list." He looked around the room. "James mentioned something that may steer us in another direction, and possibly to a stronger motive. James' uncle, Geoff's dad, had been playing around—including an attempted seduction of his brother's wife—which resulted in his being ordered to get out of town."

"So, you think James' father may be our murderer?"

"He couldn't be. He drowned in February this year. I'm not ruling James' involvement out, but there's another with even more of a motive. A prior seduction evidently resulted in a woman's suicide."

Bouton frowned. "You're thinking this was a revenge murder?"

"It's a possibility."

Evans whistled. "Do we know who she was?"

"No, but we're going to find out. I want you and Constable Nelson working the community, looking for any story involving such a suicide, prior to 1953." He waited while his constables wrote the information in their notebooks. When they looked up from their task, he continued, "Monty, I'd like you to find a man Miss Chambers met on Lismer Beach. His name was Steve and he told her he saw Geoff on the path walking back to the inn about three o'clock on Saturday morning."

"Last name?" Bouton asked.

"She didn't know his last name. I was hoping to use Constable Nelson on this, as he's familiar with the local Indian communities."

Bouton looked over at the constable. "Do you think you could find out who this Steve is?"

Nelson sat up. "Yes, sir."

"Then do it."

Moore relaxed back in his chair. "If this is a confirmed sighting, then our estimated time of death narrows to between three and five o'clock on Saturday morning."

Bouton flipped through his notes. "When did the couple from the inn say they returned from Ucluelet?"

"Mr. Robinson was quite vague about the time, but Miss Phillips put it about three o'clock." Moore nodded at Bouton. "Which puts them on that road about the same time as the victim."

"We need to re-interview them." Bouton wrote their names on the board. "Has anyone run their names through the system?" When no one answered, his eyes flashed. Okay, Evans, you do it." Bouton paced in front of the chalkboard. "Moving on to the second murder victim, have we tracked his movements that day? If he was hired for the evening shift, who worked the day shift? Was that person present when he was attacked? Or, was that person the one who attacked him? Mr. Brown was found by Corporal Moore and Constable Nelson late Monday afternoon. His wife indicated he went off to work Sunday night as usual, so we need to track his movements from the moment he walked out of their home. We need to find out if he made it to work for his shift, or if he was attacked on the way."

Moore frowned. "He was buried under a prospector's cast-off pile behind the shack he was to guard."

"Of course." Bouton nodded as he reexamined the board. "We need to find the day-shift guard. If he was a witness, then we need to know why he didn't report the beating. If he had a part in the beating, we need to know why."

He nodded at Nelson. "Constable Nelson, you follow up. Oh. Has anyone found the owner of the prospector's shack?"

Nelson flipped through his notebook, found the page he wanted, and met Bouton's gaze. "When I contacted the land office in Port Alberni, they insisted they have no record of any shacks existing in the locations described. So, the shack's owners are squatters. I did learn a survey had been done in the early 1900s with plans to develop the area into beach-side lots, but nothing seems to have come of it."

"Have you done a physical search of the second prospector's shack?"

Moore groaned. "We didn't go further up the creek once we found Danny's body. I'll grab Nelson and do that as soon as we can."

"Very good. I guess that's it. Unless you have something to add, Corporal Moore?"

"No. We're good."

"Sir?" McAteer called. "I just want to let everyone know I've finished processing Johnston's van. It's been sealed and Owens' agreed to keep it in his fenced back lot."

"Good."

33.

Sandy drained the last of her coffee and glanced at her watch. Ten minutes past eight and no sign of Conny. *Did she sleep in?* Roxanne and Edan were both up and out to work by seven. She and Conny should have been close behind them. Maybe Conny had risen and left early without telling her. After moving into Tish's old room the night before, Sandy had enjoyed her first deep sleep since arriving on the coast. She could easily have slept through Conny leaving for work. She set her mug in the kitchen sink and walked to Conny's room. Stopping outside the door, she paused to listen. No sounds came from inside. She rapped on the door and walked in. "Good morning!"

The room was empty. Sandy spun around and ran outside. Rounding the hedge, she saw no Mustang parked in the laneway. *Crap!* She headed straight to Tom's room, calling his name as she opened his bedroom door.

The tangle of sheets moved and Tom's face appeared from beneath them. "Sandy? What's up?"

"Conny's gone, and she's taken your car."

Tom sat up. "What are you talking about?"

Sandy took a deep breath. "Conny took your car."

Tom flopped back on his pillow. "I know, but she returned it."

"No. Tom, that's not what happened." She grabbed his shoulder and pulled him into a sitting position. "I found her packing last night. When I asked what she was doing, she said she was just housecleaning." Sandy started pacing. "I knew she was lying to me. I should have forced her to talk to me! Instead, I was too focused on getting my stuff to the police station."

"You went into town? How'd you get there?"

"Conny changed her mind about going and gave me your car keys."

"So, she…didn't go into town last night?"

"No, I did. But"—Sandy stopped pacing—"I think she took your car sometime after I came back."

Tom sat up and threw off his covers, revealing his very nude body. Sandy blushed and turned away. "Give me a minute, and I'll go check her room."

Sandy spun around, her eyes finding his. "I've just done that! It's empty."

"What time is it? She's probably at the inn."

"I don't think so." Sandy didn't want to admit that she hadn't checked the inn before rushing in and waking him up.

Tom crossed to his dresser. Pulling the top drawer open, he withdrew a pair of briefs, and slipped into them. "The car's probably parked outside—"

Sandy shook her head.

"Or somewhere else." He charged out of the room.

Sandy followed him into Conny's room. He stopped at the foot of the bed, staring at a piece of folded paper resting on the pillow. His name was printed across the front in clear, bold letters.

How did I miss that? Sandy plucked up the sheet and unfolded it. She read it quickly before handing it to Tom.

Dear Tom,

I've borrowed your car. I had to get away. I can't tell you why or where I'm going.
I'll leave it in Nanaimo at the Tally Ho Travelodge. The keys will be in the back-left wheel well.
Thanks for everything. Take care.

Conny

Emotions played across Tom's face as he read the note. Sandy couldn't begin to imagine what he was feeling. She was angry at herself for not doing more to stop Conny, and angry at Conny for betraying Tom's trust. But worry ran right alongside that anger. "At least she told you where to find your car."

Tom looked up at Sandy. "I don't understand. Why'd she run away?"

"I don't know. She wouldn't tell me."

"You spoke with her about it?"

"I told you."

Tom walked around the room. Conny's collection of shot glasses was arranged along the back of the dresser next to the cheesy snow globe with the Hollywood sign glowing out from a plastic hill. "Conny was so happy when we discovered this in a Tofino junk shop," Tom explained. "She must be coming back."

Sandy followed his gaze but came to a different conclusion. Conny had cleaned up the mess she'd seen the night before, and the room appeared too neat. Sandy opened the dresser drawers one at a time. They were empty. She could almost hear Tom deflate. The closet was empty, too, except for a suitcase. Sandy picked up the suitcase and laid it on the bed. Opening it, she saw two stacks of neatly folded clothes and a note with her name printed boldly on the front, like Tom's.

Sandy,

> *Take what you want. I think most of these will fit you. Give the rest away.*
> *I won't be back.*

Conny

She handed the paper to Tom. "I think we need to call the police."

"No!" Tom protested. "She said she would leave the car in the Tally Ho's parking lot."

"Do you trust that she will?"

"Conny has her issues, but she's always kept her word."

Sandy wasn't quick enough to hide her doubt, and Tom read it on her face. He interrupted her just as she was about to speak. "No. She left me this note so I wouldn't worry. And I'm not going to worry. I'll thumb down to Nanaimo and get my car."

He turned and left the room.

Sandy rushed after him. "Tom, no. Stop!" She clutched at his shoulders and forced him to face her. "We need to call the police and report this. Tish was already worried about her. What if Conny's in danger? What if she took the car because someone else told her to? I don't know her that well, but something happened, and Rod's involved."

"Her boyfriend?"

"Yes. She hasn't been the same since she went off with him on Sunday. Let's talk with the police first," she pleaded. "Just in case."

"You really think she might be in danger?"

"Yes."

Tom inhaled deeply and pressed his fingers to his forehead. "All right, but you'll need to be the one to call them. Me and the police, we don't get along."

Sandy smiled. "Okay." She pushed herself away. "Maybe you should get dressed, and we'll phone from the inn."

34.

Sandy stood beneath a sky struggling to rid itself of persistent clouds and watched the police car pull up to the front of the Wickaninnish Inn. *Nine o'clock*. It had been a very long thirty minutes waiting for them. She sucked in a deep breath of the cool morning air to clear the anxiety gripping her shoulders.

Corporal Moore, or David as he'd told her to call him, got out of the driver's side and walked around the front of the car just as the passenger door opened. An older man unfolded himself from the vehicle. Unlike Moore, this newcomer wasn't in uniform, but even in brown corduroys and black leather jacket he was obviously a cop. He held himself with all the rigid formality of someone used to living within military discipline. His stiff posture emphasised the extra four or five inches he had on Moore, and Sandy wondered if it was deliberate.

"Miss Chambers"—Moore stepped forward—"this is Corporal Merle Bouton. He's from the Major Crimes Unit in Victoria and is conducting the investigation into Geoff Johnston's murder."

Up close, Sandy could see the crow's feet etched into the corners of the new cop's green eyes, which almost glowed. Bouton's hair, on the other hand, looked like a doll's wig. The deep auburn didn't match the grey specks in his five o'clock shadow, and she wondered if he'd dyed it himself. He accepted her extended hand, his long fingers wrapping over hers in a gentle yet firm handshake that lasted a bit too long.

"Thanks for coming," she said, tucking both hands into her pockets, afraid she wouldn't be able to resist the urge to wipe them.

"We were on our way out here to speak with Mr. Robinson and Miss Phillips about Friday night when dispatch contacted us about an incident," Bouton explained.

"Robinson? Phillips? Who—"

"Tom and Tish," Moore interjected.

"Oh." Sandy paused, then pointed toward the inn. "Tom's inside, but Tish left for Calgary."

Both men fell into step behind her as she led them to the inn.

Moore looked at Bouton, then back at Sandy. "When did she leave?"

"Sometime after supper yesterday."

"Get someone to follow up on that." Bouton's instruction, Sandy noticed, was delivered with the harsh authority of someone who assumed obedience. She glanced across at Moore. He appeared unaffected by the officer's tone, and continued his casual, easy stride.

"You reported a car theft?"

Sandy paused at the lobby door and turned to face the older officer. "Yes. Conny took Tom's car sometime early this morning. She left a note telling him where she was going to leave it."

"Conny Lee?" Moore opened and held the lobby door for Sandy, then Bouton to pass through before he stepped in. "She was helping at the front desk on Saturday. I spoke with her there. The chambermaids' supervisor?"

"Yes."

"She also stopped in to check on you when I took your fingerprints."

"Yes." Sandy was surprised he remembered that. The officers followed her down the hall to the lounge, where Tom sat at a table, nursing a glass of orange juice. No one else was in the room.

"Tom, you know Corporal David Moore from the Ucluelet detachment," she said. "And this is Corporal Merle Bouton from Major Crimes in Victoria."

Tom acknowledged Moore with a quick incline of his head. "We've met."

Sandy waited as the officers took their seats. "Would you like coffee or juice?"

"No, thank you, we're fine." Moore indicated that Sandy should take a seat, which she did.

Bouton leaned forward and looked first at Tom, then Sandy. "So, how does a stolen vehicle relate to our investigations?"

"We're not sure that it does." She glanced at Tom, then realized what the officer had said "Investigations? There's more than one?"

"Yes. A body was discovered by Lost Shoe Creek."

Sandy's heart skipped a beat. "Mark?"

"No." Moore reached for her hand but stopped when Bouton spoke.

"The victim was a local Indian named Danny Brown."

Moore's hand dropped to the table as if that had been its destination all along. Sandy sat back in her chair, unsettled by the contrast between the officers. *Are they playing good cop, bad cop with me?* She'd heard some cops did that. She shifted in her seat, unsure which she should turn her attention to. Both were staring intently at her. She cleared her throat. "Danny Brown? I don't know anyone by that name."

Tom shrugged.

"He was brutally murdered the day after Mr. Johnston," Bouton snapped. "Two days. Two murders."

Sandy glanced at Tom, then back at Bouton. She was beginning to understand Tom's hesitancy at speaking with cops. "I-I called because Conny's gone missing, and she took Tom's car," she explained. "We're worried she may be in danger."

"In danger? How?" Moore flipped open his notebook and was waiting with his pen ready.

"It's hard to explain." Sandy twisted in her seat to look squarely at Tom. When he shook his head, she faced Moore. "She seemed upset, jumpy, when I talked to her."

"When was this?"

"About six-thirty last night."

"Where did you have this conversation?"

"In her room at the lodge. I asked why she was packing. She denied that's what she was doing. I told her not to go."

Bouton's brows drew together. "Why did you do that?"

An image of Conny standing in the doorway of the inn's guest room on Monday, late for work, stinking and obviously shaken, was burned into Sandy's memory. She looked down at her lap where she had twisted the fringe edging of her blouse into a tangled mess. "Over the last couple of days—since Sunday—she's been abrupt whenever I asked about Rod, her boyfriend." Sandy glanced up, meeting Moore's eyes. The formality of his uniform made it impossible for her to think of calling him David, no matter how warm his brown eyes appeared. Windows to the soul, or not, he was still a cop. Sandy flushed and brought both hands up to rest on the table. Moore sent a smile but she returned her attention to Bouton, repeating, "I told her not to go."

"Yes, you said." Bouton pointed out.

Sandy looked across at Tom, challenging him.

He took the hint. "She didn't come back to the bar. I assumed she had gone into Ucluelet like she told me she was going to. I had no idea she'd passed the car on to Sandy."

"When'd you discover it was missing?"

"This morning," Tom took a deep breath and rushed on. "I closed the bar about eleven last night, cleaned up, and was back at the lodge around eleven-thirty. I pulled a double yesterday, so I went straight to bed."

"You didn't speak with Miss Lee?"

Tom hesitated for a moment, as if confused, then shook his head. "I didn't even see her. My car was parked outside, so I assumed she was in bed."

Sandy noticed the pause. "Everything okay?"

"I didn't know Conny's last name."

She shot a quick smile at Tom, then asked if he'd picked up the keys.

"Keys?"

"I left them on the table when I came back from Ucluelet."

Tom stared at her. "There weren't any keys on the table."

Of course! She winced as she realized what must have happened. "Conny told me to leave the keys on the table so you would see them when you got off work." She shook her head. "But, no, she actually wanted me to leave them there so she could avoid having to rummage around looking for them in the middle of the night. I'm such an idiot! I should have caught that."

Moore looked up from his note-taking. "Don't berate yourself. Everyone learns to listen to their instincts by ignoring them at first. Mistakes are the way we learn."

Sandy frowned. Was this more good cop? "If I'd just returned the keys directly to Tom, she wouldn't have been able to leave!"

Moore shook his head. "Or she would have found another way."

"So." Bouton sighed. "I understand from our morning meeting that you dropped off your new statement with the officer on duty last night. About seven? What time did you get back to the lodge?"

"Around eight."

"Did you speak with Miss Lee again?"

"No.…well, yes…I tried to. She was finishing her supper when I got in but refused to talk. Said she was tired and went to her room."

"She didn't mention anything about leaving?"

"No."

"What did you do then?"

"I made a cup of tea and moved my stuff from the living room into Tish's old room. Then went to sleep."

The officers leaned back in their chairs as if taking a moment to consider what they'd learned. Sandy was just about to ask a question of her own when Bouton said, "You didn't answer my question. What makes you think the stolen car has anything to do with our investigations?"

Sandy looked at Tom, then at the officer. "Tom doesn't agree with me, but I think Conny's disappearance has something to do with her boyfriend. Tish said he's bad."

Bouton motioned for her to stop. "Tish. Miss Phillips. The one who left the same day as Miss Lee?"

"No. Tish left yesterday. Conny left this morning." Sandy looked from one officer to the other. "If you're thinking they're together, they're not."

"How are you so sure?"

"I just am." When Bouton continued to stare at her, Sandy groaned. "Look. They had different reasons for leaving. Tish quit her job and moved back to Calgary to get away from"—She glanced at Tom—"a relationship." The heat of Tom's displeasure oozed across the table toward her. "And Conny wanted to get away from Rod because I think he hurt her."

"You know this for a fact?"

"Not exactly. I just listen really well." Sandy turned to Tom for support, but he just glared at her, obviously still irritated by the mention of his involvement with Tish. "Two murders...Two murders in such a short period, and now she's gone. It's strange."

Bouton leaned back in his chair, his eyes on Sandy.

"Well, it's strange to me as well," Moore said, ignoring the look Bouton shot his way. "This isn't a big city. We're remote, isolated. The communities are spread out.

Logging and fishing are tough industries. Accidents are common and sometimes happen in clusters. But murder? It has no place here."

Sandy jumped in. "What if Conny witnessed the second murder? Or she knew Rod was somehow involved?" Even to her own ears, it sounded like she was grasping at straws. "I think Conny left because she was afraid of Rod, not because she murdered anyone."

"Again, you know this how?"

Sandy glared at Bouton. *Same way I know you're an ass,* she almost mumbled out loud.

"Look, don't worry about it." Tom stood. "I'll get the car back myself. I didn't want to involve you in the first place." He stormed out of the lounge.

Sandy leapt to her feet. "Tom! Don't go!" She ran after him, catching him just as he exited the inn.

He turned to face her. "Look, Sandy, I understand you want to do things this way, but I've got to go get my car. It's not a police matter."

"What about Conny?"

"We don't know anything for sure." He put his hands on her shoulders. "If she's running away from her boyfriend, we should let her. She's a resourceful person. She wouldn't have left without a plan. That's Conny." He dropped his hands. "Now, I've got to go."

Sandy watched him stride across the parking lot, wishing she knew these people better. Maybe she wouldn't feel so out of sync. If Tom believed Conny was okay, then she should believe Conny was okay. He'd known her longer than she had. But Sandy couldn't shake the feeling that Conny was the furthest thing from okay.

When Sandy turned back to the inn, the two officers were just pushing through the lobby doors. "I'm sorry for wasting your time," she said.

"You didn't waste our time." Moore smiled. "Like I told you, we were coming out to interview Mr. Robinson and Miss Phillips. Where'd he go, by the way? He didn't leave, did he?"

"He's about to. He's going to get his car."

Both officers looked at her blankly. "I thought it was stolen," Moore said.

"Conny left a note. Remember?" Sandy pulled Tom's note from her pocket and handed it to Moore. "She said she was going to leave his car in a hotel parking lot in Nanaimo."

Moore examined the note and handed it to Bouton, who passed it back to Sandy without looking at it. "I don't see how this relates to either of our investigations. If at some point it does, we'll be in touch." He glanced around. "Now, where did Mr. Robinson go?"

Sandy hesitated, then pointed. "The lodge. You cross the parking lot and take the lane to the first cabin on the left. You can't miss it. It's the largest building over there."

Bouton started walking, then stopped and looked back. "Moore! Are you coming?"

Sandy grabbed Moore's arm. "We don't even know if she made it to Nanaimo. I just…I just know something's wrong."

Moore waved at Bouton. "I'll catch up with you." Turning to Sandy, he said, "How about I get dispatch to contact the hotel and see if there's any sign of her, or the car?"

Sandy released her grip on his arm as relief swept over her. "Thank you."

Moore nodded and headed for his vehicle.

Just as Sandy walked through the doors, Paula poked her head out of the office and shouted, "What the hell have you been up to? And where's Conny? The rooms won't clean themselves!"

Sandy stopped in her tracks. With Conny and Tish gone, she was the only one left to do the rooms. She had completely forgotten.

"Sorry!" she shouted, and ran for the stairs.

35.

Tom watched the cop as he surveyed the room. What would it be like to be in a position where others had to do what you told them or risk going to jail? It was a lot of power. He studied the cop's well-defined profile, sharp against the sunlit walls of the lodge's living room. *Even his shadow tells me he's a cop.* Tom shook his head. *He'd never make it undercover.* "Do you want a coffee?" he asked.

The cop and his shadow turned to focus on Tom. "Yes, thank you."

"I'll be right back." Tom left the cop where he stood at the edge of the entry and headed into the kitchen. Tom had run into the guy just as he was leaving the lodge. The cop was standing on the porch, his hand raised, fist clenched in anticipation of the harshness of the weathered wood on his knuckles. The sight had so startled Tom that he had momentarily forgotten who the man was. Then he'd blurted in a jumbled rush that he was going to hitchhike to Nanaimo. The cop told him to turn around because he wasn't going anywhere until he answered some questions.

Tom filled the kettle and set it on the stove to boil. He searched the cupboards for the instant coffee but couldn't find it. A half-full box of tea sat on the middle shelf, offering an option. "Sorry, we seem to be out of coffee. Will tea do?"

"Sure. Milk. No sugar."

Tom chanced a peek over his shoulder. The cop had moved to the pool table and was rolling the cue ball across the green felt. Tom turned back to the kettle, worrying he hadn't poured enough water in it for two cups. He would just do without.

"Do you play?"

Tom turned and saw the cop holding a pool cue, pondering its weight. "No, I don't," Tom lied. No way was he going to encourage the Fuzz to hang around any longer than he had to.

The kettle finally boiled, and Tom poured the steaming liquid over the tea bags. There proved to be enough in the kettle for two cups after all. "It's ready," he announced, setting the mugs on the table. Then he went for the milk in the fridge.

The cop removed his leather jacket and draped it over the back of the chair at one end of the table, then casually took a seat, leaving Tom the choice of sitting at the other end, blinded by the sunlight streaming through the living-room window, or on one of the four remaining chairs, two on each side of the table. Tom chose a side seat, the furthest from the cop. "What did you want to know?"

The cop leaned back in his chair as if he had all the time in the world. He sipped his tea, then sat forward. "Tell me about your drive home from Ucluelet on Saturday morning."

Tom took a moment to consider his answer. He'd already told the other cop. Was this one trying to catch him in a lie? Tom studied the other man. Despite his relaxed manner, the cop's eyes gave him away. They were hunter's eyes, green like a cat's. Maybe that was why he dyed his hair, to throw people off. If it was to attract younger women, Tom could've told him he was wasting his money. Although some chicks went for older men, especially physically fit ones like this guy, he didn't know any who'd be turned on by a dye job, especially such a poor one. Tom chuckled.

"What's so funny?"

Tom shook his head. "Just thinking of some of the things I've heard as a bartender. People talk, you know?" The cop's cat eyes narrowed, and Tom turned his focus on recalling his trip into town Friday night. "I went into Ucluelet after my shift here ended. I dropped into the bar and had a beer."

"What bar was this?"

"There's only one in town. It's in the hotel." Tom rolled his shoulders, trying to relax. "That's where I ran into Tish."

"Had you arranged to meet there?"

"No. We just ran into each other and started, you know, talking." The guy leaned forward, his elbows on the table and his mug cradled in his hands like he was keeping them warm. Tom's shoulders tightened again. "We walked over to a house party, and I had a couple of drinks. At about two in the morning, things started to wind down, so Tish offered to drive me home. I was... quite drunk by then."

"Had she been drinking?"

Tom hesitated. "She had had a couple at the bar, but she only drank soda and lime at the party. Tish rarely gets drunk."

"So, she drove you back to the inn using your car?"

"To the lodge, yeah. We both rent rooms here."

"Does she usually drive you home from parties?"

Tom hesitated, uncertain of what the cop was trying to get at. "If you're asking if we were in a relationship, we weren't. Not in the usual sense, anyway." A memory from the morning before flooded over him. The sun filtering through her hair as she leaned down to kiss him. He had climaxed inside her while tasting the sweetness of that kiss. Tom shook his head to clear the memory. He gripped his mug. "It was casual."

"And you don't remember seeing or hearing anything on the road?"

"I slept most of the way back, but I'm sure I would have noticed if we had hit someone."

"We no longer consider this a hit-and-run case." The cop paused and looked directly at Tom. "Did Miss Phillips mention seeing anything strange on the way back?"

Pinned by the full intensity of those luminous green eyes, Tom shivered. "Not…not that she mentioned to me."

The cop set his mug to the side, twisted in his chair to pull a notebook and pen from his jacket's pocket, and scribbled a note. Tom couldn't read anything and wondered if the guy was writing in shorthand. The cop glanced up and caught Tom looking at the page. A slow smile spread over his face, and it was enough to send another shiver up Tom's spine. "I've read your sheet. You've had quite an interesting time of it the last couple of years, haven't you? A couple of break-and-enters, several drunk driving and speeding violations…and then there are the possession charges."

Tom's heart skipped a beat. He cleared his throat. "All water under the bridge."

"Is it? The people you were hanging out with in West Van certainly have some interesting connections. Makes me wonder. Is it a coincidence that you show up, and the local drug scene suddenly takes a turn toward the major leagues?"

"I'm not involved." Tom could feel his throat constrict. "None of it is me."

"Oh, I'll be very surprised if you aren't in this up to your ears, Tom." Bouton's smile didn't reach his eyes. The inferred threat broadcast loud and clear. "So, tell me about last night."

Sweat soaked through the fabric of his denim shirt as Tom shifted uncomfortably. "There's nothing much to tell. Conny came into the bar and asked to borrow the car. I gave her the keys. A few minutes later, Sandy came in and asked to borrow the car. I told her Conny had already asked, and that she should talk to Conny."

"Is that a common thing, loaning out your car?"

"This is a remote location, and not all the staff have cars. I don't usually loan my car because—" Tom paused, struggling to express his attachment to his Mustang. "I just don't."

"Why did you loan it to Miss Lee, then?"

"I trust her." Tom saw the skeptical look in the officer's eyes. "She takes her job seriously. She makes sure the inn's rooms are clean and made up to a precise standard. She carries that same standard into her own space at the lodge. I knew she would take care of my Mustang."

"But you also offered it to Miss Chambers."

"I figured they'd go together, and, like I said, I trust Conny."

"What happened when you discovered Miss Lee had not returned the car?"

"She left me a note telling me where she would leave it, and I was prepared to go get it."

"What stopped you?"

"Sandy was worried. She convinced me that we should speak with you cops first." Tom almost added that it was a decision he regretted, swallowing the words at the last moment.

"You had no idea Conny planned to take off with your car?"

"If I had, I wouldn't have loaned it to her, would I?" Impatience seeped into his voice. "Are we almost done here?"

"Almost. You weren't clear in your answer when we asked you and Miss Chambers if you knew a Danny Brown. Do you know him?"

"No."

"Do you know anything about a theft over the weekend from an old prospector's shack on Lost Shoe Creek?"

Tom had no idea where the guy was going with this, but he had been questioned by enough cops to know when he was being pushed into dangerous territory. "No," he growled. "And I'm not answering any more questions without my lawyer present."

Pounding on the front door jolted Tom, and he saw a similar reaction in the cop. Their eyes met, each silently asking the other who it could be. When the pounding continued, Tom rose to answer it.

Corporal Moore stood on the porch, radiating excitement. "Is Corporal Bouton still here?"

Bouton. That's the asshole's name. Tom waved Moore through and shut the door.

Moore strode to the kitchen table and sat. "When I contacted Evans to send him out to search Highway 4 for the car, he told me Danny's wife had called to say she remembered the name of the guy who hired Danny. Rod. His name's Rod. She didn't know his surname."

"Conny's boyfriend?" Tom was suddenly concerned.

"Do you know his last name?" Bouton asked.

When Tom shook his head, Moore stood. "I'll run over to the inn and see if Sandy knows. I mean, Miss Chambers."

Tom stood as well and reached for the cop's cup. Bouton covered it with his hand. "Maybe you should put the kettle on. I'm sure Corporal Moore would like some when he returns."

It took a moment for Tom to get his emotions under control. Once he was sure he could move without punching Bouton's smug face, he stepped away. *Don't screw this up. It's just tea.* He slowly let out a breath and crossed to the stove.

He had just pulled down another cup from the cupboard when Moore burst in.

"It's been found!" Moore shouted. "Dispatch just radioed a report of an abandoned car, a Mustang, on Highway 4.

"What? Is it damaged?" At the officers' shocked stares, he realized his mistake. "I mean, is Conny all right?"

"It's resting halfway in the ditch just west of Taylor River bridge but appears undamaged, except for a couple of flat tires, according to the caller." Moore dropped into a seat at the table. "No sign of Miss Lee." Moore turned his attention to Bouton. "Dispatch contacted Owens' Garage to get a tow truck out there but was told it would be at least an hour, as the truck was out on another job. I pulled Constable Nelson back on shift to head out and remain with the vehicle, which will free up Evans to look for Miss Lee. Hopefully, she's on foot and no one's picked her up."

Bouton nodded his approval, then turned a smug smile on Tom. "Looks like we'll be keeping your car for a while."

"What? Why?"

"We need to be satisfied that it wasn't being used to transport drugs."

"I told you, I'm not involved in any of that!"

"We'll see." Bouton stood. "I think we need to look in Miss Lee's room."

Tom jumped up. "What are you looking for?"

Moore raised his hands to stop Tom from approaching Bouton. "Calm down, Tom. We just need to see if she left any clues as to where she might be heading. Now, which room is hers?"

Tom led the two officers to Conny's room, opened it, and stood back to watch as they searched. There wasn't much to see. Conny had done a thorough job of cleaning it out, except for the cheap tourist crap and fan magazines she left behind.

The officers found and opened the suitcase in the closet. The clothes Conny had left for Sandy were tossed across the bed. Bouton ripped open the lining of the suitcase, revealing nothing more than a few dust bunnies.

When they started on the dresser drawers, Tom left the room and headed to the kitchen to deal with the screaming kettle. He removed it from the flame and turned off the stove, but he wasn't in the mood for tea. He grabbed himself a beer and moved to the living room, slouching on the couch. *The cops want tea? They can make it themselves.*

His beer bottle was long empty by the time the officers entered the living room with frustration written all over their faces. Tom raised his eyebrows. "What's up?"

"Nothing," Bouton growled, and stalked out of the lodge, Moore following close behind.

Tom rose and quickly crossed the kitchen to Conny's room. It seemed somehow disrespectful to leave her door open. As he was about to close it, his eye caught the snow globe. *What were you so afraid of Conny that you'd leave your dreams behind?*

36.

Conny heard a car approaching from behind and turned to face it, sticking out her thumb in the universal sign of hitchhikers. Too late, she realized it was a cop car. The officer behind the wheel broke into a huge grin. She dropped her arm. *Damn!* She glanced around, but found nowhere to run. She had just started climbing the second arm of a switchback that wound up the shoulder of Mount Porter. The gravel road was bordered on the upside by a clearcut forest filled with hidden pitfalls that could shred a leg or pierce a body, and on the downside by a hedge of thick brush. She'd face fewer perils on the brush side, but the steepness of the terrain as it dropped to the first arm of the switchback would make it difficult to remain upright. She could not have been discovered at a worse spot. She raised her chin and stood her ground as the cop brought his car to a stop in front of her.

"I've been looking for you," the officer said as he stepped from the car.

"Well, here I am."

The cop smiled. "And aren't you a sight for sore eyes?" He ran his gaze over her wind-whipped hair, the dust-covered clothes, and the dry blood coating the ripped knee of her jeans. "Looks like you had a fall."

"Hurts like a bugger."

"Come on, let's take care of it then."

Conny switched her suitcase to her right hand and gripped her jean jacket in her left, before hobbling after him. The officer opened the passenger-side door for her. "Make yourself comfortable." Taking the suitcase, he moved to the rear of the car and opened the trunk. Conny heard him shuffling things around, then a *thunk* as he dropped her suitcase inside. The car shuddered when he slammed the trunk shut. He returned with a first-aid kit cradled in his hand.

Kneeling on one knee, he set the kit on the gravel beside him and opened it. Looking up, he said, "My name's Halden, by the way. Constable Halden Evans out of Ucluelet."

She'd seen him before. He was one of the cops who'd done interviews at the inn on Saturday morning. Before that, she'd seen him around town, his confident stride always catching her eye. Up close, the warm caramel of his eyes hypnotized her. The spell didn't break until he dipped his head and Conny heard her jeans rip.

At her intake of breath, he looked up. "Sorry. I couldn't see where you were hurt." He pulled a small brown bottle from his kit and bent to his task once more.

She ran her gaze over his short-cropped, chocolate-brown hair as it rippled in the afternoon breeze. "You can't take me back, Halden," she whispered.

Halden ignored her, opening the bottle of iodine instead, and pouring a little on a gauze pad. He carefully placed the gauze on Conny's sliced knee.

She flinched and clamped her jaw shut.

Halden wrapped a hand around her arm and held her in her seat. "The sting will ease," he said. When she relaxed, he released her arm but kept the gauze on her knee. "So, how'd this happen? I didn't see any blood in the car."

Conny shot back, "You searched the car?"

"Of course I searched the car, Conny. I thought maybe you were inside, hurt. When I didn't find any evidence of that, I searched for clues as to where you might be headed. I figured you'd spent the night in the car, so I had some hope you weren't far away."

"So you came rushing to my rescue."

"Not quite." His lips turned up in a faint smile. "I had to stay with the car until Constable Nelson arrived." He paused as if waiting for her to comment. When she didn't, he asked, "Why shouldn't I take you back?"

"B-because he'll kill me."

"Who will kill you, Conny?"

Conny looked away. "I can't tell you."

Halden removed the gauze and used it to gently wipe the blood and dirt away from her damaged skin. He tossed it to the side of the road, where it fluttered away in the breeze. He chose a fresh piece of gauze and taped it over the wound. "That takes care of your knee, but I'm afraid I can't do anything about your jeans."

Conny looked down at her bandaged knee, trying to figure out if his comment was an attempt at a joke. She fingered the frayed edge of the tear. "Let me go."

"I can't do that, Conny. You stole a car."

"I didn't. Tom said I could use it."

Halden stood and gazed out over the remote landscape. After a moment, he looked down at her. "I'll tell you what. I'll radio in and tell them I've found you. If this Tom isn't laying charges, I'll give you a ride down to the Sproat Lake campground. I'm already in the Port Alberni detachment's jurisdiction, so a few more miles won't matter. You should be able to catch a ride from there."

"He won't press charges! I know he won't."

Halden held up his hand to stop her saying any more. "But if he does, I'll have to take you back."

Conny nodded her agreement. He reached for the radio's handset, and she listened as he made his call. As nice as he'd been so far, she found it hard to trust him. He was a cop. Yet compared to what Rod would do to her, she knew her only choice was convincing Halden to let her go.

The answer delivered over the radio was filled with static, yet the message was clear. Constable Evans was to bring her back to Ucluelet for questioning.

"No!" Conny yelled as she sprang off the seat and out the open door. She misjudged the width of the road's shoulder and found herself sliding down the steep hill, brush and branches ripping her clothing and gravity tossing her around like a spinning top. Then, suddenly, she dropped into the ditch edging the switchback below.

Dazed, she lay stunned, confused and afraid to move, her whole body screaming in pain. A car slid to a stop at the edge of the ditch, spraying her with dust and gravel. A string of curses followed as Halden scrambled down beside her. "What the hell'd you do that for?"

Conny couldn't find the strength to answer.

Halden knelt at her head. "Jesus! How badly are you hurt?"

Conny groaned and tried to sit up.

"Don't move," he instructed. "Let me check to make sure nothing's broken."

Hands moved over her, testing for breaks or cuts. Conny let it happen. She swallowed the pain, afraid of making him angry, even so he seemed to sense whenever he came to a source of agony, and his probing fingers became gentler. "I don't think anything's broken." He sat back on his heels. "Let's get you out of this ditch."

Conny nodded, allowing him to take her weight as they stood. Slowly, he eased her up the bank of the ditch. He released her when he opened the back door, and then took her arms as she haltingly lowered herself into the back seat. "Stay," he commanded, shutting the door.

She watched as he slipped around to the other side and opened the front passenger door, then rooted around for the medical supplies he must have tossed inside before driving off after her. He found the iodine, gauze, and tape, and had just shut the door when a logging rig came barrelling down the switchback, narrowly missing him. A loud blast of the horn expressed the driver's opinion of finding the road made even narrower by the parked car. Halden waited until it passed, then ran around to the driver's side and jumped inside. "It's too dangerous to stay here." He threw the car in reverse, and they sped backward toward the curve between the two switchbacks.

Conny closed her eyes, hoping no one came around the switchback as he backed up the narrow road and into the rutted entrance of an adjoining logging road. He slammed on the brakes, and they came to rest with the nose of the car a foot off the edge of the main road. Halden shut off the ignition, got out of the car, and walked around to open the back-seat door. "We should be okay here for a while. It doesn't look as if this access road is used much." He gently moved her until she faced him, her legs hanging out the door, before he reached down and gathered the supplies that had rolled under the front seat. When he had them in order, he winked. "You seem to have accumulated a bit more damage."

This time it was clear he was joking, and Conny smiled, breaking the split in her lip. She tasted blood. The cop handed her a small strip of gauze to dab the blood and turned his attention to finding new scrapes and cuts. "Your jeans seem to have done a good job protecting you. Your top? Not so good," he teased, as he examined the wounds exposed by shredded cotton. Lifting his eyes to hers, he indicated the buttons. "May I?"

At Conny's quick nod, he cautiously slipped one arm at a time out of her blouse. She felt vulnerable under his scrutiny, especially when the look in his eyes made it obvious he'd found evidence of her evening with Rod's goons. At the first of the old bruises, he implored, "If your boyfriend is hurting you, you need to report him."

She turned her face away, and he continued his ministrations. A tear escaped and trailed down her cheek, advertising its journey through the dust in defiance of her attempt at pretending it wasn't there. "Please," she whispered. "Don't take me back. Ask your questions here." She shifted and tried to square her back. "I'll tell you what you want to know."

His hands stilled. She looked at him and saw in his eyes an ambition that matched her own. This surprised her, and she turned away again. He did the same, as if something had passed between them. He pulled her blouse closed, leaving her to button it. "I think that should take care of things." He gathered his supplies and stood.

Conny nodded and forced herself to look up at him. "Thank you."

Halden paused, then pointed at her feet. "You'd better pull those inside so I can shut the door."

Taking a deep breath, Conny did as he asked. He shut the door and tossed his supplies into the trunk. When Halden slid back into the driver's seat, she leaned forward. "Do I have to ride in the back?"

"I don't want to have to chase you again."

Conny followed his gaze to her side door panel. No handle. She swivelled to check the opposite door. Also, handleless. *I'm locked in!* Her heart hammered her ribs and her throat constricted. *Stop it!* This isn't the same situation. There's no goons and Halden's a cop. I'm safe. Then she heard the engine start.

"Wait!" she pleaded. "Wait. Please!"

Halden shut off the ignition and turned to face her.

Conny's mind raced. If she returned to Ucluelet in the back of a police car, Rod would think she had squealed about his drug operation. She knew what the consequences of that would be. "What if I could tell you who killed the hippie?"

"You know who killed him?"

"Yes."

Halden remained facing her, but Conny could tell he was thinking about something else. The tension between them built. She turned to the window and waited for him to break the silence.

"What's the deal?"

Conny inhaled deeply. "I want you to let me go."

"Why should I? If I bring you in, you'll end up giving us the information anyway."

Conny's eyes narrowed. "I heard you have some out-of-town officers strutting around. They probably think you local guys are nothing but backwoods nobodies. Even if you bring me in, do you think you'll get credit for any information they get from me? They'll take the credit and leave you behind." If she had correctly judged the level of his ambition, he would take the bait. "I bet you watch those officers, and you want what they have. You want out of the end-of-the-world detachment you're in right now. I'm offering you an opportunity that will do just that."

He glanced away.

Bingo! "If I give you the hippie's murderer here and now, you can claim you interrogated me or maybe drew some brilliant deductive conclusions. I'll leave the explaining up to you. Either way, the credit will be yours and yours alone. They won't have any way to claim it, because they aren't here." Conny paused, allowing her words to sink in. "Think of where it'll take you."

37.

Sandy and Roxanne surveyed the mess the cops had made of Conny's room. The shredded fabric of the suitcase's lining exposed nothing but the cheap plastic casing underneath. The clothing that had been folded neatly inside was tossed haphazardly across the bed. "What were they looking for?" Sandy wondered aloud.

Roxanne shook her head. "Who let them in?"

"I didn't have a choice," grumbled Tom. He was slumped in one of the overstuffed chairs by the fireplace, a half-finished beer resting precariously on the armrest.

Roxanne left Sandy and wandered into the living room, stopping behind the armchair opposite Tom. "You just let them search Conny's room? Did they have a warrant?"

"I didn't *let* them do anything," Tom protested, catching the beer bottle before it tumbled into his lap. "Mr. High and Mighty from Major Crimes pushed his way in here, demanding I answer more questions—which I did, by the way. Then he told that other officer, the one from Ucluelet—"

"David," Sandy offered as she joined Roxanne.

Tom shot her a worried look. "David Moore, right. They decided to search Conny's room for clues as to where she went, but I was also told they were going to keep my car and search it for evidence of drugs."

"Drugs?"

"Yes, drugs."

The sharp look Tom shot Sandy made her flinch. Was he accusing her of somehow causing the police to impound his car? "Why would there be drugs in your car?"

"I have no idea." Tom sighed. "Cops are cops. They make up their mind about you and that's it, you're a crook forever in their eyes."

Sandy frowned. The state of Conny's room worried her. "I'm sorry, Tom."

Roxanne lifted an eyebrow. "What are you sorry for?"

"If I hadn't insisted on calling the cops when we found Conny gone, Tom would still have his car."

"And Conny would be free," added Tom. "As it is, that Moore cop sent one of his gofers out to find her and bring her back."

"What?" Sandy dropped onto the couch. "Oh." The implications of what she'd set in motion brought on a wave of nausea.

"They also asked if I knew a Danny Brown—"

"The guy who was killed Sunday?"

Tom jumped up. "That was the guy's name?" Tom paced the small space between the two armchairs, then stopped to face Sandy. "When they asked us about a theft from a prospector's shack at Lost Shoe Creek, was that where they found that guy?"

Sandy shrugged.

"I remember hearing something on the radio about a body found at the creek," Roxanne said. "We could call the Tofino station."

Tom returned to his chair and collapsed into it. "I'm done. My ol' man is going to kill me."

"Why?" Roxanne moved around the armchair. "Did you rob that hut?"

"What? No! But from the way the cops tore Conny's room apart, not to mention how the head cop questioned me about my past, I'd say they think I'm involved somehow. Did they find drugs in the hut?" He covered his face with his hands and groaned.

Roxanne looked at Sandy. "Were there?"

Sandy frowned. "I don't know."

Lowering his hands, Tom looked directly at Roxanne. "Doesn't matter. My father won't believe me. He'll yank me out of here by tomorrow, and I'll be working for his real estate firm by the end of the week. All his friends will believe he rescued me once again. He'll have me right where he wants me—under his thumb."

Roxanne knelt beside Tom and took his right hand in both of hers. "It does not matter what others believe, Tom. You can't control that. You can only control how you react. Stay strong. Things will work out."

Tom visibly relaxed, and Sandy only wished she could do the same. *What have I done?*

"Let's go for a walk." Roxanne rose, pulling Tom up with her, and together they left the lodge.

Thirty minutes had passed and the two had not returned. Sandy shifted her position on the couch and pulled her aching foot out from where it'd fallen asleep under her left leg. Setting her book down on the coffee table, she wondered how much longer Tom and Roxanne would be. It was close to five o'clock. They had promised to pick up supper from the inn on their way back.

She told herself not to worry. Although it had been a crazy day, things would work out. They already had once already. She had started her shift alone and late, but Brent had called his sister, Emily, to drive in from Ucluelet and help her. Emily had worked at the inn the previous summer as a waitress and a chambermaid, so she was able to seamlessly pitch in. She did, however, make it clear that she was only working the remainder of the week and was not interested in filling in for the rest of the season. She had a boyfriend who expected her to be free when he was.

Sandy reached for her book but stopped, no longer interested in the pill-popping Hollywood wannabes portrayed in the book Conny left behind. Her mind was too full of the twists and turns of the madness being played out in her real life.

The painful tingling in her foot had stopped, so she rose and crossed to Conny's room. It was heartbreaking to see the mess the cops had made. Conny wouldn't want her room left in such a state. She picked up the ruined suitcase and carried it through the kitchen to the garbage bin outdoors, then returned to fold and stack the clothes in the dresser drawers. If Conny returned, they would be there for her. If she didn't, Sandy would move the ones she wanted to the dresser in her room and give the rest away, as Conny had asked her to do.

She straightened the rumpled bed linens then surveyed the room, replaying the moment when she had discovered Conny packing. Sandy set down the pillow she was fluffing and crossed to where the closet doors stood open. She could see Conny's expression like she was standing in front of her. *Fear. Or was it guilt?* What had she been afraid, or guilty of? Sandy scanned the interior of the closet. It looked normal, but empty.

Sandy stepped into the closet and looked at the wall above and around the doors. Everything looked as she'd expected. But Conny had been up to something in the closet that she hadn't wanted Sandy to know about. Sandy was sure of it.

She investigated the joints of the walls and the top shelf. Then—yes, a crack running along the bottom of the top shelf where it met the back wall. Sandy reached up and tested the top shelf. It moved. She pushed up, and the shelf lifted. Slowly she slid it toward the front of the closet, stopping halfway, and left it resting on its brackets. As she examined the wall the hidden panel became obvious. She carefully slid the panel up and out and set it on the floor. A hole about ten inches square was revealed. Standing on her tiptoes, she looked inside. A black chocolate box stood on its end between two framing studs. Sandy reached in and pulled it out.

After carrying her prize to the living room, she sat on the couch and placed the chocolate box on the coffee table. She doubted there were chocolates inside, but she was hesitant to discover its true contents.

"Hello!"

Sandy jumped.

Roxanne stood in the front entrance. "Sorry, did I startle you?"

Sandy dropped onto the couch and tried to slow her pounding heart. "Sort of. Yes."

"I didn't mean to." Roxanne crossed the room and stood behind the couch, looking down at Sandy. "Did someone give you chocolates?"

"No. I...I found this in a secret compartment in Conny's room."

"Oh!" Roxanne slipped around the couch and sat beside Sandy.

"I don't think it's chocolates," Sandy said.

"Well, open it!"

Sandy leaned forward and lifted the lid. Inside were sheets with little coloured squares on them, a couple of marijuana joints, two small tinfoil packets, and two syringes.

Roxanne gasped.

Sandy looked at Roxanne. "This can't all be hers, can it? Was she selling?"

"I don't know. I've never seen her do drugs other than the odd joint, so selling would be a big step. They could belong to someone else." Roxanne hesitated. "I wonder if they belong to the guy in the restaurant?"

"What guy?"

"Yesterday there was this creepy guy who came into the restaurant for lunch. When I cleared his plates, he pointed at the window and asked me if I knew the girl on the beach. When I looked, it was Conny. She must've spent her lunch break outside."

"Did you tell him?"

"I told him she was my roommate. He told me to tell her 'Hello, from Dwayne'."

"What'd she say when you told her?"

"I didn't. I forgot."

"Do you think these could be his?"

"I don't know. He just gave off this weird vibe, you know." Roxanne poked at a syringe. "If they are, I don't want to be here when he comes looking for them. He was seriously creepy."

Sandy hoped it wasn't the creepy guy. "What if it belongs to the person who rented the room before Conny?"

Roxanne sat back. "Conny's been in that room since she first came to work here, right after the inn was built in 1964. Before that this building and the cabins were operated as the Wickaninnish Lodge by the local magistrate and his wife. I don't think they'd be hiding drugs in the closet."

Sandy frowned at the box. "What do you think I should do?"

"Well, ratting her out to the cops wouldn't be cool."

"Right." Sandy was beginning to wish she'd never found the box. "What if it's not hers? What if it's Rod's or the creepy guy's?"

"Maybe that's why she left it. So neither of them could find it."

The thought of Rod or the other one coming to the lodge to search for the drugs terrified her. Sandy jammed the lid down. She wasn't sure she agreed with Roxanne about not telling the cops, but she wasn't ready to make that decision. "I'm going to put it back."

Roxanne stood. "Well, I've got to go. I'm meeting my boyfriend at the inn." She grabbed her sweater off the back of the couch. "Tom's bringing supper for you."

"Did you have a good talk?"

Roxanne waved and left.

Sandy picked up the chocolate box and put it back where she had found it. She was just stepping out of the closet when she heard Tom walk in the front door.

"Supper's here!"

38.

Conny watched Halden pace outside the car. He had remained silent after she'd made her proposal—the hippie's killer for her freedom. Then he had suddenly got out, slamming the door behind him. She was getting impatient for his answer. Soon it would be dark and too dangerous to hitchhike.

She leaned over the front seat and was about to honk the horn when a white panel truck came down and around the corner too fast, sliding on the gravel, coming dangerously close to Halden, who leaped out of the way. The truck continued past, disappearing behind a cloud of dust. Halden caught her staring and gave her a lopsided grin. Conny fell back against the back seat, heart racing. He returned to the car and slid in behind the wheel, laughing. "Wasn't that a heart-stopper?"

Conny didn't join him in laughing "Do we have a deal?"

"Where will you go?"

"It doesn't matter where I go. It'll be away from here. You won't see me again."

His eyes searched for hers through the rear-view mirror. "I can't guarantee others won't pick you up."

"I know." Conny looked directly into his eyes, but she didn't find what she'd seen before—the spark of bravery. The naked ambition was still there, and she could use that, but he was just a man beneath the uniform, not the champion she realized she sought. "If I go back with you, he will kill me. At least this way, I'll have a chance."

"We could protect you—"

His words triggered a memory from when she'd worked the West End district of Vancouver. She'd seen a fourteen-year-old prostitute, tossed like a rag doll on the corner of Davie and Jarvis Streets, her throat slit. The cops never found who did it and the street had gone silent, accepting the gruesome murder's blatant display as a warning to anyone who thought they could accept a cop's promises. Conny began to shake. "No, you couldn't."

Halden turned in his seat, looking directly at her. "Did Rod cause all that old bruising I saw, Conny?"

The shaking spread down her arms to her hands. Conny stuck her palms beneath her thighs, hoping the pressure would calm them. *Keep it together. Just keep it together.* She didn't look up. "No."

It seemed forever before he spoke again, but the time seemed to work for her and her shivers were subsiding.

"Who did?"

Conny took a deep breath and let it out slowly, gradually the shaking stopped, and she removed her hands from under her legs. "It doesn't matter."

"Yes, it does! Assault's a crime. And those bruises were made by someone who knew what he was doing."

Yes, they did. Conny squared her shoulders and faced his anger. "I'm not going to tell you. It's my body." The brown eyes she'd found so attractive such a short time earlier inspired only disappointment now. "It's my body."

The clack and rumble of an approaching vehicle scattered the birds from nearby trees but didn't break Conny's steadfast glare.

He blinked first. "And you know who killed Geoff?"

Her stomach tightened at the mention of the longhair's name. "Yes."

The sound of small grains of sand and gravel settling over the car broke their attention and they both turned to watch a black transport truck whiz by. "Can you clear the windows?"

Halden sent her a confused look. "They'll only get dirty again when the next truck comes past."

He was right, and it wasn't as if she couldn't see out. She could. Nothing to panic about. She slipped her jacket on and gathered it close for comfort.

Halden opened his door and fresh air flooded in. She took a deep breath and relaxed.

"Okay. Let's do this," he said, reaching over the seat. "Shake."

Conny ignored the offered hand. "Let me out of here first."

He withdrew. "No."

"I feel trapped."

"Too bad."

Conny studied him. "How do I know you'll keep your word after I give you what you want?"

"You'll have to trust me. I have to trust you."

But I don't trust you. She rubbed at her temples, letting her eyes meet his. There really was no choice. "Okay," she said.

Halden leaned over to the passenger side of the front seat, opened the cubbyhole, and removed a notebook and pen. The smooth wood of a gun's grip was revealed before he flipped the cubbyhole door shut. Conny blinked rapidly. He already had a gun in his hip holster. *What's this one—an extra?*

The soft drone of a vehicle's engine labouring up the switchback made Conny pause, waiting for another dust cloud to deposit more grit on the car. When it didn't come, she was puzzled. Then she realized Halden had spoken. "Sorry, I didn't hear you."

"Who killed Geoff?"

"First off," she said, "it was an accident."

Surprise registered in the cop's eyes as he looked at her across the back of his seat. "Are you saying you killed him?"

She was about to answer when movement outside the windshield caught her attention. "Duck!" she screamed, diving for the floor. Bullets slammed into the hood and windshield, one boring through, zipping past Conny's ear to disappear into the back of the seat behind her. Two more gunshots popped, and a bullet bore into the backseat upholstery a good three inches lower than the first. "No! No! No!" she cried, cowering against the floor.

"I know you're in there, bitch!" Rod bellowed.

How'd he find me? Another bullet bore through the windshield, this time coming slightly left of the last ones, going high and exiting through the back window, shattering it. She wondered if Rod was moving around the car. Then she heard Halden, who had ducked upon command, speaking into his radio, asking for assistance and giving directions.

"Tell them to hurry," she whispered.

Another bullet whizzed past, this time smashing through the driver's side window and exiting out the already shattered rear window, causing a burst of movement in the front seat. The passenger door clicked open and swung wide. Bullets slammed into the metal of the door as Halden stood and returned fire.

Suddenly, silence.

Conny held her breath. Slowly, she rose from her hiding place and risked a peek.

Rod stood in the middle of the road, gun drawn, focusing on the side of the car. Halden had walked out from behind the protection of the passenger door, a gun in each hand, both pointed at Rod. "Put down your weapon!" he demanded.

"I just want the girl!" Rod shouted back.

Conny didn't wait for Halden's response, she dived over the seat, flung herself out the open driver's door, and ran, nearly tripping over the deep ruts in the logging road. She disappeared into the bush as fresh gunfire erupted behind her.

"Officer under fire!" the dispatcher's voice blasted through the crackle coming from the office radio. Moore, who had been about to slip next door for supper with his family, froze. Bouton, eating take-out fish and chips, tossed the remainder in the bin and stood. Both men listened with silent intensity as the dispatcher read out the location.

Halden! It's Halden. Moore raced to the door.

Bouton grabbed his coat. "I'll pick up Liam and meet you there!"

In moments, Moore was tearing out of town with his siren and lights engaged. It wasn't until he hit the junction of Highway 4 and the Tofino–Ucluelet Highway five miles later that he realized the scene was deep in the Port Alberni detachment's jurisdiction. Cursing a blue streak, he picked up his radio's handset and called dispatch. The car's backend fishtailed on the gravel as he travelled Highway 4 too fast. By the time dispatch answered, Moore had both his vehicle and temper under control. "This is Corporal Moore. It's my constable under fire. I'm on my way there with special officers Corporal Bouton and Corporal McAteer, who are investigating a murder that may be connected to this incident. Has the Port Alberni detachment been informed? We will be entering their jurisdiction."

"They *have* been informed, sir." The extra emphasis added to the formal address signalled that she had taken exception to his question and Moore didn't blame her. He hadn't meant to question her ability to do her job; the call had just unnerved him. This was the first time he'd had an officer in such a situation, and the emotional impact coiled in his gut. He searched his memory for the dispatcher's name, feeling an apology would be better received if it was given with the familiarity of a first name.

"Sir?"

Her name continued to evade him, leaving him with a simple, "Go ahead."

"Three of Port Alberni's constables are on their way to the scene. Constable Nelson has also responded and is expected on-scene within fifteen minutes. And I've informed Tofino of the situation."

He thanked her and signed off. The Tofino detachment would cover both their and Ucluelet's areas while he and his officers were away. He tried to focus on the road. Highway 4 from the Tofino–Ucluelet Highway junction to Port Alberni was little more than a series of pieced-together logging roads, dangerously narrow, with no shoulders, deep ditches, and a hair-raising set of switchbacks that zigzagged up the west and down the east sides of a small mountain ridge that ran along the north side of Sproat Lake. The crime scene was at the top of the west set of switchbacks. It was also several miles past the Taylor River bridge, which was the dividing line between the Ucluelet and Port Alberni detachments' jurisdictions. He had to calm down, focus. It would take him close to an hour to get to the scene, and that was only if all the gods were on his side. If the road hadn't been graded recently, the ruts would certainly impact his arrival time.

The early evening sun was casting long shadows when Moore took the first corner of the switchbacks fifty minutes later and caught sight of Constable Nelson's patrol car parked across the road, its lights flashing. Moore pulled to the side and parked. He glanced at his watch. *Seven o'clock.* He had made good time, but a lot had happened since receiving that first call. Updates from dispatch told him the gunfire had ended with one man dead, and two injured. Luckily, Evans was one of the injured, having taken a bullet to his arm. Also, Nelson and two Port Alberni officers had arrived to secure the scene.

Moore grabbed his flashlight. Though nightfall was a couple of hours away, he liked to be prepared. The crunch of gravel and voices in hushed conversation made him look up. His breath caught. Nelson was approaching with purposeful, unhurried strides. Evans kept pace, but his struggle was etched on his face. Evans' bandaged left arm was in a sling partially hidden by his uniform jacket; the empty sleeve swung to the rhythm of his step.

Nelson smiled. "I'm taking him to Tofino Hospital."

"How bad?" Moore asked, changing direction and matching his stride to theirs.

"My arm…caught…a bullet…fine."

Moore fought to keep the fear from his voice. Bullet wounds could be tricky. "Of course you'll be fine." Evans' obvious struggle deepened Moore's concern. "Would it be closer to go into Port Alberni?"

"It's about the same distance either way." Nelson indicated Evans. "He wants to go back to Tofino."

Moore considered using one of the Port Alberni officer's vehicles, which would surely be on the other side of the rig, but decided it would be easier to interview Evans in Tofino. "Fine," he said.

When they reached the vehicles, Nelson opened the passenger door of his patrol car and assisted Evans into the seat. Once he was settled and the door shut, Nelson pulled Moore to the back of the vehicle and handed him some folded papers that looked like they'd been ripped out of a notebook. "He wrote down what happened. It's not a formal statement, but I figured it would give you the basics of what went down here."

"Dispatch said there were two injured."

Nelson sneered. "Yeah. Rod's the other one. A flesh wound where a bullet sliced his thumb. Halden's wound is more serious. The bullet went through but the truck driver, who cleaned and wrapped both, said Halden was lucky as it appeared the bullet had not hit any major vessels, and he was able to control the blood loss. He wasn't sure about the bone, so we're to keep his arm as still as possible until it's x-rayed."

Nelson nodded to indicate Evans. "He said he arrested and cautioned Rod at the scene."

"Okay, so twenty-four hours is when?"

"About six o'clock tomorrow night, but the court doesn't sit in Ucluelet until Friday."

"Well, we have him an extra sixteen hours then." Moore folded the papers and slipped them in his jacket pocket. "Look, there's no way you're going to be able to do the scheduled short-shift change into a day shift tomorrow. By the time you get Halden to hospital and yourself back, you'll have done close to a double shift. You'll be dead on your feet."

"It's okay—"

"No, Monty, it's not." Moore grabbed Nelson's shoulder. "After you deliver Halden to the hospital, you go home and sleep. Halden's going to be out of commission for at least a couple of days. The specialist officers are here so we've got the day shift covered. I want you to stay on night shift…for now."

"Yes, sir."

Satisfied, Moore let go. "You'd better get going."

As Nelson headed to the driver's side, Moore moved to where Evans was leaning back in the passenger seat, his eyes half-closed. He opened the door, his gaze automatically dropping to the wrapped arm, inspecting it for signs of fresh blood. He could see none, and gave Evans' shoulder a gentle pat. "Glad to see you made it through. I'll check in with you later."

Evans looked up at him. "I had her, sir. I had her."

Moore nodded. "What matters is that you get to the hospital and get patched up."

Evans laid his head back, whispering, "She confessed. I had her, and she confessed."

Moore closed the door and stepped back. Nelson pulled away, his lights and siren broadcasting the urgency of his mission, just as Bouton and McAteer arrived. Moore jumped in his patrol car and waited for the specialists to pull over to the side of the road before moving his vehicle to replace Nelson's as a roadblock. He turned on his lights and the flashing strobes, adding drama to the scene.

"Was that Constables Evans and Nelson leaving?" Bouton asked.

"They're headed for Tofino."

Moore pulled Evans' notes from his pocket and used them to update the specialists as they walked to the scene. "Three officers from Port Alberni responded. One set up a roadblock on the Port Alberni end, turning back traffic coming west. The other two officers turned away any cars they found on the road along the ridge between that roadblock and the scene. When they arrived here, they set up a second roadblock at the top of this switchback, and one officer stayed to turn back any cars they'd missed. The third officer made his way on foot around a logging rig that had jackknifed when it came on the scene." Moore nodded a greeting as they passed the constable leaning against the front grill of a white panel truck. "That officer is now guarding the prisoner, who is Miss Lee's boyfriend, Rod Ouellet." They ignored the scowling man handcuffed to the passenger door mirror. "The other gunman is dead."

"Where's Miss Lee?"

"She's gone. Halden said she took off when Rod showed up."

When they came to Evans' patrol car, backed into a logging road entrance, all three stopped to take in the gravity of the scene. The sight hit Moore like a sucker punch. Bullet holes riddled the hood, windshield, and passenger-side door, their sharp ridges emphasized by the evening light's high-contrast shadows. The shattered glass from the blown-out rear and driver's side windows reflected the rosy hues of the setting sun like thousands of tiny jewels.

"Reminds one how dangerous this job really is, doesn't it?" Bouton said.

Moore forced himself to look away. The mud-encrusted bulk of a logging rig blocked the road about fifteen feet up, halfway through the hair-pin curve of the first switchback descending the mountain. Its driver appeared to be inspecting the front grill. Moore heard the two specialist officers move off, and he turned to see where they were going.

They stopped beside the body lying face-down near the left front fender of Evans' vehicle. Bouton remained standing while McAteer took photos, then knelt and examined the dead man. Moore joined them.

"Recognize him?" McAteer asked.

Moore squatted and examined the dead man's face, its features scrunched against the sharp gravel of the road. "No."

"Okay, let's see what he has to say for himself." McAteer searched the man's pockets, pulling a wallet from the right hip pocket. Flipping it open he dug out a driver's licence. "Finn Lehmann, 28, of Vancouver." He handed the licence to Moore. "Ring any bells?"

Moore shook his head and passed it back to McAteer, who tucked the wallet into an evidence bag he pulled from his toolbox. Moore surveyed the area around the body looking for blood splatter.

"What about that tattoo?" McAteer asked, pointing at the dead man's right arm.

Moore squatted down once again. The victim wore a long-sleeved, plaid shirt with both sleeves rolled to the elbow. At first, Moore couldn't see any sign of a tattoo, then he caught what looked like a black smudge on the right wrist. He carefully turned the man's hand to expose the underside of the wrist, where a four-inch, black-inked, mink-like creature, entwined in battle with a cobra snake, was etched into the skin. The image was professionally done, every detail sharp. "No, I don't recognize it. Do you?"

"It's the tag of a gang known as the Mangosta that showed up in Vancouver last year," Bouton explained. "A report said they came up through the States from Mexico. There have been several skirmishes between them and various Vancouver park gangs. Their appearance could mark the beginning of a battle for the local drug trade operated by the park gangs, or it could prove to be a play for the international trade coming through Vancouver's docks. I have no idea why they would be on the island, especially in such a remote location as this." Bouton signalled McAteer, who had risen and stepped a few feet behind them to enjoy a smoke. "Liam, get him processed as fast as you can. We can't keep the road closed much longer."

McAteer tossed his cigarette into the bush, his intense blue eyes scanning the scene. "There's a lot to process. Has anyone touched the body?"

Bouton's eyebrow arched as he looked at Moore.

"Just to test for signs of life," Moore answered automatically.

McAteer knelt once more beside the body and opened his toolbox. Bouton remained standing. Soon, the specialists were engaged in the same closed, whispered conversation Moore had witnessed over Danny's body. Fighting a sense of exclusion, he stepped back, pulled out his notebook, and began writing down the details as he saw them. The man lay face-down, both arms flung out as if he had tried to brace himself but died halfway down, his arms unable to stop his impact with the road. His gun, a steel-framed, ten-shot .22 Browning revolver, lay just out of reach of the splayed fingers of his right hand. A wide fan of dried blood spray covered the man's upper left arm and nearby road gravel.

When McAteer pulled aside the blood-stained collar of the man's polo shirt, Moore noted the damage where a bullet had ripped through the left side of the man's neck. McAteer leaned over the body to scrutinize the wound. "Looks like the bullet shredded both vein and artery." He lifted the shoulder to peer underneath.

Moore squatted to see what the corporal saw. Blood had drained through the road gravel into the dirt beneath. "I sure hope this guy fired first," he said as McAteer lowered the dead man's shoulder to the ground.

"It may take some time to determine that," McAteer muttered. "In the meantime, you can map this area."

Moore was surprised by the corporal's tone of voice. He had thought McAteer was the friendlier of the two specialists. He straightened and looked around the scene. It was going to be a complicated one.

"Do you have something other than a Polaroid?" Bouton asked.

Moore gave a quick nod and headed off to fetch his SLR from the trunk of his car, as well as the supplies he'd need. The evening light disappeared as he moved into the shade of the trees lining the downward side of the switchbacks and Moore slowed his pace to allow his eyes to adjust.

"Where are you off to, sir?"

Startled, Moore turned to the speaker. "Sorry. What'd you say?"

The Port Alberni officer pushed away from where he'd been leaning against the back fender of the van and faced him. "Just curious, sir. Are you leaving?"

"No. I'm going to get my camera to map the scene."

"I photographed the scene, sir."

Moore stared at the officer, the implications sinking in slowly. "And you are?"

"Constable Robert Bailey, sir."

"Corporal David Moore." Stepping forward, Moore accepted the constable's extended hand. He glanced at Rod. "How'd you do that if you were guarding the prisoner?"

"My partner, Constable Greg Whittaker, was guarding him, sir. I was helping people turn their cars around when they couldn't get past the logging rig. It was a good thing that rig jackknifed. It acted as a natural roadblock. Otherwise, there'd have been people and cars all over the scene." The constable took a deep breath. "There were only a couple of cars, so I walked down to the scene. I was told by the injured officer—"

"Constable Evans."

The Port Alberni officer paused, absorbing this. "Constable Evans asked me to photograph the scene."

"So, why are you on guard duty now?"

"Constable Evans wanted someone to search for the missing girl." Bailey scanned the surrounding forest. "I'm a city boy and Greg knew it. So, when I finished with the scene, we switched. I got guard duty."

Moore nodded and eyed the prisoner. He was a big man, in height as well as girth, but the way the red plaid shirt and black T-shirt beneath stretched over his upper body, Moore figured Rod came by his size through hard work rather than a gym. If he'd wanted to, Rod could've made short work of freeing himself from the mirror brace he was cuffed to, but for some reason, he hadn't attempted to escape. *He's been in custody before, or he knows something we don't.* Moore turned his attention back to the constable. "Did you use a Polaroid?"

"No." The constable pointed at the backpack sitting on the ground beside him. "I had my camera in the car."

"An SLR?"

"Yes, sir."

Moore indicated he'd be back shortly, and ran off to grab the supplies he needed. When he returned he was out of breath. "Uncuff him," he wheezed. "We've got to move him…so you…can help me."

The constable pulled a keyring from his breast pocket, shouldered his backpack, and unlocked the prisoner's cuffs. After instructing the prisoner to turn to face the van and present his hands behind his back, the constable re-cuffed him, showing little care for the bandaged right hand. Rod didn't flinch at the rough treatment. His fierce glare had settled on Moore.

The constable pulled the prisoner away from the vehicle and, with a firm grip on the prisoner's right arm, marched him forward.

Taking hold of the prisoner's left arm, Moore matched his pace to Bailey's.

"I need to take a leak," Rod growled.

Moore took in the dark shadows bordering the road. The bush was thick and the trees sparse. Moore had a strange feeling about the request. He stopped and unsnapped the cover of his holster, resting his hand on the grip of his gun. "Okay, but you do it here."

"What? In the middle of the road?"

Moore ignored Rod's protests and stood silently beside him. Bailey moved behind Rod and released Rod's left wrist from the cuff, quickly snapping the open cuff around his own left wrist before returning to his previous position, his expression neutral. Scowling, Rod used his freed hand to unzip and soon a stream of urine shot out toward the side of the road. Moore relaxed. He was about to ask Bailey how long he'd been with the Port Alberni detachment when the officer jumped back.

"Hey!" A wet stain trailed down the left leg of Bailey's pants.

Rod laughed and swung to the left, directing the stream of urine like a water hose, narrowly missing Moore's pant legs.

Bailey used Rod's distraction to buckle his knees, dropping him to the wet gravel. Moore and Bailey quickly re-cuffed their seething prisoner. Moore tightened his grip, nodded to Bailey, and they hauled Rod to a standing position.

The commotion attracted the attention of the specialist officers. McAteer stood. Bouton ran toward them. "Stop!"

Bouton's shout caught Bailey mid-stride. He let his foot fall and turned to face Bouton.

"What are you doing moving the prisoner, Constable?"

"It's Bailey, sir. Constable Robert Bailey."

Bouton glared at Moore. "You were given a task. Moving the prisoner was not part of it."

"Yes, sir. But I found out Constable Evans had asked Constable Bailey to photograph the scene," Moore explained. "All the initial scene photos are on his film. I thought it best to keep all the photos on the same roll of film."

"Well, when he's done there, get him to give you the film and any notes he has on the scene. Then I want him back on the prisoner and you bringing me the bagged evidence before it gets any darker." Bouton turned and stalked back to McAteer.

Moore faced Bailey. "Are you all right?"

"Yeah. I just won't be anyone's favourite dance partner."

Moore grinned. "Call me David."

"Bob," Bailey replied.

"Shall we find a place to secure our prisoner again?"

Bailey agreed and pointed to a young Douglas fir close to the edge of the road. It was strong enough to keep the prisoner in place, yet close enough to keep him in sight while they worked the scene. They shuffled Rod over, then cuffed him with his arms wrapped around the trunk. His shouted obscenities followed them as they strode to the bullet-riddled patrol car.

Moore glanced over at the specialist officers and noticed they'd been joined by a man in a tan overcoat and wearing a dark fedora. They seemed to be in deep discussion over the dead gunman. "Who's the newcomer?" he asked Bailey.

"Dr. Spicer. Our coroner."

"Of course." The coroner would be pulled from Port Alberni since they were deep in the Port Alberni detachment's jurisdictional area. Moore redirected his attention to the subject at hand. "Since you have photographs of the scene on your camera already, I'd like you to photograph the evidence as we find it. Do you have enough film?"

"Yes, sir." Bailey patted his knapsack.

"We'll start with an inward spiral search, starting"—Moore led the constable to the still-open passenger door of Evans' vehicle—"here."

Stepping away from the vehicle, they played their flashlights across the gravel now deep in early evening shadow, their eyes peeled for shell casings. What they found first was blood. *Halden's*. Moore forced himself to concentrate on accurate note-taking, while Bailey photographed the splatter. Then they continued at a steady, measured pace, stopping only to mark, photograph and bag evidence. Moore did his best to ignore the pungent smell that followed Bailey. When they finished, Moore felt confident he had a clear record of the scene in the gathered blood scrapings, spent shell casings, and the three guns. He was glad. They would need every piece of evidence they could gather if they were going to make sense of the gun battle. Any shooting involving a police officer become a nightmare of political power plays, and Moore wasn't looking forward to the paperwork required for this one.

"Should I return to the prisoner, sir?"

Disturbed from his thoughts, Moore looked up to see an expression on the constable's face that clearly indicated he did not wish to return to guard duty. "When you photographed the scene," Moore asked, "did you do any detailed closeups of Halden's—I mean Constable Evans' vehicle?"

"No, sir."

Moore glanced over to where Rod continued to hug the Douglas fir. The coroner was examining the dressing on Rod's hand while McAteer observed. Moore returned his attention to Bailey. "Then, I will cover the prisoner while you take detailed photographs of Constable Evans' vehicle, the panel truck, and the rig."

Bailey's excitement with the assignment reminded Moore of a child given permission to stay up late. "But first," Moore instructed, "take the bagged evidence to Corporal McAteer."

After Bailey left, Moore crossed the narrow stretch of grass between the road's edge and the tree line where Rod remained cuffed. The coroner and McAteer were in deep discussion as they walked away. Moore found a large, flat rock and sat. It felt good to be off his feet. He pulled out a pack of Player's, lit one, and inhaled deeply. *Sam'll understand*, he told himself, knowing she wouldn't.

He pulled his notebook out and reviewed his notes on the evidence gathered and was struck by the first entry. There had been two types of shell casings gathered near the patrol car's passenger door. What was a single .22 calibre long-rifle shell doing there? The casing had been one of several found near the open passenger door of Halden's vehicle, evidence of his constable's part in the gun battle. Moore frowned. The standard issue Force service revolver was a Smith and Wesson MP-10, which took .38 calibre ammunition.

The sound of gravel crunching announced Constable Bailey's return. Moore quickly stubbed out the cigarette. "All finished?"

"Yes." Bailey pulled his camera away from where it hung against his hip. He started to rewind the film, hesitated, and glanced at Moore. "The driver said a bullet hit his grill. He hasn't been able to find it. He thinks it's lodged in the engine somewhere."

"Were you able to get a shot of where the bullet went in?"

"The driver held a marker, while I took the shot." Bailey finished rewinding the film, removed the canister from the camera, and handed it to Moore. "This is the first time I've used my SLR at a crime scene. I took several shots at different settings, just to make sure I didn't mess up."

"I'm sure you did fine," Moore reassured Bailey. "Did you keep notes on the settings you used?"

Bailey nodded.

"I'll tell you what, when we get them developed, I'll let you know how they turned out so you can figure out which settings worked best."

"That would be great!"

"Okay, I'll take this over to Corporal Mac—"

"That won't be necessary," Bouton said. "I'll take it to the corporal."

Moore, surprised by how silently Bouton had appeared, handed the cannister over.

Bouton turned to Bailey. "I saw you at the rig. Did you take a statement from the driver?"

Bailey frowned. "N-no, I didn't." He looked quickly at Moore. "I didn't realize—"

"I'll do it," Moore said.

Bouton stomped off, mumbling under his breath.

"I don't seem to be impressing him."

"I don't think he's impressed with any of us." When Bailey offered him a lopsided grin, Moore indicated the prisoner. "Before you resume your guard duties, have you heard anything from your partner? Has he found Conny?"

"The girl? No. But Greg's a bit of a bulldog, doesn't give up easily. He's probably halfway up the mountain searching for her."

"Are there many cabins at this end of the lake?"

"Most are on the east end. Do you think she could've made it that far?"

"No." Moore looked past Evans' patrol car to the logging road beyond. "Not unless she caught a ride from someone on that road. Where does it lead?"

"It's an old logging road, sir. It must go up the mountain, but the crew's moved on. I think they're working closer to Kennedy Lake. Besides it's too dangerous. You can see how it joins this road right at the turn. Look what happened to that rig when it tried to stop coming down that hill."

"Could she have gone down through the bush?"

"I'm not sure. The terrain is pretty steep." Bailey paused as if considering the possibility. "She'll probably just bed down somewhere and we'll find her easy enough in the morning."

"Okay. If you hear anything from him, let me know." Moore stood up and stretched, before heading to the jackknifed logging rig.

Bailey took Moore's seat on the rock and pulled out his pack of Marlboros.

The truck driver spied Moore's approach from his perch behind the wheel, swung himself out and down from the rig, and landed just as Moore came even with the cab. "Can I help you?"

From the way he bounced down, Moore expected the driver to be younger, but the man had to be in his late forties, early fifties. Moore extended his hand and introduced himself.

The driver accepted Moore's greeting with a confident grip. "Wayne Thompson."

"I understand you saw what happened here."

"Never seen anything like it." Thompson led Moore to the front of his vehicle. "They came out of there." He indicated the point where the road switched back on itself, the lower arm hidden by the brush covering the slope between. "They walked bold as brass across the road in front of me. Expected me to stop on a dime, coming downhill!" He shook his head. "I thought for sure they were going under my tires." He patted the nose of his rig. "We came close, I tell ya!"

Pulling out his notebook, Moore quickly sketched the scene from the rig's perspective. "So, what'd they do?"

"They both had their guns out, focused on the cop and the girl in the car, but when I slammed on my brakes and started sliding, the little one turned, cool as blazes, and fired at me!" The trucker pointed to his rig's grill. "Either he was a piss-poor shot or he wasn't aiming at me. Either way, I was lucky to come away with nothing more than a hole in my radiator."

Moore glanced at the green river of coolant tracing a path down the centre of the road, then to where the gunman must've stood when he fired at the rig. It was outside the search area he and Bailey had done. Turning to Thompson, he nodded at the scene below. "What happened next?"

"Both men were shooting at the cop car as they're walking towards it. Then they stopped and the tall one shouted something."

"You didn't hear what it was?"

The trucker looked down and kicked his rig's front tire. "Something about knowing they're there." He looked sideways at Moore. "They didn't wait for an answer, just started shooting again. I grabbed my mic and sent a call out over the CB right quick."

"Could you see where the officer or girl were?"

"She was hunkered down, I expect. But the cop, the cop comes out the passenger side guns blazing! Killed the short guy."

"Is that when the officer was injured?"

"No. Everyone stopped shooting for a sec, like a stand off. The cop shouted for the last gunman to put his weapon down, but he doesn't. He just shouts back that all he wanted was the girl; for the cop to hand over the girl. That's when the girl sprung out of the driver's door and tore off outta there!"

"Did you see where she went?"

Thompson shook his head. "All hell broke loose. Lucky for me they were shooting at each other and not in my direction. Suddenly, the gunman's gun drops to the ground and the cop has his trained on him. They were both bleeding, so I grabbed my kit and went to assist."

"Kit?"

"First-aid."

"Of course. They told me you helped Constable Evans."

"Well, yeah, but I took care of the gunman first. Didn't want him reaching for his gun while I was tending the officer."

"No, of course not." Moore closed his notebook. "Thank you for assisting my officer. Once your rig is towed, I need you to drop into the station with a written statement."

"Sure."

Moore left Thompson and saw McAteer searching the trunk of Evans' patrol car, evidently deep in thought, as he didn't respond to his approach. "Constable Bailey photographed the vehicles. Everything should be on the film I gave Bouton earlier."

McAteer looked up. "Did he take any of the interior of the car?"

As he drew up to the car Moore realized McAteer was searching through a suitcase inside the vehicle's trunk, not the trunk itself. "No, just the exterior."

"Okay, I'll do it."

"The trucker says a bullet hit his grill and punctured the radiator. Constable Bailey took a photo of that as well." Moore paused, unsure how to proceed. He cleared his throat, which caused the corporal to look up. "Did you know the truck had been hit?"

"Not until now, no." McAteer looked up the hill at the truck. "I guess I have more work to do."

Moore nodded. "Me too."

When McAteer didn't respond, Moore scanned the area. "Where's Corporal Bouton?"

"He's gone to the car to arrange for tow trucks."

"Where from? I don't think Terry—"

"Terry?"

"Terry Owens, the owner. I don't think he has more than one truck and it may still be tied up with Tom's car." When McAteer just shrugged, Moore asked, "Do you need a hand with this?"

"No. Thanks. I prefer to do it myself. Helps with the memory when it comes time to write the reports."

Moore nodded. "I understand. I'll leave you to it."

"Corporal Moore."

Moore turned to see Bouton striding toward him. "Yes?"

"I've arranged to have all three vehicles towed to Owens' Garage in Ucluelet."

"May I ask where the tows are coming from, sir?"

"Mr. Owens from the Ucluelet garage is coming to pick up the panel, another truck is coming out from Port Alberni for Constable Evans' vehicle, and MacMillan Bloedel is sending one of theirs out to haul the rig." Bouton looked from McAteer to Moore. "Corporal McAteer is going to have to escort the body to Nanaimo. Will Constable Nelson be returning?"

"No, sir. I told him to go home."

"Very well, then. You and I will escort the prisoner back to Ucluelet as soon as Corporal McAteer leaves for Nanaimo. I want the prisoner in a cell as soon as possible." Then, as an afterthought, he added, "You can tell Constable Bailey we need him to stay until the tow trucks arrive. Has his partner returned?"

"Not yet, sir."

"Are we going to need to send a search party out for him, too?"

Moore frowned and looked up at the rutted road where it disappeared into the deepening shadows of the forest. "I hope not, sir."

Turning at the sound of new voices, Bouton's face brightened. "Ah, the Port Alberni men are here, Liam."

The undertaker and an assistant were struggling to squeeze around the jackknifed rig without dropping the heavy, coffin-sized box they carried between them. Corporals McAteer and Bouton strode over to assist. Together they brought the box to rest beside the body and stood back with a collective sigh.

Moore left them to the loading of the body and returned to Bailey's side. "Do you have any short-rolls of film?"

"How short?"

"Ten, maybe twelve shots."

"Yes. I have a 10-shot roll, but I think it's black and white."

"That'll have to do." Moore stood for a moment deep in thought. Where he needed to search for the shell casing for the bullet that went into the rig's grill, he would have no sight line on the prisoner. He looked back where McAteer was busy with the undertaker and Bouton logging the evidence in his notebook. "Look," he said. "I'm going to go do a quick search for shell casings. If I find anything, I'll mark them, then come back and relieve you. You'll then take photos of the casings and their position within the scene."

"Yes, sir."

Moore gave a quick nod and left.

Fifteen minutes later, he was back. "There was only one casing, which supports what the driver told me. I marked it well. When you're done mark it as black and white film, then give what you have to Corporal Bouton." Moore settled on the rock and examined his sketches of the scene.

"Sir?"

Moore looked up to see Bailey approaching and stood up. "You're finished?"

"Yes, sir."

Moore looked across at the prisoner. He was leaning into the tree, his head down on his left arm. *His arms must be numb by now.* "Give me a minute," he told Bailey. "I have to check on something and then we'll move the prisoner back to the panel."

Bailey pulled out his cigarette pack as Moore headed to the far side of the road. Once there, Moore turned back and looked at Halden's vehicle, trying to imagine the scene as described by the trucker. He then aligned himself with where he guessed Halden and the dead gunman would have stood. He spun around and instantly realized the task he had hoped to accomplish would be impossible. A vast, tangled mass of brush and tree stumps spread out before him, offering nothing a bullet could be retrieved from.

He marched back to Bailey.

"Let's get him back to the panel," Moore said. "Have you heard from your partner?"

"No. But he'll show up, sir."

"Corporal Bouton and I will be escorting the prisoner to Ucluelet detachment. He wants you to stay until the tow trucks get here. They shouldn't be long."

THURSDAY, MAY 16, 1968

39.

The morning fog had cleared with the sunrise. Moore, standing at the detachment's window, could see across Ucluelet Inlet to Port Albion. The decision to hold the briefing at seven instead of six, giving everyone an extra hour of sleep, had helped, but he was still feeling the impact of the long, rough day before. Evans' bullet-riddled car had haunted his sleep, and the watery sludge offered by the office percolator lacked the kick needed to erase that image.

"Are you still with us, Corporal Moore?"

Moore jumped at the interruption of his thoughts. Taking a deep breath, he turned to face Bouton. "Of course," he answered, forcing a smile. Bouton sent him a look full of reprimand, which Moore ignored. He was too tired to care if Bouton liked him. Moore left the window and crossed to his desk, set down his coffee cup, and slumped into the chair.

"First off," Bouton said, "Corporal McAteer is still in Nanaimo after escorting Mr. Lehmann's body to the pathologist. He will rejoin us this afternoon." Turning to Moore, he added, "He and I would like to send our wish for a speedy recovery to Constable Evans, and we hope to see him out of the hospital soon. He did himself and his team proud yesterday."

Well, thought Moore, *Halden's goal of transferring into the big leagues just got a step closer.*

Bouton turned to include Nelson, the only other member of the team in the room. "As for Miss Lee, she has not been seen since dramatically exiting Constable Evans' vehicle at approximately five-thirty yesterday afternoon. The Port Alberni constable who was sent in search of her—"

"Greg Whittaker."

"What?"

"The constable's name is Greg Whittaker," Moore explained.

"Ah. Yes. Constable Whittaker came up empty. His corporal has informed me that they're sending a couple of officers out later this morning to continue searching the area. If that's not successful, they're planning a house-to-house canvas of the cabins along that end of the lake. Since it's a Thursday and not a weekend, they hope a strange girl wandering around will standout. With any luck, we will have Miss Lee back with us soon. I've notified both the Nanaimo and Vancouver detachments in case she somehow makes it that far. I explained that she's wanted for questioning concerning Mr. Johnston's murder."

Bouton turned to the chalkboard and wrote SUITCASE in bold letters. "We do, however, have her suitcase, which was in the back of Constable Evans' vehicle." Facing his small audience, Bouton tapped his desk with the chalk. "Corporal McAteer did a quick inventory of its contents at the scene. There were the usual clothes and toiletries necessary for a trip. No drugs. No syringes. He'll take a closer look when he gets back from Nanaimo." He paused. "Basically, this means Miss Lee is travelling rough. With any luck, she won't have the resources to change her appearance or be comfortable, making her easier to spot and catch."

After a moment of silence, he nodded at Nelson. "Constable Nelson, I understand you gave Constable Evans' notes to Corporal Moore?"

"Yes."

Bouton paused. "At what point did you learn Miss Lee had confessed to the murder of Mr. Johnston?"

"In the car, sir. On the way to the hospital." Nelson sent a furtive glance at Moore before focusing on the major crimes officer. "Constable Evans was semi-conscious when he said it, so I'm not sure of its accuracy. There was nothing in the notes he'd showed me."

"Either she did or she didn't, Constable," Bouton admonished.

"I'm just passing on what he told me—or, um, mumbled. He wasn't making a lot of sense. Said something about it being an accident."

"Accident or not, she has a lot to explain."

Nelson nodded and glanced again at Moore.

"Corporal Moore, do you have anything to add?"

Moore considered telling Bouton what Evans had whispered before Nelson took him to the hospital, but decided to keep it to himself until Evans made an official statement. Instead, he just shook his head.

"Okay then. Let's look at what our only witness saw." Bouton picked up his notebook from his desk. "According to Mr. Thompson's statement, Ouellet and Lehmann fired first. Constable Evans responded in self-defence."

Nelson let out a sigh of relief.

Bouton glanced at Moore. "Yes, we can all breathe easier now." He turned to write on the chalkboard. "While several bullets were fired, the sequence of the important ones is Constable Evans shooting Mr. Lehmann, killing him; Mr. Ouellet shooting Constable Evans, wounding him; and Constable Evans shooting Mr. Ouellet, wounding him. Our witness had a clear and continuous view from the cab of his rig. I feel confident Evans' shooting will be found as justified. The other witness, Miss Lee, may be able to provide some information about Mr. Lehmann's death when she's found, but not the rest, as she'd fled the scene. She will, however, be able to provide some answers as to why Mr. Ouellet demanded that Constable Evans hand her over to him."

"Lucky for Evans that Mr. Thompson knew first aid," Moore said, once again seeing the bullet-riddled car in his mind's eye.

"Very lucky." Bouton agreed. "The pathologist's report will give us an official cause of death for Mr. Lehmann." He paused, then added, "The guns, as well as the spent shell casings and other evidence gathered at the scene went with Corporal McAteer to Nanaimo last night." He wrote the name and ownership of the three vehicles involved in the scene. "Corporal Evans' and Mr. Ouellet's vehicles, as well as the logging rig, have been towed to Ucluelet. Corporal McAteer will be examining them over the next few days."

"I should point out," Moore said. "I received a message from Mr. and Mrs. Johnston, stating they checked out of the inn yesterday. They flew back to Nanaimo to await the release of their son's body. Any idea when that'll be?"

"I'll see if I can find out. Make sure their contact information is in the file and I'll get back to them." Bouton shifted papers on his desk until he found what he was looking for and jotted a quick note. "Getting back to the Brown murder, the lab report on the steel box came in. There were traces of methamphetamine and LSD, but there's no way of knowing how much of these drugs were inside the box at the time of the theft."

Bouton looked across at Moore. "If you or your officers have community resources who might know if a large amount of methamphetamine or LSD has become available on the street, you should tap them."

"We'll keep that in mind, sir."

Bouton returned to shifting the papers on his desk, then pulled out another. "The pathologist has confirmed that Danny Brown died of blunt force to the right side of his head, where the skull is weakest. He ruled out natural weapons, like rocks or blocks of wood, and said we should look for an item with a small, round, flat surface, like a hammer. The beating, he said, was administered by more than one person—"

"It would have taken more than one person to bring Danny down," Nelson remarked.

"—who meant to cause maximum damage."

Bouton raised his voice. "Also, the missing hand may be part of the violent circumstances of Mr. Brown's death. The pathologist determined that evidence of a scavenging animal, possibly a wolf, had obscured what looked like marks from the teeth of a saw." He looked at Nelson. "I understand you're close to the family. You may want to let them know, in case they want to organize a search for the missing hand. I'm not sure what their beliefs are. Some cultures, I've found, become quite upset when we can't deliver a whole body for burial."

"I'll look into it," Nelson said.

"Mr. Brown was murdered, brutally." Bouton stepped back from the chalkboard. "So, two murders and a police shooting incident. Are they related? Let's find out." He nodded to Moore. "Corporal Moore, we have a guest cooling his heels in the cell. Shall we go have a chat?"

"Yes, sir." Moore went to follow Bouton as he left the room, but stopped in front of Nelson's desk. "Please tell the man in the office entry to follow us."

As soon as Moore opened the door to the interview room, Rod bellowed, "Where's my lawyer?" Moore stopped so suddenly that Bouton, following him, ran into his back. Embarrassed, Moore stepped to the side, allowing Bouton to continue to the table, where Rod stood glaring at them.

"Sit down, Mr. Ouellet," Bouton commanded. "Your lawyer's on his way, but as you know, getting here from Vancouver takes considerable time." Bouton indicated the man who had followed them into the room. "Your lawyer has authorized local lawyer Mr. Wood to act as your counsel until he arrives."

Moore and Bouton chose chairs facing Rod and sat. The lawyer strode around to Rod's side of the table, tossed his coat over the back of the chair next to him and the file he carried onto the table, before taking his seat. Rod remained standing for another defiant moment before dropping into his seat. Moore considered the two men sitting across from him. They couldn't have been more different, though they were likely close enough in age to have been in the same grade in school.

Rod's slouched position didn't diminish the physical power evidenced by the heavily muscled body beneath the black T-shirt and the corded muscles of the arms crossed over his chest. His black hair, clipped close to the scalp, framed his harsh, angular face, from which brown, almost black, eyes broadcast his anger to anyone who dared look his way. He was now offering the resistance Moore had expected at the scene. The lawyer, on the other hand, was a redhead—fair, freckled, and fine-boned. His dark grey suit looked fresh off the store hanger. An odd couple.

Moore reached over to the reel-to-reel tape machine on the table and pressed the record button. "Interview with Mr. Rodrique Ouellet, eight forty-five A.M., Thursday, May 16, 1968, Ucluelet RCMP detachment, E-Division. Present are myself, Corporal David Moore; MCU Corporal Merle Bouton; and the prisoner's counsel, Mr. Rick Wood." He paused and waited for Bouton to begin the questioning.

Wood leaned forward, his elbows on the table, hands clasped. "Speaking for Mr. Ouellet and myself, I would like to protest the early hour of this interview."

Bouton sent a long, slow appraising look at the lawyer. "And I would like to remind counsel we're in Canada, not America. The accused has a right to seek legal advice, but counsel need not be present during interviews. Your presence here is a courtesy."

Wood sat back and nodded. Moore suspected the lawyer had been testing boundaries. Moore made a note to find out more about the young lawyer. All he knew was that he had recently moved to Ucluelet.

Wood cleared his throat. "I understand that a doctor has not examined my client since he was brought in last night—"

"The flesh wound was cleaned and treated at the scene," David broke in.

"Still, a doctor—"

Bouton slapped his hand down on the table. "Enough!" he shouted. "I'd like to point out for the tape that Mr. Ouellet was arrested and cautioned by Constable Evans at the scene last night on Highway 4, during which shots were fired. Could you tell us what you were doing there, Mr. Ouellet?"

Rod looked at the lawyer. Wood sat forward and addressed Bouton. "My client will not be answering any questions about that incident this morning."

Bouton looked from the lawyer to his client. "That's too bad, because your client is facing some serious charges, including the attempted murder of a police officer."

Rod jumped up from his chair. Wood grabbed him before he fully came out of his seat, and firmly pulled him back down with a muttered warning to keep his mouth shut.

Moore was impressed. Though the lawyer looked like a teenager, he obviously had the maturity and confidence needed to deal with clients like Rod.

"Is there anything else?" Wood looked at Bouton.

Moore watched as Bouton considered his next move. Moore knew they had enough to support the attempted murder charges, but they were hoping to connect him to Danny Brown's murder. "We're considering other charges," Bouton said. "In the meantime, we have a missing girl running through some pretty rough country, and we would look favourably on any assistance your client could provide in locating her."

Rod slouched into his chair and folded his arms across his chest once more. "I don't know where the bitch is."

Moore grimaced, not liking Rod's language or attitude. "I understand you were in a relationship with Miss Lee?"

"Yeah. So what?"

"Well, I would think you'd be interested in finding her."

A slow smile spread across Rod's face. "That I am."

Moore refused to react to the implied threat. "How long have you known Miss Lee?"

Rod stared at Moore for a long time. Wood leaned in and whispered something, but Rod swatted him away. "About six months."

"How'd you meet?"

"She approached me at a party."

"Was the relationship solely of a romantic nature?"

Rod laughed. "Was she givin' it up, you mean? Yeah. She was an eager beaver."

Moore gritted his teeth. "Did you and Miss Lee have a business relationship?"

"Ah"—Rod snickered—"and what type of business do you think we would be in?"

Bouton opened the file sitting on the table in front of him. "There's drug trafficking, running prostitutes, protection racketeering."

Rod looked at Wood, then back at Bouton. "So? You can read," he said. "If you check around town, you'll learn I'm here to provide an opportunity for the local fishermen, giving them quicker access to Vancouver's market. All that other stuff is history."

Moore and Bouton exchanged a look. Moore figured they now had a possible link to Danny's murder, and Rod's relationship with Conny established a possible link to Geoff's as well. He masked his excitement with a feigned cough. "So." Bouton smirked. "That's what we'll find when we search your panel truck? Fish?"

"No. I was on my way back after dropping my first load in Vancouver."

"Fish?"

"Yeah, fish."

"So, your truck's empty? Nothing to worry about if we search it?" Moore asked.

Wood grabbed Rod's arm again, stopping him from responding. Then he faced the officers across the table. "Mr. Ouellet has answered your question. Shall we move on??"

Moore and Bouton settled in their seats. Moore spoke first. "So, why the gun battle with our officer?"

"I said no—"

Rod put a hand on his lawyer's shoulder, silencing the man, then withdrew it and faced Moore. "He had something of mine."

"The girl?"

"Yeah. He had no business with her in the car."

Bouton leaned forward, holding his hand up to interrupt Moore. "She must've been very important for you to risk the death penalty that comes with killing a cop."

All emotion drained from Rod's face. "She wasn't," he snapped.

The hair on the back of Moore's neck stood up. His gut told him he was sitting across from someone who would think nothing of snuffing out someone's life. A cold-blooded killer. He cursed the recent change in the definition of capital murder. Before the end of 1967, capital murder was defined as the premeditated murder of anyone, not just enforcement officers, and it carried the death penalty. But as the law stood, Rod would only receive a life term in prison if convicted of Geoff or Danny's murders. Moore doubted prison would hinder his or his affiliates' business. He glanced down at Rod's bandaged hand and the tattoo partially exposed there. "Tell me about the tattoo," he said.

Rod leapt from his seat before Wood could stop him. "We're done here."

Bouton slowly rose and faced Rod. Though they were evenly matched in height, Rod clearly outweighed the officer.

Moore and Wood rose from their seats as if they'd been unwillingly thrust onto the same team. Wood slowly turned to his client. "Rod, sit down."

Bouton held up his hand. "No need," he said. "Corporal Moore, please escort Mr. Ouellet back to his cell."

Moore turned to the recorder. "Termination of interview, nine-fifteen A.M.." Standing, he approached Rod, but when he reached for his arm, Rod jerked it away.

"Don't touch me, pig," Rod growled.

Bouton marched around the table, pushed Wood aside, and grabbed Rod's arm before he could move away. "Get comfortable Mr. Ouellet, you'll be spending the night in a cell."

Wood sputtered in protest. "You can't hold him more than twenty-four hours"

"The magistrate, as you should know, doesn't sit until tomorrow morning. We're keeping him."

40.

When Moore opened the door to Constable Evans' hospital room, he was struck by how young and vulnerable Halden looked. A wave of parental protectionism washed over him. He squared his shoulders. Halden was not his son. He was a fully qualified officer of the law, who was presently looking at him, wearing a smart-ass grin.

"Wipe that grin off your face, Halden," Moore said. "We've got work to do."

The grin disappeared. "Sir?"

Moore set the yellow legal notepad he carried on the bedside table, pulled the visitor's chair away from the wall, and sat. "We need to talk."

"Do I need a lawyer?"

"Maybe later."

When Evans shifted position in an attempt to sit straighter against the pillows and a grimace of pain crossed his face, Moore had to stop himself from assisting. Instead, he leaned forward, resting his elbows on his knees, and fixed his gaze on the younger man. "The doctor tells me the bullet missed everything important and you'll be released soon."

"They wanted to keep me a little longer, but I told them I have to get out of this place."

Moore understood. Hospitals, for a cop, were often a source of tragic and traumatic memories they carried for life. He drew a deep breath and jumped into the purpose of his visit. "For now, this is an informal conversation and will not be recorded or witnessed." He paused, waiting for Evans to look at him directly. When he did, Moore asked, "What happened yesterday?"

"I already told you."

"Yes, you did." Moore nodded. "But I'm hoping you might be able to expand a bit, fill in a few more details."

Evans dropped the eye contact, then seemed to realize it was a mistake and re-established it. "I was in the middle of taking a confession when these guys showed up and just started shooting."

"You were in the middle of nowhere, backed into a logging road access halfway up the west-end switchbacks, taking a statement from a suspect?"

Evans opened his mouth. Shut it. Then tried again. "She wasn't a suspect at the time. I was sent to pick her up for questioning, remember. I asked a couple of preliminary questions when she became quite upset about returning to Ucluelet. She was afraid for her life." His eyes locked on Moore's. "Seems like her concern's been validated."

Moore shook his head.

Evans caught his reaction and blurted, "She said she killed Geoff."

"You mentioned that last night." He reached for the small notebook in his breast pocket and flipped through its pages. "Why would Conny kill Geoff? It doesn't make sense. We haven't found any connection between them."

Evans set his free hand on Moore's notepad, stopping his search. "She said it was an accident."

"An accident?"

"Yes." Evans withdrew his hand. "She was about to explain when we were interrupted by flying bullets."

"So, her boyfriend and this Finn guy just started shooting? Why would someone like Rod chance a shootout with a cop to kill a girlfriend?"

"I don't know, but Conny was terrified of him." He looked down at his injured arm then back up at Moore. "She had some pretty nasty bruises in areas where they wouldn't be easily visible."

Leaving aside the obvious question about how Evans would know about hidden bruising, Moore searched his notebook for a free page. "So, you suspect an assault?"

"Yes."

"Did she say who did the beating?"

"No."

Moore sighed and collected his thoughts. "Look, Halden, there's another reason I wanted to talk to you." A frown creased Evans' brow. *Good. He needs to be concerned.* "I found a long-rifle shell at the scene close to where you would've been firing from. At first, I thought it was probably unrelated, possibly from a hunter, but then I remembered you mentioning a while back that you had a personal gun that used that type of ammunition. Did you have that gun at the scene?"

Evans' chin dipped in a quick nod. "I kept meaning to take it into the house, but we've been so busy, I just never did."

Moore held up his hand to silence him. It wasn't uncommon for officers to own personal guns. Many belonged to gun clubs and took part in local competitions. Shooting a gun accurately required regular practice, and the Force held annual competitions to encourage the continued development of that skill. But personal guns were not to be carried in an officer's work vehicle. "Where is it?"

"I gave it to Monty, along with the spent shells I picked up."

Moore was shocked. *Monty? Not Monty.* "Are you telling me that you gave the gun and shells to Constable Nelson to keep them from becoming part of the evidence gathered at the scene?"

"I realize—"

"Enough!" Moore shouted. "When did this happen?"

"Just before you showed up."

"So, you two conspired to keep the existence of the fourth gun from me." Moore had to stop speaking. He didn't trust his voice or what he would say with it. He stood and crossed to the door, overcome by a need for fresh air. He stopped with his hand on the door and turned around. "What did he do with them?"

"Don't know."

"What type of gun was it?"

"A Colt Woodsman."

"How many shots fired?"

"Two." Evans paused. "No, three."

Moore wrestled with his temper. Finally, he returned to the bedside table, picked up the legal pad, and dropped it in Evans' lap, setting a pen on top. He glanced at his watch. His hand still shook slightly from anger. "It's ten-thirty now. I'll be back at six. You are going to write out exactly what happened from the moment you found Conny, including an account of every shot fired, this time from both of your guns. And you may want to contact a lawyer."

41.

In the staleness of the interview room, Moore cursed the room's windowless design. Driving the twenty-six miles between Ucluelet and Tofino to discipline both his constables in one day had done nothing to improve his mood. He felt very much like a tired and disappointed parent.

"What the hell did you think you were doing?" Moore demanded.

Nelson, sitting ramrod straight in the chair usually reserved for suspects, opened his mouth to protest, but Moore held up his hand, silencing him. "I've changed my mind. I don't want to know. Here is what you're *going* to do now." His pulse pounded in his neck, making it difficult to concentrate. He pushed away from the table and started pacing.

The small confines of the room restricted his pacing to a few feet around the central table, which only increased his frustration. He turned to face his silent constable, catching him blinking away welled tears. Moore averted his gaze momentarily before refocusing on the constable. "Halden is writing a revised statement," he said, forcing himself to look directly into Nelson's eyes. "Monty, you're going to do likewise. I want a detailed account of what happened from the moment you arrived on-scene to when you entered Halden's second gun and shells in the evidence locker."

"But I haven't—" Nelson protested.

"Yes. You did. Right after dropping Halden at the hospital," Moore insisted with a meaningful look. "You took the gun and shells you should have given to Corporal McAteer at the scene and placed them in the evidence locker at the office." Moore pressed his fingertips to his pounding temples. "I don't care what excuse you come up with for neglecting to give them over at the scene, but it better be convincing. Once you've written your statement and I've reviewed it, we will remove the gun and shells from the evidence locker"—Moore held up his hand, once again silencing Nelson—"and send them to Regina for whatever testing they need to do."

Moore motioned for Nelson to stand. "Right now, you're going to show me where you put the gun and shells Halden gave you. Then, they're going into the evidence locker."

As they left the interview room, Moore whispered, "And this bloody well better stay between us."

Moore watched Bouton usher Ouellet's Vancouver lawyer through the office and to the interview room. Unlike his predecessor, this lawyer was big in size as well as attitude. His displeasure over being kept waiting a few short minutes in the office entry was evident in the way he clenched the stub of cigar between his teeth, leaving great puffs of smoke in his wake. Given the cut and style of his suit, Moore wondered how Rod could afford to bring such a man all the way from Vancouver. When they were out of sight, Moore returned to reading the pink message slips that had accumulated on his desk while picking at the remaining half of the cheese sandwich Sam had made him. Dealing with his constables had unsettled him. The gun and shells were now safely tucked into the evidence locker, and he was expecting to see revised statements on his desk before the end of his shift.

The sharp trill of his phone broke through his reflection. "Yes?" he growled.

"Corporal Moore, we just had a call from a trucker travelling to Victoria who says he thinks he picked up your missing girl last night, east of Port Alberni."

Moore waited for the dispatcher to get on with the message. When she didn't, he asked, "He's just calling now?" Moore glanced at his watch. *One o'clock.*

"He says he didn't know we were looking for her until this morning, when he stopped at a diner and heard it from another trucker."

"Where is she now?"

"He doesn't know. She got out at Duncan."

"What's the guy's name and number?" Moore searched the mess on the top of his desk for a notepad. When he found it, he had to ask the dispatch clerk to repeat the information. He was told the trucker would be out of town until the weekend. Moore hung up and dialled the Duncan detachment.

The officer who answered didn't offer much in the way of additional information, and Moore rang off with no confirmation that the girl was even Conny. He was jotting a quick list of possible means of follow up, when he heard his name called.

Bouton indicated that he wanted Moore to join him. Moore grabbed his notebook and crossed the office. Bouton stopped him. "Time to see what else Mr. Ouellet has to say. This time I just want you to observe, nothing else."

Moore frowned. "You don't want me to assist?"

"No. Just take notes."

When they entered the interview room and took their seats, Rod appeared calm, while the new lawyer was as tense as a cobra with his hood flattened. He was by far the ugliest man Moore had ever seen. Pudgy features were crisscrossed with spider veins, and red welts crawled from beneath his crisp white shirt collar to spread up his neck and lower cheeks

"Maybe we can get started, Corporal?" Bouton asked.

"Yes, of course." Moore reached for the recorder. "Interview with Mr. Rodrique Ouellet, one-thirty p.m., Thursday, May 16, 1968. Ucluelet RCMP detachment, E-Division. Present are myself, Corporal David Moore; MCU Corporal Merle Bouton; and the prisoner's counsel, Mr. Kent Klein." He paused and turned to Bouton, waiting for him to begin the questioning.

Bouton looked up from the notes he was studying. "Mr. Ouellet, you mentioned in our earlier conversation that you operate a business delivering fish to the mainland. What do you bring back?"

Rod seemed startled by the question. He glanced at his lawyer, and back. "Nothing."

"Do you expect me to believe that you, as a businessman, would make the long journey back from Vancouver without a payload?"

Rod shrugged.

"So, the fish deliveries either provide a large enough profit margin to cover ferry fees and gas to and from Vancouver, or you're lying."

Klein leaned forward. Cool. Confident. "Are we here to question my client's business practices? Because if that's what you're doing, I'd suggest you check the sign outside this building. It identifies you as a policing agency, not a branch of the Better Business Bureau."

Moore looked up from his notes, opened his mouth, remembered Bouton's instructions, and closed it again.

A smirk played at the edges of Bouton's lips. "Thank you for pointing that out, Mr. Klein." Turning to Rod, he asked, "Do you know a Danny Brown?"

"No."

"Are you sure?"

Rod glared at Bouton. "I've never heard of him."

Moore studied Rod. He was lying. While his answer seemed quite firm, his eyes had done a brief flicker.

"That's interesting." Bouton tilted his head. "We found Mr. Brown buried in a cast-off pile behind an old prospector's shack."

Moore noticed a slight shift in Rod's posture and another quick glance at Klein.

"Did you not know Mr. Brown was dead?"

Rod raised his hands. "What's that got to do with me?"

Moore's eyes narrowed. He was about to ask a question, but Bouton shot him a warning glare.

"We learned that Mr. Brown had recently been hired as security for a company shipping fish to Vancouver," Bouton said.

"So what? I'm sure I'm not the only one shipping fish."

"That may be true, Mr. Ouellet, but we also learned the name of this company's boss. It was the same as yours. Rod."

Klein paused in his note-taking. "Asked and answered. Move on."

Bouton studied Rod before leaning forward and resting his elbows on the table. "We believe Danny Brown's murder is related to the Highway 4 incident, and that you are involved."

Rod leaned back, his eyes narrowing as he glared at Bouton.

"Where were you Saturday night, Mr. Ouellet?"

"The beer parlour."

"Which one?"

"There's only one in town. The Innlet."

"All night?"

"Until closing."

"And then where?"

"To bed."

"Anyone with you?"

Rod snorted.

Klein rested his hand on Rod's shoulder and faced Bouton. "Are you fishing, Corporal?"

Bouton rolled his head releasing soft snapping sounds as vertebrae shifted, then slowly turned his focus back on Rod. "Mr. Ouellet, I need you to explain to us, for the record, why a businessman and his associate would open fire on an RCMP officer?"

Klein sat up, but Rod placed a hand on his arm, stopping his protest. "No comment," he growled.

"Our previous conversation established that you knew Miss Lee was inside the officer's vehicle and that you wanted the constable to hand her over to you. But what we don't get is why?"

"No comment."

"What made you stop at that particular location?"

"No comment."

"There must have been some reason you stopped. You couldn't have known Constable Evans was going to be there at that time. So, what did you see that made you so angry you turned your vehicle around and, drove half-way back up the switchback before slamming on your brakes so hard your vehicle ended up sideways on the road? What was it that made you and Mr. Lehmann approach Constable Evans' patrol car, clearly marked as an RCMP vehicle, with guns raised?"

"No comment."

"Were you having a bad day? Decided to work it off with some pistol practice on a lone police officer?"

"He wasn't alone!"

"Miss Lee wasn't armed, so, Constable Evans was alone in protecting her."

"No comment."

Bouton leaned back in his chair. "Mr. Ouellet, along with your voluntary statements this morning, we have witness statements that indicate you not only knew Miss Lee was in the officer's vehicle, but that you wanted her out of it and brought to you. I ask you, Mr. Ouellet, what were Constable Evans and Miss Lee doing that prompted such an angry response?" He paused. "Are you the jealous type, Mr. Ouellet? Was the thought of your girlfriend—"

"Ex-girlfriend!"

"Excuse me, ex-girlfriend. Was the thought of her in a car with another man, parked in the middle of nowhere, just too much for you? Did you just have to teach her a lesson, even if she was with a cop? Maybe even *because* she was with a cop?"

"I don't care who she's fucking, okay? We were done! It was business! Just business. It didn't involve the cop. He's the one who came storming out of the car like we were in some cheap Western movie!"

"So, you claim you were just defending yourself?"

"No comment."

"We found several bullet holes in the constable's car, three matching where Constable Evans and Miss Lee were likely sitting and five in the door Constable Evans used to shield himself. I'd say that indicates they were deliberately shot at. Would that be a fair observation, Mr. Ouellet?"

"No comment."

"What do you mean by your statement, and I quote, 'It was just business?' Do you make a habit of shooting your business associates?"

"No comment."

Bouton shook his head, then stood. "Mr. Ouellet, I remind you that you have been charged under Section 210 of the Criminal Code of Canada, that on the fifteenth day of May 1968, you did attempt to murder Constable Halden Evans and Miss Conny Lee. You will continue to be held in custody until tomorrow morning when you will be brought before a magistrate to offer a plea."

Rod jumped out of his seat. "You can't—"

His lawyer rose as well. "Rod, shut up!"

Bouton stepped away from the table. "Corporal Moore, please escort Mr. Ouellet to his cell."

Moore turned to the recorder and terminated the interview before escorting Rod to his cell.

"I'll need time to consult with my client," Klein hissed.

42.

The late afternoon's warmth stayed with Sandy as she entered the lodge after her shift. Slipping out of her shoes, she gave a sigh of relief and padded across the kitchen floor to pour herself a large glass of water. She still hadn't gotten used to the taste of well water but had been assured by her roommates she would. After draining the glass, she returned to the entry where she pulled a *Victoria Daily Times* out of her purse and moved into the living room to drop onto the couch.

Silence. Taking a moment to enjoy being alone, she closed her eyes, and let the day's tension slip away. It had been difficult all day to focus on her job after hearing the gossip about what had happened on the switchbacks. With Robin's no radio, television, or newspapers policy, she had been unable to dispel the wild scenarios whirling through her mind. Then she'd found an abandoned newspaper in a guest's room with a brief story on the incident and brought it back to the lodge with her.

As she read, the main points of the gossip she'd overheard were supported but she was shocked to see Conny's name mentioned. The journalist gave no details about how Conny was involved, only that the police were asking for the public's help in locating her. Sandy couldn't fathom what Conny had gotten involved with, but she didn't want whatever it was to come back to the lodge. If Sandy left the drugs in their hiding spot, the police might end up suspecting that everyone in the lodge was involved in Conny's mess. Or worse, if Conny was holding the drugs for someone else and that person came looking for them—

Flippin' hell! She was beginning to hate Conny. Sandy stood, determined. She had to get rid of the drugs.

She was in the middle of removing the panel when she heard a knock on the lodge's front door. Sandy tried to slide the panel back in place, but it jammed halfway and defied her every attempt to unstick it. The knock came again. She heard the door open. *Crap!* She stepped out of Conny's room as Mark came around the corner. "Oh!"

"Hi." Mark smiled and held up a bottle. "I brought wine."

Sandy blinked at him, confused. "Did we make plans for tonight?"

A faint blush rose in Mark's cheeks. "No. It's just…I thought I'd chance it and see if you were in." His eyes flicked over Sandy's shoulder. "Are you in the middle of something?"

Sandy turned and realized he could see the jammed panel. "No…well, yes." She eyed the bottle he carried. "How about we open that first?"

"Sure." Mark stood back to allow her to lead the way into the kitchen.

Sandy dug through the dirty dishes in the sink to find the wine glasses she knew were there. "Ah-ha!" She freed the glasses and quickly washed them while Mark searched the cutlery drawer for the corkscrew.

Setting the glasses on the counter, Sandy waited while Mark opened the wine and poured generous helpings. "Did you know that Conny has run off?"

Mark tipped up the bottle. "I didn't. But I read about yesterday's shooting on the switchbacks. Apparently, the police are looking for her."

"M-m-m," she sighed. "This is much better than the last one."

"I figured that if I was going to introduce you to grown-up wine, I needed to offer a variety so you could find your own favourite. This is a merlot. Still full-bodied, but smoother on the tongue." He swirled the burgundy liquid in his glass. "So, what are you up to in the closet?"

Sandy considered not telling him, but after a moment's deliberation led Mark into Conny's room. She filled him in on the events that led to Conny's disappearance. "I thought I'd convinced her to stay, but she was gone by early yesterday morning. She took Tom's Mustang."

"I'm sure he appreciated that!"

"She'd sort of asked to borrow it earlier. Long story. Anyway, I was sure she was hiding something."

Mark laughed. "So, you went snooping."

Sandy blushed.

"What'd you find?"

Sandy handed her glass to Mark and stepped into the closet. "I found a hidden compartment with a stash of drugs." She pushed up on the panel, but it wouldn't budge.

Mark stepped forward, holding out both glasses. "Here, let me try."

Sandy took the glasses. "I put everything back because Roxanne said taking it to the police would be betraying Conny. But after hearing about the shooting and her involvement, I'm worried that Conny leaving this stuff here could cause more problems. I'm taking it in."

Mark worked the panel free and set it on the floor. "I agree with you." He looked in the hole. "Have you touched it?"

"Yes." Sandy frowned. "I pulled it out and looked through it. So did Roxanne."

"So, too late to worry about smudging fingerprints."

"Well, Conny would have done that already, if you're thinking about the prints from the person who sold her the drugs."

"Let's see." Mark opened the chocolate box and examined its contents. "Okay, you are definitely giving this to the cops." He raised his eyebrows. "She left? Without these?"

"Yes."

"Then she either left them for someone to pick up, or she abandoned them for some reason. Either way, you need them out of here."

"Conny was frightened of someone. Terrified. I think it was her boyfriend, Rod."

"The guy we met at the bar?"

Sandy nodded.

Mark closed the chocolate box and handed it to her.

Sandy sighed. "My dad used to get mom a box of these every Mother's Day. She would let me and my brother each choose one. I really wish it'd been chocolates inside."

"Do you have a phone here?"

"No. But there's one at the inn."

Mark returned the box to its hole. When he was finished, he reached for his glass and downed the remaining wine. "I'll run up to the inn and call the cops. Will you be all right here?"

She smiled and nodded.

"I'll be back in five minutes." He gave her hand a quick squeeze then left.

Sandy was curled up on the couch next to Mark when the knock at the door broke into their discussion about Andy Warhol's worth as an artist. Instead of getting up, she called out, "Come in!"

As expected, it was Corporal Moore, David, who walked in. He stopped when he saw them on the couch. "You called about some drugs you found?"

"I'll show you." Sandy led him to Conny's room and pointed out the hole in the back of the closet. "I found them after Conny left."

Moore stepped around Sandy and walked up to the closet. "We searched this room. How'd you find this? Did you already know it existed?"

"N-n-no. I just…I just got curious. I remembered the look on her face when I caught her packing Tuesday night. She seemed upset that I'd seen her in the closet."

Moore slipped a hankie out of his pocket and wrapped it around the end of the chocolate box as he pulled it out of the hole. He eased open the lid using the edge of the hankie and stared at the contents for a long time. "You have no idea how these got here?"

Seeing the way the officer handled the box, Sandy groaned. "You should know that I touched it. So did Roxanne and Mark. Our fingerprints will be all over it, as will Conny's."

Her comment seemed to amuse him. "Don't worry, Sandy. We'll figure it out."

His use of her first name and casual manner suddenly bothered her. *Was he making fun of her?* She straightened her shoulders and studied his face. She could read no cruelty there, but she saw disappointment. *What was he expecting?* "It was the syringes," she blurted. "I—I thought they could be connected to Geoff's murder."

Moore looked up at her. "Yes, good point." He shook his head. "I thought maybe…never mind." He pointed at the syringes. "Do you have any idea what they're used for?"

"No," Sandy said.

"They could be for heroin," Mark suggested. "It depends on what's wrapped in the tinfoil. I know there was heroin at last weekend's party."

Moore looked at Mark. "Did you notice any methamphetamine?"

"Speed? Not that I saw, but it was a large party, and I wasn't mixing." His expression turned soft when he glanced at Sandy. "I stuck to my own camp."

Moore returned the lid to the chocolate box and put it back where he'd found it. "I need to get my camera. I'll be right back."

Sandy and Mark moved back to the couch, each deep in their own thoughts. Mark refreshed their glasses. They heard Moore return and walk through to Conny's room.

Mark turned to Sandy. "Where are Roxanne and the others?"

"I think Roxanne's out with her boyfriend. I saw her get into a car as I left the inn." Sandy paused to sip her wine. "As far as I know, Edan and Tom are working."

"What were you going to do for supper?"

"There are leftovers in the fridge."

"How about I buy you supper at the inn?"

"Oh, well, I-I'm not sure."

"No pressure." Mark tilted his head toward the sound of Moore moving around in Conny's room. "It's kind of amazing how you figured out the drugs were there."

Sandy grinned. "I can't believe it myself. It was just this weird certainty that if I looked, I'd find something."

"Well, I'm impressed."

They sat in companionable silence, enjoying their wine, until Moore emerged, carrying the chocolate box wrapped in a plastic bag. "I'm going to take this into the office," he said. "I've sealed the room. No one is to go in there." He looked pointedly at Sandy. "Including you."

Sandy gave a mock salute. Moore rolled his eyes, then left.

Mark set his empty glass on the table. "How about that supper?"

43.

Moore found a bleary-eyed Nelson waiting at the office when he returned from Tofino. "You look terrible," he said. "Are you going to be okay for the rest of your shift?"

"Yeah." Nelson stood, holding out a sheet of paper. "My amended statement, as requested, sir."

The formality surprised Moore, but he understood the reason for it. Recovery from a superior officer's dressing down was never easy. "Thank you, Constable. I've just picked up Halden's."

"How is he?"

"Anxious to get out of there." Moore looked around the office. "The others leave?"

Nelson glanced at the auxiliary officer sitting at Evan' desk, then back at Moore. "Corporal Bouton left a while ago to meet Corporal McAteer at the hotel."

"I'll just drop this into the evidence locker and head next door." Moore tucked the chocolate box inside the evidence locker, next to Evans gun and shell casings. He pocketed the statements to read through later. Once again, he was late for supper.

The two-storey officers' residence next door was attached to the single-storey detachment office, the equivalent of a business owner living above his shop. The same advantages and disadvantages. No commute to work. Family close by. The flipside was the closeness made separating work and home life difficult. Then there was the building itself. Gary thought it looked as if two bricks were set together: one standing on end, the other lying on its side. Sam said the stark lines gave the building an institutional air. Moore agreed with both. Built in 1957, there had been no attempt by a string of resident officers to soften the exterior brick with landscaping or decorative features. After all, they rarely stayed longer than two years before being reassigned elsewhere.

As Moore opened the front door, sensory overload instantly engulfed him: the guttural bass of rock music boomed from Gary's bedroom, the pungent odour of dirty diapers mixed with the delectable scent of roasting chicken, and the screams of infant frustration was erupting from the kitchen.

"I'm home," he shouted into the chaos.

Sam poked her head out from the kitchen and laughed. "Welcome to paradise!"

Moore joined Sam just as Matthew, strapped into a highchair, released another ear-piercing scream. "What's your problem, little man?" Moore asked the pint-sized mix of his and Sam's features. He pressed a gentle kiss on the over-heated bundle of angry energy's soft head.

Sam gave up trying to coax Matthew into accepting his supper of mushy peas and dropped the spoon into the bowl. "He doesn't want to eat. He wants to keep playing with the new toy your mother sent him."

Moore leaned in and caught the pink softness of her lips in a kiss. "Don't give up. Stay strong," he whispered. When he pulled away, he was surprised to see a tear glistening on her eyelashes. She playfully swatted at him with her free hand.

He jumped aside, then went to the bottom of the staircase. "Gary! Turn off the music and come down for supper."

FRIDAY,
MAY 17, 1968

44.

Although a clear, bright sky was outside the office, the mood inside was as dense as low-hanging clouds. Everyone was in a foul mood and seemed determined to ignore everyone else by immersing themselves in the paperwork cluttering their desks. Neither of the specialist officers were in any hurry to rise and lead the morning's briefing. Moore reached for his coffee and then thought better of it. Whoever had made the pot that morning had taken their frustration out on the percolator, and it had spit forth black tar in response. He pushed away the mug. It was already six-fifteen, well past the time the morning briefing should have begun.

He squared his shoulders and rose. "Good morning, everyone."

Bouton started to rise, decided against it, and settled back again.

Momentarily distracted by Bouton's actions, Moore paused before proceeding. "As you can see, Constable Evans has rejoined us. He will be on desk duty until his doctor signs off on a return to regular duty." Pausing, he picked up a folder. "I'm going to kick off this morning by introducing a couple of revised statements provided by my constables." He held up the statements and glanced at Evans and Nelson. "The revisions describe Wednesday's incident on Highway 4 in greater detail, with the inclusion of a fourth gun."

"Fourth gun?" Bouton jumped up. "Whose?"

"Constable Evans', sir." Moore held up his hand to silence the inevitable protest. "I have discussed the implications of the situation with *my* constables and the matter has been settled." Moore stressed the possessive to re-establish his jurisdiction over his staff. "The gun and the spent shells are in the evidence locker and will be sent to Regina for processing as soon as possible."

"What was he doing with a second gun?" Bouton glared at Evans, who answered the silent challenge by lifting his chin and sitting up straighter.

Moore crossed the room to stand in front of Bouton, blocking the man's view of Evans. He placed the statements on Bouton's desk. "Constable Evans is a member of a Port Alberni gun club and had recently used the gun to practice at the local gravel pit. The events of the past week distracted him, and he had not yet returned the gun to its proper storage at home. He has already been reprimanded for that oversight," Moore said. "On Wednesday, he was under attack by two gunmen in a remote location, with an unarmed woman in the back seat of his vehicle. He can hardly be blamed for wanting to use every asset at his disposal to protect her."

Bouton scowled at Moore. "That doesn't forgive the fact he had the personal weapon in his patrol car in the first place."

"No, it doesn't. But, like I said, I've dealt with it." Turning away from Bouton, Moore returned to his desk, sending a reassuring smile to Evans on the way. *Maybe you won't be leaving us after all.*

Moore reached for his chair then changed his mind. He picked up a poster from his desktop and held it up.

"There is something else I need to bring up before we get back to discussing the cases." He faced the specialist officers. "My officers are aware of this event, but you may not be. A surfing competition is being held this weekend and there will be several officers from area detachments arriving later today to assist us with the expected long-weekend crowds, as well as those drawn to the competition. Tofino and this detachment will also be making use of available volunteer auxiliary officers. Auxiliary Officer Tim Owens, of course, will continue on night-shift guard duty of our prisoner."

Bouton looked at McAteer. "Sounds like we're on our own for the weekend."

Moore settled in his seat. "We'll assist where we can, but the weekend will strain our resources."

Bouton stood and walked to the chalkboard. "We all know how easily resources become strained. So, let's get through this." He wrote MISSING on the chalkboard beside Conny's name. "The Port Alberni officers' search for Miss Lee yesterday turned up nothing. Where the devil is she?"

"The only plausible report we've had came yesterday from a trucker who said he picked up someone matching her description late Wednesday night, just east of Port Alberni. He dropped her at a gas station in Duncan," Moore said. "We've alerted the Cowichan Valley and Victoria detachments. They'll hold her if she's found."

"I'm surprised—"

"There's been another development related to Miss Lee." Moore talked over Bouton's comment. "Last night, I was called out to the staff lodge at the inn by Mr. Mark

Wilson, who was there visiting Miss Chambers. Miss Chambers found a secret stash of drugs in Miss Lee's room."

A frown creased Bouton's brow. "Where? We searched her room."

"Well, we missed it." Moore shrugged. "There was a cut-away section in the back wall of her closet." He paused. "I went out hoping for something related to the box at the prospector's shack, but I don't think it is. Miss Lee didn't have nearly the amount suggested by the size of the metal box. It appears to be more of a dealer's package. Miss Lee may have been holding the package for a local dealer, or perhaps she was dealing herself. The package is in the evidence locker, awaiting transfer to the lab."

"We shouldn't assume it's hers," Nelson mumbled, but the comment was ignored as the conversation continued.

"What exactly did it contain?" McAteer asked. "And why didn't you take me with you?"

Moore sighed. "I understood you had your hands full at the garage processing the vehicles from the scene. But, you're right, I should have informed you. I apologize." He flipped through his notebook until he found the list. "To answer your question, I found five marijuana joints, ten blotter sheets of LSD tabs, two tinfoil packets containing a powder of some sort, and two syringes. All were stored inside a chocolate box. According to Miss Chambers, she and her roommate, Miss Roxanne Clark, examined the product inside the box. Mr. Wilson did not. Their fingerprints will also be all over the closet. I sealed the room for you."

McAteer pulled out his notebook. "I'll take a look. I doubt I'll get anything usable. Are you thinking we may have found a link to the injection site on the first murder victim?"

"It's possible. Neither of these syringes appears to have been used, so I don't think we've found the one used on our first victim. But if we find traces of meth inside either syringe, we can infer a connection, yes." Moore looked over at Evans, then back to Bouton. "Corporal Bouton, you will notice that in Constable Evans' statement, he said he received a verbal confession from Miss Lee relating to Mr. Johnston's death. She told the constable that the victim's death was accidental."

"You know that any statement she made to Constable Evans could be considered involuntarily compelled and therefore iffy as evidence."

Moore ignored Bouton's tone. "I'm confident that she'll confirm what she told Constable Evans when we apprehend her. If the death was an accident, the sloppy attempt to hide its cause makes sense."

"In the meantime, we're wasting time spinning our wheels."

The irreverent interaction halted conversation and an uncomfortable silence filled the room until Moore broke it. "Has anyone found the keys?"

"Keys?"

"The keys to Mr. Johnston's van."

"No."

Moore referred to his notebook. "We need to find the keys and the used syringe."

"Was the area around the van searched?" asked McAteer.

Moore took a moment before answering. "Unfortunately, not as a murder scene. At the time, remember, I was proceeding on the basis that this was a hit-and-run incident."

McAteer sighed. "It's probably too late now."

Moore frowned. "After a week's worth of traffic, there's no way we could take anything we found to court without them bringing up the question of contamination." He paused, thinking things through. "However, maybe we could use it to get a suspect talking." He considered his scribbled notes. "We've let people know to keep an eye open for the keys."

Evans cleared his throat. "It may be nothing, but since we're discussing loose ends, I feel I should bring it up." He waited to ensure he had everyone's attention before holding up Sandy's drawing of the scene. "I think I might have found what was used to beat Mr. Johnston's legs." Moore and the other officers gathered around Evans' desk. "I was looking at the way she'd drawn the body in the water and comparing it to my photographs when I noticed this." Evans pointed to the tip of a stick clearly sticking out of the ditch water in Sandy's sketch. "See how the tip is curved? Isn't that a familiar shape?"

"A paddle!" Moore cried out. "That's the grip of a paddle."

"Yes." Evans smiled. "That's what I think too."

Moore took the drawing from Evans. The blade of a paddle would have a curved edge, which could very well match the bruising on the victim's legs. "I'll take this and see if the paddle's still there. And…I'll have another conversation with Miss Chambers."

"You can take Liam with you. He needs to see if he can pick up anything from the closet." Bouton's look told Moore the company wasn't optional.

Moore took the drawing back to his desk and sat, watching as the others returned to their desks. He wondered if anyone else noticed that Bouton had been using McAteer's first name. *Is it a signal that the team can refer to them by their first names?*

Bouton looked over at Nelson. "You're awfully quiet this morning, Constable Nelson. Have you been able to find the missing Indian?"

Nelson looked over at Moore, face crumpled in confusion.

Moore smiled. "He means Steve."

Nelson nodded. "Oh. Right. Yes, I think I know who he is, but I haven't had the opportunity to speak with him. I plan on doing that this evening."

"Ask him if he recognized anyone else on the path at that time." Moore picked up his pen, then set it back down, forgetting what he'd intended to write. "If we're lucky, maybe our killer was skulking along, twisting his moustache in that telltale manner of all proper villains."

Nelson offered a tentative smile. "Will do."

Bouton looked out at the group. "As you may know, Mr. Ouellet has been charged with the attempted murders of Constable Evans and Miss Lee. I feel confident these charges will stand up in court." He paused. "What we haven't got is evidence connecting him to the murder of Mr. Brown."

"Are we sure?" Moore asked. "Mr. Ouellet admitted to operating a business that hauls fish to the Vancouver market. Danny's wife said a man named Rod, who was shipping fish to Vancouver, hired him."

"And how does shipping fish to Vancouver relate to a prospector's shack or the suspected theft of drugs from that shack or the beaten body found there?"

Moore walked up to the chalkboard. "Miss Lee is a known associate of Mr. Ouellet's. She's connected to the drug trade through the dealer's kit hidden in her closet. I'm sure if we make some inquiries on the beach, we'll find out whether the kit was hers or her boyfriend's. Either way, we know Mr. Ouellet was in the company of a member—and, from what I saw of the tattoo on his wrist, is a member himself—of the Mangosta, who are, if they're a typical gang, suppliers."

"So, you're saying drugs are the connection?" Bouton challenged; frustration written all over his face. "Who stole the drugs? Or are you saying that Ouellet and his crew just moved them?"

"Then why kill Danny?" Nelson asked.

Evans jumped in. "Then there are Miss Lee's bruises. She was beaten, I would swear to it. Not like Danny. I don't think the intent was to kill her." He glanced from Bouton to Moore. "I think it was a warning…and that could be why she's taken off."

"The trouble is, we need proof—hard evidence—to make the connections stand up in court," Bouton pointed out.

Evans pushed on. "When we find Miss Lee, I'm sure she'll provide that proof."

"Figuring out if those syringes contained meth will go a long way to helping us get that proof," McAteer offered.

"Especially if we can connect them to whatever was in that metal box. We need to get the rest of the evidence to the lab as soon as possible."

"I'll take it," Evans volunteered. "I'm no good for much else. I can sit behind a desk, or I can sit behind the wheel of a car."

Bouton shot an incredulous look at Evans. "You don't have a car, and you can't drive your own evidence—"

"Oh. Right." With a flush burning his cheeks, Evans sank further into his chair.

"You also need to rewrite the report you're presenting to the magistrate this morning." Bouton turned to Moore. "I'll accompany Constable Evans and Mr. Ouellet to court."

Moore tried not to show his disappointment. He had hoped to accompany the prisoner. "When you get back, Constable Evans, you can go through the messages we received in response to the ad placed in the paper," Moore said. "It came out yesterday and the messages are piling up."

Evans stood and gathered the stack from Moore's desk.

Moore wrote and underlined THE DRUG SQUAD in his notebook. "Has the new drug squad heard anything about a large amount of methamphetamine or LSD being shipped this way?"

"I don't know." Bouton rolled a piece of chalk between his palms. "I'm not sure if they're that organized yet. I'll find out."

"Was there anything in Rod's panel truck?" Moore asked.

"I've only just started on Constable Evans' vehicle. I sent in a request for help processing the vehicles, but I'll be lucky if I get any. Nanaimo's still running short-staffed. I'll know later today if anyone shows up."

Moore sighed, rolling his shoulders to release the tension knotting his muscles. The logistics of the double murder investigation and the time involved was draining his energy and patience.

Bouton scanned the notes scrawled across the chalkboard. "Has anyone checked out the other prospector's shack, the one Mr. Ricci said was occupied?"

Moore felt his shoulder muscles tighten once more. "I'll add it to my list."

"I'll join you, sir," Nelson offered.

"No, Monty, you're on night shift, remember? You'll be busy with the insanity of the long weekend and the surfing competition."

"I'll come with you Corporal Moore," Bouton announced. "Corporal McAteer, you shouldn't need more than half an hour to process Miss Lee's closet. How about you drive out with Corporal Moore, and I'll join you after court. That way, you can take my vehicle and get back to processing the vehicles while Corporal Moore and I locate the other shack."

"Sir, I won't be riding out with Corporal Moore." McAteer stepped forward. "I processed Mr. Robinson's car and found no sign of drugs."

Bouton frowned. "I'm surprised by that, given his past and the people he's associated with in Vancouver."

"I can only tell you what I found. Or didn't find, in this case. His car is clean. If I'm going out to the lodge, I might as well return it."

Moore placed Sandy's drawing and a pad of lined paper in a file folder. "Fine, then," he said. "Let's get started."

"Hold on," Bouton cautioned. "We haven't had breakfast yet." He motioned to McAteer. "We'll be back in an hour."

Moore dropped into his chair as he watched the two corporals head out the door. Sam had fixed him breakfast, as she did every morning, so it wasn't hunger that made his stomach churn. It was the obvious snub. Was it deliberate?

"You okay, sir?"

Moore waved Evans' concern away and pulled the phone forward.

45.

A bank of cool air had slid in off the Pacific Ocean, erasing the promise of what had been shaping up to be a beautiful spring day as Moore pulled into the Wickaninnish Inn's parking lot. A moment later, he caught the guttural rumble of Tom's Mustang. McAteer cruised up the driveway and into the space beside him. "It's just after eleven o'clock," Moore shouted across to McAteer. "Mr. Robinson should still be at the lodge. How about I meet you over there after I deal with Miss Chambers? I shouldn't be more than fifteen minutes." McAteer nodded and headed toward the laneway leading to the lodge.

Moore sucked in a deep breath, determined to dispel the negative energy lingering from the morning's briefing. After a quick stop at the front office, he bounded up the stairs to the second floor. A chambermaid's cart in the hallway provided him with a clue to which room she was in. He tapped on the open door beside it. "Hello?"

Sandy poked her head out of the bathroom. "Hi."

"Do you have a minute to answer a couple of questions?"

"Sure." Sandy threw the rag she'd been cleaning with into the bucket by the tub and stepped into the main room.

Moore opened the file he carried and pulled out her drawing. "Could you explain something you drew?" He pointed to the object sticking out of the water. "What is this?"

"Oh. It's a paddle I saw in the ditch." Concern clouded her eyes. "You told me to draw everything I remembered about the scene."

"Yes. Yes, I did. And thank you. You did a great job." Moore turned the drawing back to its original position and closed the file folder. "I stopped on the way here to see if I could find it, but I couldn't. You didn't happen to move it?"

"No." Sandy closed her eyes briefly, as if trying to recall something. "Um, it wasn't there when I took Geoff's parents to the place."

"When was that?"

"Tuesday. About four."

Moore considered this new information. "Do you think it just got pushed further into the brush?"

Sandy shook her head. "I don't think so. I looked. I even walked up and down that road. Without the paddle, I had trouble remembering exactly where I found Geoff."

"But you found the spot eventually?"

"Yes…At least, that's what I told the Johnstons."

"But you're not one hundred percent sure you were looking in the right place?"

"It was so foggy Saturday morning, remember? And a lot was going on."

Moore considered what the absence of the paddle meant to the case. Not much. It wasn't the murder weapon. They knew that. If it was underwater, maybe it was worth pulling on a pair of wading boots and searching. If he was lucky enough to find it, would any fingerprints remain intact? He scratched his neck in frustration and noticed

Sandy was watching him. "I understand the parents have left," he said.

"Yes. They went to Nanaimo to wait until Geoff's body is released."

"Do you know the name of the hotel?"

"The Hyatt House Motel. Near the airport."

After entering the name in his notebook, Moore made a note for himself to ask McAteer if fingerprints survived submersion in water.

"Did you see the whole paddle? Or just the part extending from the water?"

"I saw most of it. I had to move it out of the way to pull Geoff out of the water."

So her prints would be on it too. Moore frowned. "Did the blade of the paddle have—"

"I just realized"—Sandy flapped her hands excitedly—"the paddle was from Geoff's van!"

"What?"

Eyes dancing, Sandy beamed. "I knew it! There was something about that paddle. It hung on the inside wall of his van, over the bed! Someone had painted on it. Surfers. There were surfers, waves, and a sun."

Moore was stunned. If the paddle was from Geoff's van, then that changed things. He started to pace as he ran through the implications, then realizing Sandy was staring at him, he mumbled a quick apology and made to leave but stopped and turned to face her. "Did Geoff ever mention that he was diabetic?"

"No. He only said he had to watch what he ate and drank." She paused, tilting her head. "So, he was diabetic? Is it fatal?"

"Not with proper treatment."

Sandy's brows drew together. "Is that what happened? Conny gave him something that caused it?"

"That's not how it works. Why do you think Conny had anything to do with it?"

Sandy quickly glanced past Moore's shoulder to the outer hallway then back at him. "She just acted strange about a couple of things."

"What things?"

"I can't really remember, but at the time, I thought she was being weird."

They stood in silence, both deep in thought, until Sandy blurted, "I've got to get back to work."

"Of course." Moore left the room and headed for the stairs.

46.

Moore was troubled by the differences between the two murders. Geoff's seemed chaotic, almost amateur, compared to Danny's. As he stepped onto the porch at the lodge, he remembered how excited he'd been at having his first murder case and his expectations of career advancement. Now, after experiencing the reality of trying to solve not just one, but two murders, he felt humbled by how much he still had to learn.

He found McAteer in Conny's closet. "Find anything?"

"There's too much here." McAteer scowled. "Too many people have been in here. I haven't been able to pick up a single clear print."

Moore offered him a sympathetic smile. He was beginning to understand the level of concentration it must take to do the specialist officer's job. "Well, I'll get out of your way."

In the kitchen, Tom stood at the counter munching a bowl of Cocoa Puffs.

"Did Corporal McAteer tell you he brought your car back?"

Mouth still full, Tom nodded.

"Terry fixed the punctured tires."

"I noticed."

"He runs a top-notch garage."

Tom shovelled another spoonful of cereal into his mouth.

Moore watched him for a moment before asking, "Have you heard anything about a large supply of methamphetamine or other drugs coming into the area?"

Tom paused mid-chew. "No. Why?"

Moore took a moment to consider what he was about to do. Tom was friendly, charming; and if his history was to be believed, he had the background to move easily between social circles. Moore pegged him as a bored, spoiled rich kid, not a murderer. Still, it was a big risk. He'd never had to develop a source; it always seemed like something reserved for a big-city scene. But then, he'd never had to deal with a murder investigation before, let alone two. He decided to take a chance. "We believe a new supply in the area was stolen. We're not sure if it's being offered locally, or if this location is nothing more than a transportation stopover point."

Tom's eyes narrowed. "Why should I care?"

"Rumour has it that you want to return to the mainland. I figured that helping the police with a murder investigation might be one way to convince your father you've changed since coming here."

Tom set down his cereal bowl, his eyes fixed on Moore. "Do you want some coffee?"

Moore glanced at the cluttered counter and empty stove. "Is it fresh?"

"It will be." Tom disappeared into one of the bedrooms. When he came out, he was holding a packet of coffee. "My private stash," he said. "Columbian. Arabica beans. Roasted with care. *Not* instant."

Moore couldn't hide his grin of anticipation. They slipped into a companionable silence as Tom set up the electric percolator. When the coffee began to drip the room filled with the sweet, satisfying scent of a rich coffee. Tom broke the spell. "Just how much of a supply are you talking about?"

"We're not sure. The container was approximately the size of a small suitcase."

Tom whistled. "That's a lot of meth. Could it have held something else, as well?"

"What are you thinking?"

"Guns."

It took effort not to show his shock. *I really am a small-town cop.* "That's possible. What made you think of guns?"

"If serious drugs are coming into the area, you'd better believe the muscle and weapons needed to protect them will come too."

Of course. He may not have had much experience with the drug trade, but he knew it was competitive. If Rod and his associates were here, others would follow—if they hadn't already. Moore shook his head. He had wanted the West Coast to remain wild and, in a way, innocent. The residents were always telling him that when the road from the east coast of the island opened in 1959, everything had changed. Peace. Innocence. They were slipping through the fingers of the long-time locals. He just hadn't wanted to believe it. Guns. Of course there'd be guns. It had been right there in Rod's eyes when they interviewed him. "You're saying whatever was in there was worth killing for."

Tom leaned against the counter and studied the floor for a minute. "Are you talking about the guy you found behind the prospector's shack?"

Moore sighed. *Small towns.*

"From what I heard, he was a nice guy. He didn't deserve to die like that."

"Don't stick your neck out, but if you hear anything, I'd appreciate you letting me know." Moore reached into his breast pocket and pulled out a business card. "Call any time. We need to get these guys."

"I smell coffee," said McAteer, wandering out of Conny's room with hope in his eyes. "Good coffee."

"It's perking," Tom said.

"Are you ready to go?" Moore couldn't keep the disappointment out of his voice. The coffee smelled wonderful.

"No. I've a bit more to do."

Moore smiled. "Great."

"Great?"

"I meant—"

"It's okay. I know what you meant." McAteer gazed longingly at the percolator. "Just bring me a cup when it's done."

Moore noticed the dark shadows under the IS officer's eyes. He should have realized the specialist officers were under just as much, if not more, pressure than he was—and all those drives to and from Nanaimo couldn't have helped. "You've got a lot on your plate. Is there anything I can do to help?"

"No." McAteer dismissed the offer with a wave of his hand. "I'm hoping the identification specialist I requested will show up this afternoon, but the department's stretched thin, so who knows."

As McAteer headed back to Conny's room, Moore turned to Tom and smiled. "How's the coffee coming?"

47.

Fog shrouded the forest lining the Tofino–Ucluelet Highway as Moore pulled his patrol car into the narrow opening between the tangled brush crowding the Lost Shoe Creek trailhead. "The shack we're looking for, according to Jim, should be to the right of the path, about fifteen minutes in," Moore explained.

Bouton nodded and opened the passenger door, unfolding his six-foot-five-inch frame and took a deep breath. His brow furrowed as he looked to where the path disappeared into a darkening forest.

Seeing Bouton's uncertainty, Moore realized the other man wasn't comfortable in the forest. This, he hoped, meant he wouldn't have a repeat of the humiliating trek he'd had with Monty. "You've probably noticed how Mother Nature can be quite moody on the West Coast!"

"Are you sure this is the same path we took on Monday?"

"It's the same path. You just approached from the beach on Monday. We're approaching from the highway end today because Mr. Ricci described the second prospector's shack as being closer to this end of the trail." Moore paused. "I never asked you, sir, where are you from?"

Taken aback, Bouton looked across the vehicle's roof at Moore. "Toronto."

Moore hid his smile as he walked around the back of the car. *That explains a lot.* "How long have you been posted in Victoria?"

"A year."

Moore took the lead and moved down the path, Bouton following close behind. "I grew up in Calgary. Dad was a city cop and never had any desire to move away. I didn't understand it when I was younger. Couldn't wait to get away. That's why I joined the RCMP rather than following in my father's footsteps. I liked the idea that the Force moved its people around, never too long in one place." He stepped over a fallen log, watchful for any broken branches sticking up through the undergrowth. "Now that I have kids, I understand the choice he made."

Bouton was silent for so long that Moore looked over his shoulder just to make sure the man was still following him. Bouton caught him looking and smiled. "My father was a Toronto city councillor. He was strongly opposed to my joining the Force and used his influence to keep my postings nearby."

"Toronto?"

"Toronto, London, Hamilton—"

"All cities?"

"Didn't want his son mixing with the hicks."

"I've had the opposite. All small towns so far."

The path led them through the fringe of brush to a border of Sitka Spruce, Douglas fir, and hemlock. Wisps of ghost-like fog drifted around the dark trunks and a jumble of rotting logs abandoned where they fell, evidence of an earlier harvest of the area's marketable lumber. Moore walked in silence, thinking of how each of their fathers had impacted their careers. He had no regrets. The decisions he had made had led him to this wet, magical place. A light tap on his shoulder pulled him from his thoughts.

"There," Bouton whispered, pointing to their right.

At first, Moore could see nothing. Then, between the drooping boughs of a western hemlock, he picked out the rough-cut cedar shingles of a small shack. He motioned for them to carry on and searched for access across the creek running along the deep trench between them and the shack. Gradually working down through the trees, they found a narrow path winding along the water that led to a bridge made of rough-cut planks nailed to two logs laid across the creek. It proved stronger than it looked and they quickly crossed.

Signalling for Bouton to stop, Moore pointed to where the shack's south-facing wall appeared over the ridge shelf above them. "Jim said he was warned off by a shotgun."

At Bouton's silent nod, Moore led them up the slope through a thicket of salal bush. As they drew even with the shack, Moore unclipped the cover of his holster and heard Bouton do the same. Slowly they moved around to the front, where they discovered a man leaned back in his porch chair, a cup of steaming coffee in one hand and a shotgun in the other.

"What do you want?" the man demanded.

With the business end of shotgun pointed at them Moore turned to face the man directly, his brown eyes boring into the blue-green depths of the older man's. "Are you Marco?"

"Who wants to know?"

"I'm RCMP Corporal David Moore and this is MCU Corporal Merle Bouton. We wanted to talk to you about Danny Brown."

Lifting the shotgun from its defense position, the old man leaned it against the wall of the shack and rose from his chair. "I'd better put more coffee on," he said, before disappearing into the shack.

Moore reclipped the strap over his gun and looked at Bouton, who was doing the same. He then climbed the porch steps, noticing a half-eaten peanut butter sandwich sitting on a stump used as an outside table. The paperback resting face down next to it was Ian Flemming's *For Your Eyes Only*. An interesting choice.

Moore stepped through the door. The man was pouring water from a jug into a pan sitting on the wood stove. A jar of instant coffee sat on the counter. Moore glanced around the shack's interior. The furnishings were practical, like the other shack, but didn't have the same feel. Instead of mismatched found objects thrown together, the space held handcrafted cabinets and cupboards. Even the table and chairs, though simple in design, displayed a quality of workmanship that impressed Moore. "Did you know Danny Brown?" he asked.

The old man turned and nodded. "Heard what happened to him too." His brow furrowed as he returned to preparing the coffee.

Moore pushed on. "I understand from his wife that you told him to quit the job."

"Yeah, I did."

"Why?"

"He said he was guardin' office supplies, furniture and stuff, meant for a business goin' into that boathouse that burned down." He shook his head slowly. "No way anyone screws windows shut for furniture."

"You saw the windows?" Bouton joined Moore in the doorway.

Turning to face them, Marco nodded. "Yeah, just like I saw the size of the padlock on the door and the blacked-out windows."

"When was this?" Bouton asked.

Marco pulled the boiling water off the stove and poured the steaming liquid into two mugs sitting on the wooden counter, then topped up his own. After adding coffee crystals, he handed a mug to each man and motioned for them to take the two chairs at the table. Moore and Bouton sat while the old man leaned against the counter. No sugar or milk was offered. Bouton repeated his question.

Marco shifted his gaze to the forest outside the still-open door. "When I was on my way back here from the beach on Saturday mornin', I spotted a spiral of smoke comin' from the area of the old Johnston shack and decided to check it out. That's when I saw Danny."

"The Johnston shack?"

"Yeah, Aaron Johnston. He came here about the same time I did—1928 or '29."

Moore pulled out his notebook. "Related to James Johnston?"

"Grandad."

"So, the shack was owned by Aaron Johnston, James' grandfather."

"That's what I said, 'cept it ain't owned. Like mine. I don't own nothin' but the right to search for gold, minerals. We're squatters, same as those hippies on the beach."

"Who owns the land?"

"Some developer back in 1914 subdivided the land, even sold a couple of lots, but not many. Don't know if he still owns the strip Johnston and I are on, or if ours were sold. He had a tough time gettin' rid of it. Nobody wanted to live way out here, 'specially when you had to bushwhack your way in. Now, of course, everyone's waitin' to see what the government does with the park they want to bring in."

Moore's mind raced. "What time on Saturday?"

Marco looked down at the floor and then back at Moore. "Must've been about two-thirty, three, sometime thereabouts."

"In the morning?"

"Yeah."

"You were at the beach party?"

Moore looked up from his note-taking and caught the look of disbelief on Bouton's face, and he smiled.

"Yeah. I'd gone to get supplies for my arthritis. It's been givin' me horrible trouble the last month."

Bouton sent a quick look across the table to Moore. "Supplies?"

"Marijuana. There's a strong belief in natural medicine up here," Moore explained. Turning to face Marco, he asked, "You hadn't noticed anyone at the Johnston place before that? I ask because Lisa Brown said her husband took the job about two weeks prior to his death. It seems strange that you wouldn't have spotted Danny, or a day guard, before Saturday."

"Don't usually come that way." He waved his hand to the right. "I come across the top."

Moore noted that Marco was indicating the hill beside his shack.

"Or from the highway."

"So, you were curious about the campfire?" Bouton prompted.

"And that's where I found Danny, sittin' by the fire."

"What'd you do?"

"Well, I sat down and asked what he was doin', didn't I?" Marco sipped his coffee. "He told me about the guardin' business."

Moore looked at Bouton. "Did he mention a name?"

"Nah, but I think it must've been the same guy I saw in the woods a couple weeks back. Rod somebody."

Bouton leaned forward, and Moore almost copied him but checked himself in time. "What made you think that?"

Marco looked from one to the other. "I was workin' up a vein about ten minutes from here and heard voices. It was strange. The voices were all serious like. Not…you know, hippie talk. Besides hippies don't usually come across the top. I wanted to check it out, but I made sure I wasn't seen." He placed his mug on the counter. "They were on that trail that comes from that old road that cuts off Long Beach Road." He looked at Moore. "You must know the one. Runs along the small bog and gets too muddy to pass through in the winter."

Moore nodded.

"There were three of them: two men and a girl. One was a guy named Rod. He was in charge—or at least the one the other two were trying to please. They were talkin' about havin' found the perfect place to stash somethin'. I didn't catch what that was or anythin' like that. I got the sense that it would do me no good to be discovered. I skedaddled back here."

"You're sure about the name Rod?"

"Yeah. I didn't recognize the girl at the time. Knew her voice, just couldn't place it. Then Saturday mornin' at the bonfire, I saw her and realized who she was. Don't know her name, but she works at the inn. I've seen her in the lounge. I don't think she's a waitress. When she's been there, it's as if she's finished her shift and was enjoyin' a bit of relaxation afterward."

"How do you know she works there?"

"Because the bartender would ask her how her shift went, or they'd comment on their work day. You know, insider jokes." Marco paused. "He'd know her name."

Moore didn't have to ask the bartender; he knew exactly who she was. Conny.

Bouton pulled out his notebook. "Can you describe her?"

"In the woods? Naw. She wore a rain slicker, and she was turned away from me. But she's always done up real nice in the lounge. Auburn hair styled and stiff. You know, like the girls do now. Shoulder-length. Even in jeans and a T-shirt, she's a looker."

"Did you get the impression they planned to use the Johnston shack for whatever it was they wanted to stash?" Bouton asked.

"Yeah." Marco looked Moore in the eye. "When I saw Danny there, I knew that's what it was. That's why

I warned him to leave that job. This Rod guy wasn't the type someone like Danny should be workin' for."

Moore nodded, deep in thought.

Bouton stood and handed Marco his empty mug. "Do you think Rod killed Danny?"

Marco hesitated. "Can't say for sure. When did he die?"

As Moore placed his empty mug on the counter, he caught sight of a cereal box tucked against the side of the open-shelf cupboard to Marco's left. It had a ripped top. Moore stared at it, the tiny wires in his brain sizzling.

"Somethin' wrong with your coffee?"

Startled from his thoughts, Moore found Marco scrutinizing him, a frown creasing his brow. "No. The coffee was fine." He shook his head. "What was I saying? Oh yeah. After what you've described, we'll have to say he died sometime early Sunday. Did you know him well?"

"To see around, yeah. I knew what he did for the local kids, though. A nice guy."

"He was," Moore started to leave, then turned back. "Why hadn't you seen his campfire smoke before?"

Marco tilted his head to indicate the single bed tucked up against the windowless side wall. "I'm usually in bed right after supper. The mornin' comes early for me."

"Then Saturday morning was an exception?"

Marco gave a sharp nod of his head. "Gets lonely here sometime, and I gives myself a treat of company by goin' to the inn for a drink, or hangin' down at the beach with the young people once in a while."

Moore gave one last, quick glance around. "Thanks again for the coffee and the information." He handed the old man his card. "Drop in if you think of anything else."

When they reached the makeshift bridge, Bouton stopped, pulled out a cigarette and offered the pack to Moore. Moore shook his head and stepped onto the bridge. "Sounds as if we've got our connection," he said.

"Um."

Once he was safely on the other side of the creek, Moore turned to study Bouton. "You don't think so?"

"I'm not sure. We still don't know what was in the steel box. The traces imply there were drugs at one point, but when? And why kill Danny?" Bouton passed Moore and led the way up the path to the highway.

Moore followed in silence, then stopped. "Do we know if there's a rival gang to the Mangosta?"

Bouton snorted. "There are always rival gangs, but I'll check if any specific one has made a move on the Mangosta."

"At least we've narrowed the window for Danny's time of death."

48.

The fog had rolled in by the time Tom left the lodge. It made everything seem timeless, but a quick glance at his watch showed it was already halfway through the day. He headed across the parking lot, looking for his Mustang. As he approached, the sight of it almost overwhelmed him. *His* car. Bought and paid for with money he had earned working at a bar in Gastown, Vancouver. It was the first car his father had not bought for him and, because of that, it was a weapon each had used to hurt the other.

Tom didn't want to think about what he would have done if it hadn't come back to him.

The afternoon light, filtered through the fog, muted his reflection in the side-door panel, but he smiled at his image as if it were glossy and sharp. Owen had washed it for him, good man. He opened the door and sank into his seat. The interior had been cleaned, too; no trace of the police search remained. Owen had outdone himself.

Feeling better than he had in a while, Tom turned the key in the ignition and felt the rumble of the engine vibrate through the car. He had decided to drive into Ucluelet the moment the cop mentioned the suitcase-sized box. Tom was familiar with such packages. He had seen them being carried into the back rooms of various downtown Vancouver bars. If such a package was here, and the contents stolen, something slimy had just oozed into paradise.

He backed out of the parking spot and spun the Mustang around to head up Long Beach Road to the highway and Ucluelet.

Fifteen minutes later, Tom pulled up in front of Janet's place in Ucluelet. Known for nightly parties and a premium supply of BC Bud, Janet's had become the closest the small town had to an institution. He was surprised at how shabby it looked in the daylight, then realized he'd never visited the place except after the beer parlour closed. The paint was peeling off the porch planks, the siding, and the door. The windows were cloudy and smeared. Obviously, Janet wasn't worried about curb appeal. Tom stopped in his tracks. *I'm starting to sound like my dad!*

After pounding on the door three times, the familiar hulk of Janet's regular bouncer opened it. "What do you want, Tom?" He waved to the sign tacked by the door. "We're closed."

Tom couldn't remember the man's name. "Janet? Is she up?"

"Yeah, she's up. What d'ya want?"

"I just want to talk." Tom glanced around to make sure no one on the street could overhear him. "Have you heard about Danny?"

The hulk didn't acknowledge the question, just stood back and motioned for Tom to enter. The shabbiness of the exterior continued inside. Tom waited until the bouncer closed the door and indicated for him to follow.

When the man turned right and started climbing the stairs to the second storey, Tom raised his eyebrows in surprise. He had expected to be led to the kitchen.

Following the mass of muscle up the stairs, Tom decided to admit his faulty memory. "Hey, man, I'm sorry. I can't remember your name."

The hulk stopped and slowly turned to look down at Tom. "Jay," he said, reaching out a hand.

Tom hesitated before extending his own hand, afraid it would be crushed in a powerful establishment of male dominance, but Jay's handshake was almost gentle. Tom was speechless.

After releasing Tom's hand, Jay turned and continued climbing the stairs. At the landing, he tapped lightly on a door to the right. "Janet," he said softly. "It's Jay. I have Tom here. He's heard about Danny."

Tom couldn't make out the muffled reply, but Jay opened the door and motioned for Tom to enter. Janet lay in bed, propped into a half-sitting position by a mound of pillows. A white gauze bandage encircled her head and covered her right eye, giving her a lopsided appearance. She offered Tom a quick smile, then grimaced, touching her hand to her split lip.

Jay grabbed a tissue from the bed-side table and handed it to her.

Tom shifted his gaze away from her face, swallowing the lump in his throat. This wasn't the brash, ball-buster, party-house hostess he knew. This girl was vulnerable and he instinctively wanted to protect her. Janet's right arm was encased in a plaster cast up to the elbow and was supported by a sling. The skin of her upper arm that peeked out from underneath the short sleeve of her pink nightshirt was marbled with the blue and yellow of healing bruises, as was the skin at her neck and chest. "What happened to you?"

"They picked her up on her way back from the store." Jay answered for her.

"They?"

"The new shit in town."

Tom frowned. "I don't—"

"They didn't identify themselves. They just brought her back here and, well—"

Tom didn't have to imagine what they'd done to her; he could see it. "What did they want?"

"They kept asking her about a stolen shipment."

"Why did they think she had anything to do with it?" Too late, Tom realized he'd given away his prior knowledge of the shipment.

The bouncer gave him a strange look and was about to say something when Janet spoke. "Don't…know." The words came out in short bursts. "Thought…Danny and I…had taken it."

Glancing quickly at Jay, now slouched at Janet's bedside, Tom asked, "Danny? What's Danny got to do with it? Why would they think you two were linked? Are you involved with Danny?"

"Of course not!" boomed the bouncer. "She's with me. They were just morons! Someone must've told them Danny was bringing in stuff for Janet on his boat."

"Danny would never…have done that," Janet croaked. "They had…the wrong guy."

Tom's stomach twisted with sudden nausea. *This is worse than I imagined.*

"They left her a bloody mess. I didn't find her until that night." Jay leaned in and kissed her bandaged brow, whispering, "I should have been here, babe."

"When was this?"

"Sunday."

The day before they discovered Danny. Tom tried to keep his voice neutral, even. "Where were you?"

"It was my day to visit my kid."

Janet reached out with her good hand and touched Jay's arm. "It's…okay."

Tom considered what he knew as he ran a hand through his hair. "They wouldn't have done this unless it was a serious stash and they thought you knew where it'd been taken. Do you?"

Janet started to shake her head but froze, pain clear on her face.

Jay gripped Janet's hand. "She told them Danny would never steal anything, especially drugs. And she had only referred Danny to Conny when she came looking for a guard. She had no idea about any stolen shipment." He closed his eyes and Tom could tell he was struggling to keep his emotions in check. "But no matter what they did to her, she wouldn't give them Danny's last name or where he was from. She didn't want them going after Lisa. You know, Danny's wife."

"How big of a stash are we talking about?"

"They kept demanding she owed them ten grand."

Tom was stunned. "That's a serious stash. And you have no idea who they were?"

"We've seen them around town. They've got some deal with the fishermen to truck their fish to Vancouver, but everyone knows there's more to it."

Tom closed his eyes. *Do I want to stick out my neck this far for you, Conny?* If this led where he thought it was obviously leading, it was serious. He took a deep breath. They needed to spell things out pretty damn clear if he was going to jump into this pile of shit. "What do you mean?"

"They have that…look," Janet whispered. "You know. Connected."

Tom swallowed, knowing exactly what she meant. "Any idea who they're connected with?"

Janet and Jay both shook their heads.

"Shit," Jay said. "They're connected to city shit."

Janet reached for a glass of water on her side table. Jay picked it up and held it to her lips while she drank. When she'd had her fill, he placed it back on the table. Janet sighed. "Tattoo…like a mink…killing a snake."

Tom rubbed his hands over his face. He didn't know much about gangs. His involvement in Vancouver's drug scene had been strictly as a customer. Privileged West Vancouver partiers never thought about the dirty underbelly of their party treats. "Do you think they're making a move?"

"If they're going to the trouble of establishing a transport company, they're doing more than selling to tourists on the beach," Jay said.

"A friend said…Jackals…partying on the beach last weekend," Janet whispered.

"Jackals?"

Jay touched Janet's shoulder. "They were probably just checking out the beach like all the other tourists, babe."

Tom didn't like the sound of this. "Have you heard about any large amounts of meth coming in?"

Janet glanced at Jay, who answered. "We've had requests for it. Same as heroin. But we don't hold with that stuff. MJ, a bit of acid. That's all."

Tom remembered how he'd felt after the party Saturday night. "Has there been any changes to your supply lately?"

"No…I don't—"

"We hired a new driver," Jay pointed out. "Why?"

"There was a difference in the feel of a hit I took at the party last weekend."

"You think someone's messing with our stuff?"

Tom shrugged. "What are you going to do?"

"We haven't decided yet." Jay kissed Janet's hand. "First, she has to heal."

"What about your business?" Tom couldn't imagine Ucluelet without Janet. She and the community were entwined. Illegal or not, people trusted her and her supply. That didn't happen in the city. People there played a game of Russian Roulette every time they toked, popped a pill, or shot up.

Jay stood and indicated that it was time for Tom to leave. As he led Tom to the door, he said, "I don't think they're interested in competition. This was more than a warning. This was a shutdown."

"What are you going to do?"

Jay held open the door. "I can't go too far from my kid. We'll probably stay on the island, just not here."

"Do you think they'll be back?"

"Don't want to know. They made their point."

Tom nodded. "Have you considered going to the cops?"

Jay snorted. "You joking?"

Tom turned and crossed the porch, calling back over his shoulder. "Take care."

49.

Tom took a deep breath. What he was about to do would betray the trust of a friend. It was the right thing to do. It just felt wrong. He stood on the corner, sucking on his cigarette, staring across the street at the cop shop. "Okay," he whispered. He tossed his cigarette to the ground and stepped off the curb.

The creak of the door shutting behind him announced Tom's entry. A cop he recognized from the previous Saturday rose from his desk and approached the counter. "I'm Constable Evans. Can I help you?"

Tom stared at the cop's slinged arm. "You're the one who got shot."

"Can I help you?" the officer repeated.

Unnerved by the sight of the injured officer, Tom scanned the room. It was empty except for the cop in front of him. "I'm looking for Corporal Moore."

"He's not here. Is there anything I can help you with?"

"No. I need to speak with him. When will he be back?"

"I'm not sure." The cop slid a notepad across the counter. "You can leave a message."

Tom considered the option, then decided not to. He pushed the notepad away, shook his head, and walked out the door.

Moore's stomach grumbled as he entered the detachment. The chili-dog he'd grabbed for lunch at the beer parlour was threatening to embarrass him in front of Bouton, who followed behind.

Constable Evans looked up. "Is something wrong, sir?"

"My lunch is just giving me a bit of a hard time," Moore groaned as he passed. When he reached his desk, he searched its drawers for mints left over from a dinner out with his wife.

Bouton, who had invited Moore to the beer parlour when they arrived back in Ucluelet, laughed as he took his seat. "A sensitive stomach is one of the first signs of old age, David."

Moore smiled at the jab and the use of his first name. He had almost turned the invitation down. Looking across at Bouton's relaxed smile, Moore was glad he'd accepted, even with the resulting upset stomach. "Ah, well, you would know, Merle."

Bouton chuckled as he looked through messages left on his desk.

After shrugging off his jacket, Moore threw it over the back of his chair and dropped onto the polished wood seat. The springs in the swivel joint protested as he leaned back. He closed his eyes and waited for the mints he was chewing to do their work.

"Sir?"

Moore opened his eyes to find Evans standing at the corner of his desk. "What is it, Evans?"

"A Constable Norman Addington showed up, saying he was here to help Corporal McAteer. I sent him to the garage."

"When was this?"

"About forty-five minutes ago."

"I'm sure he'll be welcome news for the corporal."

"Sir, I looked through the messages and have started calling back the ones that sounded promising, but I thought I should bring this one to your attention." He separated one of the slips from the two he had gripped in his hand and passed it to Moore. "It wasn't a response to the ad, sir. It was a complaint that came in over last weekend."

Moore examined the slip. Along with a name and number, the words BIKE GANG and LONG BEACH were scrawled across it. "Have you followed up?"

"No, sir. It was Tofino's to deal with since the problem occurred on the other side of the airport road. The complaint involved a group of bikers partying hard on the beach. Tofino sent Alex, I mean Auxiliary Officer Doukas, out with Constable Romani, who gave them a warning. Doukas passed it on to us because of what we were talking about at the briefing he attended." Evans glanced quickly at Bouton's desk. "Doukas said Romani believed the group seemed like more than friends taking their bikes out for a spin. A couple looked, um, patched. Romani hadn't seen them before and felt we should be made aware of them. They were polite, he said. Almost too polite."

"Did he get a good look at the patch?" Bouton stood and joined them. "Can I have that?"

Moore passed the message over. "Do you think there's something to it?"

"I was going to contact the Vancouver drug squad anyway, so I might as well ask about this." He picked up a pen off Moore's desk and wrote the information on the back of the message slip. "How'd he describe the patch?"

"Doukas said it was like a mad dog encircled with some writing. He didn't catch what it said." Evans waited for Bouton to finish writing. "He also said they sounded like they were celebrating. Like it was a special occasion, not just a weekend blowout."

Bouton straightened and handed back Moore's pen. "Thanks. I'll follow this up."

Evans waited until Bouton had returned to his desk and started dialling before bringing forward the other message slip. "There was also this."

Moore looked down at the slip and jumped up. "Keys! A set of keys have been found on the beach? Did you call them back?"

"No, because she didn't call it in, she came in. Corporal McAteer spoke with her, then took the keys with him to test against the van."

"And?"

"And he's still got them."

"Where were they found?"

"I'm not sure."

"Did he get her address?" Moore stood and grabbed his coat off the back of his chair.

"It's written on the back. She lives near the airport."

"Great." He grabbed a slip of paper and wrote the woman's phone number on it before passing it to Evans. "Call her back and tell her I'm on my way." He paused. "No, better yet, see if she can meet me at the inn. I need her to show me where she found the keys. Here's hoping the syringe will be in the same place." Moore strode off toward the door.

"Wait, sir!" Evans called out. "I nearly forgot, you had a visitor. I think it was the bartender from the inn."

"Tom? Did he say what he wanted?"

"No. He just asked for you."

"Okay, well, I'll drop in at the lodge and speak with him while I'm there."

The moment Moore stepped into the bay of Owens' Garage, the smell of oil and grease transported him back to a childhood spent in his grandfather's garage. That single-bay garage, sitting in the middle of a small, prairie town north of Calgary, had provided more of an education than he ever received in a schoolhouse. The memory was bittersweet as his grandfather had passed away three years earlier and only his son Gary had had the opportunity to build his own cherished memories with the old man. Matthew would know him only through the memories of others.

Moore maneuvered around Rod's panel truck, which was wedged in between Evans' patrol car and the hippie's van. Space was tight in Owens' Garage. The logging rig was left to brood in the side yard. "Corporal!" Moore called, as McAteer appeared from behind Rod's truck.

McAteer looked up from his clipboard and waited for Moore to approach. "Are you here about the keys?"

"Yes. Were they a match?"

"Yes, they were."

"Were you able to lift any prints?"

"None that were usable." McAteer passed Moore the clipboard, with the keys resting on top. "We've also completed processing Mr. Ouellet's panel and, as you can see, I haven't found any drugs. Only traces of fish."

Moore pocketed the keys and glanced down at McAteer's notes. His heart sank. "So, we have no evidence other than witness testimony that he was moving drugs."

"Not so far."

"Sir?"

Both Moore and McAteer turned toward the speaker. Moore stifled a grin. The constable, who appeared to be in his early twenties, was as gangly as a puppy with paws and head out of proportion to the rest of his body. He would be tall if he grew into his feet and Moore hoped there were future muscles growing under the uniform that hung on his thin frame. His voice, though, was deep and strong. "I was wondering if you wanted me to start on the patrol car."

"Ah, Constable Addington come meet Corporal David Moore."

Moore accepted the constable's offered hand and was impressed by the strength in his grip.

"He was sent up from Nanaimo to give me a hand processing the vehicles and whatever else I need assistance with." McAteer reached for his wallet and pulled out a couple of bills. Turning to Addington, he passed him the money. "Go get us a couple of coffees—"

"None for me. I have to head out to the inn."

"Okay, just you and me, Constable. Cream and sugar."

Once Addington was sent on his errand, Moore asked, "From the lab?"

"Well, no. It's all hands on deck down there. Very busy." McAteer accepted his clipboard back. "They pulled him from their *possibilities* list. Apparently, he's interested in learning forensic science. They sent him up here figuring it would kill two birds with one stone. I'd get the help I needed and he would be field-tested for aptitude."

Moore smiled. "How's he doing?"

"I'm enjoying the gift of his enthusiasm and not worrying about the rest."

50.

The heavy fog clung to Moore like a moist blanket as he struck out across the now-familiar parking lot of the Wickaninnish Inn. He was finding it difficult to keep his excitement in check. The woman from the airport turned out to be the mother of three fidgety boys. Moore had to consign them to the restraints of her car with the promise of ice cream just to get five minutes alone with their parent. It proved to be enough time for the woman to show him where she'd found the keys, and for him to hand over the cash for the promised treats. Once she and her boys left, Moore searched for a used syringe but found none.

Disappointed, Moore headed for the lodge to find out what it was Tom had come to the office to tell him. He was momentarily taken aback when Sandy answered the door. "Is Tom here?"

"Yes. Come in." She stepped back to allow Moore to enter.

Feeling as if he'd been a bit gruff, Moore reached out and touched Sandy's arm as he passed. "How are you doing?"

"Fine."

Moore nodded and continued on to where Tom rose from the couch.

"You wanted to speak with me?" Moore asked.

Tom looked quickly at Sandy.

"I'll just go to my room," she said.

"Is anyone else here?"

"No." Tom motioned for him to sit. "Edan and Roxanne are still at work."

"You came to the office to see me?" Moore chose the overstuffed armchair next to the fireplace, the warmth helped to counter the fog's chill which had leached heat from his bones.

"Things may be worse than you thought." Tom said, settling back on the couch.

Moore rushed across the parking lot and jumped into his car. Tom's description of his visit to Janet's and his concern over the implications of what he learned there had glued Moore to his seat for the past hour. Now, he was consumed with the urgency to update his team. He radioed the Ucluelet office and got Evans. "I know it's short notice, but I need to pull everyone in for a briefing. If Corporal Bouton is on board, set it up for five o'clock."

"Yes, sir."

"I'm just leaving the inn now. I should be at the office before five."

Sandy lay on her bed, eyes closed. It had been hard to say goodbye to Emily at the end of their shift. Brent's sister had not been convinced to stay for the rest of the season, but one of the weekend girls agreed to fill in until they hired someone new. Sandy was finding it hard to accept the change.

But the day had brought a bit of luck her way, by way of a twenty-dollar bill folded inside her jeans' front pocket—an unexpected bonus from a guest she'd chased down after she discovered a document folder tucked behind the bed. The guest had already checked out, but as she descended the stairs to the lobby, she spotted him on his way to his car and rushed after him. He was so grateful that he gave her the twenty-dollar tip on the spot. The extra cash meant she could finally contribute to the grocery fund her roommates kept in a jar on top of the kitchen cupboard.

The sound of the front door shutting turned her attention to the men she'd left talking in the living room. When Sandy arrived after her shift, Tom had been on the couch, brooding, and rebuffed every attempt she'd made at drawing him into a conversation. She had been about to give up when David showed up. She shook her head. It was becoming easier to think of him as David. She wasn't sure if it was a small-town thing or his personality. Now, it sounded as if maybe David had left. She was trying to decide whether she wanted to join Tom in the living room when a soft tap came at her door.

"Sandy?"

When she opened the door, she found a Tom buzzing with energy. "Yes?"

"We need to talk." Tom stepped back. "Do you want a beer?"

"Sure." She slipped past him, taking up a post at the kitchen counter while he pulled two beers from the fridge. "What's this about, Tom?"

He motioned for her to follow him across the kitchen to his bedroom door. He gently pushed it open, and Sandy was shocked by who was asleep on his bed.

"Conny!" she gasped.

"Shh-h-h!" Tom quickly shut the door. "Keep it down."

"What?" Sandy stared at him. "What are you—"

"She came back," Tom said.

"I can see that! What happened? Where was she?" Sandy crossed to the table and dropped into the first chair she came to. "I don't understand."

Tom slid onto the chair next to her. "She showed up about two hours ago—"

"Is that what you were talking about with David?"

"No!" Tom shot a worried look at his bedroom door, then turned to face Sandy. "I didn't tell him about Conny. This has got to be our secret until she tells us what she plans."

"She didn't tell you?"

"No. But I do need to tell you about my visit to Janet's."

"Who's Janet?"

"She operates a—ah, um, a place you'd go if you want to score. Good stuff. Not the crap you'd get on some city street corner."

Sandy took a swig of her beer. "A dealer?"

"Not really. She's more of a hostess who makes sure her guests have what they need to enjoy the evening. It's a place you go to party after the bar shuts down."

Sandy frowned. "Tom, I don't want to know about Janet's place. I want to know what Conny's doing in your bedroom."

"Shush!" Tom put his hand over her mouth.

She swiped it away, glowering at him.

"Keep your voice down! I'm trying to tell you because it relates to Conny, and Danny, and you."

"Me?"

"Yes, because of the drugs you found in Conny's room."

"But I gave them to the police." She looked at his closed bedroom door. "Is that why Conny's back?"

"I'm not sure why she's back." Tom leaned forward, resting his elbows on his knees, his beer cupped between his hands. "She looked like hell, Sandy. I almost didn't recognize her. She must've been sleeping rough."

"Did she say where she's been?"

"No. She just wanted a shower and to sleep. I took her to my room because I didn't think her room would be safe if word got out that she's back."

"Then there's the mess the police left."

"Yeah. There's that. That's why I need to tell you about Janet." Tom pulled his chair closer to hers. "Janet had a visitor, actually three visitors, on Sunday—"

"Sunday?"

"Yes. One was Rod. They worked her over trying to get her to tell them where she had hidden a stolen shipment of meth."

The mention of the meth, frightened Sandy. At university, she had witnessed how an addiction to hard drugs could change a person and pull them into a dark world they seemed unable to escape. Although she felt sympathy for this woman, she worried about her roommates' involvement. "Is she okay?"

"She's alive—"

"Who's alive?"

Sandy and Tom looked up to see Conny standing in the doorway of Tom's bedroom, wearing one of Tom's shirts, and it appeared nothing else. "Janet," Tom said. "I was explaining what had happened to Janet." He stood, pulling out his chair and motioning for her to take it.

"Just a minute." Conny disappeared into Tom's bedroom and came out wrapped in a blanket. She shuffled over to the chair he'd pulled out for her.

Once she was comfortable, Tom went to the stove and put the kettle on.

Sandy didn't understand what Tom meant when he said she looked like hell. Sandy looked different, but not in a bad way. Scrubbed bare of makeup, Conny looked like a much younger, more vulnerable version of herself. Gone were the backcombing and hairspray. Her hair curled softly against her cheek and shoulders. "Where were you, Conny?"

Conny ignored the question and kept her attention on Tom. "What happened to Janet?"

Tom motioned for her to wait a moment. When he finished making the tea, he carried a steaming mug to her, then pulled a chair over to sit next to her. "I started to tell Sandy," he said, "about Rod and his two thugs beating up Janet on Sunday—"

Conny, who had lifted her mug to take a sip of her tea, abruptly set it down, as if it had already burned her.

Sandy reached out for her. "Are you okay?"

"Y-yes." Conny waived Sandy's concern away. "Yes, of course."

Sandy remembered Conny, late for work, looking and smelling awful, standing in the doorway of the room she'd been cleaning. "Did Rod beat you up on Sunday, too?"

"Fuck!" Tom jerked out of his chair and started pacing. "The bastard!"

Conny's blanket dropped to the floor as she tried to stop Tom's pacing. "Tom! Wait. It wasn't Rod." She grabbed his arm. "And when did you start using that word? I thought you never used that word."

Tom waved her away and continued to pace.

Sandy rose, mouth agape at the sight of Conny's legs. Purple and deep blue bruises marred the backs of both her thighs and half-circles around her ankles. Tom caught Sandy's stare and stopped pacing. He bent and picked up the blanket, wrapping it around Conny before guiding her back to her seat. When she was settled, he said, "Jesus, Conny, you told me you'd rolled down a hill! Now…Why didn't you…If it wasn't Rod, who was it?"

"It doesn't matter." She waved her hand dismissively. "And I did roll down a hill."

"Jesus!" Tom stormed off to stand by the living room's picture window.

Sandy reclaimed her seat and reached for her beer, mind racing. Flashes of memory filled in the vacant look in Conny's eyes that day. The smell of sex. "You weren't just beaten," she whispered. "You were raped."

"What?" Tom rushed to the table. "Why didn't you tell me?"

When he reached for her, Conny pushed him away. "Don't," she growled, and held up her hands, warning them both to stop. The blanket slid from her shoulders, and she didn't bother retrieving it. "Look. It's done. It's over."

"But—"

She shot a warning glare at Tom. "No. It's done. Stop!"

Conny looked from one to the other. "It's my fault. All of it's my fault."

"No, it's—"

"Stop it!" Closing her eyes, Conny took a couple of deep breaths. "Look. I did a lot of thinking while I was out there." She motioned to indicate the scene outside the window. "I don't want to run anymore. This is my home. I…I don't want to leave. Besides, no matter where I go, Rod will find me."

"No, he-he's in jail," Tom blurted.

"That doesn't change what I did."

Tom looked at Sandy, then back at Conny. "What did you do?"

Conny slowly raised her eyes to meet Sandy's. "I'm so sorry…I-I killed Geoff."

"What?" Sandy and Tom chorused.

51.

Though Constable Evans had done his best to get everyone to the meeting on time, in the end, they had to wait for the specialist officers to show. Moore tried to keep his impatience in check when he asked how long they'd be.

"About ten minutes," Evans said. "They'd left their cars here and walked to Owens'. Corporal Bouton drove over to fetch them."

Moore nodded absently and looked at his constables sitting alert at their desks. Since his blow-up over the hidden gun, they had become very attentive—almost too attentive. He missed Constable Nelson's casual ease and Evans' brash confidence. "So, how has our prisoner been today?"

"I haven't paid much attention, sir. Should I have?"

Ah, there he is. Moore smiled. "You fed him, I presume?" Moore could almost see the smart remark forming. He decided to intercept it before Evans could verbalize it. "Well, we'll be dealing with him tomorrow."

"I hope so, sir. The dog needs to be put down."

The sound of voices and the clomping of boots tramping across the entry hallway announced the return of the specialists. Full of apologies, the group filed in and took their seats. The newest member dragging in a chair from the front entry. When everyone was settled, Moore walked to the chalkboard. "I felt we should meet because a lot of information has been gathered over the day and I want to see if we could connect some dots."

He wrote KEYS and SYRINGE on the board. "Okay. Let's start with our first murder. The keys for Mr. Johnston's van were found, but I was unable to find a syringe. The keys are now with the van. There were no clear prints on them." He glanced at McAteer. "So, no link yet between Miss Lee and the van."

He pulled Sandy's drawing from the file. "Miss Chambers, however, not only confirmed that the item she drew in the water was a paddle, she also identified it as being from Mr. Johnston's van. It had hung on the inside wall of the van, over the bed. She remembered it because it had a surf scene painted on it."

"Does she know where the paddle is now?" McAteer asked.

"No. Apparently she looked for it Tuesday, when she took the Johnstons to see where their son died. She didn't find it."

"So, if the paddle was pulled from the van, used on the victim, then tossed into the ditch, the side of the road may be part of the crime scene." McAteer pulled out his notebook. "There's no way I can process the road after all this time."

"He probably died inside the van," Evans mumbled.

Bouton pointed at Evans. "You're going to have to go over your photos again and pull all you can from them. Make sure we didn't miss anything else." Bouton turned to McAteer. "You're confident you got everything you could from the van?"

"Yes."

"There were no signs of drugs?" Moore asked.

"Not a trace, but I did find what looked like a secret storage hole hidden in the side wall of the back wall panel. It was too small to hold the box we found in the prospector's shack though."

"Could be for transporting cash," Moore suggested.

"Okay." Bouton sighed. "We keep the vehicle sealed and where it is."

McAteer nodded. "I could see if I'm able to find the paddle."

"Let your assistant do it." Bouton turned to Evans. "You can show him where you found the body?"

Evans glanced at Moore before shrugging. "I think so."

Moore tapped the chalk against the board then pointed at where TRUCKER had been written. He crossed it out. "Unfortunately, our one lead on Miss Lee's whereabouts has turned out to be false. Dispatch radioed as I was on my way here to say the Duncan detachment had located the woman the trucker picked up. Although she bore a close resemblance to Miss Lee, she isn't our girl."

"So, Conny might still be around here somewhere," Evans said.

"Yes," Moore acknowledged. "We should put a new request over the radio."

"I'll take care of that," Bouton said.

"We've discovered a link between Miss Lee and the prospector's shack where Mr. Brown was killed." Moore cleared his throat. "She was seen a couple of weeks ago in the company of Mr. Ouellet trying to convince him to use the shack as storage. How this links to Mr. Johnston's death, I'm not sure. Anything to add?"

Evans leaned forward and tapped his notebook. "From the fishermen I spoke with today, the fish transport business seems legit. They said a guy named Thanos had been actively recruiting customers for it over the last couple of months, and the business was registered in March. The address attached to it, however, is of the boathouse that burned down."

Bouton made quick notes and thanked the constable. "Gangs often hide illegal activities within legal ones."

"We've had no more sightings of Conny?" Nelson asked.

"Nothing remotely credible since the Duncan call," Evans said.

"Now"—Moore pointed to Rod's name on the board—"Merle, do you have any more information on Mr. Ouellet?"

Bouton stood and took Moore's place at the chalkboard. Moore returned to his desk, conscious of Nelson and Evans' eyes following him. When he sat down and pulled his notebook from his pocket, his eyes flicked between them. He mouthed a silent, *What?*

Evans raised an eyebrow and mouthed, *Merle?*

Moore shot him a warning glare before turning his attention to what Bouton was writing on the board.

"I contacted the Vancouver drug squad this afternoon and asked if they knew of any recent large shipments of meth or other drugs moving to or from the island, specifically in this area. I was told there had been some movement, but the officer wouldn't get into the details until I filled him in on my reasons for asking. That's when I was told a warrant had been issued for Mr. Ouellet in connection with an incident in Nanaimo on Tuesday night." Turning away from the surprise expressed by his audience, he mumbled, "More about that later." Pointing at where he'd written METH and LSD, he continued. "Reports from the drug squad indicate that meth and LSD have been showing up on the island in larger quantities. This matches what the Tofino officers observed on Long Beach."

Bouton drew two arrows out from the word GANGS, writing MANGOSTA and JACKALS at the end points. "Thanks to Constable Romani and Auxiliary Officer Doukas' observations, we now know the Jackals gang was in the area at the time of Mr. Brown's death."

Bouton glanced down at his open notebook. "My contact confirmed the existence of a gang called The Jackals, whose patch bears a stylized image of a jackal, which they say looks very much like a dog. Evidently, the Jackals are actively trying to expand from Eastern Canada, so they're after the same Western market as the Mangosta. My inquiry interested my contact because Thanos Andino, 23, a known member of the Mangosta, was found dead in the middle of a Nanaimo mall parking lot on Monday night, his throat slit."

"The same Thanos who's been approaching area fishermen to ship their fish to Vancouver with Rod's company?" Evans asked.

"He was a known associate of Mr. Ouellet's," Bouton continued, ignoring Evans. "My contact said they figured the body was dumped in such a public space to send a message to the Mangosta, if not to Mr. Ouellet himself." Bouton stopped to take a long draw from a glass of water before continuing. "I took a quick drive out to the beach this afternoon and couldn't spot any sign of either of these gangs. Their absence was confirmed by the patrolling officers I spoke with. They figured a combination of the increased police presence and the cool weather kept the number of long-weekend visitors down, including those coming for the surf competition." He turned back to the chalk board and tapped where he'd written MANGOSTA. "While the Mangosta's main clubhouse is in Langley on the mainland, they did set up a satellite clubhouse in Nanaimo last September. Last month the Jackals set up their own clubhouse in Nanaimo." He drew a bold line between the two names. "My contact believes that this was meant as a direct challenge to the Mangosta, who were staking the island as their territory." He paused, his right hand tapping the table. Then he looked directly at Moore. "I also learned that an undercover RCMP officer had been imbedded in the Jackals since before they came west. There had been no word from him since the gang set up in Nanaimo."

Moore's stomach turned over. "Do they feel the officer has been compromised? Is this the beginning of what? A gang war?"

"It could've been the officer hadn't found an opportunity to check in. Unfortunately, he was killed during a brawl between the two gangs Tuesday night in Nanaimo." Bouton paused. "This brings us back to the new arrest warrant against Mr. Ouellet. The Nanaimo detachment learned that we had him in custody, thanks to his court appearance in Ucluelet court this morning. The sheriff's service has been contacted and will be here tomorrow to transport him to the Nanaimo Correctional Centre."

Evans shifted in his seat, drawing the corporal's attention. "For the attempted murder charges?"

"Yes. The not-guilty plea he entered in court this morning means he's going to trial. It'll be interesting to hear the defence his lawyer puts forward." Bouton drew a line from Rod's name to where he'd written JACKALS, before facing his audience. "He will also be down there to face a murder charge from Tuesday's brawl."

"Capital or non-capital?" Evans asked.

"I don't know. I haven't seen the judge's order or warrant."

Nelson sat up and glanced at Evans. "Did Rod know the guy was a cop?"

Bouton shook his head. "I'm not sure. It'll be up to the MCU officer assigned to the case to find out. But no matter what happens to Mr. Ouellet, it sounds like we're going to see a lot more gang activity on the island."

"Well." Moore felt his world shift. "It seems what I learned this afternoon from Mr. Robinson would support that. He visited a place known as Janet's this afternoon. It operates as some sort of party house here in Ucluelet. This was in response to my asking him earlier to keep his eyes open for increased drug activity in the area—"

"You asked for his help?"

Bouton's tone caused Moore to momentarily lose his train of thought. Giving his head a shake, he ignored the question, and refocused. "Mr. Robinson went directly to Janet's because he knew the hostess as a friend."

"I bet he did."

Moore ignored the sarcasm and continued. "He found Miss Janet White in a poor state, having suffered significant injuries during a beating she received from Mr. Ouellet and two others on Sunday afternoon. According to Miss White, Mr. Ouellet was looking for a stolen shipment of drugs. He referred to Danny Brown as Miss White's partner in this alleged theft. Miss White denied stealing the drugs and Danny's involvement. Unfortunately, Ouellet didn't believe her. But it was during the subsequent attack Miss White got a clear view of the tattoo we now know as a membership tag of the Mangosta: a mongoose entwined with a cobra." Moore caught McAteer's eye. "Like the victim from the Highway 4 shooting."

"Okay," Bouton said, "that connects Mr. Ouellet to the box inside the shack and to our second victim. And given what we got out of the old man this morning, we have a connection to Miss Lee."

"Sir?" Nelson asked. "If Mr. Ouellet and his men thought Janet and Danny were working together, and they beat her hoping she'd give up Danny's location, doesn't that indicate Rod's not Danny's murderer?" The question drew everyone's attention and Nelson visibly shrank into his chair.

Moore jumped in before Bouton could respond. "Good catch, Monty. We've been so focused on trying to connect him to everything, we didn't consider the possibility he didn't do all of it. We'll follow up on that when we speak to him again." Everyone relaxed, and Moore scribbled a quick reminder in his notebook.

"What did you learn from Marco?" Evans asked.

"About two weeks ago, he saw Conny, Rod, and another man in the woods above his place. They were talking about using the abandoned prospector's shack next door to stash something. He also told us that the neighbouring shack belonged to Geoff Johnston's grandfather, which is another connection."

"Doesn't that—" Evans jumped up, swayed, and dropped back into his seat. Moore started to rush over but Evans waved away his concern. "It's okay. Just dizzy. Got up too fast." He self-consciously cradled his slinged left arm as he shifted to face Moore. "Sorry. I was going to say that everything you're describing indicates that Conny is deeply involved, which would explain why she took off."

"Yes." Bouton turned to the chalkboard. "But it doesn't explain why she told you she killed Mr. Johnston…unless it was under orders from Mr. Ouellet. I wonder if he saw the cousins snooping around the area. Does anyone know if either of the Johnstons have been to the shack since Mr. Ouellet took possession?"

Moore searched through his notes, stopping when he found the page he was looking for. "James said he checked to see if the claim was still valid. He'd invited Geoff for supper at his place the next night, Saturday." He flipped to the next page. "I don't have him saying anything about the shack."

"We need to confirm that. Constable Evans, can you give him a call?"

"Should we be interviewing Mr. Ouellet again?" Moore asked.

"Yes, but let's get Miss White's statement first."

Evans' hand shot up. "I can do that on the way home, sir."

"Very good."

Moore scanned the chalkboard. "With the sheriffs coming up tomorrow, we should talk to Mr. Ouellet tonight."

"I think we'd do better first thing in the morning. I want tonight to review the case notes again. Aren't you going to be busy with the surfing competition?"

"So far, things are under control."

Bouton looked at Evans. "How confident are you that Miss Lee is Mr. Johnston's killer?"

Evans glanced at Moore, then back at Bouton. "I don't know, sir. We can't find a connection or a motive."

"Then we need to locate her fast because if it wasn't her, and Ouellet was the killer, then we need to know that before he's taken. Let's get that plea for information over the radio as soon as possible. We won't bother with the smaller papers. I'll send a photo to the large dailies in Victoria and Vancouver. We need to find her now." Bouton faced the chalkboard. "She could be protecting someone, and if it's Mr. Ouellet—"

Moore held up his notebook. "When we started asking about Danny's murder, Mr. Ouellet's counsel shut it down because he hadn't discussed anything except the Highway 4 shooting with his client, but I believe he had that discussion when they met after our interview. It'll be interesting to see how Mr. Ouellet reacts to the questions tomorrow."

Bouton grabbed his notebook and flipped through it. "No matter how he reacts, we need to find out if he was involved with Mr. Brown's murder before we lose him."

52.

Fog darkened the windows of the lodge and muffled outside noise, cocooning the three people gathered at the kitchen table from the outside world. With her tea growing cold, Conny bore the weight of Sandy and Tom's silent stares. She was rocking slightly to the pounding of her heart, and she braced her arm against the edge of the table to stop it. "I killed Geoff," she repeated.

"You killed the hippie?" Tom took the seat beside her. "I don't believe it. You didn't even know him! Why would you kill him?"

"B-but I did," Conny said. "It was an accident, but I did…kill him."

Suddenly, Sandy inhaled so sharply that Conny thought she'd choked. "You came over and helped me after I found Geoff," she said. "Why would you do that if you'd killed him?"

"I-I-I needed to know if you believed he'd been hit by a car."

"You—"

The sound of Tom pushing his chair away from the table surprised her. "Tom?"

"I need a minute." Tom spun and headed for the door.

She watched him leave, wondering where he'd go.

"So…we were never friends?" Sandy whispered.

Conny forced herself to face Sandy. "No…I mean, yes." Conny released a puff of air and stood. She'd been so naïve, thinking that by coming back and accepting responsibility for her actions, she could make things right. She had only made things worse. "I just came back to sort things out. I didn't mean to hurt you." She headed to Tom's bedroom.

Sandy brushed past her and flopped down on the edge of the bed, arms crossed and expression defiant. "Are you going to tell me what happened?"

Conny left the door open and joined Sandy on the bed. "I saw him at the bonfire on Friday night. He seemed so excited about the idea of prospecting with his cousin." She shot a quick glance at Sandy. "You know how I feel about longhairs. Well, that night I couldn't stop watching him." She scrubbed her fingers across her scalp and shook her head. "I guess it was the passion in his voice.... Anyway, when I heard him tell his story about prospecting in the area above the cliffs I worried he might be talking about the area where we'd hid our stash."

"We?"

"Rod, me, and two guys who"—she searched for the right word—"help Rod."

Sandy shook her head. "You had drugs hidden somewhere at Wreck Bay?"

"Yes. But only because the place Rod bought earlier had burned down. He arrived the next day with the first shipment from Vancouver and no place to store it."

"When was this?"

"A couple of weeks ago." Conny sighed, amazed her life had changed so dramatically in such a short time. "Rod called me at work and asked if I knew somewhere he could store the stuff until he sorted out a new place."

"And you put them in an old shack?"

"Well, it was the best I could do. Since the new road came in, businesses have been popping up everywhere. All the commercial space was gone. That's why Rod purchased the old boathouse."

"What about people selling their homes? Wouldn't that have worked?"

"Yes, if there was anything to buy, or at least at a reasonable price. Everyone's in limbo, waiting to hear what the government plans for the national park. Anyway, the new place needed to be a storefront because Rod had set up a transport business." Rod had been so full of promises when she first met him. The office was hers to run, he'd promised, giving her valuable experience for when she moved to California. A secretary would outrank a chambermaid on any application form.

"Why didn't he just keep the drugs hidden in whatever he brought them up in?" Sandy asked.

"He was worried about the cops stopping him. Plus, the truck was already contracted to transport fish to Vancouver."

"So, you chose the shack?" Sandy prompted.

"I knew of a couple empty buildings around, but it turned out the hippies had already found them. Then someone told me about an abandoned prospector's shack along Lost Shoe Creek."

"And that's how Danny got involved," Tom said from the doorway. "And now he's dead." Tom moved into the room and shut the door.

Conny nodded.

"Tell me what happened to Geoff," Sandy demanded.

Fake Out

When Conny looked at Sandy, she saw the life she could have had if she'd been born anywhere but in a backwoods dirt town to a family full of monsters. Pain shot through her chest, momentarily silencing her. She squeezed her eyes shut and sucked in a deep breath. When she opened her eyes, she found Sandy's on her, and she raised her chin "He was waving around this beat-up old prospector's pan, bragging about how he and his cousin were going to work their grandfather's claim. If only I'd walked away."

"You were alone?" Tom asked.

"Yeah. I was trying to get rid of some product." Suddenly, she pushed off the bed. "I have to check on something."

Sandy sent a furtive glance at Tom. "Don't!" she shouted. "It's not there."

Conny stopped, bracing her palms against the door. "What do you mean it's not there?"

"The police have it." Sandy threw up her hands. "I found the chocolate box and turned it in."

A chill ran up Conny's spine.

Tom rushed to add, "They searched your room. It's a mess."

Conny looked at Sandy. "What about the rest of my stuff?"

"Your clothes? They're still there."

When Conny lowered a hand to the doorknob, Sandy jumped up. "How about I bring you what you need?"

Conny shuffled back to the bed and dropped down on the edge of the mattress. "I need everything. I tossed everything I was wearing into the garbage after my shower." She glanced up when Sandy left the room and caught Tom staring at her. "The cop put my suitcase in the trunk of his car."

"When was this?" he asked.

"Wednesday."

"The day of the shooting."

A deep frown creased Conny's brow as she studied Tom. "The cop found me hitchhiking on the switchbacks. He put my suitcase in his trunk. He was going to take me back to Ucluelet."

"What happened?"

"Wait!" Sandy gasped as she rushed through the door carrying a stack of Conny's clothes. "Here." She set them on the bed and stepped back. "Okay, continue."

"I was trying to convince him to let me go—"

Sandy held up a hand to stop her. "I meant with Geoff. What happened to him?"

Images flashed and vertigo flooded over her. "Sick. I'm going to be sick!" She bent forward placing her head in her hands, breathing deeply.

Tom grabbed the garbage can and brought it over.

Conny waved it away. The vertigo leaving as quickly as it had come. Looking up at Tom and Sandy, she saw how frightened they were. Were they frightened for her, or of her? She couldn't tell. Taking a deep breath, she sat up and faced them. "It was an accident. I'm not a murderer."

"But you said you killed Geoff," Sandy said.

"I know. I did." Conny looked down at the pile of clothes stacked on the bed beside her. "Look, I need to get some clothes on."

"Of course!" Tom took Sandy by the arm and led her out of the room.

Conny quickly slipped into a set of underwear and a pair of jeans. She kept Tom's T-shirt on but slipped a long-sleeved shirt over top. She immediately felt less vulnerable. Dropping down on the bed, she pulled on a pair of woolly socks and called to the others. When they joined her, she continued her story. "The claim Geoff talked about sounded like the land where I'd found the prospector's shack. I wanted to find out if it was."

"Because Rod stored his drugs there?" Sandy prompted.

"Yes—"

Sandy scratched her head. "But wasn't he worried about someone stealing them?"

"That's why he hired Danny," Tom said.

"I hired Danny," Conny corrected. "Rod hired Thanos."

"And Thanos is who raped you—" Sandy suggested.

"Don't!" Conny snapped at Tom before he could rush to her side. She glared at Sandy. "You're wrong."

"Oh. But I-I didn't—"

The sound of the lodge's front door opening made them all freeze. Tom shushed them as he got up and walked to the door. With one last glance back at them, he slipped through the door and shut it quickly behind him. "Oh, hi, Edan."

An awkward silence settled over Conny and Sandy as they listened to Tom joke about hosting a special guest in his room and apologize for any strange noises he might hear. Edan's hearty laugh came clearly through the door, as did his comment that Tom needn't worry as he was just changing into a fresh uniform before returning to the inn.

The door opened a crack and Tom slid through. "Coast is clear," he whispered.

Sandy confronted Conny. "Were you following Geoff when he walked back to the inn?"

"Halfway back, I decided I wasn't going to bother asking him anything. I was tired, and he seemed drunk or maybe high."

"What do you mean? He told me he had to stay away from drugs and alcohol."

"Yeah? Well, he told me he didn't do drugs, but he must've changed his mind, because he was stumbling around as if he was drunk or stoned. He fell bad just before I was going to turn off at our walkway." Conny shook her head at the memory. He had tripped over a root and gone down so fast he hadn't had time to break his fall. She'd rushed over, sure he'd done some major damage to his face, but when she gently rolled him over, he was hardly marked.

"Is that when you killed him?"

"No!" Conny snorted.

"Then when? When did you kill him, Conny?"

"He begged me to take him to his van. Said he needed to get to his van. He was…he was just so out of it. So, I picked up his flashlight—"

"Flashlight?"

"Yeah. He lost it when he fell." Conny remembered how panicked she had felt fumbling for the switch. "I found it. Then I took him to his van."

"Why'd you move the van?"

"I had to. Later." Conny looked across at Tom. "When we got there, he couldn't even get his key in the lock, he was so blotto."

"He was going to drive?" Tom asked.

"No. The side door. He wanted in the back." Shaking, she sought Tom's bed cover, wrapping it around her. "When I got the door open, he fell in. I couldn't believe it. I tried helping him sit up, but he grabbed me and started mumbling about a needle. He wouldn't let me go. He just kept going on and on about a needle." She searched for understanding from Tom, but he looked away. She dropped her gaze, took a deep breath, then continued. "From the way he was acting, I thought he was crashing, in need of another fix…but when I pulled the cold shot out of my purse—"

"You carried a loaded needle in your purse?"

Conny turned to Sandy. "Did you look inside the chocolate box?" At Sandy's reluctant nod, Conny huffed. "Well, you know what I had then." She felt guilt bite into her. Telling her story brought back her reluctance at trying the new cold-shot product Rod had pushed on her. It had been her first attempt at pre-loading a syringe and selling the drug in a ready-to-use state. It had felt dangerous. She'd only loaded one of the syringes he'd given her. And in spite of his assurances that the package would be an easy sale, no one had wanted it. Turning to Tom, she said. "Geoff went berserk, sending it flying to the other side of the van."

"So, you fought over it?" Tom said.

"And that's when I accidentally pricked him." If only she hadn't taken the protective cover off in anticipation of Geoff using it. "I pulled it out right away and didn't think anything had been injected, but suddenly he starts convulsing."

"Is that when he died?" Sandy moaned.

"No. I tried to help but nothing I did stopped the convulsions, so I shut him in the back and jumped in the front to drive him to a doctor I knew lived near Ucluelet."

"What about the inn?"

"It was four in the morning. No one would've been up, and it would have wasted too much time trying to find out if anyone was a doctor. I just wanted him to stop convulsing." Conny shouted. "Then he did."

"You need to go to the police." All three turned toward the door. Edan stood there, his hands planted on his hips. "You need to go to the police now."

SATURDAY, MAY 18, 1968

53.

The tension in the office was so intense the air vibrated with it. Not even the freshly-baked scones Samantha had brought in as a treat for the team soothed it. Although they'd expressed gratitude while she was in the office, everyone had immediately returned to their desks to sit in solemn silence the moment she left. The scones disappeared, leaving only crumbs and grease marks where bits of pastry had escaped inattentive mouths, as brains struggled to solidify a link between the murders.

Moore stretched and glanced at his watch. *Six-thirty.* Time to refocus. "Without Miss Lee's confession, can we establish a link between her and Mr. Johnston's murder?"

McAteer leaned against his desk, his arms crossed. "We have prints from the back of Constable Evans' vehicle that we know are hers. When I'm in Nanaimo, I'll compare them to prints we found in the victim's van. If they're there, we have a link."

"Any news about her whereabouts?" Bouton asked.

Evans quickly swallowed the bit of scone he'd shoved in his mouth and answered. "None so far, sir."

"I contacted Steve Brown last night, sir," Nelson said. "He confirmed what Miss Chambers told us. He saw Mr. Johnston walking along the path from Wreck Bay in the direction of the inn."

"Any relation to Danny Brown?"

"None, sir."

"Did he see anyone else he recognized on the path?"

"Other than the transients, it's a small community up here, sir. He recognized several people, including Miss Lee."

"Did he say what she was doing and when?"

"He assumed she was going back to the inn. He did say that he saw her just after seeing Mr. Johnston." Nelson glanced at Moore, who gave him a reassuring nod.

"So, it could be a coincidence, or it could be a link between our cases." Bouton moved to the chalkboard and wrote the time and place below Conny's name.

"We may also have a witness." Evans sent a quick glance at Moore. "It was one of the messages you asked me to sort through. A guest at the inn claims she heard an argument in the inn's parking lot. She had the window open because she loves the sound of the ocean, but she got up when she heard a couple arguing. By the time she opened the patio door she could see no sign of the guy, but she saw a woman slide shut a van door and get in to drive away."

"Would she be able to identify this woman?" Bouton wrote WITNESS below Conny's name.

"She says it was too dark and too far away, but she knows it was around four A.M. last Saturday, which fits our timeline."

"Is she local?"

"No. She checked out of the inn on Sunday. She lives in Kelowna."

"Hold on to the information." Bouton turned back to the group and asked, "Anything else?"

"You asked me to get a statement from Miss White," Evans said.

"Yes?"

"Well, I stopped by on the way home last night and it looks like she's left town. The place was locked, and a closed sign hung on the door. I canvassed the neighbourhood. No one I spoke with knew anything about their leaving or where they might have gone, until I spoke with a newspaper boy delivering in the neighbourhood." Evans referred to his notebook. "He told me they'd packed up their car and left about three yesterday afternoon."

"Do you think their leaving was in response to Mr. Ouellet's earlier visit?"

"I do, sir."

"Then let the Port Alberni and Nanaimo detachments know to keep an eye out for them. I'd love to add assault to the charges against Ouellet. We need that statement from Miss White." Bouton looked around. "Anyone else?"

"We've processed the logging rig and can release it to MacMillan Bloedel," McAteer stated. "I think they've already arranged with the garage to have the radiator fixed. As for Constable Evans' car, we were unable to finish processing it yesterday, but hope to do so this morning. Have you ordered a replacement vehicle for him? This one will be a write-off."

"I've already let purchasing at S Division know and expect a reply soon," Moore explained.

McAteer jotted a note in his book, then closed it. "As you know, the Sheriff Service will be arriving sometime today to transport Mr. Ouellet to Nanaimo Correctional Centre. I will drive down separately to drop the new evidence at the lab so it can be processed quickly."

"Sir?" Nelson rose from behind his desk. "I just wanted to give an update on the long-weekend crowd and surfing competition. My shift was pretty normal last night. Racing on the beach. Underage drinking. Nothing out of the ordinary. The extra officers and the colder weather seem to have kept things manageable."

"Thank you, Constable." Bouton waited as Nelson to retake his seat. "If that's all, let's get to it." When Moore was about to walk by, he held up his hand to stop him. "How about we run through what we're going to do with Mr. Ouellet."

Moore knew the moment he opened the interview room door to Evans that the coffee filling the mugs on the tray he carried was not from the office percolator. The rich, heady scent could only have come from his own kitchen. Evans winked as he brushed passed, his right hand holding the edge of a mug-filled tray while the other end balanced on top of his slinged arm.

Moore resisted the urge to help. Instead, he left the door open and returned to his seat at the interview table, trusting Evans to solve the problem of setting the tray and full mugs on the table without spilling everything. Evans smiled and bent from the waist like he was serving at a high-end restaurant, waiting as each of them in turn removed a mug from the proffered tray. Once everyone had a coffee, Evans straightened and left the room, tray swinging jauntily from his right hand.

As the door closed, Bouton indicated to Moore that they should begin.

Moore started the recorder. "Interview with Mr. Rodrique Ouellet, eight-fifteen A.M., Saturday, May 18, 1968. Ucluelet RCMP detachment, E-Division. Present are myself, Corporal David Moore; MCU Corporal Merle Bouton; and the prisoner's counsel representative, Mr. Rick Wood."

Bouton took a long, appreciative sip of his coffee before speaking. "I understand Mr. Ouellet spoke with his counsel, Mr. Klein, last night before that gentleman returned to Vancouver."

"Nanaimo."

"What?"

"He's in Nanaimo," Wood stated, "in anticipation of Mr. Ouellet's appearance in court there on charges regarding an incident Tuesday night. Mr. Klein will meet with Mr. Ouellet once he's at the Nanaimo Correctional Centre.

Moore could see by the intensity of his focus on Bouton, the effort the lawyer was making to be sure he was understood.

"I trust Mr. Klein has updated you."

Wood leaned forward, resting his elbows on the table, and gave a quick nod. "Yes."

"Mr. Ouellet, you're still under caution. You've had a chance to speak with your lawyer, and his representative is present at this interview. You should be set to answer the questions we have for you." Moore waited; pen poised above his notebook, his eyes fixed on Rod, who was glaring at Bouton.

"Mr. Ouellet, where were you in the early morning hours of Sunday, the twelfth of May?"

Rod's eyes narrowed as he leaned forward, mimicking his lawyer's earlier pose. "Sunday? I was sleeping."

"Were you with anyone? Can anyone verify your movements?"

Ignoring Wood's attempts to attract his attention, Rod smiled. "Naw. You might've heard I'm between girlfriends at the moment. Mine's done a runner."

"Is there anyone else who can—"

"Provide an alibi?" Rod leaned back and held up his hands. "My roommates, but I doubt they'd want me giving you their names. They don't like cops."

"You never know. Maybe they'll reconsider when they hear there's a murder charge on the table."

Wood's hand shot out, gripping Rod's arm and stopping him from reacting. Keeping a firm grip on his client, Wood turned his clear blue eyes on Bouton. "Murder? I thought the charge was attempted murder."

"Oh, that was for Constable Evans and Miss Lee. We're now discussing Danny Brown, who was not only murdered but buried under a pile of rubble behind a shack at Lost Shoe Creek we now know your client secured to store a cache of drugs—"

"Hold on!" Wood released Rod's arm and flipped through the papers in the file in front of him. The freckles stood out on his flushed face like splatters of rust-coloured paint. "Do you have proof of this?"

Bouton ignored Wood and fixed his attention on Rod. "We understand you were looking for Mr. Brown on Sunday."

Rod's eyes flicked between Moore and Bouton. "What of it?"

"Why were you looking for him?"

"That's my business."

"Well, I hear you made it Miss White's business."

"Miss White? Who the hell's she?"

"She runs a local party house referred to locally as Janet's."

"Never heard of her."

"Well, you made quite an impression on her."

"I tend to have that impact on the chicks."

"Why were you asking around about Danny Brown?"

Rod leaned back and crossed his arms. "Like I said, that's my business."

A soft tap came at the door and Moore got up to answer it. "Sorry to interrupt," Evans whispered. "There's someone here you need to see."

"Now?" Moore glanced at Bouton, who didn't look pleased with the interruption.

"Yes," Evans stressed.

Moore returned to the table, leaned down to the recorder, and stated, "Interview suspended, eight-thirty A.M., Saturday, May 18, 1968."

As soon as Moore exited the interview room, he saw why Evans had pulled him out. Conny stood in the entry hall, flanked by Sandy and Tom. He almost didn't recognize her. Her hair was loose around her shoulders and her face was free of makeup. Moore grasped her arm and ushered all three quickly outside. "You can't be here!"

"Do you know who this is?" Sandy pulled at Moore's arm, trying to get him to release Conny.

"Yes! And we can't let him see her!"

"Who?" Conny stopped when they reached the sidewalk curb and faced Moore.

"Rod. Now—" Moore felt Conny's arm start to slip out of his hand, and he realized she was fainting. He caught her just as she was about to hit the ground and held her upright as she recovered. "Let's get you out of sight." Taking a firm grip of her hand Moore sprinted down the street.

Sandy and Tom ran after them.

When they reached the entrance to the The Innlet's coffee shop, Moore pushed through the door and guided his reluctant followers to a booth at the back. "Make yourselves comfortable. Do not go anywhere. Order breakfast, my treat."

Pulling bills from his wallet he handed them to Tom. "Make sure she doesn't leave. I need to interview her."

54.

Bouton looked up from the file he was examining as Moore walked into the office. "I hear the prodigal daughter has returned."

Moore gave a quick nod. "I put her over at the hotel coffee shop. What happened when I left?"

"I left them in the interview room. Figured the lawyer could use the time to speak with his client." Bouton indicated Evans. "He filled me in on what happened. Did you speak with her at all?"

"Only to explain why she couldn't come into the office right now." Moore took a deep breath. "I thought she was going to faint right there in the street."

"Well, we certainly don't have the room to interview two suspects. I'd forgotten how small these outpost detachments are." He sighed. "It must get difficult juggling people at times."

"Believe it or not, this is the first time we've had the problem."

"How do you figure we should handle it?"

Moore looked back the way he'd come, then to Evans and Bouton. "How about we finish our interview with Mr. Ouellet before returning him to his cage? Then we can bring in Miss Lee and see what she has to say."

"Right. We can't run too long. The Sheriff Service will be arriving to pick up Mr. Ouellet today." Bouton marched down the hallway to the interview room, bursting though the door without knocking. "The interview will continue," he announced.

Moore followed Bouton in, and they each reclaimed their seats. Moore flipped open his notebook then started the recorder. "Interview with Mr. Rodrique Ouellet, nine-ten A.M., Saturday, May 18, 1968. Ucluelet RCMP detachment, E-Division. Present are myself, Corporal David Moore; MCU Corporal Merle Bouton; and prisoner's counsel, Mr. Rick Wood."

Bouton leaned back in his chair, tipping it onto its back legs, and stared at the prisoner. "I can't help but notice from your earlier comments that you consider yourself a businessman. Would that be a fair assessment Mr. Ouellet?"

"No comment."

Bouton dropped forward, causing his chair to level out with a scrap and a clang. Moore cringed. "Is it the illegal drug trade that you, as a businessman, profit from, Mr. Ouellet?" Bouton asked. "Because the metal box we found inside the old prospector's shack you'd hired Mr. Brown to guard had been used to store meth and LSD."

Rod smirked as he leaned forward, challenging Bouton. "No comment."

"That is your business, isn't it, Mr. Ouellet? Drugs. That's where the real money is. Not in fish. Drugs are more your style. That and prostitution."

Rod's eyes narrowed. "No comment."

Moore felt Bouton's frustration. Ever since Nelson had pointed out that Rod's questioning of Janet removed him from being Danny's murderer, they found themselves stumbling around in the dark, unable to find a suspect to replace him for the brutal killing. Then a thought occurred to him. Taking a quick glance at Bouton, Moore asked, "Do you suspect the Jackals of stealing the stash from the prospector's shack, Mr. Ouellet?"

Rod's gaze swiveled to Moore. "No comment."

Moore ignored the heat of Bouton's glare and pushed on. "Did you know the Jackals were partying at Long Beach that weekend?"

Rod's eyes blazed under the dark shadows of his furrowed brows, but he remained silent.

"Is that what the brawl at the Jackal's clubhouse was all about Tuesday night?" Bouton interjected.

Rod continued his silence.

"What about the guy left in the parking lot?" Moore flipped through his notes.

"Thanos," Rod growled. "That traitorous piece of shit?"

"That's enough!" The lawyer shouted. "You're obviously fishing. We're done here unless you've got further charges to lay on him."

Bouton stood. "That's all for now."

Sandy fidgeted with her coffee cup, accidentally spilling a bit over the rim onto the saucer. She glanced at Tom then Conny. Neither had spoken since giving their orders to the waitress. "Look," she said. "I don't want to be here any more than you do, but David said—"

"Yeah, yeah. We know what *David* said," Tom snapped. "I just don't like having her out in the open like this."

"Well, I'm sure he'll be back soon." Sandy downed a quick sip of coffee, wondering what they'd do if he wasn't.

Her thoughts were interrupted by the waitress appearing with their orders. As everyone tucked into their breakfasts, the sounds of the busy restaurant settled around them, but Sandy found it hard to relax. As she reached for her coffee she caught Conny staring, her face a frozen mask drained of colour. Sandy spun around to see what had caused such a reaction.

A man stood in the entrance to the café, a wicked grin spreading across his face. "There you are," he said. "Rod wants me to look after you—"

Conny bolted from her seat and tore off into the kitchen. The man pushed past a waitress and raced after her.

Sandy sprang up, grabbing her plate and swung around, bashing it into the man's face as he came parallel with their booth. Momentarily stunned, egg yoke and bacon grease running down his face, the man wabbled and slid to one knee in the pool of breakfast waste on the floor.

Tom and Sandy pushed past and ran to the entrance, apologizing as they bumped customers on the way. Outside, they paused, searching for Conny, then spotted her as she came around the side of the hotel and dashed across Main Street. They raced after her.

"She's heading to the police!" Sandy shouted to Tom.

Moore paused, his hand on the office's exit door. *What was that?* He thought he'd heard his name called. Looking over his shoulder into the office he saw no one looking his way.

"David!"

It's outside! Pushing through the door he searched for its source.

"David!"

Turning to his right he saw Sandy running down the street toward him, Conny in front, Tom behind, and in hot pursuit was a large man he didn't recognize waving a gun and shouting.

Moore unsnapped his holster and whipped out his gun. "Halt! Put your gun down, now!"

The man slid to a stop, then ducked to the left and disappeared down an alleyway.

Bouton and Evans rushed out of the office, Bouton with his gun drawn. Moore waved them to stand down. "He's taken off down that alley."

Conny, Sandy and Tom lurched up to Moore, arms dangling, mouths gasping. Sandy dropped to the lawn holding her side. "Holy cow! I didn't think we were going to make it."

"Who the hell was that?" Moore demanded.

"Dwayne." Conny gasped as she sank down beside Sandy. "That was Dwayne."

Bouton signaled Moore and they dashed across the lawn to Moore's vehicle, then tore off down the road, lights and siren engaged.

"Oh, no," cried Tom.

Sandy looked up from where she lay flat on the grass. "What?"

Tom pulled his right hand out of his jeans pocket, it held a bundle of cash. "I forgot to pay for our breakfast!"

55.

Conny arched her back and twisted one shoulder forward, then the other. "My butt's going to sleep from sitting so long on this bench." She stood up and stiffly paced the narrow confines of the public entry of the cop shop. "It's ten-thirty! How much longer do we have to wait?" She shot a quick glance at Halden who remained hunched over his desk on the other side of the counter. He seemed intent on ignoring her and continued writing in his notebook. Conny found it hard to understand the man. Ever since she arrived an hour ago, he had treated her as if she were some stranger off the street. There had been no spark, no recognition of experience shared. She lifted her chin and announced, "They should've just asked me. I could've told them where to find Dwayne."

Halden offered no response. Conny fought the urge to storm over and slap him, anything to have those caramel eyes focused on her.

"Do you really want to find him, Conny?" Sandy asked.

Looking back at the two sitting on the hard bench, bored and miserable, she shrugged.

Tom caught her look and chortled. "You took off pretty fast last time you saw him."

Conny waved away his tease. "Look, why don't we just go back to the lodge?"

Halden jumped up, jolting them. "You can't."

"What do you mean, we can't?" Tom rose from the bench. "We're not under arrest."

Conny swallowed her own retort as she spotted the two senior cops crossing the parking lot. "They're here."

Bouton pushed through the office door, swinging it wide enough it forced Tom to jump out of the way. Moore followed behind. Neither appeared happy.

"You didn't find him?" Conny moaned.

Bouton brushed past, ignoring her. Moore stopped and answered. "No. He must've had a car close by."

Tom crossed his arms. "Conny believes she knows where he is."

"Where?"

Conny found it hard to face the hope in the cop's eyes. "Maybe."

"Where?" Moore repeated.

Looking back at Sandy and Tom, Conny swallowed her fear. "The clubhouse."

Bouton's hand froze half-way through discarding a message and he turned from his desk to face Conny. "There's a clubhouse here?"

Conny hesitated, she wasn't completely sure that was what was going on but from what she'd seen of the house she felt it was too big for what Rod told her it was to be used for. "I don't think it is now but I'm sure that's what it will be in time."

"Where?" Bouton demanded.

"I need a map."

From the way Moore brushed past her, Conny felt she was meant to follow, and did. When he reached his desk, he rummaged through each drawer, finally pulling a map from the bottom one. "Will this do?"

Stepping forward, Conny opened and flattened it across his desk before scanning it for the route she'd walked back to the inn after her night with Rod's goons. "There!" She tapped a spot on a rural road just south of the intersection of the two highways. "It's along that road. About a mile in."

"Okay. Let's go." Bouton grabbed Conny's arm and started leading her out of the room.

Conny jerked out of his grip. "Let go!"

Moore stepped in. "We need you to show us where this is, Conny." He pointed to the map.

"I know that! Just keep your paws off me!"

Moore signalled for her to lead the way. Bouton scowled at Moore then grabbed the map off the desk and followed.

As she approached the entryway, Sandy and Tom stopped their pacing and turned to face her. "Are we leaving?" Sandy asked.

Moore stepped forward. "Miss Lee is going to be assisting us. Maybe you two should head back to the lodge."

Conny gasped. "Can't they wait? I don't want to hitchhike back to the inn—"

Sandy rushed forward. "We're not going anywhere. We'll wait in the car."

Conny nodded and chanced a quick glance at Halden, who had stepped up to the counter and was watching, concern etched on his face. She squared her shoulders and turned away to follow the officers out the door.

They crossed the street to what was obviously an unmarked cop car, where Moore stepped forward to open the back door for her. Conny stopped and backed up. "No. I'm not going in the back."

"Well, you can't ride in the front," Bouton said, stepping past her to open the driver's door.

"No." Conny continued to back away.

Tom rushed forward. "It's okay. She can ride with us and you can follow."

Bouton inhaled sharply.

Moore quickly shut the door and stepped between Conny and Bouton. "That sounds like a plan." He tipped his head to Tom. "We'll follow and when Miss Lee sees the right house you touch your brakes twice to signal us. Then I want you to keep driving, Tom. Do you understand? Keep driving. Do not stop. We'll see you back at the office."

Moore peered at the thick hedge bordering the property Tom's double tap had indicated where they'd find the man they were after. They'd pulled to the shoulder of Willowbrae Road as Tom carried on. It was impossible to tell what was happening behind the thick, green curtain of leaves without turning into the drive and making their presence known. "What do you think? Is he there?"

Bouton sat back and put the car in gear. "There's only one way to find out."

Turning into the gravel driveway, the car's left front tire immediately dropped into a pothole. Bouton cursed, then eased the vehicle out of the hazard only to have it rumble and rattle along the heavily rutted dirt trail leading to a grey, wood-paneled, two-storey house. Scaffolding climbed the right-side wall and roof. The high-pitched whine of a table saw told Moore and Bouton they weren't alone.

Stepping out of the car they scanned the property. A simple, unadorned front lawn wrapped around the modern Cape Cod style home, ending at a six-foot cedar fence that hid the backyard from view. The front facade of the house presented five double-hung, sash windows on the ground floor and four on the upper storey but revealed nothing of the interior. The driveway swept past the house and ended at a three-car garage sitting about ten feet to the right. It was there, inside the garage, that the noise emanated.

As the two officers came abreast of the garage door they were nearly knocked over by the appearance an eight-foot, two-by-four being carried by a pony-tailed, lanky, man in brown coveralls. "Who the hell are you?" he growled.

Bouton stepped around the protrusion and extended his hand. "Corporal Merle Bouton and this is Corporal David Moore."

The man ignored Bouton's hand and boldly looked them over, his gaze lingering on their holstered side arms.

Bouton dropped his hand. "Is this your place?"

The man set the plank on its end and fixed Bouton with a defiant glare. "Nah, I run the reno crew."

The whine of the saw suddenly stopped, and three very large, very buff men walked out from the garage. Dressed in matching black dress shirts and pants, they moved with the discipline of the military and made no secret of the guns they carried in shoulder holsters. "Is there a problem, Luke?" the one in front asked as they approached.

Luke turned his gaze back to Bouton. "Is there a problem?"

Bouton hesitated a moment, causing Moore's heart to race. It would take very little to set off a gun battle he feared they wouldn't win.

Bouton slowly spread his hands and smiled. "We were just checking out a noise complaint."

"This is private property, gentlemen," the lead enforcer snarled. "Unless you have a warrant, it's time to leave."

Bouton turned his back on the group and returned to the car. Moore followed, the back of his neck twitching. Once inside the car, Moore dropped his head against the seat and closed his eyes. Bouton spun the vehicle around, leaving a set of fresh ruts in the lawn.

56.

Watching from where he'd parked the Mustang a half-block from the cop shop, Tom had a clear view of the unmarked vehicle's approach. When it turned into the driveway that led to the back parking lot he could see only the two officers inside.

"It doesn't look like they found him," Sandy declared, leaning forward from the backseat, her elbows braced against each of the front bucket seats.

Tom shifted to look past Sandy to Conny, who had pushed herself forward from the passenger seat to get a better view. "Did you see anyone else in the car?" he asked.

Conny shook her head and sat back in the seat.

Absently tapping his fingers on the steering wheel, Tom struggled with ending the heated discussion they'd been having while waiting for the cops to return. "Look, I know I went along with Edan's wanting you to talk to the cops, but, like I said, after what's happened, I no longer think you should." He didn't mention that Roxanne's viewpoint against taking Conny to the cops had started to make sense to him. Her discovery of their wayward roommate sitting at the breakfast table that morning, then learning their destination had prompted an uncharacteristic outburst from the dark beauty. Now, he was beginning to think she was right.

Her face still flushed from the heat of their exchange, Conny snapped. "Why not? This is why we came here."

"I know. But that was when I thought you'd be safer with them." He glanced quickly at the detachment office across the street. "If they were unable to find this Dwayne character even after you pointed them in the right direction, and if they were so concerned about you and Rod being in the same building together that they ushered you out to a café, then I no longer believe you'll be safe with them."

"That was when Rod was in the interview room and there was a chance he'd see me when they moved him back to his cell. He's in his cell now."

"Are you sure?" Tom asked.

"Well, I think she'd be safer in there than out here." Sandy settled back into the backseat. "Dwayne's still running around out here somewhere."

An uncomfortable silence settled over them, until Conny turned to face Sandy. "Do you trust this David?"

"Yes. Yes, I do."

"Well, then." Conny opened her door.

Tom grabbed her arm. "You could go down for seven years on the trafficking charge alone," he stressed. "If they decide what you did to Geoff was murder, you could go down for life."

Conny avoided looking at him. "I confessed, Tom. I confessed to that cop."

"Which cop?"

"The one who got shot trying to protect me." Pulling out of his grip, she stepped out of the car and headed for the office.

Tom ran after her, catching her arm again, and spun her to face him. "Then come to Vancouver with me. I know people. My family's loaded. I can get you a new ID. You can start again." Releasing his grip on her, he waved his arms to indicate the world around them. "Don't throw your life away because you chose the wrong guy to love."

"I didn't love him."

Tom dropped his hands, exasperated. "Then there's no reason to allow him to destroy your life."

The sound of Sandy yelling pulled their attention to the car. She was pointing wildly at the detachment office. "Look!"

Tom turned to see the local cop striding toward them. Whipping around he whispered to Conny. "Go back to the car."

Forcing a smile, Tom turned to Moore, whose eyes tracked Conny's quick return to the Mustang. "You didn't find him?"

Moore swiveled his focus on Tom. "Yes and no. We feel confident the house Miss Lee indicated is where we'll find him. We just didn't see him while we were there."

Tom wondered why he was getting cop double-talk. "Do you mean you couldn't find him?"

"We hadn't prepared for what we found. We need to speak with a judge about a warrant." Moore replied. "Right now, we're waiting for the Sheriff Service to pick up Mr. Ouellet and take him to Nanaimo. Once he's gone, we'll pull Conny in. We have some questions for her." He paused as if considering what he was about to say. "If the sheriffs arrive too late in the day to allow for an interview, we'd like to place her in custody—"

"Charged with what?"

"—for her own safety."

Safety? Tom didn't believe that. He knew from experience that once cops had you in custody, they worked hard to find a way of keeping you there. "No," he said, and backed away.

Moore held up his hands. "Tom, stop! Dwayne is still out there!"

"I don't care! We'll look after her." He spun on his heels and left Moore standing in the road.

Entering the office Moore pressed his fingers to his temples. He had offered what he thought was a perfect solution to the problem of keeping Conny safe while giving them a chance to interview her, but it appeared that wasn't going to happen.

Bouton set aside the report he was writing. "Where is she?"

"With her friends."

Bouton burst from his chair and rushed for the door. Moore took a moment to consider before he followed. When he joined Bouton on the entry steps and scanned the street, the Mustang had gone.

"You shouldn't have let them go!" Bouton scolded.

"How could I keep her? Without a confession, we don't have anything to tie her to the first victim."

"I was hoping to speak with her; to give her a chance to tell us what happened with Mr. Johnston *and* with Mr. Ouellet," Bouton shouted. "Where were they going?"

"I'm not sure. Probably back to the lodge."

Bouton spun on his heels and re-entered the detachment. Moore checked the street one more time before following Bouton.

"We need clean, clear fingerprints." Bouton stated. "If we don't have a confession, then we need her fingerprints in the van. If her prints are on any of the contents of the chocolate box, we can hold her on a trafficking charge."

Moore left Bouton at the chalkboard and sought his desk, where he dropped into his chair and closed his eyes. He took a deep breath and exhaled slowly. He felt as if his head would explode.

"Sir?"

Moore opened his eyes to find his constable and the major crimes officer staring across his desk at him. With a deep sigh, he sat up. "What?"

Evans motioned to the office entrance. "The sheriffs are here for Mr. Ouellet."

Moore stood inside the back entry of the detachment watching Rod being loaded into the sheriff's van. He was glad to see the back of him, even if it meant his departure left a few loose ends. *Let the lawyers battle it out in court.* He was sick of the guy.

"He's a dead man," Bouton said.

Moore looked across at where the corporal leaned against the door jamb. "What makes you so sure?"

"They've got a solid case on the murder charge. I heard there's a witness. So, between our attempted murder charges and Nanaimo's murder charge, Rod won't be seeing too many more Christmases."

"Good riddance," Moore mumbled.

"I agree." Bouton patted Moore lightly on the shoulder before heading down the hall to the front office. Moore shut the door and followed.

When Moore caught up, Bouton had just picked up his keys from his desk. "I'm going over to the café for lunch. Liam and his gofer should still be there. Feel like joining us?"

Moore glanced at his watch. "No. My lunch will be waiting for me next door."

Bouton gave a quick nod. "I'll see you afterward, then."

Moore stood and crossed to the chalkboard, where he tried to make sense of the chaos. *If the assailant, or assailants cut off Danny's hand before burying him in the prospector's cast-off pile, then what would they have done with the hand? Would it become their trophy? Or would they toss it?*

Moore frowned.

Or was it scene dressing?

Moore picked up a piece of chalk and wrote Dwayne's name on the board. Could he be Danny's killer? The man certainly displayed an intent to cause harm when he'd chased Conny and the others.

His eyes landed on Thanos' name and he remembered Rod's response when he was asked about him. He'd called Thanos a traitorous piece of shit! Was Thanos the day-shift guard?

Moore grabbed his coat. He may have just figured out why Thanos had showed up in Nanaimo with his throat cut!

57.

The pencil slipped from her fingers and speared the sand at her feet. Sandy looked down at the dart and sighed. She had hoped that time spent sketching at the beach south of the inn would help solve the problem of Conny. But her thoughts remained as muddled as the pencil scratches she'd discarded and were now rolling across the sand to the edge of the water.

It had not been easy listening to Tom's impassioned description of plans he hoped to pull together to change Conny's life. During the drive back to the inn from Ucluelet Tom had pitched one outlandish idea after another, while Sandy shouted for him to watch the road and Conny sat pressed up against the passenger door, her eyes glued on Tom.

When they had finally arrived at the beach, Tom ran into the inn and returned with a key which he pressed into Conny's hand and told her to pack her things. She was to move into one of the cabins, where she'd be safe for the night. He'd then made Sandy promise not to tell anyone where Conny would be. "I have to work my shift," he told her. "Brent can't cover me because he's got some family thing he's got to go to."

Sandy left for the beach, not waiting to see where Tom led Conny. The onshore sea breeze was filled with the scent of wild things, and Sandy found herself collapsing on the nearest log, her brain racing. She no longer felt comfortable with what she was doing with Conny. Supporting her decision to tell the police what had happened to Geoff was one thing, helping her to run away was another. The image of Geoff's parents standing on the side of the road, where she'd told them their son died, haunted her. Their grief was so graphic. Could she really help the person responsible for his death disappear, leaving them to live the rest of their lives in limbo, not knowing why their son died?

"There you are!"

Sandy sprang up, her heart pounding. Mark walked down the beach toward her. "You scared me half to death!"

Raising his hands, Mark apologized. "I stopped at the lodge and was told you were out." Sliding in next to where she'd reclaimed her spot on the log, Mark leaned in and planted a kiss on her forehead. "I figured you'd be sketching." He glanced down at the sketch pad resting on her knees. The page was blank. He laughed and waved his hand at the crunched-up rolls of paper cluttering the beach. "Not going so well?"

She searched his eyes for any trace of sarcasm and found only kindness. "I-I—" A tear broke free and traced a path down her cheek.

Mark's smile disappeared. "Sandy? What's wrong? Tell me."

Looking away, she quickly wiped the tear from her cheek, remembering her promise to Tom. "I can't. I promised."

Mark's eyes searched hers. "If the promise is causing you pain, then keeping it isn't worth it."

"I just don't know what to do."

"Let's talk. Maybe between us we can figure that out."

Sandy reached down and plucked the pencil from the sand, then told him. As she spoke she felt a calmness settle over her, and when she finished they sat in companionable silence while watching the waves creep up the beach. When she was ready, Sandy rose, set the sketch pad and pencil on the log, and began gathering the wads of paper from the beach. Mark joined her.

"You need to tell Conny how you feel," Mark said.

"But—"

Touching his finger to her lips, he shook his head. "She needs to know." He paused, then took her hand and led her back toward the lodge.

They came upon Tom suddenly when he stepped out from a break in the salal hedge bordering the beach path. The surprise encounter stopped all three in their tracks.

"I was just headed back to the lodge," Tom explained, and indicated his wish to continue along the path.

Sandy glanced to her right, down the rough pathway Tom had come from. A small cabin sat back against a fringe of trees hiding it from the beach beyond. *He's got her hidden away already?*

Mark stepped forward. "We'll join you."

Sandy reached out to lightly touch Mark's arm. "I'm going to stop here," she said. "I need to talk with Conny."

"What?" Tom's eyes whipped between Sandy and Mark.

Mark stepped between them. "It's okay. I know."

"Sandy you promised!" Tom shouted over Mark's shoulder.

Mark placed his hand on Tom's chest to keep him from moving past him to Sandy. "Look, it's okay. Let her go. I have something to discuss with you."

Sandy watched Mark lead Tom away. "I'll see you at the lodge. I won't be long," she called.

Tom was angry and disappointed with Sandy. How could she betray them so quickly and easily? Whatever her hippie boyfriend wanted to discuss, he wasn't interested. He had too many things on his mind as it was.

But Mark was not to be put off. He caught up with Tom and started questioning his plans. "I don't think it's a good idea for you to drive Conny to Vancouver using your Mustang. It's too recognizable. The cops, or Rod's gang, will have you before you even make it out of town."

Tom spun and challenged him. "What right do you have to say that? You don't know us. What we do is none of your business!"

The hippie stopped and folded his arms, his eyes sending a clear message that he wasn't backing off. "I've got a better plan."

Giving a dismissive wave, Tom turned his back on Mark and started walking again. "Well, I don't want to hear it."

Mark set off after him. "Do you have all the arrangements made on the other end? A place to stay? A new identity? A job?"

Tom walked on in silence, considering the calls he'd made earlier from the inn. "I'm working on it."

"Okay," Mark exhaled. "I have a friend who might be willing to deliver Conny to Vancouver, for the right price. And nobody, the cops or the others, will even notice them."

Tom continued walking, deep in thought, until his arm was grabbed. "What?"

"Sh-h-h," Mark pulled Tom back from the exposed exit of the laneway they were about to enter and pointed.

Two cops were standing on the lodge's porch. Roxanne was in the doorway explaining that Conny was not there.

"Corporal Bouton and Moore," Mark whispered. "We've got to warn the girls." He let go of Tom and started running back down the path. Tom hesitated. Then the crack of a gun shot split the air, and he tore after Sandy's hippie.

The first thing Sandy noticed when she approached the cabin was the sound of voices. She hadn't expected Conny to have company. *No, the first thing was the door being ajar.* "Conny?" she called, gently pushing the door open further. Silence greeted her.

"Conny? It's Sandy. Are you here?" The voices had stopped, leaving a strange hollowness to the narrow hallway stretching the length of the cabin. Sandy stepped through the doorway, her eyes flitting from left to right. The small pantry kitchen to the left was empty, as well the small bedroom on the right. "Conny?"

Sandy moved down the hallway, hoping this wasn't some stranger's cabin and Tom had stashed Conny somewhere else. "Conny, it's Sandy. Just checking to make sure you're okay." The hollowness of the silence began to raise goosebumps along Sandy's arms as she continued toward what looked like a living room with patio doors opened to the beach. *Maybe, the voices had travelled in from tourists strolling the beach.* "Conny? We need to talk—"

"Stay where you are!"

Sandy froze. She recognized the voice. It was the man from the café. *Dwayne.* "I'm looking for Conny," she called out, her throat suddenly dry. Slowly, she turned her head to the left, where she found Dwayne pointing a gun at her. His nose and forehead were purple with bruising, adding a sinister darkness to the scowl creasing his face. She raised her shaking hands. "Please, don't shoot."

Conny, who was backed up against the couch, sent an anxious glance her way before returning her focus on the gunman. "Let her go. This is between you and me, Dwayne."

Dwayne ignored Conny. His eyes bore into Sandy's. "It just ain't your day. Kneel."

"What?"

"Kneel!" He shouted. "I don't want you getting any ideas about running."

Sandy sank to her knees.

Dwayne returned his attention to Conny, who Sandy noticed had backed further along the couch and was standing at its end. "You must've thought you were so smart," he sneered, "keeping your deal with Thanos from us?"

"I didn't have any deal with Thanos." Conny took another step back and Sandy saw what she was working her way toward. A pair of canoe paddles rested against the arm of the couch. Sandy sent a furtive glance at Dwayne. He didn't appear to have noticed. Sandy lowered her arms and silently prayed.

Dwayne shook his head slowly. "It was hard for me, you know." His gun wavered. "I liked you. I thought Rod had hit the jackpot with you. I didn't want to do what we did to you." He took another step toward her. Conny stepped back. "It was business." He took a deep breath and raised the gun again. "Just like this is business."

"No!" Sandy sprang, her toe catching on the frayed hem of her bell bottoms just as Dwayne swung the gun and fired. A whisper of wind brushed her cheek as the bullet whizzed past, and she landed hard at his feet.

Leaning down, his face level with hers, he calmly put the muzzle of the gun against her forehead. "I guess you go f—"

Suddenly his head was jerked back, Conny's fingers ensnared in his hair. He swung his gun hand wildly and it caught the side of her head, sending her flying. She landed half-on-half-off the couch. "Bitch!" he screamed, rubbing his scalp. He made to approach her, but a noise at the hall entrance made him stop and look.

The hippie burst through the cabin door with no thought of what lay beyond, causing Tom to hesitate and pull to the side of the door, out of sight. The sound of Mark pounding down the tiled hallway suddenly stopped. Tom chanced a cautionary glance inside.

Mark stood at the entrance to the living room, his hands slowly rising. The room was backlit by the afternoon sun flooding through the open patio doors, making it difficult for Tom to see things clearly. He squinted against the light, making out Sandy kneeling in the centre of the floor. The gunman, whose features were cast into dark shadow by the sun, stood commando-style, his gun pointing directly at Mark. Tom guessed he was the same guy who'd chased them from the café and rolled back against the cabin's rough wood exterior. It was then he noticed the two policemen, in crouched position, cautiously approaching along the cabin's path.

Bouton motioned for Tom to move further to the side, and he and Moore slipped into the vacated space; each, in turn, glancing inside.

Sandy stayed perfectly still, afraid that any movement would set Dwayne off. He had spun away from Conny to face the new intruder and now stood above her, the same creepy smile from the café stretching across his face.

Mark stood at the hall entrance to the living room with a deer-in-the-headlights look in his eyes. Sandy hoped he wasn't alone.

Dwayne raised his gun and pointed it at the newcomer. "Drop to your knees," he growled.

Panic gripped Sandy as she watched her friend kneel. *How are we going to get out of this now?* She turned to see if Conny had recovered when she caught a flash of motion, a loud *thunk*. Dwayne dropped on top of her, his gun skittering across the floor.

Conny stood trembling above her, gripping the paddle like a baseball bat.

Suddenly the room filled with the sound of running feet. "Police! Put down your—"

Conny dropped the paddle and raised her hands.

"Get him off me!" Sandy shouted. "Get him off me!"

The sound and vibration of pounding feet flooded Sandy's senses, then suddenly she could breathe. The pressure of Dwayne's dead weight had been lifted from her. She pushed herself into a kneeling position. Dwayne lay face down on the floor next to her, out cold. David stood at his head, the major crimes officer at his feet.

"Thank you," she croaked.

Mark dropped into a squat beside her. "Are you okay?"

Sandy gave a quick nod, and glanced back at Conny who was huddled against the side of the couch, one hand holding the side of her head, blood seeping between her fingers. Sandy's view was momentarily blocked when Bouton approached Conny with a hanky pulled from his pocket. He knelt to inspect the wound and wipe the blood from her face. When he stepped back, Sandy found Conny's gaze on her and a smile spreading across her lips.

THE END

ACKNOWLEDGEMENTS

Researching this dynamic period of our history was challenging, but I was fortunate in having tremendous support from the staff and volunteers of organizations such as the historical societies of Ucluelet, Tofino, and the Alberni District, as well as the Royal BC Museum and Archives, the University of British Columbia libraries, BC Registries, Library and Archives Canada, and members of the RCMP Veterans' Association.

I am also grateful for the assistance of the many individuals who offered me insight into their specific areas of expertise.

And, of course, the task of writing this story would not have been possible without the insights and guidance offered by editors Arlene Prunkl and Tara Avery, both members of the BC branch of Editors Canada, and my friend and former newspaper editor, Carl Hahn.

But most of all, I would like to thank Robin Fells for taking the time to speak with me on several occasions about his experience building and operating the original Wickaninnish Inn, and for allowing me to set this mystery series in and around his unique inn.